BEFORE SERIES
BOOK TWO

Before I Saw You

A LOVE STORY BY

ASHLEY ELIZABETH

To the girls afraid to look in the mirror: I promise it's not as scary as society makes us believe.

You are beautiful just the way you are.

And to the man who stood behind me while we looked in the mirror together, thank you.

AUTHOR'S NOTE

Before I Saw You takes place *almost* a year after Before I Tell You. It is strongly recommended but not necessary to read Before I Tell You first.

This book contains references to abuse, Alzheimer's disease, disordered weight and body thoughts, eating disorders, panic attacks, sexual assault, sexually explicit scenes, violence, and topics that may be sensitive to some readers.

Reading is an escape for many of us, so if you feel that the mention of any of the above will upset you, please put this book down.

I present to you Jason and Vanessa's love story.

xoxo Ashley Elizabeth

Prologue

Vanessa

Have you ever heard someone say something about you that you wish you could forget?

Something that keeps you up at night—gnawing away at your mind as you play it on an endless loop over and over again, like a broken record you can't seem to shut off.

And no matter how many shots of tequila you throw back or how many pints of Ben and Jerry's you devour, you can't forget.

Not the pain.

Not the guilt.

Not even the heartache.

But the worst part about hearing those three words is that you have to pretend as if you never heard them. You have to go on with your daily life acting like they don't affect you, because you just happened to be in the wrong place at the wrong time, and you don't want him to know the power he holds over you.

The power he has *always* held over you.

So you tuck those three words away like a secret. A secret he can never know.

"She's not him!"

"No, but she sure as hell is related to him. He's her fucking brother, Nate. Her brother!"

"That doesn't mean shit. You need to stop looking at her like she's him. She's not. She's your sister's fucking best friend, Jason! She used to be your friend too!"

"How are you okay with this? Tell me you don't look at her and instantly feel sick to your stomach, because I do. Every single time I see her face, I'm overcome with anger, knowing what that monster tried to do to my sister. And now everyone is okay with letting her walk around as if everything has gone back to normal? Like her brother didn't try to fucking rape my sister?"

I hear the raised voices, immediately realizing who they are arguing about.

Me.

I only left the graduation party to grab a sweater from Natalie's bedroom, but the voices coming from across the hall—from Jason's bedroom—stopped me in my tracks. And the second I realized that Nate and Jason were fighting about *me*, I found myself frozen on the other side of the door, my heart pounding so loudly in my chest that I had to press my ear against the smooth wood surface to hear them over the sound of my erratic heartbeat.

"That monster is currently rotting in a jail cell, and trust me, I understand your anger toward him, but I won't let you take it out on Vanessa. She doesn't deserve this!"

I don't think I've ever heard Nate sound so upset.

"I'm not going to pretend I'm okay with all of this when I'm not."

I can practically hear the venom protruding from Jason's mouth with each word he spits out.

"Then do it for Natalie," Nate pleads. "She needs her best friend after everything she went through. And the way you've been treating Vanessa is stressing Natalie the fuck out, which is why I can't stand back and not say anything any longer. You're giving her the silent treatment. Walking out of rooms when she enters them. Pretending she doesn't even exist.

It's not okay, and it's not fucking up to you if they're friends again. That's Natalie and Vanessa's decision. Not yours."

I hear Jason breathing heavily on the other side of the door, knowing it could fly open any second, but I can't find it in me to move my feet. Suddenly, the door vibrates against my head with a loud bang, and I find myself backing away, rubbing my fingers at the point of impact on my forehead.

That's going to leave a mark.

Jason must have struck the door.

I've never seen Jason lose his cool before, which tells me he's angrier about me being back in the picture than I realized.

"We're all going to the same fucking school in just a few months." Nate sounds exasperated. "You need to pull your shit together."

"I. Hate. Her."

Jason's words stab right through me, shattering my heart into a thousand pieces. A pain consumes my chest like I've never felt before. My eyes fill with tears, begging me to release them, and—unwillingly—I do.

There's no stopping the salty, narrow streams cascading down my cheeks. My throat tightens as a silent sob escapes me, knowing there's no going back to how things used to be between us.

The guy who promised me we'd always be friends just broke that promise in the same moment he broke my heart.

The handle on Jason's door turns, and the next thing I know, I'm gasping for air as I clutch my chest, sitting upright in my bed, panicked. I glance at the clock on my nightstand, noting it's just after midnight, as I wrap my arms around my bare legs tucked against my chest, breathing erratically. The rain flowing down the glass French doors to my patio matches the tears sliding down my face. Tears that I have become quite familiar with over the past few months.

After wiping my face dry with the oversized T-shirt I'm wearing, I push my damp hair away from my forehead, realizing it was a nightmare.

It was just a nightmare, Vanessa.

Only it wasn't a nightmare.

It was a memory. A memory of that night.

The night I heard the man, that I have loved my whole life, say that he hates me.

One

VANESSA

S EPTEMBER 1ST

It's the perfect summer day.

The warmth from the sun kisses my body like it's worshiping me.

The birds chirp pleasantries back and forth to each other, perched among the neighboring trees.

And there's a slight breeze cascading over my bare, flushed skin, sending a shiver up my spine.

Everything is perfect.

But as much as I love the feeling of the afternoon sun embracing my skin, I'd much rather be looking up at the night sky. Because at least then, I could stare endlessly at the stars above me, getting lost in the natural beauty they provide to a world that runs off of superficial facades.

A world I don't feel like I belong in.

"I wish every day was this beautiful." Natalie removes her oversized sunglasses and peers up at the, almost, cloud-free, blue sky. Her long silky blonde hair flows behind her as her toned, slightly tanned legs stretch before her.

Jealous of my best friend? Never.

Envious? Maybe a little.

Growing up with a best friend who ranks a solid ten out of ten on any hotness radar, means I have always dreamed of what it would be like to look like her. To walk a mile in her shoes—watching all the guys get whiplash from how fast their necks turn to gawk.

The two of us couldn't look more opposite from each other, but maybe that's why we've been best friends for so long. What is the saying? Opposites attract?

Well, that's me and Natalie.

Where she has straight blonde hair, I have thick, dark chestnut strands that fall in waves around my face. Where she has a gorgeous, toned and tanned body, I have a softer figure with a pale complexion. And as we both lay side-by-side on chaise lounge chairs by her family's pool, wearing bikinis, and soaking in every last ray of sunshine, it's hard not to compare myself to her.

Even harder not to hate what I see when looking at my own body—a body I no longer even recognize. And on the rare occasion, I get brave—or drunk enough—to look in a mirror, I don't see a beautiful twenty-year-old girl, but instead a monster. A girl who went from being a perfect size two most of her life to developing curves and extra weight, making her a few sizes bigger.

A few sizes *too* big.

Of course, it's my mother who likes to remind me how much my body has changed over the years, with the occasional side comment or crash diets she would put me on, telling me she was only doing it so I would be happy. It's funny, though, because every time she put me on one of her special diets, it only made me miserable.

Because no diet should remove chocolate from your life.

But I wanted to make her happy—to make her feel proud of her daughter. So, whenever she pushed a salad my way, I ate it. When she removed all the carbs from the kitchen, I'd grab a celery stick for a snack instead. And after she'd make me stand on the scale in front of her to see the lack of progress in my weight loss, I'd go upstairs and cry silently into my pillow, wishing I could be skinny enough for her.

Because in her eyes, to be skinny means to be beautiful.

A word she has never once used to describe me.

"Hey, what are you thinking about?" Natalie's soft voice liberates me from my thoughts. Her brows furrow as she looks at me with concern etched in her light grey eyes.

I wave along the length of my body. "Oh, nothing. I just noticed I'm getting a little pink and should get more sunscreen." I sit up, but she gently places her hand on my forearm to stop me.

"No, you stay. I have to pee anyway. I'll get it—be right back!" She hops up from her side of the chaise and struts into the back of her family's home.

I let out a deep breath.

Don't go down that path, Vanessa. Not today. Today is your day to relax and not give a fuck about what size you are.

I decide my front has had enough of the blazing sun, so I look around to make sure no one is nearby and untie the back of my bikini top before I lay back on my stomach, letting the strings hang by my side.

God forbid I get an ugly outline from the bikini top string on my back. That's the last thing I need.

I stretch my arms above my head and instantly relax into the sun's warmth, hoping I don't get too burnt before Natalie returns with the sunscreen. I can't even imagine how uncomfortable it would be moving into my new apartment tomorrow, being red as a lobster.

My new apartment.

The day I've been waiting for is here.

Because after the past couple of years, I needed, more than anything, to be close to my best friend again, which is precisely why last spring, I decided to leave my school in New York City to transfer to Linrey University for my sophomore year in Boston, and be roommates with

Natalie. It wasn't something I had to think about. It made complete sense to me, seeing that I was tired of always feeling alone.

To my parents, it made no sense. But nothing I do appeases them anyway, so I tried not to take it too personally that they feel—without saying—that after everything that happened this past year, I should keep my distance from Natalie and that, in *not* doing so, I took a side in this whole, uncomfortable situation between our families.

Awkward? Abso-fucking-lutely.

But I won't let anything get between Natalie and I again.

Never.

I stretch my legs out and twist my body the slightest bit, bringing my arms up and folding them under my head like a pillow, feeling ready to take a little cat nap.

Nothing could ruin this day.

"Here."

My cheerful mood quickly fades when I hear the very recognizable, and deep voice of Jason Spencer, Natalie's younger brother.

The man that hates my guts.

This entire past summer, he's made his feelings pretty clear toward me.

I enter a room; he leaves it.

I join his family for dinner; he eats in his bedroom.

I stand in his presence; he acts like I don't exist.

You get the point.

Not that I can really blame him. Although it's not me he's personally mad at, it's my brother.

Remember that abso-fucking-lutely awkward thing between our families I mentioned? Well, the thing is, my brother, Brian, is currently sitting in a jail cell for sexually assaulting Natalie almost two years ago.

Yeah, like I said, it's an uncomfortable situation.

Natalie and I were able to put what happened behind us, but it would appear that Jason doesn't share the same feelings as his sister.

So I try not to take his not-so-subtle hints that he hates me to heart. I pretend it doesn't bother me. But sometimes, his behavior toward me stabs me a little harder than I can manage.

I've always been the girl who comes off put together, able to handle everything that comes my way, but at times—especially lately—I feel like a piece of glass ready to shatter.

There's only so much one person can take before they break. Especially from the man who has always had my heart.

He just never knew that little secret and never will.

I. Hate. Her.

I open my eyes and peek up to find Jason staring down at me, holding a bottle of sunscreen for me to take. He's wearing a pair of blue swim shorts and nothing else.

God, I wish he didn't look like freaking Jeremy Burns. Yeah, the same, gorgeous quarterback for the Cincinnati Bengals that brings every girl out to their living room on game day to watch football.

From the tousled dirty blonde hair and grey eyes, that come off blue in the right light, to the placement of every perfectly sculpted muscle on his body.

Did I mention he's also a quarterback like his unofficial twin, Jeremy?

Oh, and I saved the best part for last. He's Linrey University's rookie quarterback *and* my new neighbor.

Fuck me.

"Just leave it on the table." I place my head back on the chaise and close my eyes, waiting for him to leave. Usually, I would take the bottle from him, but that would require me to move, and well, with the top of my bikini untied, that's not happening.

This man is not getting a free show today.

Besides, no one, and I mean no one, is allowed to see me in a bikini. The only person I have ever felt one hundred percent myself in front of is Natalie, who promised me no one would be home today, but I guess she didn't consider that her brother would be here. Or maybe she didn't think I would care if he saw me like this since we'd spent our whole lives together.

Wrong.

Because he is, in fact, the last person who I want to see me like this.

"You're going to burn Vanessa. I can see the pink starting to appear on your skin."

"Well, then, don't look at me," I respond casually, but inside I'm slightly dying, knowing his eyes are on me.

Please leave. Please leave. Please leave.

"God, you are so irritating sometimes."

I'm not even looking at him, but I know he's running an exasperated hand through his hair because that's what he does when he gets frustrated—especially with me, which lately doesn't take much.

"Jason, just leave it and go. I'll put it on in a few minutes."

Silence.

Thank the heavens he left—or at least I thought he left. That is until I hear a metal lounge chair scraping across the cement floor and stopping right beside me. Next, I hear the familiar sound of lotion squeezing out of the bottle. And finally, I feel that same lotion being rubbed on my back, causing me to freeze.

"Jason ... what are you doing?" Every muscle in my body locks up, hyper-aware of his rough hands rubbing lotion tenderly all over my skin.

"I said you were burning, but you're too stubborn to listen to me."

"Gee, stubborn? Who does that sound like?"

"Vanessa," he warns.

"Why do you care anyway?" I wanted it to come out confident, but my voice became too soft at the end. Maybe because this is the first time we've spoken to each other in a very long time.

It never used to be like this between us. There was even a time when I used to feel closer to him than Natalie. Although, I would never admit that out loud.

"Just let me do this." His voice sounds less hostile.

Jason's large hands rub the lotion all over my back very slowly. Almost too slowly.

"You feel so tense. Relax. It's just me."

It's just me.

He says it like it's supposed to calm me down, but it only has the opposite effect on me.

There used to be a day when he would say, *it's you and me.*

But not anymore.

"I'm not tense."

"Oh yeah?" His thumbs work their way into my upper back like he's giving me a deep tissue massage. Wow, that feels amazing. "Now, take a deep breath."

"Why?"

"Can you ever just do something without asking me why?"

I purse my lips but do what he tells me to do.

"Now let it out," he orders.

At the exact moment I let out a deep breath, he pushes down on the upper part of my back, and it feels so good that an unwarranted moan slips out between my lips.

Oh. My. God. Please tell me he didn't hear that.

But from how his hands have stilled on my body, I'm going to guess he most definitely did. My body heats up from my head to my toes, and I know it's not from the sun.

Well, this is fucking awkward.

Thankfully, Jason's hands go back to rubbing the lotion over my skin, acting as if nothing happened. His fingers gently stroke the skin under my breast, at the top of my ribcage, and I realize he's tracing my tattoo.

"When did you get this?" he asks, referring to the outline of stars.

"Umm..." I'm having an impossible time thinking with his hands on me. "Last year."

Last year when I felt the loneliest I've ever felt in my life.

"I like it," he says softly.

"Thanks."

As his hands go lower onto my back, I feel something simmer in my core. Something that no man has ever made me feel. I clench my thighs together, trying to dissolve this feeling, but his hands caressing my skin make it impossible.

What the fuck is wrong with me?

I shouldn't feel this way with him. He hates me.

"The back of your legs is starting to get pink. Want me to apply it there too?" His voice sounds husky, almost unrecognizable.

I don't know why, but my head just nods. It just fucking does.

He starts at the back of my calves but then slowly works his way up each thigh, lightly squeezing my muscles.

Holy Lord, am I dreaming?

My bikini bottom covers only about half of each ass cheek, and realizing this, I suddenly feel incredibly self-conscious. I'm practically lying naked in front of Jason, giving him a full view of all of my cellulite and stretch marks. I curl my hands into fists at my side, my nails digging into the palm of my skin, insecurities suffocating me.

"You're getting tense again," Jason notes.

"Sorry..." My voice is barely a whisper as I unclench my fists, taking a relaxed breath.

His hands glide over the back of my thighs before hovering below my ass. Oh, God.

"Is this okay?" he asks.

Again, I nod my head because, for some reason, I can't even remember what my name is. I'm pretty sure it starts with a V, but I could be wrong.

A sudden pulse strums between my legs, begging to be touched, begging for attention. But above all, begging for a release that I somehow know he could provide me with, unlike the others.

What the hell are we doing? This is a line we've never crossed before.

And where the hell is Natalie?

I hear his breath hitch as he slides his hands up my body, and knowing this is affecting him as much as it is affecting me only turns that aching pulse between my legs into an insufferable pounding I can't stop. But suddenly, he freezes and promptly removes his hands, causing my skin to instantly feel cold even with the sun beating down on me. I hear people's voices coming from inside his house, and I open my eyes to find Jason with furrowed brows.

"Shit. They're here," he says, sounding like he's talking to himself.

His fingers find the strings of my bikini top, and he quickly ties my suit back into place. He moves away from me and grabs a towel. "You need to cover yourself. Now."

"What?" I sit up and cross my arms over my chest, accidentally pushing up my boobs.

His eyes darken as they travel from my breasts up to my eyes. "Now, Vanessa. Don't play games."

I look toward his house and see a few of Jason's friends walking through the opened glass door, making their way toward the pool. One person has a cake in their hands, and I narrow my eyes when it occurs to me what day it is.

It's Jason's birthday.

My eyes return to Jason, and I realize then that he doesn't want his friends to see me. He's embarrassed by me and doesn't want his friends to see someone like *me* next to *him*.

I jump from the chaise, humiliation engulfing me, and snatch the towel from Jason's hands, wrapping it around my body. "Fuck you, Jason! Don't worry. I'm covered now. You don't need to feel embarrassed to be seen next to someone like me." I shove past him, storming off toward the house.

"Vanessa, wait!" I hear from behind me, but I don't stop as the tears threaten to escape. I march into the house, ignoring the pleasantries from Jason's buddies as they make their way outside, and I head straight up the stairs to Natalie's room.

I can't believe I let him touch me.
What the fuck was I thinking?
Never again.

Two

JASON

After a full day spent moving into my new apartment, my body screams in agony as I melt into the sofa like molten lava, feeling every muscle burn in relief.

Of course, it was nothing compared to the past few weeks of football, where I learned college football differs significantly from high school football. But I feel ready—mentally and physically. I've worked my whole life for this opportunity, and I'm not going to blow it.

"I think you have more stuff than Natalie does," Nate says as he molds into the chair in the corner of the room, wiping sweat from his brow. "Maybe Vanessa should have just roomed with you. It would have been less work for all of us."

I glare at him, narrowing my eyes.

He smirks. "Just saying."

I now live in Natalie's apartment, or I should say her *former* apartment. She needed a two-bedroom unit so that she and Vanessa could room together, and there happened to be an available apartment down the hall for them to take.

Vanessa.

I fucking made a mistake when I touched her yesterday because now that's all I can think about. But what was I supposed to do? She was lying there, practically naked, looking like every guy's wet dream, and I couldn't stop myself. I mean, I would have if she had told me to, but every time I asked, she just kept nodding away, letting me explore parts of her I had only ever dreamed of. She wasn't supposed to feel that damn good in my hands. And her moan, fuck me, it made my dick instantly hard. And I know she didn't mean for it to slip from her perfect pout, which made it even better. Don't even get me started on how hard I could feel her clenching her thighs together. She was just as fucking turned on as I was.

Even if she would never admit it, she wanted it too. Her body was giving her secrets away, begging to be touched. And I happily obliged, even if there was a voice in the back of my head screaming at me to stop, trying desperately to remind me why I shouldn't be touching her. But I couldn't. My hands began moving on their own as I ensured every square inch of her backside was doused in lotion, enjoying having a reason to touch her like that for the first time.

I was so damn distracted by the feeling of her under my hands that I had completely forgotten my friends were on their way to my house for a little birthday celebration. And it was a damn good thing that my friends showed up when they did, or who knows what might have happened.

How far would we have taken it?

The door swings open, and in walks Nate's friend, and current roommate, Paul. "Well, the girls are all moved in and just going through their stuff now." He has one of my boxes in his hands marked *"private"* and tosses it beside me. "What the hell is in there?" He doesn't even make it to any of the pieces of furniture. He just plops down on the ground and lets his abnormally long body flop on the floor like a fish out of water.

"My sex toys. Want to see?" It's not sex toys, but I say it so he'll lose interest in the box now resting beside me.

"No, thanks." His massive hands cover his face. "What goes on in the privacy of your bedroom is between you and your hand."

We all laugh.

"God, I'm wiped." Paul rolls onto his stomach and places his arms under his head.

"Me too," I agree, tucking the box under my arm and getting up from the couch to bring it into my new room, where I slide it under my bed for safekeeping. I look around, viewing the Charles River that resides outside the large window across from my bed. The sun is just starting to set, casting an amber glow over the river, making it look peaceful and serene. Convincingly giving the appearance of a river you'd want to jump into on a hot day like today. But there's a reason its nickname is *Dirty Water*.

I'll just stick to my family's pool.

My basic bed has white sheets, a grey comforter, and matching grey pillows. The furniture in my room sits in front of exposed brick walls, and my TV hangs in the corner at the perfect angle so I can lay in bed without hurting my neck as I watch it. I turn on the light in the bathroom. It's pretty bare, and I'll have to run to the store later to get some essentials: shampoo, a toothbrush, and a bar of soap.

What else does a guy need?

Yeah, I think I'll be fine here.

It was a good choice.

Well, it was the *only* choice.

Because Natalie and my parents can never find out about The University of Southern California—the dream school I always wanted to go to. The school that offered me a starting position—

Nope.

I shake my head because I am not going down that path right now.

You made the right choice.

I turn off the light and return to the living room, finding Nate and Paul exactly how I left them.

"So ... Vanessa is pretty cute," Paul remarks, making me pause my step. There's unease sweeping through me. But why? She's single, as far as I know, and free to do whatever she wants. But the thought of Paul touching her the way I did yesterday is doing something to my sanity. Just as I open my mouth to tell him to forget about her, Nate speaks.

"Don't even think about it." Nate rubs a hand over his temple, and Paul's eyes widen in shock. Did Nate really tell Paul not to go for her? The same guy that every girl refers to as a freaking teddy bear, for Christ's sake. Now I'm curious. "Don't get me wrong. You're a great guy, but that girl is a sister to me, and she's been through enough the past couple of years. She needs time for herself."

I wonder who Nate would approve of for her. Not that it matters to me.

As if he can read my thoughts, Nate looks directly at me with a sour expression. If he actually could read my mind, he would hear me saying, "*I'm not interested!*"

"Understood," Paul replies glumly. "I'll just remain single for the rest of my life." He turns his face, pressing it into the carpet.

"Hey, don't stain my carpet with your tears, big guy," I say.

Nate laughs. "You'll find someone. What about that girl you were telling me about? No luck finding her?"

Paul responds with a frustrated groan.

I guess that's a no.

"So, how long until you think one of the girls needs us to do something for them again?" Nate asks, stretching his long legs out from the chair. "I'm beat."

"I give it—" I start to say before being interrupted by a quiet knock on the door. My lips curl up. "Well, I have to admit that was faster than I thought."

Natalie pokes her head inside. "Hey, guys!"

"Natalie, you know I have a special place in my heart for you, but I can't lift anything else. I can't even feel my arms," Paul mumbles into the carpet as he quickly lifts his arms and then drops them smack back down on the floor beside him.

Nate lightly kicks him with his foot on the side of his torso. "The only person with a special place in their heart for her is me." He laughs and looks over at the door where Natalie stands. "What can I help you with, beautiful?"

She blushes. You'd think the two of them just started dating when it's been almost a whole year. Besides the fact, they've known each other for years, even before that.

"Well, Vanessa and I wanted to thank you guys for helping us move everything, so we ordered pizzas, and they should be here any minute," she says.

"Fuck yes. I'm starving." I walk toward the door, feeling motivated by the thought of shoving some pizza in my face.

"Someone is going to have to carry me. My legs aren't working." Paul attempts to get up but then falls back down. "Or just leave me here. I think my time has come." He closes his eyes for dramatic effect.

"Oh, Paul." I hear her voice, causing my heart rate to surge. Somehow Vanessa and I were able to avoid each other the entire day, until now. One of us would be inside while the other was outside. But I knew avoiding her couldn't last forever. I look over at her, standing behind Natalie in the entryway. She's wearing a white oversized T-shirt and a denim pair of shorts that show off her round ass. That same ass my hands were so close to squeezing yesterday. *Goddamn.* She tucks a piece of her long brown hair behind her ear. "Has anyone ever told you, you look like a much taller Michael B. Jordan?"

Paul jumps up as if shot by lightning. "What? Me. You think so?"

Is she ... flirting with him?

Nate laughs. "Well, what do you know? He can walk again. It's a miracle." He slaps Paul's back. "Come on, Mr. Jordan, let's get you some food."

Vanessa looks up with a smile, locking eyes with me, and that's when her smile falters.

"Oh, Vanessa. The guy just texted saying he'll be right up with our food." Natalie grabs Vanessa's hand, dragging her across the hall, causing Vanessa to look away from me.

"What guy is texting you?" Nate asks, walking quickly behind them with Paul beside him.

Natalie smiles at him and then pats his chest. "It's cute when you're jealous."

"Natalie Spencer?" Our heads turn, and we see an older man standing in the hall holding pizza boxes and a couple of bags.

"That's me!" Natalie takes the bag from the delivery guy's hands while Nate grabs the pizza boxes. "Thank you."

We all make our way into the girl's apartment.

It's pretty identical to my own, just a lot bigger. And I mean a lot bigger.

Knock. Knock.

I turn, finding a familiar face at the doorway.

Sarah Fleur.

I met her last year when I finally made it over to visit Natalie during her spring semester. She's hot in the obvious way if you like girls with long dark black hair, floral tattoos, curves that look hard to resist, and a pair of emerald Disney Princess eyes. You know, if you like that sort of thing. But I tend to prefer perfect chocolate brown eyes surrounded by long thick black lashes, a full pouty set of pink lips begging to be kissed, and chestnut brown hair that settles just below a perfect set of—

What the fuck? No. I internally shake my head.

Get it together, Jason.

I am not attracted to Vanessa.

Maybe if you repeat it enough times, you'll convince yourself just that.

"Sarah! Perfect timing. We were just about to have some pizza. Did you want some?" Natalie beams at the sight of her friend and neighbor walking over to her and wrapping her arms around her quickly before letting go. Looking at Vanessa from the corner of my eye, I could swear she appears a little green.

Is she jealous?

"Oh, that's so nice of you! But I was just on my way out and wanted to say hi." She smiles and waves at everyone in the room, her eyes wavering on Paul's back where he stands by the kitchen island, placing the food down, completely oblivious to our guest. No wonder he has such a hard time finding someone. The man has no game.

"Let me introduce you to the gang." Natalie takes a step away and lightly pulls on Vanessa's arm, dragging her over. "This is my best friend, Vanessa."

Vanessa does a little awkward wave before Sarah walks right up to her and squeezes her in an embrace that has Vanessa looking panicked. Sarah is definitely a good few inches taller than her, making Vanessa look even smaller than usual.

"I am so glad to finally meet you!" Sarah exclaims.

"You are?" Vanessa breathes out.

Sarah unwraps her arms from around Vanessa's smokin' body.

I mean from around her body!

Jesus Christ, what is wrong with me?

"Yes! I knew the moment I met Natalie that something was missing from her life. And"—she looks over at Nate—"no offense Nate, but it was you."

"None taken," Nate responds, reaching into the fridge to pull out a cold beer.

Vanessa's cheeks turn the slightest shade of pink before looking away. She hates attention.

Natalie knows this, so she quickly resumes the introductions.

"And you know Nate, of course. And you met Jason last time he was here."

"Hey," I add with a quick nod.

"And Sarah, this is—"

"Paul." Paul walks over and reaches a hand toward Sarah.

Sarah's head tilts to the side, her eyes grazing up his body until they lock with his. "Paul," she says breathlessly, taking his hand in her own.

The two stare at each other for a beat too long before Sarah finally blinks and shakes her head, removing her hand from Paul's and taking a step back.

That was interesting.

If I didn't know any better, I'd say this wasn't the first time they met...

"Well, it was really nice to finally meet the rest of you, but I better be going." She smiles and turns, making her way out the door, but not before I notice the double take she does at Paul, who hasn't taken his eyes off her.

After a few seconds of us all looking at each other in confusion, Nate finally asks the question on everyone's mind.

"What the hell was that?"

"What was what?" Paul finally emerges from his daze and steps toward the fridge, reaching for a drink.

"That!" Nate waves his hands between Paul and the now vacant door entryway.

"I don't know what you're talking about," Paul responds before guzzling the soda in his hand. After almost drinking half of it, he places the cold can against his cheek. "Natalie, is the heat on in here? It feels like I'm in a sauna."

She smiles, knowing exactly why he suddenly developed an immense fever. "Nope. I think it's just you, TB."

"Oh, Jesus, you gave him a nickname?" Nate pinches the bridge of his nose.

"Of course, I gave him a nickname."

"What's TB stand for?" I ask, feeling extremely confused.

Nate sighs and then rolls his eyes. "Teddy Bear."

Paul bursts out laughing. "Oh, Natalie. You are definitely my favorite."

"You think you're so funny, don't you?" Nate stands behind Natalie, wrapping his arms around her waist.

"I know I am." Her face tilts toward him, and she reaches up, kissing his cheek.

"Alright. Everyone, dig in," Vanessa announces as she organizes the food on the marble island in the kitchen. She seems to be looking at everyone except me.

I do the math and see there are five boxes of pizzas and five of us, so I grab a whole box for myself.

What? I'm a growing boy.

I plop on the sofa with the box on my lap and begin to devour this pizza as if it were my last meal.

"Is it okay if I sit here?"

I've got half a slice in my mouth when I look up to see Vanessa standing before me. Quickly looking around the room, I see that everyone else is currently occupying the only three counter stools surrounding the kitchen island, leaving only the other side of the sofa as an option for her. After gulping down what's in my mouth, I reluctantly say, "Sure."

She doesn't say anything else and takes her seat beside me. There is one cushion between us, but it still feels like she's right next to me, taking all the air in the room from me. She opens the plastic container in her hand and starts mixing the salad inside with her fork—the very bland-looking salad.

"Why aren't you having pizza?" I ask.

"Oh, I shouldn't," she responds as she stabs a piece of lettuce and then brings it to her mouth. It doesn't even look like there's any dressing on her salad.

Gross.

I furrow my brows. Is she lactose intolerant or something? Does she have a gluten allergy? If she does, this is news to me, seeing that we've known each other almost our whole lives. "And why not?"

She opens her mouth but immediately closes it, as if she doesn't know what to say. "I, umm…" Her free hand squeezes into itself, her nails digging into her palm as her knuckles turn white. She doesn't even notice when she does it. But I do. I've always noticed. She does it when she's nervous. When she's feeling self-conscious, which is a lot of the time. My hand wants to reach out to hold hers, reassuring her she has nothing to be self-conscious about, but I remind myself I can't. Not anymore. "I just don't like—"

"Hey Jason," Natalie interrupts us, causing Vanessa to jump a little, finally releasing her hand from the death grip. "Can you adjust the curtain rod in Vanessa's room? We both couldn't reach it."

"No, it's fine." Vanessa shakes her head. "I was going to fix it later. I have a step stool I can use. It's not a big deal."

"Don't be ridiculous." Natalie looks from Vanessa to me. "You'll help her, won't you?"

Natalie's not dumb. She's felt the tension between Vanessa and me this past year and has been trying anything she can to make it dissipate.

Newsflash. Unless you can rewind time, it won't be happening. There's no going back to the way things were before. But if my sister asks me to jump off a bridge with her, I jump fucking first to ensure she has my body to land on.

I sigh. "Which room is it?"

"The room down the hall on the left," Vanessa quietly responds. "But you really don't have to. I can fix it myself."

I place the pizza box on the coffee table, ignoring Vanessa, and go to her bedroom. Walking inside, I immediately see the curtain rod dangling out of place. It's an easy fix. But not something either Natalie or Vanessa would have been able to fix without a step stool or even a full-on ladder. I place the rod on the hook and make sure it's secure before I back away and observe it, confirming it's even along the top of the window frame.

"You know, if football doesn't work out for you, maybe you can be a professional curtain hanger."

I turn to see Vanessa smiling, leaning against the wall next to the door. Her arms are crossed in front of her, pushing up those perfect tits I find myself unable to stop thinking about.

"Funny." Looking away from her and at her room, I notice her walls are pretty bare. Maybe she just hasn't hung up any pictures yet. I thought all girls do that, but perhaps I was wrong. "No pictures?"

Her smile falls. "I have a couple of me and Natalie in one of those boxes in the corner."

I don't miss the fact that she doesn't mention anything about having any pictures of her family in those boxes. But the thought of her family, specifically her brother, immediately puts me in a foul mood.

I can feel my pulse accelerate, my blood seething beneath my skin.

"So," she takes a step toward me, "I was hoping we could talk."

"About what?" I'm getting frustrated and wish she wasn't standing so close to me. Why does she smell so damn delicious? Is it some kind of floral scent? Rose? Lavender? Or maybe it's something edible, like honey. Because all I want to do is taste her, and it's driving me fucking mad. My hands clench into fists at my sides as I take a deep breath, steadying my pounding heart.

"With us being neighbors, I was hoping we could try to get along." She shrugs her shoulders. "It's not a secret you're not my biggest fan, but I was just hoping that we—"

"Listen." I step toward her, backing her up against the wall, looking down into her big damn beautiful brown eyes. They're almost enough for me to melt, but not right now. Not while the reminder of who her brother is, plays in my head—a constant infuriating reminder on an endless loop. "You stay out of my way, and I'll stay out of yours. Okay?"

She looks at me like a deer caught in headlights. Her chest heaves with each breath she takes, and the way she's biting her full, bottom lip is doing something to me. But just as quickly, she shakes her head, escaping her slight trance. Her eyes glaze over as she nods in understanding, a slight tremble in her bottom lip as she pushes herself away from the wall, and then walks out of her room, leaving me feeling like a piece of shit.

I run an irritated hand down my face and take a deep breath. Why the fuck did I think coming to Boston would be a good idea? Oh, right. Because when I got the call from my dream school in California offering me a starting position on their team, my first thought was my sister. After what happened to her, how could I not feel guilty living on the other side of the country? I know she has Nate, but it's not enough. I need to be here to protect her because almost two years ago, I wasn't there, and she was almost fucking raped.

I want to hit the wall, but I don't want to destroy Vanessa's room. I'm not that much of an asshole. So I turn around and pummel the pillow on her bed, instantly releasing some pent-up frustrations.

But as I look down at Vanessa's bed, my mind flashes to the events that took place yesterday. To the way she felt in my hands and how fucking sexy she—

No! I shake my head to clear my thoughts, pulling at the ends of my hair.

What happened yesterday can't happen again. I never should have touched her. I know that now. And it won't happen again.

Never fucking again.

Three

VANESSA

I think I'm the most socially awkward person in the world.

No, let me rephrase that. I *know* I'm the most socially awkward person in the world.

It's not that I don't want to meet new people, because I do. But anytime someone new approaches me, I worry about what they'll think of me.

Will they judge me based on appearances alone?

Will they notice my jeans look a little too tight, wrapped around my thunder thighs?

Will the sight of me repulse them?

It makes me sweat under their glare, leaving me too nervous to make conversation, which is why I got the not-so-subtle nickname in high school of Queen Bitch. When really, I was just the most self-conscious girl in my class, scared of having anyone's cruel eyes on me.

But I'm determined not to let that unpleasant title follow me to Linrey University.

I can do this.

I take a deep breath, straighten my shoulders, and—

The buzzing of my phone in my coat pocket stops me. Grabbing it, I see *"Connecticut State Prison"* displayed on the screen. My stomach immediately plummets, knowing who it is.

Brian.

Guilt takes hold of me as I press decline with a shaky thumb—something I've done every time he's called these past few months.

"I hope you can live with the guilt."

I can't talk to him.

Not after what he did.

Not after what *I* did.

It's too much for me to wrap my head around right now.

Shoving my phone back in my pocket, I take a deep breath and walk into the large classroom, taking one of the empty seats in the last row next to the enormous windows overlooking the campus, trying to forget about what just happened.

The subtle hints of fall are just starting to show around campus. Leaves are transcending from greens to reds as an early chill in the air forces students to retire their summer attire and opt for their hoodies and light coats instead.

But that's September in New England—my favorite time of the year. Mainly because it means I get to start wearing layers again, using clothes as my own personal defense from judgmental eyes. But still, one can't grow up in New England and not feel nostalgic at the change of seasons. Not to mention, I'm a huge fan of pumpkin spice everything.

That reminds me. I pull out my phone from my coat pocket.

Vanessa: Meet for coffee after class?
Natalie: Yes! See you then!

"Good morning, class." My head snaps up from my phone to find the professor standing in front of her desk, ready to start class. "I'm so excited to begin this semester with you. My name is Professor Fabuleuse, and I plan on teaching you everything I know about fashion!" She speaks with a slight French accent making everything she says sound even more exciting than it probably is. "This course will provide you with everything you need to know about textiles, patterns, shapes, sewing techniques, and most importantly, the history behind fashion." She finds a marker and begins to write her name on the whiteboard behind her. "And as you all know, you had to provide samples of designs in a well-executed portfolio to be accepted into the fashion program here at Linrey University, as our fashion design program is sought after by those all over the world, and we only accept the best of the best. So, to be sitting here is an accomplishment in itself. Take a moment to really let that sink in." She looks around the room giving off a warm smile, like a proud mom would be doing.

Not something I'm used to.

But maybe that's why I find myself sitting in this classroom. Because fashion has always been my escape when things became too much for me. It provided me with an escape from life. An escape from ... My throat tightens, knowing the pathetic truth is I used fashion as an escape from my mom.

As a kid, I'd hide in my room for hours, creating anything I could think of just to stay hidden from her look of shame every time she saw me. I would do anything I could to avoid the disapproving look her eyes would give me as they traveled up and down my body, withholding dinner from me when she noticed even a few pounds gained.

Brian would always make sure I had something to eat, though. Sneaking takeout in my room late at night or texting me to let me know he hid something in the back of the fridge for me. I swallow a hard lump, internally shaking my head at this memory.

You don't have a brother anymore.

You don't have anyone to stand up to your mom for you anymore.

It's just you.

Deep breath.

So, I guess it's thanks to my mom that I became pretty talented at designing. A complete wizard with a needle and a piece of thread, if I say so myself.

Gee, thanks, Mom.

From a young age, I knew I wanted to spend my life surrounded by fashion. I dreamed of someday seeing my designs on the cover of Vogue or worn by models walking down runways at Paris fashion week. But as I got older and my body started developing, I realized my true passion. It's creating a line of clothes that all women would feel beautiful wearing. They wouldn't feel ashamed of their size but instead would feel confident.

Empowered.

Beautiful.

It's how I wish *I* could feel, which is why it's my goal to bring that feeling to someone like me who needs to be reminded how beautiful they are. To remind them that they are more than a size or a number on a scale. They are perfect just the way they are.

"Now, every year, we have a friendly competition between our students, and this year is no different." Her stunning smile widens. "I take it you are all familiar with The Metropolitan Museum of Art?" We all eagerly nod our heads, and I'm pretty sure I already know where this is going because anyone and everyone in the fashion world knows about the upcoming event in New York, *The Met Future of Fashion*. It's an event held once a year, recognizing ten, talented fashion students from selected schools worldwide. Anyone who is anyone in the fashion world will be there, and having your designs displayed that night with the eyes of the world on your pieces would guarantee you a place in that same world. My heart races, waiting for the professor to continue.

"This year, for The Met Future of Fashion event, they have decided to hold it on Valentine's Day, with this year's theme centered around *'love.'* It will be up to you to wow the judges with your designs, as the winner will not only be gifted a generous scholarship from the university but will also be chosen to feature their designs at the event." She claps her hands together in excitement as students whisper enthusiastically around everyone.

"Wow. I can't even imagine having my designs displayed at The Met." I look to my right to see a guy relaxed in the seat beside me. His face is almost too pretty, with a chiseled jaw, big hazel eyes, and shaggy brown hair that falls perfectly just above his eyes. "I think I would pass out. No, I would cry. Actually, I would probably cry and then pass out."

I find myself laughing in his presence. There's something very approachable about this guy, and I instantly like him.

"I'm Brady, by the way. I'm known to be a little dramatic, but since it looks like we will be desk buddies for the semester, I thought I would give you a fair warning." He reaches his hand toward me, and I immediately notice all the beautiful silver rings on his fingers.

"I appreciate the heads up." I return the smile, shaking his hand. "I'm Vanessa."

"Well, Vanessa, I must say, you are perfection in that beautiful, double crepe, red peacoat." His bright hazel eyes glide over me, but not in a sexual way at all. More in the way of wondering where the hell he can get his hands on a coat like this.

"Oh, I didn't even realize I still had it on." I hesitantly unbutton it before letting it slide off my shoulders and over the top of my chair. "But thank you." Remember how I mentioned that wearing layers is my way of putting up a defense between me and people? Well, if layers are my defense, then this red peacoat is my titanium shield, the most essential piece of armor I've had for a very long time. It buttons the length of my body, just below my knees, and slightly flares out at my waist, keeping me hidden beneath the thick layer of fabric.

Ironic, seeing that I'm extremely claustrophobic.

"I can tell right away that you and I will get along just fine." He inches his chair closer to mine. "Friends?"

"We just met five seconds ago, but sure. Why not?" I respond, causing us both to laugh.

The professor clears her throat to get everyone's attention. "Now, if you are interested in contributing to this year's competition, you will be responsible for providing three completed garments, along with your sketches, a name for your collection, and an essay explaining the significance of your mini collection. The sketches, name of your collection, and essay will be submitted first before you leave for Thanksgiving break. The five students I deem worthy enough to be featured at The Met will be announced after the break. Those students will then be responsible for creating those designs and leaving them with me the week before Christmas break. Judges from The Met will have the final say regarding which student will be the winner from Linrey University and the winner will be notified the day after Christmas. But the details and guidelines can be found here in these packets."

She holds them high, catching our attention, and then places them on her desk. "Make sure you grab one on your way out, and if you have any questions, feel free to ask me." She claps her hands together, gazing over the classroom. "But for today, being that it is our first class, I want you to pull out your sketchbooks and use this time to let your imagination run free with predictions of upcoming trends."

Everyone in the class places their sketchbooks on their desks. I look for my pencil case in my bag but can't seem to find it. "Shoot."

"What's wrong, new friend?" Brady asks.

"I guess I forgot to pack my pencils." I continue digging through my bag, hoping one might magically appear.

"Well, here, I have plenty." He hands me a box to take.

"No, really. I only need one."

"Nonsense. I have too many anyway. Take them, I insist." He pushes them toward me.

"Well, since you insist." I smile at him, taking them. "Thank you."

We spend an hour silently letting our imaginations get to work as we sketch until our hearts are content and the campus bell tower rings twelve times, letting us know it's twelve p.m. and class has ended. Brady shoves his sketchbook in his bag and then buttons his navy, double-breasted peacoat.

"So, any other classes today?" he asks.

"Just two more, then work tonight. I'm already looking forward to going to bed." I sigh, still feeling exhausted from moving in and also because I am not looking forward to my first day at work. The only thing I *am* looking forward to is the tips that I heard are insane, and the only reason I applied to this place in the first place.

"Where do you work?" Brady throws his bag over his shoulder.

"Well, umm, it's my first day, but it's…" Might as well tell him. "It's a sports bar near campus called Winners."

Brady's mouth falls wide open. "Holy shit. That's my brother, Rob's, bar!" He laughs, shaking his head. "What a small world. I help cover shifts sometimes, so I'll definitely be seeing you there."

Relief fills me. "Is your brother like you?" I ask, hoping he says yes.

"Oh, no. No. No." He shakes his head. "He's gruff, rough, and tough around the edges." He chuckles. "I'm the good one in the family," he says with a wink. "He's also ten years older than me with a wife and kids and the whole package, so you could say we're polar opposites, but we're family." He runs his fingers through his hair and looks at me like I'm supposed to know what *"but we're family"* means—but I don't. "Well, I won't keep you, but good luck tonight at the bar. Get those tips!"

He turns and heads to the professor's desk, grabbing a packet for the competition before leaving the classroom. I realize I'm the last one left, so I put my coat back on and swing my bag over my shoulder, but just as I step toward the professor's desk, something outside the window catches my eye.

Or more like someone.

It's Jason.

The guy who hates me.

He's leaning against a tree, with his burly arms crossed in front of his chest. His hair is slightly tousled, which only adds to the sexiness he exudes, and his damn smile is making every girl stop and stare at him—especially the two girls standing right next to him talking to him now.

They're beautiful.

One has long red hair flowing down her back, and the other has a short, chic, brown bob emphasizing her jawline. Neither of them has love handles or a tummy. They look toned and ready to gain the attention of any man they want, including Jason.

Every time he laughs at something they say, my insides twist into tiny knots, and I don't understand why. He's free to talk or flirt with anyone he likes. It doesn't bother me. Nope. Not in the slightest.

I shake my head and walk toward the professor's desk, grabbing the packet more forcefully than I had planned, and then hurry out the classroom door, fighting back a weird urge to cry.

At six on the dot, I walk into Winners, feeling pretty drained from my first day of classes, but I remind myself how much I need this job, so I take a deep breath and plaster a fake smile on my face as I approach the bar.

"Hi, I'm looking for Rob. Is he around?"

The girl on the other side tells me to wait here while she gets him. Only a moment later, a guy, I can only assume—from Brady's description—is Rob, walks from the back of the bar, heading my way. He's big and tall, with a thick, black beard covering his face. He's got tattoos covering both arms that are on full display since he's only wearing a black T-shirt. To most people, he probably appears intimidating, ready to scare the shit out of them.

It's me.

I'm most people.

But as he gets closer, he smiles, erasing any frightened thoughts I might have had about him five seconds ago. "Hey, you must be Vanessa." He puts his hand out for me to shake, and I do.

"Hi, yes. That's me."

"Well, Brady already called me and told me he made a new friend in class and that I'm not allowed to scare you away, so I don't plan on doing that." He chuckles, shaking his head. "In case you can't tell, we're pretty different, but we're family."

But we're family.

Again, they say this as if I'm supposed to know what that means.

"Yeah." I nod as if I understand.

"I have your uniform in the back, so once you get changed and meet me out here, I can start showing you around. It's pretty straightforward. There's nothing fancy here to learn." He points up at the old-school chalkboard above him, displaying some food options. "The menu is basic, but it's really good food, and the drinks are simple. Since it's a Monday, we won't be busy, so this is a great night to get you started."

"Ok, great." I try to feel excited about this. Really, I do. But ten minutes later, after putting on what would be considered my uniform, I'm dreading this already.

Think of the tips, Vanessa.

I walk from the breakroom to the front bar, where Rob is waiting for me. My hands pull at the bottom of the black skirt, trying to bring it down further as I'm pretty positive it's barely covering my ass, but it's as low as I can get it to go without revealing my stomach. I could be imagining it, but I feel like every eye in the place is on me.

"Ok, ready to get started?" he asks as I approach the bar.

"Ready," I respond, feeling anything but. This uniform is making me second-guess everything. It's not that I'm not covered because I am. It's just that the skirt does nothing to hide my round ass from everyone here. If anything, it just emphasizes it. And the small apron that ties around the tight black top underneath my double D's, only makes them more noticeable.

I hate this.

But after two hours of Rob showing me the fairly basic procedures of serving at a bar with a minimal menu, I feel that I've gotten the hang of it.

"What do you say? How about the next group that comes in, you help?" I know we've only spent two hours together, but I swear Rob is looking at me like a child he just dropped off at school on their first day, convincing them they can do it!

I take a deep breath, straightening out my apron. "Yeah, okay. I can do this." I smile, trying to show him I'm not scared, while every cell in my body screams at me to run out the front door.

"Great! Because it looks like they just walked in."

I turn around and see a group of guys make their way inside, escaping the downpour currently going on outside, and my smile instantly drops.

You have to be shitting me.

"Vanessa?" I glance to my left to see Rob looking at me, concerned. "Everything okay? Do you want to wait for a different table?"

"No. No. I've got this." I plaster that damn, fake smile back on my face and head straight to the corner booth where the five, rather large guys have seated themselves. It's not until I make my way up to the table that a pair of light grey eyes look up from the menu, widening in surprise. "Hi, boys. What can I get you tonight?"

I'm met with five pairs of hungry eyes, but it's the pair furthest away from me that won't even blink.

Good. I hope he's as uncomfortable as I am.

"Well, aren't you a sight for sore eyes," the one closest to me says. His eyes glance over my uniform, creeping me the fuck out before finally landing back on my face. "I'm Zach, and you might want to remember that because that's the name you'll be moaning tonight when you think about me." He winks, making me want to vomit whatever is left in my stomach all over the table.

Normally I would slap someone for saying something like that or even just walk away, but seeing as it's my first day at this place, I start to giggle awkwardly, feeling heat spread across my chest.

Suddenly, Jason's large hand smacks the back of Zach's head.

"Ow. What the fuck was that for?" Zach rubs the back of his head while sneering over at Jason.

"Apologize." Jason's eyes stare unwaveringly at him.

"What?"

"You heard me. Fucking apologize." Jason's eyes, once light grey, are now dark and demanding.

The guy beside Jason commands the same thing. "Apologize, Zach. You don't want to make this one unhappy. He'll be your future captain soon enough." He runs his fingers through his dark brown hair, narrowing his brown eyes on Zach.

Jason and the guy beside him look like two guys you don't want to piss off, which is probably why Zach ends his little pissing contest with Jason, glancing at me and giving me his full, unwanted attention.

"Sorry," he grits out before picking up the menu, cowering behind it and slouching in his seat.

"We'll just have five burgers with fries, please." Jason only has eyes for the menu in his hands as he places everyone's order.

"Sure thing." I turn around and hear the guys begin to talk.

"Did you see that ass?" one of them whispers.

"Don't fucking make me hit you, too," Jason responds as I make my way to the kitchen to give the chef the orders. As I wait for their food, I stand by the counter, loading napkins into the containers that sit on every table. Well, I was, until I feel a significant, dominating presence behind me.

Turning slowly, I find Jason standing only a few feet away, towering over me.

"Did you need something?" I ask.

"Why the hell are you working here?" His muscular arms cross over his chest as his eyes narrow down on me.

I'm caught off guard. "Excuse me?"

"Here. This place." He gestures around wildly with his hands before facing me again. "Why the hell are you working here?"

"Why does it matter, Jason." I'm tired. I'm tired of him always being mad at me when I haven't even done anything wrong. "If you have a problem with my service, talk to my boss. Otherwise, just leave me the fuck alone."

He steps into my space. He's so close that I feel his hot, minty breath wash over my skin, sending shivers down my body. "I asked you a question, Vanessa."

"And I gave you an answer, Jason." I sigh, but I'm not backing down. "Why do you have a problem with me working here, anyway?"

He runs a frustrated hand through his messy hair, and for a moment, I wish it was my hand running through it. I bite my bottom lip, wishing I could—

NOPE!

"I have a problem with you, working at a place where perverts come to gawk at the girls who work here wearing slutty uniforms." He looks at my uniform disapprovingly, making me want to disappear under the bar until my shift ends. I turn around, ready for this conversation to be over, but Jason grips my arm, stopping me.

Our eyes meet, and he looks almost ... concerned? No, Jason doesn't give a fuck about me, so I don't give a fuck about him. I shake my arm out of his grip, and he lets go.

"Wait. Why are you ... working?" he asks.

I shake my head, knowing he won't understand. How could he when he has two amazing parents who support him financially with whatever he needs?

Not me though. Not after what I did.

But it was the right thing to do.

I know it was.

"I need money. And if you must know, this place is known for its tips, which is why I am currently standing here in this slutty uniform so that perverts like your buddy over there who come here to make crude comments and gawk at me will tip me."

He scowls. "But your family—"

"What family, Jason?" I cut him off and slam the napkin holder on the counter, breathing heavily. "I have no one. In case you haven't noticed, I'm alone. Always alone." Gazing into his eyes that soften with pity, I instantly regret letting those words slip out of my mouth. I don't need his pity or want it. "Listen, I'm tired. I have twenty minutes left of my first shift, and all I want to do is go to bed. So please..." I look away, not wanting him to see me like this any longer. "Leave me alone," I say softly.

He looks at me for a few seconds before eventually nodding and saying, "We're going to take our burgers to go if that's ok?"

"Yeah. Sure. Fine." I turn and walk away toward the kitchen, praying the damn burgers are cooked, and I praise the Lord when they are. I pack each one in a box with fries and then put each box in a bag, making it easier for them to carry.

As I exit the kitchen, Jason stands there waiting for me. I hand him the bags, and he gives me just enough money to cover the food—perfect, not even a tip.

Asshole.

I watch as Jason leads the guys out of the bar toward his big, black pickup truck that sits out front. As he pulls away, he glances out his window, locking eyes with me for the briefest moment.

When did things unravel between us?

When was the exact moment that we were no longer friends?

Was it the moment he found out about my brother?

Was that the same moment he decided to hate me?

Making my way over to the table they sat at, I pull out the rag from my apron, ready to wipe it down, when I see some bills in the center. Actually, I see five bills in the center of the table. And each one of those bills is a hundred-dollar bill.

What the fuck?

I pick them up, looking them over to make sure they're not fake. Although let's be honest, I don't even know what a phony bill would look like.

Holding the money between my fingers, I contain the urge to scream at the top of my lungs. How dare he?

I look up at the clock on the wall, relieved to see I'm free to go. I change in the back and thank Rob before exiting, letting him know I'll see him in a few days for my next shift. Getting into my car, I turn it on and put it in drive, squealing out of the parking lot. When I get to my apartment building, I park, enter the building, and practically run up the five flights of stairs before finally stopping in front of Jason's door.

My fist slams on his door, pounding frantically. He opens it up slowly and stands before me, wearing nothing but black boxer briefs. He leans against the door frame with his arms crossed over his chest, causing his thoroughly impressive biceps to stand out, momentarily distracting me from my mission.

Holy shit, he looks so freaking delic—

I shake my head. *Not the time.* "Take your money back. I don't want it." I push the cash toward him, but he just tilts his head, staring at me, not reaching for the money.

"That's not my money." He shrugs his shoulders.

"I'm not a fucking charity case!" I'm breathing hard and feel the tears wanting to escape, but I won't let them—not in front of him.

"I never said you were." His brows furrow as his face softens.

I take a deep breath. "Then why did you leave me a five hundred dollar tip?"

"I didn't." He shakes his head. "Zach did."

I look at him, feeling confused.

"I told him it was his job to leave the tip tonight after the comment he made. And that if he didn't want to run extra laps tomorrow, he better make it worthwhile."

I look down at the money in my hand, feeling slightly better knowing it came from that asshole's wallet, not Jason's.

"You can do that? I mean, you're only a freshman."

A mischievous smile appears on his face. "I have my ways."

"But, why?"

He glares down at me. "No one is allowed to talk to you like that. So even though he tipped you well, he'll still be making up for his comment tomorrow on the field."

"Oh..." Why would he care about some stupid remark from some asshole who clearly doesn't know his ass from his elbow?

"Yeah, so if you don't mind, I'm going to be getting back to bed now." He turns but then stops, glancing back at me over his shoulder. "Unless you want to join me?"

"Wh-what?" My heart pounds erratically inside my chest. Did he just say what I think he said?

Jason's lips curl up. "Goodnight, Vanessa." He then shuts the door in my face, leaving me so fucking confused.

Four

JASON

Winning the first home game of the season is a fucking incredible feeling. Granted, I didn't get a single minute of playing time, and I spent half of the game questioning why I didn't accept the offer from California, where I was guaranteed the QB1 spot, but still, we won.

The cheers from the crowd, the flashing lights from reporters, and the slaps on your back from proud coaches only add to the high you experience as you see the score plastered brightly on the scoreboard for all to admire. The smile on my face must have made me look like a little kid on Christmas morning, but I didn't care because this was the feeling I chased after every week on the football field.

A feeling of pure, unaltered bliss that left me with just enough endorphins in my system to make it to the next game before I needed another hit to my system.

It's what keeps me going.

But when I looked up in the stands at the friends and family section, that feeling of bliss didn't feel quite whole tonight. Yeah, I saw my proud parents cheering along with everyone else, and I saw Nate and Natalie jumping up and down at the sound of the band solidifying our win, but I couldn't help but feel like one person was missing from the stands.

A girl with long strands of chestnut hair and big, chocolate brown eyes I used to get lost in. A girl with a smile that would erase my bad day and who fit perfectly in my arms. A girl I had been trying to make myself hate for the past year, but no matter what I did, I couldn't find it in me to do so.

That girl wasn't here.

And I can't say that I blame her.

"Why so down, freshman? We won!" Grant, the senior starting quarterback and the current captain, slaps me on the back as he comes up beside me, giving me a beer as I stand against the counter in the kitchen.

It's tradition after wins to celebrate at the football house on campus, where I find myself with the rest of the team, surrounded by cheap booze, loud music, and sweaty bodies.

"Yeah, you should be pumped!" Chris, the sophomore linebacker, adds, walking up to us with a fresh beer in his hands.

I take the cap off the beer and guzzle down a few sips. "I'm not down. I'm just tired."

"Sure." Grant doesn't sound so convinced.

"You know"—Chris tilts his head toward the main room—"that hot blonde, in those tight jeans, has been giving you sex eyes all night. Bet she could wake you up." He wiggles his brows.

Yeah, I'm not blind, I've noticed her staring at me all night, but I'm also not interested. "Has she? I haven't noticed."

Grant shakes his head with a smirk. "This wouldn't have anything to do with that waitress the other night, would it?"

"I don't know what you're talking about." I bring my drink to my lips and look at the party, in full swing, around us.

"Ohhh," Chris exaggerates. "So you *do* know her. And all this time, I thought you were just a fucking gentleman when you were actually just being territorial." Chris starts laughing. "Who is she?"

"Nobody."

The only girl I've ever given my heart to.

"Well, then, you wouldn't mind giving me her name, right?" Chris asks, innocently. "That girl had curves in all the right places. I sure would love to see her out of that uniform."

I narrow my eyes at him, feeling my blood boiling inside every inch of my body. I know he's fucking with me, but it still pisses me off.

"She doesn't have a name," I grit out.

"Hmm. No name. That's odd," Grant ponders. "Guess we'll just have to go back some night for drinks and ask her ourselves, right Chris?"

Chris smiles triumphantly. "Right, captain."

"The fuck you will," I say a little too forcefully. The both of them start laughing, which only pisses me off more. "Can we just drop it?"

The last thing I want to do is talk about Vanessa right now.

"Fine. Fine. But you should probably know Zach sprained his ankle tonight. Said something about running too much this week during practice. You wouldn't have had anything to do with that, right?" Grant's eyebrows raise.

Good. I hope he's out for the rest of the season after what he said to Vanessa.

"Nope. Not me, captain."

Grant's hand lands on my shoulder. "You're going to make a great captain one of these days." He smiles, but something to his side catches his attention, so he turns to find a tall brunette walking this way. "Baby, come here. Let me introduce you to someone."

She saunters up, wearing a tight short black dress. "Hi, guys." She gives a little wave and a slight smile.

"This is Kayleigh, my sexy as fuck girlfriend," Grant announces. She blushes, bites her bottom lip, and smacks Grant on the chest. "What? It's true." He laughs. "Anyway, you know Chris from last year, and this is Jason." His head tilts toward me as he wraps his arms around Kayleigh's waist, pulling her toward him. "He'll be taking my starting spot soon enough."

"So *you're* the fresh meat with amazing skills I keep hearing about." She smiles, looking at Grant over her shoulder. "It's all he's been talking about."

"What can I say? I'm just excited knowing the team will be in good hands when I leave." He kisses the side of her neck before looking up at me. "This may be our best year yet."

"You say that every year," she remarks. "But I hope you're right. I love when you come home after a win." She winks at him, and he smiles, looking into her eyes.

"Yup, well, that's my cue to go, boys. See you guys on Monday." Grant looks like he's ready to devour this girl in one sitting.

Chris and I nod as Grant quickly leads the way out of the house, keeping Kayleigh closely beside him.

"I think I'm going to get going anyway." I look at my phone and see it's just after midnight.

"Alright, man. I'll see you," Chris says, heading to the main room. It doesn't go unnoticed that he's heading directly toward the blonde in the tight jeans.

I'm about to unlock the door to my apartment when I turn around and take a few steps to knock on the door down the hall from mine instead.

Natalie opens it, wearing her pink flannel pajamas. She tilts her head and says, "Jason? What are you doing here? I thought you would be out celebrating your win."

"I was, but it was getting a little too crowded for me, so I thought I'd see if you were up."

"We were just watching *Stranger Things*. Come in!" She eagerly motions for me to follow her.

We?

I walk in behind her to find Nate sitting on the new oversized chair the girls purchased last week, Paul sitting on one side of the couch, and Vanessa, who appears to be sound asleep, on the other side.

I don't know why, but I don't like seeing Paul and Vanessa sharing a couch, even if they are on opposite sides.

Natalie sits beside Nate on the chair, and I plop myself between Paul and Vanessa on the couch. It's a little tight, seeing as Paul and I take up most of the couch, but as long as I'm between them, that's all that matters.

"Hey, good game tonight." Paul raises his fist, waiting for a fist bump from me, which I return with a smile. "Wish I could have been there, but basketball practice ran late tonight."

"No worries. Thanks, man."

"Yeah, Mom and Dad were so happy they made it." Natalie beams.

"But I didn't even play," I remark. I can't believe my parents would drive three hours just to watch me sit on the bench.

"That doesn't matter. Besides, you will play eventually." She shrugs her shoulders. "They had to leave right after, but they wanted to make sure you knew they were there."

"Yeah, I saw them."

"Did you see the face paint your sister made me wear? Because that is the one and only time I am ever doing that." Nate glares at Natalie.

"What? I thought you looked really cute with it on." She bites her bottom lip, holding in a laugh.

"Never again." He smiles before giving her a quick kiss. "But good game, Jason. We're all proud of you.

"Thanks, guys." I don't know what they have to be proud of since, again, I didn't get a single, fucking minute of playing time, but I sigh, letting it go. I look over to my right, at the girl sleeping soundly beside me. "Is she okay?"

"Vanessa?" Natalie asks. "Yeah, she had a long day. Classes and then a project she had to work on, and then she ended a night with a long shift at work. She said she wanted to watch the show with us but fell asleep the second she curled up. I don't think she's been sleeping well."

I look over at Natalie. "Why not?"

"I don't know." She shrugs her shoulders. "Just a feeling."

I look down at Vanessa more closely, noticing slight bags under her eyes that concern me. When we were teenagers, Vanessa stood out from all the other girls in her class. She was curvy and she was every guy's goddamn dream. But when Vanessa saw herself in a mirror, you'd think she was looking at a monster, not the most beautiful girl in the school. So many times, I witnessed her starving herself, thinking no one noticed when she threw away her lunch or only ate an apple for breakfast.

But I did.

I always notice everything about her.

Looking at her now, I'm overcome with worry that she's not taking care of herself, and I'm not about to sit by and let that happen.

"Has she been eating?" I ask Natalie quietly, not looking away from Vanessa.

"I think so. Maybe not enough, though. I know she's been busy with work and school, and she doesn't eat when she's stressed." I look at Natalie, and she bites her bottom lip before saying, "Do you think…"

Shaking my head, I say, "Like you said, she had a long day. That's probably all it is."

I know it's not, but I don't want my sister to worry about her. I'll keep an eye on Vanessa.

"Wait, guys, you have to watch this!" Paul whisper-yells to get everyone's attention.

"Haven't you seen this scene like a hundred times?" Nate asks.

"You just don't get it! Joyce and everyone else thought that Hopper had died. Now here he is, and they're finally reuniting. Don't you have a heart?" Paul asks, pinching the bridge of his nose.

"Yeah, but it's currently with this girl right here." Nate places a soft kiss on Natalie's forehead.

"That was the corniest fucking line I've ever heard." I roll my eyes.

"Shhh!" Paul emphasizes. "I'm getting goosebumps."

"Well, keep your goosebumps to yourself on that side of the couch." I inch closer to Vanessa, and her body shifts more into me, feeling so damn warm and soft. I reach for the blanket falling off her shoulder and bring it up to cover her. That same, damn, floral aroma surrounds me, making me want to press my face into the side of her exposed neck, inhaling every ounce of her natural fragrance.

"Paul, I never knew you had this side to you." Natalie observes Paul, who can't take his eyes away from the TV.

"What side?" he asks, not looking away.

"A nerdy side," I answer for her.

This gets Paul to look away from the TV. "I am not a nerd."

Nate laughs. "Says the guy who dressed up as a character from Game of Thrones last Halloween, has not one, but two, lightsabers in his room, and has watched every Marvel movie known to mankind."

"Please tell me why you have two lightsabers?" I ask, grinning.

He shoves at my shoulder. "I prefer not to answer that."

Natalie laughs. "We need to find you a girl, Paul."

"Trust me, I know." He runs a hand down his face. "I'm surrounded by them everywhere I go."

"Then what's the problem?" I ask.

"It's not what I'm looking for." He shrugs his shoulders. "Because of my name, I'm like the light moths flock to. The moths being the girls in this situation." He crosses his arms and sits back further on the couch. "But all those girls see when they look at me are dollar signs. I want someone who sees me for me and not the amount on my future NBA contract. Someone who doesn't compare me to who my—" He stops, shaking his head, frustrated. "Never mind."

It can't be easy living in someone's shadow, but that's exactly what Paul goes through every day.

I give him a sympathetic look. "You'll find someone. Maybe when you least expect it."

"Yeah, I hope so."

"What about you, Jason?" Natalie asks.

"What about me?"

"I mean..." She looks at Nate before looking back at me. "You haven't dated anyone since Grace. You're a freshman in college, playing on the football team. It shouldn't be too difficult for you to find someone, right?"

My sister's been dying to know why Grace and I broke up last year, and as much as I don't like keeping secrets from Natalie, I haven't felt like talking about it with anyone.

I scowl. "I'm too busy right now to start dating."

"Hmm." She ponders.

"What?" I ask.

"Earlier, I mentioned to Vanessa that I thought she should start dating too, and she said the same thing as you."

Looks like Vanessa and I have more in common than I thought.

Paul looks over at Natalie. "You know I'm always—"

"No," Nate cuts him off before he can finish his sentence.

Paul puts his hands up in surrender. "Fine. Was just offering." He turns his attention back to the TV.

I quickly notice Nate looking over at me before returning his gaze to the TV screen. What was that about?

"Paul, are you ... crying?" I hear Natalie ask.

I look to my left and find Paul staring at the TV screen with glossy eyes. "No, I am not crying, Natalie. I just got something in my eye."

Yeah, right.

"It's okay if you're crying, Paul. Girls like a guy who isn't afraid to show their emotions," Natalie adds.

"I'm not crying." He sniffles. "It's just..." He points at the screen where Hopper and Joyce are reuniting for the first time in a year.

"Keep it together, big guy." I pat his back, biting the inside of my cheek to hold in laughter at this softy beside me.

God, I guess he really is a teddy bear.

A few minutes later, the episode ends, and everyone stretches out.

"I'm so tired." Natalie stifles a yawn curling up in Nate's arms.

"Yeah." He looks at Paul. "You want to make the couch your bed tonight? Or you know there is a neighbor down the hall I could always see if she has a spare room?" Nate displays a mischievous grin, hinting at Sarah.

The girl, who I am pretty certain has been on Paul's mind.

"The couch is fine," Paul says flatly.

"Suit yourself." Nate lifts Natalie in his arms, her legs wrapping around him, and walks toward Natalie's room. "Night, everyone."

I look down at Vanessa, who is still out cold, and then look over at my other side at Paul, who starts grabbing blankets off the ottoman in front of us.

Oh, hell no.

There's no fucking way I'm letting these two share a couch.

"Guess I'll bring her to her room," I say.

"Do you need help?" Paul asks.

And even though I know he has no ill intentions, I still get a little defensive, not wanting his hands anywhere on her. "Nope. I'll take it from here."

He smiles as if he knows something, but he doesn't.

No one understands the relationship that Vanessa and I have.

Me included.

I slide one arm under her thighs and the other around her back, lifting her easily against my chest. She nudges her head into my shoulder and whimpers, which does something to the man downstairs.

Walking into her room, it looks exactly as I would expect her room to look. Everything has been unpacked, and it now resembles a smaller replica of her bedroom at her family's house. Her bed is covered in a floral print, her walls display pictures of her and Natalie, and an old battered-looking sewing machine takes up over half of her desk. But in true Vanessa fashion, there's a mess of different colored fabrics lying everywhere and sketchbooks taking up the other half of her desk.

Her dream was always to be a fashion designer.

And I know she will be.

I gently slide back her covers and place her on the sheets before bringing the blankets to her chest. She sighs, shifting in the bed to get comfortable.

"Sweet dreams, Vee." My knuckles brush against her cheek before I turn, walking away. But at the intoxicating sound of my name, I abruptly stop and spin around to face her.

"Jason," she whimpers.

Her eyes are completely closed. Is she ... dreaming about me?

I should leave. I need to leave. But when she says my name again, I find myself unable to look away from her.

Her head turns to the side, and she moans.

She. Fucking. Moans.

God, I wish I could wake her up by putting my head between her—

No!

I shake my head and run a frustrated hand through my hair. I need to get out of here right now. When I head toward her door, which is currently closed, I see a familiar face.

Fucking Jeremy Burns.

Not this again.

I rub my temple, smirking at the sight before me.

She may get off to your face, but it's my name she's calling out in her sleep, asshole.

I look back at Vanessa and smile, remembering our old conversation about good ole' Jeremy.

You're coming with me.

I carefully take the poster down from the back of the door and roll it up, carrying it under my arm and bringing it straight to where it belongs.

The trash.

Five

VANESSA

Terrific, I have just under ten minutes to make it to campus, or I'll be late to class and have to walk into the classroom in front of everyone.

All eyes on me? I don't think so.

That's not happening.

I open the door to the stairwell, ready to run down the five flights of stairs, when I hear the ding from the elevator at the end of the hall. I'm extremely claustrophobic and avoid the elevator at all costs, but this is an emergency. So, against my better judgment, I bolt down the hall, just in time to see the elevator doors begin to close.

"Wait!" I yell, praying the person inside will hold the door open for me.

Thankfully, a large hand grasps the door, keeping it open, but as I approach, I see who it is, and immediately regret not taking the damn stairs. Of all the people in this building, it had to be him.

"Oh," slips out of my mouth. I glare at Jason, still holding the door open, as I hesitate to cross the threshold.

"Well, are you coming in or not?" he huffs, sounding inconvenienced.

I take a few steps inside, keeping my chin held high, and lean against the corner of the small space, waiting for the doors to inevitably close.

You can do this. You just need to spend thirty seconds trapped in a small space with the man who hates you. No biggie.

Except I can already feel my chest tightening at the realization that I'm about to be encased in this metal box—with no way out.

Deep breath, Vanessa.

I watch as Jason hits the button for the ground floor and then rests against the opposite wall, looking down at his phone in his hands. The doors to the death trap slowly close, and the elevator begins to descend.

It'll all be over soon.

A loud thud echoes beneath us and I lurch forward, grabbing the metal railing beside me to steady myself, and look at the screen at the top of the door, which reads "*ERROR.*"

"What ... what just happened?" My eyes roam over the small space, searching for any way out. But there isn't one.

We're trapped.

I'm trapped.

"Looks like we're stuck," Jason casually responds, not looking at me as he puts his phone in his pocket.

"Stuck?" I panic.

We can't be stuck.

No. No. No.

I watch as Jason opens a panel next to all the buttons and picks up a phone. "Hey James, my man, it's me, Jason. Yeah, it was a good game. That's for sure." He laughs, running his fingers through his hair. "Yeah, hey, listen. I'm on the elevator right now with ... another resident, and we're stuck between the fourth and third floor."

I can't breathe.

My heart thrashes wildly in my chest, my airways are starting to feel constricted, and it feels like we are in the freaking Sahara Desert as heat rushes throughout my body. I need to take my peacoat off—right fucking now. I claw at the top button on my coat, but my hands are shaking too hard.

"Shit," I hiss.

Jason's eyes jump to my face, watching me cautiously as he talks to the concierge. "So, James, if you could get someone over here to get us out, that would be great. But I need to go now." He slams the phone down and takes one giant step, standing directly in front of me. "What's wrong?" I could swear there was concern in his voice, but that's impossible.

"I can't ... I can't breathe," I gasp, beginning to feel like a fish out of water, desperate for every last bit of air in this small coffin. "I'm v-very claustrophobic." I'm still struggling with this damn top button, my hands trembling worse with each passing second. I swear all future coats I buy will have zippers.

"Shit. I should have known that. What can I do?"

I love this coat. It's my red suit of armor, making me feel comfortable in my skin. Something that not many pieces of clothing in my closet have the capability of doing. But I need it off of me as soon as possible before I pass out, so I say, "Get this off of me."

"What?" He raises his eyebrows and tilts his head, watching me.

"Rip it. Please," I beg.

"But it's your favorite coat. Let me just unbutt—"

"Jason!" A tear slides down my cheek.

Jason's hands grasp the top of my coat, where they rip the front of my peacoat, sending all the buttons flying around us. I let my coat fall off my arms, then slide down the mirrored wall. I wrap my arms around my legs, which are snug against my chest, and I rest my face against my knees, letting the tears rain down my cheeks as I press the palms of my hands against the sides of my head, rocking back and forth.

Inhale. Exhale. Inhale. Exhale.

God, the one time I decided to take the elevator, and this happened for Jason to witness. I'm so embarrassed.

I wait for Jason to laugh or make a snide comment, but instead, he surprises me.

Jason slides down the wall, sitting beside me. His arms wrap around my waist, lifting me directly onto his lap so that my side is snug against this chest. I grip his shirt and press my face into him, not caring that I'm probably soaking the fabric with my tears. He keeps one solid arm slung over my legs, and the other finds its way around my back, where his hand starts placing soothing strokes.

"You're having a panic attack," he states.

"Make it stop," I plead.

"I will. I won't let anything happen to you, Vee. I'm here."

Did he just call me, Vee?

The gentle movement of his hand starts to calm my erratically beating heart, but I can't manage to stop trembling like a leaf against his body. He places the palm of his hand firmly against my chest, anchoring me to him. "I need you to breathe, Vee. Keep your eyes closed and take a nice slow deep breath for me. They'll be here soon to get us out of here." His voice is soft, calming my racing mind.

But why does he keep calling me Vee? A nickname he hasn't used in so long.

I take a long, slow, deep breath and nuzzle my head against Jason's broad chest—his very sculpted and defined chest. The familiarity of his hold placates my anxious body.

"That's a good girl," he says.

My pulse just sped up again but for an entirely different reason.

"I'm sorry, Jason. I didn't mean to—"

"It's ok." His large hand smooths out my hair, and then he does something—something I never would have expected.

He kisses the top of my head. "You're safe."

I tilt my head up to look at him, lips parted. My eyes find his grey ones and stay there, neither of us looking away. His hand comes up gently, cupping my cheek, and his thumb glides over my skin, wiping the tears away. My tongue slides out, wetting my lips, catching Jason's attention.

And then, slowly, his thumb moves down to my bottom lip, tracing it back and forth.

My breath comes out weak, and I shudder under his gaze.

His hand slides down, lightly wrapping around my neck, his thumb pressing on my pulse point. I close my eyes, taking pleasure in the sensation of his touch scorching my skin. With a soft caress of his fingertips, he tucks his fingers under my chin and lifts it.

"Look at me, Vee."

My eyes flutter open, staring into the most beautiful eyes I've ever seen, and I'm overtaken with a lust unlike anything I've ever experienced. His hands grip me at my waist, repositioning my body so I'm straddling him. A small moan leaves my lips when his hardened length presses against my core, causing an immediate ache between my legs.

"Jason..." I breathe.

This is too much.

This isn't enough.

His fingers rake through my hair, making me lightheaded from the gentle sensation.

I want more.

I need more.

I shift on his lap, cautiously grinding against him, not knowing if he wants this. He groans, leaning his head back, closing his eyes. His hold on my hips gets tighter, dragging me over the large bulge confined beneath his jeans.

Relief fills me, knowing he wants this as much as I do.

His eyes open, a dark desire taking over him as he grips the back of my neck, pulling me toward him. Our lips have nothing more than a thread's width between us. He deliberately brushes his lips against mine, barely touching, sending shivers down my spine. I'm so close to tasting him, to having his lips thoroughly on mine, devouring me like that moment years ago when we couldn't help ourselves.

A moment when we both had finally given in to the temptation that, for years, had continuously suffocated us.

Jason's forehead presses against mine as he wraps his arms around me. "Vanessa, I—"

We're both jolted when the elevator starts moving, Jason's grasp on me becoming firmer before we suddenly stop. The door slides open to reveal James and two firefighters standing on the other side, waiting for us.

"Sorry to interrupt, lovebirds, but I figured you'd want to get out of here," James jokes. And I suddenly realize we look as if we were *enjoying* each other's company—our bodies molded together as one. Jason's hands are still gripping me around my waist, and mine are clutching the front of his shirt for dear life. When I look at our reflection in the mirrored wall, I realize we look like how an actual couple would look—lost in each other's embrace.

One of the firefighters takes a step inside and reaches out a hand for me to take. "Come on, darling. Let's get you out of here."

I reach for him, but Jason pulls me tighter against him. "I've got her," he growls.

Jason stands, noticeably adjusting his pants, lifting me in his arms and then gently placing me beside him until my feet land firmly on the ground. He sweeps my hair out of my face and looks down at me. A look of raw tenderness shines in his eyes that now appear to be a soft blue. "Are you okay?"

"I'm..." I look around, realizing everyone is staring at me and that I'm no longer wearing my suit of armor to protect me. "I'm fine." I smooth out my hair and bend down to pick up what remains of my coat. Maybe I can somehow salvage it. "I have to go." I step off the elevator and head toward the stairs.

"Vee, wait!" Jason calls after me, but I don't stop.

Vee?

No way.

Because I have no idea what the hell just happened between us. He's been nothing but a jerk to me this past year, and now suddenly, he says things like, "*I won't let anything happen to you, Vee.*"

And then he touched me like he'd waited his whole life for a moment like that between us.

Nope.

As I enter the stairway, I do the only reasonable thing. I trudge straight up the stairs and back to my apartment instead of down and toward class.

Because, as I said, I would never walk in front of a room full of people where all eyes would be on me.

JASON
TEN YEARS AGO

I hate everyone.

Tears stream down my cheeks, and I let them, feeling sorry for myself as I hide away from the world on the swing set in my backyard. Normally, on a day like today, with the sun still shining high above the sky, I would be out playing with friends, maybe even doing a backflip in the pool.

But today sucks.

And I don't want to see anyone.

Not after what happened.

I stop swinging, planting my feet on the ground, and let out a frustrated growl. My fingers pull at my hair, and my breath comes out erratically as I think about what they said to me.

Why do people have to be so mean?

A small thud grabs my attention, and I look up to see Vanessa dropping her bike on the grass and walking toward me.

Ugh, I don't want her to see me like this.

"Go away, Vaness-ss-ss-ss-a." My usual stammer is more prominent. Maybe the crying is making it worse.

But per usual, Vanessa doesn't listen to me. "I just want to swing." She takes the empty one beside me and starts kicking her legs, getting higher with each swing.

I watch her, rubbing the back of my forearm across my face, wiping away the tears and snot. "Natalie's inside."

"I know." She keeps swinging. A slight breeze washes over us, pushing her hair away from her face.

"Then why-y-y are you out here?" I didn't shower after football practice, so I run a hand through my messy hair and kick the ground, sending dirt in the air.

"I came to meet Natalie to get some ice cream." She stops, bracing her feet on the ground, holding on tightly to the two chains, looking bewildered. "But please don't tell my mom. She thinks ice cream will make me fat, so I'm not supposed to eat it."

I've never liked Vanessa's mom. She never has anything good at her house to eat. "I won't s-s-say anything."

She tilts her head to the side, observing me. "Why are you crying?"

"I'm not!" I yell, knowing my red eyes and runny nose are giving me away. I make it a point to look anywhere but at her.

"It's okay to cry." She shrugs her shoulders. "I cry all the time."

"You do?" I ask, finally looking at her.

"Yeah. Like when my parents fight or when I hear my mom tell my dad that she wishes I was prettier." She twists in her seat, facing me. "I just go to my room to cry, and it makes me feel a lot better. Sometimes I even sneak a candy bar in my room because I'm not allowed to eat candy."

"Your mom doesn't think you're pretty?" I ask. That can't be true, Vanessa is the prettiest girl I know.

She looks up at the sky. "I don't think so." Her eyes find mine. "Why won't you just admit you were crying?"

I shake my head. "I'm a boy. I'm-m-m not suposs-ss-ss-ed to cry."

"Says who?" she asks, twirling a piece of her long chestnut hair.

"Everyone."

"Just because everyone says it doesn't mean they're right."

I take a deep breath, knowing she'll never leave until I tell her the truth. "A couple of kids at football practice were making fun of m-m-my stamm-m-m-ering today."

I've always had a stammer when I talk, but Vanessa and I have spent so much time with each other over the years that I think she barely notices it. Either that, or she's just too nice to say anything. It only gets worse when I get upset, which would explain why I'm having a hard time controlling it now.

"What did they say?" she asks quietly.

"They told me I sound like a baby." I lightly kick the ground this time. "They were m-m-mocking me."

"I don't think you sound like a baby," she tells me.

"You don't?" Is she lying?

"No. And we're friends, so I would tell you the truth."

"Thanks, Vaness-ss-ss-a." I look away, embarrassed. Sometimes it's hard for me to say her name, which makes me sad.

"Is my name hard for you to say?" she asks as if reading my mind.

I nod, remaining silent as I look down at the freshly cut grass beneath us. My feet are planted firmly on the Earth, whereas hers have at least half a foot of space between her and the ground.

"Hmm. Then why don't you give me a nickname."

"A nickname?" I ask, looking at her curiously.

"Yeah. You know, something that is easy for you to say, and it has to be something that only you will call me. It'll be like a secret only we know." I watch her eyebrows scrunch together, and she purses her lips, deep in thought.

A name comes to mind. "Vee?" I ask quietly.

She looks at me. "Vee." She smiles. "I like it."

"Okay." I scratch my head. "Can you promis-s-s-e not to tell Natalie I was crying?"

"Okay. I promise." She gets off the swing and walks toward the back door.

"Hey, Vee?" I call out, practicing using her new nickname.

She smiles at this and looks back at me. "Yes?"

"Just so you know, I think you're pretty." I start swinging again, kicking my long legs in front of me. Her cheeks have turned a light shade of pink, probably from sitting in the sun for too long.

"Thanks, Jason." She turns and runs inside to find Natalie, I assume.

And I smile, suddenly not caring about the mean things the other kids said to me earlier today. Because I just told the girl I like that I think she's pretty.

Six

JASON

"It's the man of the hour!" Chris cheers, raising his cold pint up in the air as Grant walks through the bar entrance, engulfed in applause and congratulations from the rest of the team and fans.

Grant smiles, shaking hands with people throughout before finally approaching our table. "Come on, now. That win was a team effort." He takes the free seat beside me, across from Graham, a wide receiver for the team.

"What took you so long anyway? I'm already on my third beer," Graham remarks right before chugging what's left of his drink, proving that he'll be on his fourth beer soon enough.

"Easy. You know we have to be up early for our flight home." Grant motions for the waitress, signaling for a beer. "Besides, you know I call my girl after every away game."

"God, you're whipped." Chris reaches for the plate of nachos at the center of the table, shoving a handful of chips in his mouth.

"Yeah, I am." Grant removes his jacket, placing it on the back of his chair. "And I wouldn't have it any other way." He smiles at the waitress as she hands him a pint. He brings it to his lips, gulping a few sips before placing it beside my glass of water on the table.

I glide my finger around the edge of the glass, feeling annoyed.

"Not drinking tonight?" Grant asks with furrowed brows.

"Can't. They're carding." I shrug my shoulders, trying to hide my disappointment over tonight's game. It's not that we lost, because we didn't. We walloped the other team's ass, or I should say, everyone but *I* had a piece of tonight's victory, seeing that *I* spent the entirety of the game sitting on the bench, waiting for the moment the coach would choose to put me in.

But it never came.

I know it's not Grant's fault, it's how things go when you're the new freshman on the team. Plenty of other freshmen on the team are going through the same thing as me, but it's difficult going from the starting quarterback of your high school team, seeing your name plastered in the paper every week, to being the second-string quarterback who sits on the sidelines waiting for his chance to prove his worth.

I'm no longer the fish in a small pond but instead, a guppy in the fucking ocean.

And while the rest of the team celebrated in the locker room after our win, I stood under a scalding hot shower, head hung low, relaxing my muscles as I tried to remember why I accepted a position on this team. Why didn't I take the starting quarterback position in California, where I would lead one of the country's best teams?

Simple.

Because I would never let anything bad happen to my sister again.

And being on the other side of the country from her would never be an option for me.

Grant bumps my shoulder with his own as if knowing where my head is. "Hey, your moment will come, man. You just need to do your time, like we all have. And someday, you'll tell the newest freshman the same thing." He gives me a reassuring smile.

"I know. You're right." I sigh. "I just miss the action." The fucking truth is that I miss feeling valuable—needed. Like I was worth something. I miss not feeling like a constant disappointment to myself. I steal a couple of nachos from the plate in the middle of the table, eating my misery away.

"Well, if you're looking for some action, there's a hot brunette at your three o'clock who hasn't been able to keep her eyes off you all night." Chris tilts his head toward the booth packed with what looks like a bachelorette party, where girls wear mini veils with pink sashes across their chests.

My eyes scan the booth, where they lock with the eager brunette. The only problem is, she doesn't have those familiar, big, brown, doe eyes I was unknowingly searching for. She displays a seductive smile and a small wave. I politely smile but return my attention to the guys around me.

"Not interested?" Chris asks, surprised. "You know this is now the second hot girl you've turned down."

Graham looks over at the booth and then back at me, wide-eyed. "I don't get it."

"I get it," Grant answers, finishing his beer and bringing the glass to the table. A stupid knowing grin spreads over his stupid face.

God, I wish none of them knew about Vanessa.

"Not this again." I rub a frustrated hand over my face.

"Fine." Grant puts his hands up in surrender.

Thankfully, my phone begins vibrating in my pocket. I pull it out, seeing a familiar name, relieved by the distraction. "Well, that's my cue." I get up from my chair, grabbing a few more chips, before leaving a couple of bills on the table. "I'll meet you guys back at the hotel." I make my way out of the noisy bar and into the quiet street leading to the hotel where we're all staying for the night.

I bring the phone to my ear. "Hey, Mom."

"Hey, sweetie. Your dad and I watched every minute of the game and just wanted to tell you how proud we are of our favorite son." I can practically see her beaming on the other end of the phone.

"Mom, I don't know if you watched the right game because I hate to be the one to tell you this, but your favorite son didn't play tonight. Not even for a single second." I'm positive she can detect the frustration in my tone.

"We know. But that doesn't matter. You're part of a team, and it's a big deal playing for a college football team," she says matter-of-factly.

"Yeah, I guess."

"What's wrong, Jason? You sound disappointed in yourself."

Bingo.

"I don't know. I guess I'm just trying to get used to going from being the star of my team last year, to being a nobody on my team this year." I lean against the hotel's brick exterior, not ready to go inside yet. A cool breeze caresses my skin, so I zip my jacket, tucking my free hand in my pocket.

"Jason Spencer. You listen to me right now." Her voice becomes stern but soft—in a way only a mother can pull off. "You are not a nobody. You are the most amazing son I could have ever asked for, and someday, teams will be fighting over you in the NFL draft. You've worked your life to get to where you are. Don't give up now. Do you understand me?"

"Yes, Mom." She's right, but I still roll my eyes.

"Did you just roll your eyes?"

"How the hell did you know that?" I survey the area to double-check she's not secretly here.

"I'm your mother, sweetie. I have eyes in the back of my head. Besides, I could hear it in your voice."

"I never could get away with anything from you." I laugh, remembering how much shit I used to put my mom through as a kid.

"Never." She laughs too. "Your dad already went to bed, but he wanted to make sure you knew how proud he is of you. I'm pretty sure you remind him of himself from twenty years ago."

I swallow the emotions building inside me. "How is Dad doing?"

She knows what I'm really asking without having to say it. *How is his heart?*

A year ago, I thought I lost my dad forever when he had a heart attack, and I sat helplessly in the back of the ambulance, gripping his hands the whole way to the hospital, pleading for him not to leave me.

Begging him not to die.

Please don't die, Dad. I need you.

It was the worst night of my life.

But thanks to my mom, who has placed my dad, the love of her life, on a healthy regime, he's been doing better than ever. Although, sometimes I still find myself remembering that night like it was yesterday, feeling my pulse panic because, at any moment, I could be thrown back into that nightmare again with a different outcome that would destroy my world.

"He's fine, honey." Her soft voice interrupts my memory of that dark night. "We went on a nice long walk this afternoon, and he's even agreed to cut down on his hours at work soon. Owning his own business doesn't mean he needs to be there every day, and I think he's finally starting to realize that."

"I'm glad to hear that." But there is someone else I need to ask about, and it sends my blood pressure in a tizzy every time I do because I never know what the answer will be. "And Mom?"

"Yeah?"

"How's Grandpa?"

There's silence, which only intensifies my beating heart until she finally speaks. "He's ... okay." She doesn't sound confident in her words, and I know it's because she knows how much this affects me. She doesn't want to give me false hope while also trying to be truthful. "I went to see him yesterday, and he wasn't having the best day, but the nurses called me this morning to let me know he was doing better." She lets out a lengthy breath. "He has good days and bad days. You know how it goes."

"Yeah, I do." And that's the problem. I run a frustrated hand in my hair, feeling the need to get up to my room and take a hot shower, ridding myself of all the confusion I'm feeling. "Mom, I have to go, but I'll call you guys tomorrow, okay?"

"Alright, Jason. We love you. And don't forget, we're proud of you, no matter what," her voice breaks near the end.

"Thanks, Mom. I love you guys too."

I end the call and enter the hotel, pulling the keycard out of my wallet. Stepping into the elevator, I slink against the wall, feeling the world's weight on my shoulders. I feel like a disappointment, letting everyone down, including my parents. They could tell me a thousand times they're proud of me, but how can they be proud of their son while he sits on the bench for the whole game?

Proud, my ass.

I pinch the bridge of my nose, feeling a headache forming. Glancing around, I take in the small space, experiencing déjà vu, remembering the feeling of Vanessa in my arms only a few days ago in an elevator just like this one. She was terrified, as was obvious from the big tears crawling down her cheeks and her body that couldn't stop shaking in my hold. And it absolutely killed me seeing her like that. I didn't know what to fucking do to make her feel better except hold her and promise her I wouldn't let anything happen to her.

Because I would never let anything happen to her, even while I'm feeling so fucking confused.

Because Vanessa and I ... well, I shake my head. *No.* Nothing can happen between us. Because one, I made a promise to her years ago that we would always be friends. Friends. Nothing more. Nothing less. Even if I haven't kept up my end of the bargain recently, I will always be here for her. Two, her brother will always be in her life, whether I want him to be or not, and I will never be able to forgive him for what he did to my sister. And three, and most importantly, it's the thought of my grandpa that reminds me why nothing can happen between us, because I won't be responsible for hurting her. I can't put her through what my grandma went through. I won't do it.

I reach for my wallet and unknowingly take out the bracelet that hides between the leather folds.

The same bracelet I've kept with me for the past four years.

The same bracelet that reminds me of the girl who stole my heart years ago.

The same bracelet that calms my racing heart during moments like this.

I wrap my fingers around the dainty silver chain, close my eyes, and let out a deep breath just as the doors of the elevator open.

Holding onto the bracelet tightly, feeling the charms dig into the palm of my hand, I quickly walk down the empty hallway, enter my room, and head straight toward the balcony to open the sliding door. The moment the gust of cold air hits my skin, I feel my heartbeat subside and my mind relax. I step out, looking up at the perfectly clear night sky with bright stars shining and the moon looking at peace.

It's nights like these when I wonder if she still looks at the moon like it's her whole world.

SIX YEARS AGO

"What are you doing, Vee?"

Vanessa sits up, appearing startled, until she realizes it's just me. "Jason, you scared me." She lies back down on the red and black plaid blanket, separating herself from the grass.

"As I said, what are you doing?" I stroll across my backyard until I reach the edge of her blanket, looking directly down at her. It's September, but it's unseasonably warm for this time of year, so the only thing she is wearing is a red satin pajama short sleeve top and shorts with no shoes, looking so content where she is. Her dark chestnut strands of hair splayed around her head in waves, and the way the moon is casting a glow on her, makes her look like she is wearing a halo around her head.

She waves her hand at me, signaling for me to move. "You're blocking my view."

"View of what? And where's Natalie?" I look around, wondering if I missed something. Is there a firework show scheduled for tonight?

"Of the full moon," she replies, continuing to wave her hand at me, insinuating I'm in her way. "And Natalie is sleeping. I couldn't sleep, so I came out here."

My eyes wander to the night sky above us, where for the first time, I realize there is a pretty cool-looking full moon above us. I sit on the other side of the blanket and lie beside her, staring at the sky.

"What are you doing?" Her face turns toward me, watching me curiously.

"The same thing as you."

She faces the sky, both of us remaining in comfortable silence for a few minutes until she speaks.

"It's called a harvest moon. It only happens around the time of the autumnal equinox," she states. "Isn't it amazing?"

I look over at her. "How do you know that?"

"I love learning about the stars and the moon. Looking up at them reminds me of how small we are in the grand scheme of things. It helps me put things into perspective." She's silent before saying, "The stars are the most beautiful thing in the world. They make me happy."

I want to tell her she's wrong. That the most beautiful thing in the world is her, but I keep my mouth shut. Blame it on being an awkward teenage boy, but there's no way I'm telling her that.

Silence surrounds us, so I blurt the first thing that comes to mind. "Is red your favorite color?"

She smiles, still looking up at the stars. "What gave it away?"

"Oh, I don't know. Maybe because that's the color I see you wear all the time."

She laughs quietly, her pretty smile widening. "What's your favorite color?"

Without hesitation, I say, "Brown."

"Brown? That's such an ugly color," she teases.

"No, it's not."

She stares at me with wide, curious eyes. "Name one pretty thing that's brown."

"Your eyes." The words leap from my mouth faster than I can stop them, and I quickly turn my head toward the sky, avoiding her reaction, heat spreading over my chest in embarrassment. The silence between us has turned uncomfortable, and it's my fault. I shouldn't have said anything.

God, why am I so stupid?

"I like the color of your eyes, too," she whispers.

"Yeah?" I ask, relief filling me at her words.

"Yeah. Sometimes they're blue, and other times they look grey. I swear it all depends on your mood." She giggles, erasing any awkwardness between us.

"My mood, huh?"

"Mhm. Like the other day, after your football game, when we all went out for pizza, your eyes were bright blue, and it's because you were happy you won your game."

I was happy because she was there, sitting right across from me.

"You're very observant." My shoulder bumps into her playfully.

"I've known you almost my whole life." She shrugs like it's no big deal, but I notice a slight blush spreading over her cheeks.

"Does that make me your best friend?" I tease because I know the answer is obviously Natalie.

"No." She laughs. "Natalie is my best friend. You know that."

"So then, what are we?"

"We?" She thinks about this, her head turning to face me, peering at me under her dark lashes, remaining silent. Her lips part, looking like she has something to say, but she doesn't know if she should.

But I want to know.

I need to know.

The distant hooting sound from an owl momentarily distracts her as she turns her head away from me, looking off at the woods where the noise came from. Instead of looking back at me, she faces the night sky and closes her eyes. I watch as she sucks in a deep breath, trying to calm her mind from the thoughts I wish I could hear.

Maybe I'm better off not knowing the answer to this question.

I sit up, wiping invisible dirt from my pants, feeling too nervous to look at her. "We should probably go back inside. It's getting really late."

"Okay." Vanessa sits up, and after I stand, I reach out a hand for her to take, helping her up. Our fingers linger together for only a moment before she backs away, smoothing out her pajamas, and grabs the blanket from the ground, folding it against her chest. We both make our way silently into the house and up the stairs. I whisper, *"Goodnight"* as she soundlessly walks back into Natalie's room, and as I walk down the hallway, I'm left wondering if the word *friend* is the right word to describe how I feel about Vanessa.

Seven

VANESSA

The sun is just beginning to rise over Boston, casting an aesthetically pleasing, amber glow over the city. Birds are waking up, evident from the high-pitched chirping coming from the large trees lined up along the path that I find myself venturing. At this time of day, most people are sound asleep in their beds, snuggled under their blankets, but not me. Because I know it's the perfect time to run on the school track seeing that no person in their right mind would be here this early.

Clearly, I'm not in my right mind. But I'm also not one for an audience, especially not while working out.

I stretch my legs out against the bleachers, feeling the burn in my calves. I'm not really in the mood to run. Actually, I'm never in the mood to run, but after Natalie and I celebrated Girl's Night a little too hard last night with Mexican food and margaritas, I knew I would need to burn off those extra calories I consumed without a second thought.

One minute you're ordering a salad with your drink, and the next thing you know, you're three baskets deep into tortilla chips and guacamole. Margaritas can do that to a girl.

Can't say I entirely regret my tortilla chip indulging—we did have fun. Natalie and I even ended up on the little karaoke stage, giving everyone a once-in-a-lifetime show. I only wish I wasn't about to have to work my ass off because of the overindulging.

What's the saying? Do the crime, pay the time. That's exactly how I feel right now.

Twisting my body, I turn my head over my shoulder and look down at my ass. "It's because of you that we're here right now." I get into position on the track, turn the volume of my music on my phone to as high as it will go, and start running, knowing every, excruciating, hungover mile I'm about to conquer will be worth it.

Or at least I hope it will be.

After running straight for two hours, my legs begin to feel like jelly, so I sit on the grass surrounding the track. Well, more like I stumble down onto the grass, but either way, my ass is planted firmly on the grass. My whole body feels shaky, so I close my eyes and lay back, waiting for this uneasy feeling to subside. Maybe I should have eaten something this morning before I decided to run—too late now.

"How's the view from down there?"

Oh, God. *It's him.*

My eyes shoot open to find Jason standing beside me, staring down at me with his damn eyes that don't know if they want to be blue or grey today. I haven't seen him since our encounter in the elevator a couple of weeks ago, purposely avoiding him. Maybe even hiding behind a fake tree in the lobby when I had nowhere else to go.

But how could I face him after that moment?

A moment I secretly never wanted to end.

A moment I had only ever dreamed about.

Because being with him like that, wrapped in his arms, his eyes lit up with lust, felt like everything I could have imagined.

It was better than any dream I've ever had with him.

Because it was real.

I turn my head, noticing the Linrey football team heading toward the field, not too far from here. "It's fine. Just taking a little break," I respond.

"What are you doing here so early, anyway?" he asks, his eyes grazing over me, probably disgusted by how sweaty and red I must appear.

"I could ask you the same question." I pull down on my T-shirt, recalling I'm wearing spandex shorts that barely cover my ass. But I only wore them, knowing no normal person was supposed to be here at this time.

I never said I was normal.

And I guess I forgot Jason isn't normal either.

"Well, I have this thing called football practice. Otherwise, I'd still be in bed. But you didn't answer my question." He crosses his burly arms in front of his chest, raising an eyebrow as he waits for my answer.

Swiping my forearm across my forehead, I try to rid myself of some of the sweat making its way down my face. "Not that it's any of your business, but I was just getting a few miles in before anyone got here. But now that *you're here*, I guess I'll go. Wouldn't want to get in your way." I try to stand, but my legs wobble, sending me smack into Jason's solid chest. Jesus, what is he made of, titanium or something? His arms grip my shoulders, holding me firmly upright.

"How many miles did you run?" His eyebrows draw together.

"Umm..." I hold out my wrist, looking at my digital watch that had recorded my mileage, and see twelve miles displayed on the screen. Holy shit. I've never run that far before. "Twelve miles." I look back up at him to find him appearing pissed off.

What did I do wrong now?

"And what did you eat this morning? You know, before running almost half a marathon," he scolds.

"Eat?"

"Jesus, Vanessa. What were you thinking? Sit down." He firmly pushes my body to the ground, and my legs instantly feel better. Reaching into his black bag hanging on his shoulder, he pulls out a sports drink and a protein bar. "You're not leaving until you drink and eat this."

He holds out the items for me to take, and I'm tempted to be a pain in the ass and refuse, but I would love for this shaking feeling to subside, so I begrudgingly take them.

I drink half the bottle within seconds and then take a big bite of the protein bar. Without thinking, I turn the bar over, looking at the nutrition label. "Oh my God. There are five hundred calories in this little bar!"

"Vanessa, you just burned your daily intake of calories and then some. You need to eat. And if you don't finish that bar, I'll shove it right in your sassy mouth." He glares down at me, watching me as I take another bite, following his order. "That's a good girl."

I instinctively clench my thighs together, a low pulse purring at the dead center of my core from his words.

Down girl!

I narrow my eyes at him. Why the hell does him calling me a *"good girl"* have this effect on me?

I must still have tequila in my bloodstream. That's the only plausible explanation.

He deliberately smirks at me as if knowing his words affect me, so I look away, feeling heat crawling up my neck.

After finishing the whole bar and the drink, I stand up feeling the tiniest bit better. "I need to go." I'll probably soak in a tub for a bit, not thinking about Jason. Definitely not thinking about him. And then, I should reach out to Brady to see if he can meet to find a fabric for our projects.

"I'm walking you back to the building." Jason's deep voice interrupts my thoughts.

"Umm ... what?"

"I said I'm walking you back to the building." He zips up his sports bag and positions it over his shoulder, ready to leave.

"The building is only five minutes down the road, and you have practice. Besides, I don't need a babysitter." I cross my arms over my chest, inadvertently lifting my boobs.

Jason's eyes immediately notice, smoldering before he looks up at the sky, looking anywhere but at me. He takes a deep breath. "No, but if you pass out on the walk back, Natalie will be pissed at me for not walking you home. So, let's go." He doesn't even wait for me. He just turns and starts walking toward our apartment building.

Of course. It's not that he wants to walk me back and make sure I'm okay. It's that he's more concerned Natalie will be upset with him if something happens to me. *Fuck this.*

I storm off, shoving past Jason on wobbly legs, and march toward the apartment building. Jason's long, lean legs easily keep up with me. For every two steps I take, Jason only needs one to walk in unison with me.

It's infuriating.

We continue to walk in silence for a few minutes, but as we approach the building, all I can hear in my head is Jason's angry voice, yelling, making me feel worthless. His words to Nate are playing on an endless loop like a broken record.

I. Hate. Her.

Every time I remember Jason saying those words, it feels like a healed wound being reopened. It's like I'm being stabbed in the chest, over and over again, losing the ability to breathe. And I can't take it anymore.

I abruptly stop walking, which prompts Jason to do the same. He looks at me with furrowed brows, hands on his hips.

"You know what, Jason? Just leave me alone!" My hands are balled up in fists by my sides as every emotion I've tried to keep concealed claws its way out of me.

"What's your problem?" he retorts.

"You! You are my problem!" I feel my chest rising rapidly up and down as the question I've been tightly holding inside tumbles out of my mouth, breaking free for the first time in months. "Why do you hate me?"

"Hate you?" he asks, surprise evident in his voice.

"Yes!" I shout, knowing he does. I heard him that night with my own damn ears.

He steps into my space, taking all the air from my lungs. "I don't hate you. I could never hate you. Even when I've tried, I can't fucking do it!" he seethes, staring down at me.

I shake my head. "Funny, because '*I hate her*' were your exact words to Nate when discussing me." Jason's mouth gapes open, realization dawning on him that I heard everything he said to Nate, but I stop him from speaking, putting a hand up in his face. "Don't. Don't say anything. I heard every word you said to Nate the night of your graduation party, and I'll never be able to forget it." My throat constricts, and I swallow hard. "I've spent the past year walking on eggshells around you, and I have no fucking idea why. But I do know that I don't deserve to feel this way. I don't deserve to feel like a horrible person for something I never did!"

I narrow my eyes at him, not backing down. "Don't you think I feel guilty for what happened that night? For what happened to my best friend because I was passed out in my room? I wasn't there for her, and maybe—" Maybe that night would have never happened if I had just been there for her. But who am I kidding? It would have happened sooner or later. Brian is an asshole who will always be related to me by blood, which is why Jason will always hate me, no matter what I do.

"I hope you can live with the guilt."

I look right into Jason's eyes, which are no longer blue but more of the color of a cloud right before lightning strikes. My throat feels tight as I fight the slaughter of tears that want to escape, making me look weak in front of him.

"We used to be ... friends." I can no longer hold back the tears that roll down my cheeks at the word *friends*. This guy used to be my knight in shining armor, and now I'm just so fucking hurt and confused. "We used to be there for each other. I told you things that I ... I never even told Natalie." I wipe the tears before pushing loose strands of hair away from my face. "You promised me we would always be friends, but then you ... you ..." You left me. You made me feel worthless, just like so many others in my life have. But you were supposed to be different from everyone else. I look down at the ground, avoiding his glare. "Just go back to pretending like I don't exist, Jason. You're really good at that."

Turning away from him, I walk straight toward the building, but my feet come to a screeching halt. There is one last thing I forgot to mention, so I turn right back around, storming toward Jason until I'm only an inch away from his body. I look right up into his confused eyes and slam my index finger into his sculpted chest. "And *you* owe me a new Jeremy Burns poster, asshole."

As I say these words out loud, I realize that now may not have been the best time to mention this, but I also know how much it pisses him off that I keep a poster of the Bengals quarterback in my room, so I figured a little salt rubbed in the wound would make me feel better.

And from his irritated expression, which I witnessed right before turning and walking straight to my building, I do feel much better.

My fingers glide across an endless assortment of fabrics lining the walls at the fabric store, *Threads N' More*, near campus.

"What do you think of this one?" Brady holds up a ghastly, yellow, floral pattern that makes my eyes go cross.

"I'm trying to win the competition, not go down in history as the girl who had no taste," I remark.

"Oh, thank God. It was a test, and you passed." He laughs, throwing the fabric back in a large bin. "By the way, where is your adorable red coat? I don't recognize you without it."

"Oh, it umm ... I lost it. I must have left it somewhere. I'm sure it'll turn up eventually." *RIP* to my favorite coat. "What if my sketches aren't good enough for Professor Fabuleuse?" I ask. "Maybe it's pointless to be looking for a fabric now when I don't even know if I'll be entered into the final round of the competition."

"Oh, stop that negative talk right now." Brady goes headfirst into a deep bin, sorting through a selection of marked-down fabrics. His voice is muffled by the materials when he says, "Besides, I saw your sketches, and you have absolutely nothing to worry about. You're very talented." He pops out of the bin with an emerald-green satin cloth in his hand. "Got it!"

"Ugh, this is so frustrating. I need to pick something that will make my designs stand out in a good way, and nothing is wowing me." We've been here for an hour, and I feel defeated, which only adds to my sour mood.

"I don't think it's the fabric that's bothering you, babe." Brady furrows his brows. "You seem stressed."

"I am," I say flatly.

"Everything going okay at the bar?" he asks.

"Oh, yeah. Everything is fine there. Rob has been great, the shifts go by quickly, and the tips have been very generous." And it was true, thanks to the tips I've been saving, I should hopefully be able to afford a decent fabric today and maybe even a new sewing machine by Christmas.

"Then spill."

I roll my eyes. "There's nothing to spill. Don't you need to pick a fabric too?"

"Oh, I do. But this is more important." His eyes narrow at me with his hand on his hip.

I let out a deep humph. "I don't know. Well, I guess there's this guy—"

"Aha! I knew it had to do with a guy!"

"Okay, well, do you want to hear it or not?"

He pretends to zipper his lips. "I'll be quiet. Please continue."

I look around the place and notice more people walking around. "Let's go talk about this over coffee."

"Oh, this is going to be good." Brady smiles, throwing the fabric back in the bin and then looping his arm through mine, leading us toward the exit. But out of the corner of my eye, I see the fabric I have been searching for my entire life.

"Wait!" I separate myself from Brady and run over to the wall that displays the beautiful delicate black floral silk fabric. It looks like it will cost me all the money I have been saving. "This is it. This is the fabric." I pick it up, running my fingers over every detail, feeling my pulse racing excitedly.

"Well, what are you waiting for? Let's go ring this bad boy up!" Brady doesn't hesitate as he takes the fabric in one hand and my hand in the other, pulling me to the register to check out. It's not enough fabric for all three pieces I need to create, but the cashier puts in an order for me and assures me it will be here in time for me to use.

Thirty minutes later, we find ourselves sitting at a little table outside a local coffee shop, where I've just told Brady everything. And I mean *everything*, which is probably why his hands, holding his coffee cup, freeze midway to his gaping mouth.

"Are you going to say anything?" I ask.

He shakes his head as if coming back to reality. "And I thought my life was tough." He puts his mug of coffee down and runs a hand through his hair. "So, let me just make sure I didn't miss anything. Your brother is in jail for sexually assaulting your best friend, who had previously pushed you away because she didn't want you to know what happened, but now you two are closer than ever, and you even transferred schools to be with her. You got the job at the bar because, even though you come from a family with money, your parents won't help you pay for your apartment or school because they feel you chose the wrong side. Your mom, in general, is a sore topic. And your best friend's brother has the hots for you."

I choke on my coffee, having to smack my chest to get my airways cleared. "Everything was right except that last part. Jason does not have the hots for me. Didn't you hear what I said?"

"Oh, you poor naïve girl." Brady tsks and then finally takes a sip of his drink. "That boy wants you ... and bad."

"He does *not* want me. He hates me. I heard those words come straight from his mouth." I look down into my coffee, feeling the sting of those words passing through me.

Brady shrugs. "Ever heard the saying, *'there's a thin line between love and hate?'* That's you two."

Love? No way.

"Okay, now you're being ridiculous because Jason does not love me. He can barely stand being in the same room as me for more than thirty seconds."

"Do you want my advice?" he asks.

Do I?

"Maybe," I offer.

"When that boy comes crawling to you asking for forgiveness, give it."

"And why should I?"

"Because the way you talked about him, telling me everything that's happened these past few weeks, was as if he was your whole world, and you didn't even realize it." He gives a know-it-all-smile. "Every time you said his name, your eyes lit up, and the corners of your lips curved into a smile. So face it, you want him just as much as he wants you. The two of you are just too stubborn to give in to your feelings." He places his now empty cup of coffee on the table. "You two just need to fuck and get it out of your system."

"Brady!" I look around, making sure no one heard him.

"What? That's how me and my boyfriend met. I thought it would just be a one-time thing, and now look at us. Two years and still going strong, baby."

"Yeah, well, not all of us get the happily ever after like you." I roll my eyes, taking a sip of my coffee.

"No, but you can if you let that wall down. And the same goes for him. You both need to reevaluate your situation. To me, it sounds like the two of you always had a special bond. Maybe even stronger than the bond you share with Natalie, but in a different way. Am I right?" His brows raise, waiting for my response.

I purse my lips. God, he's spot on. "I guess."

"And it also sounds like the two of you always had feelings for each other but were too scared to cross that line, worried how it would end. But why do you need to worry about an ending? Why can't you just live for today, together?"

I sigh. "Because, like I said, he hates me."

He shakes his head. "He doesn't hate you, he's confused. He took his sister's side when there really shouldn't have been a side to take between the two of you." He looks at me with sympathy in his eyes. "I know we've only recently become friends, but I can say with certainty that you're not your brother. You are your own amazing self. You're Vanessa Gordon. And Jason will realize that soon enough."

My eyes water. "Are you sure you're not supposed to be a psych major? You seem pretty spot on for everything."

"Nah, I could never pull off a blazer. My shoulders are too wide."

We both laugh, and it feels so good. It feels freeing to finally have someone to talk to about this with. Getting things off my chest that have been weighing me down for months. I just hope I can trust Brady to keep what I've told him to himself, but for whatever reason, I know I can.

"Hey." He reaches across the table and squeezes my hand. "You can trust me. I'm not going to run off to the tabloids with your story. I may be a sucker for gossip, but I know when to keep my mouth shut."

I smile. "I'm really glad we met, Brady."

"Me too, Vanessa."

I look down at my phone and see the time. "Well, I need to get home to bake some cookies for … a friend's birthday, but I'll see you in class on Monday." Getting up from my seat, a breeze whips by me, and I wrap my arms around myself, wishing I had my red peacoat wrapped around me instead.

"Yes, you will! Save a cookie for me, please!" Brady gets up and wraps his arms around me before we part, walking in opposite directions.

The football field comes into view as I walk toward my building, and I can't help but look over. Could Jason possibly *want* me like Brady said?

It's hard for me to believe.

We grew up together as just friends. Always just friends.

And maybe that was my fault. I mean, I was the one who, years ago, made him promise we'd always be friends. Even when I said it, I regretted asking him that.

But I was always too scared to find out what would happen if we crossed that line together.

As kids, we played tag on the school playground, chased each other around the Spencer's yard with water guns, and even TP'd the mean neighbor's house on Halloween.

But as we got older, something started to change between us. That fine line of just being friends started disintegrating with every day that passed us.

And when we spent days lounging around his family's pool, I couldn't help but notice the way his body had practically bulked up overnight. Every defined muscle rippled as he swam back and forth, making me feel like a kid in the candy store as I watched him leap out of the pool with water flowing down his chiseled chest.

Once or twice I wondered what it would be like to be in his embrace. To be dominated by him in a way no man has ever made me feel. I was curious.

No, screw that, I was horny. More specifically, I was horny for Jason.

And all this time, I thought the feelings were one-sided, but maybe I was wrong. Maybe he started seeing me as more than just a friend, but I was too self-conscious to think someone like him would ever want someone like me. Especially in a physical way, which is why I pursued other guys in school. *Assholes*. Ones I knew were the literal definition of being a walking red flag but would give me the attention I craved and the feeling of self-worth, even if only for five minutes.

But with Jason and I, we shared things that I never even told Natalie about. They were secrets between us—one of the biggest being our first kiss. Yes, you heard that right.

Our. First. Kiss.

I thought he just wanted to get his first kiss out of the way with someone he knew, but maybe there was more to it.

He was always there for me.

Until he wasn't.

He promised me we would always be friends.

Until we weren't.

Because of my brother.

And he would never be able to look at me again without thinking about my damn brother.

I know the thought of my brother brings him to the edge. I see how his body tenses around me, alerting me to his thoughts, which kills me.

But maybe I could make him see past that. Make him see me for me. To show him I am not my brother.

I am Vanessa fucking Gordon.

But who am I kidding? Because even if there are feelings for each other now, it's not like we can act on them.

Because of Natalie, aka my best friend.

My roommate. The sister I never had. The most important person in my life.

And Jason's actual sister.

If I ever did anything with Jason, I would feel like I was betraying her. Guilt would consume me. So every time a thought of Jason popped into my head over the years, wondering if we could be more than friends, I always brushed it off, reminding myself that we couldn't be because I couldn't lose Natalie. Not again.

A whistle blows across the field, releasing me from my thoughts as the players run off the field to the side for a water break.

And as I continue walking to my apartment, I can't help but wonder if maybe Jason is just as confused as I am right now.

Eight

JASON

"Good practice, kid." Coach Bill slaps me vigorously on the shoulder.

Yeah, that's probably because I'm fucking pissed off.

"Why don't you meet me in my office in five minutes?" he asks.

"Yes, sir." What could he possibly want to talk about?

I quickly jump in the shower, relishing the feeling of the cold water on my sore muscles. I gave it my all on the field today, and my little quarrel with Vanessa earlier lit a fire under my ass that might have pushed me to play the hardest I've ever played in my life. I would thank her if I weren't so pissed at her.

Just go back to pretending like I don't exist, Jason. You're really good at that.

What gave her the right to be mad at me?

I don't know, maybe how you've treated her the past year? Ignoring her. Giving her the cold shoulder. Being hot and cold with her because you're so fucking confused.

I slam my hands on the wall, taking a deep breath. I just need to talk to Coach, and then I'm out of here to find Vanessa. Shutting off the water, I wrap a towel around my waist and mentally prepare myself for what's to come.

Five minutes later, I poke my head into the coach's office.

"You wanted to see me, Coach?"

"Yeah, take a seat." He motions at one of the chairs in front of his desk, and as I step inside, I notice Grant sitting on the couch against the wall.

What the hell is going on?

Taking a seat, I look at Grant for any clue, but he gives me nothing as he stares ahead at the coach.

"We wanted to talk to you about next week's game." He places his hands behind his head, looking between me and Grant. "We want you to start."

I raise my brows. "What?" Did I hear him right?

Coach Bill smiles. "You heard me. We want you to start."

"But I'm just a freshman. A rookie." I look over at Grant. "He's the guy you want to start."

Grant relaxes on the couch, laughing. "I've been leading this team for the past few years. It's time to switch things up—surprise the opposing team."

"And you're okay with this?" I ask him.

"It was my idea." He shrugs, taking me by surprise.

I narrow my eyes at him suspiciously and then look at Coach Bill. "Is there a catch?"

He laughs. "No catch. Just promise us you'll play like you did on the field today, and we won't have any issues."

I'm stunned. This is the moment I have been waiting for. So why don't I feel ... excited?

"Thanks, Coach." I look between him and Grant. "I won't let you guys down."

"I know you won't. Now get out of here before I change my mind." Bill smirks. "Congratulations."

I get up and walk out of the office, feeling surreal. This is everything I've wanted. It's what I've worked my whole life for. So, why isn't it sinking in? And then I remember why.

Vanessa.

Clenching my jaw, I march straight out of the locker room and to my truck, ready to give Vanessa a piece of my mind.

I don't bother knocking. I swing open the door to her apartment, barging in to find Natalie alone in the kitchen.

"Jeez, Jason, you scared me!" She puts her hand up to her chest.

"Where's Vanessa?" And why the fuck does it smell like Betty Crocker's kitchen in here? Natalie can't cook to save her life.

"She just left. She was here making cookies for a friend and then needed to ship them. Why?" She watches me cautiously as I pace back and forth in front of the sofa. "Jason, what's wrong?"

"Why are you friends with her?" I grind out, not feeling in control of my emotions. I feel so overwhelmed right now.

"What? Friends with who?"

"Vanessa!" I shout.

"I don't understand." She shakes her head. "She's my best friend. We're basically sisters, so what—"

"But she's not your sister! She's *his* sister! She's Brian's fucking sister!" I roar.

The silence that follows is insufferable. I don't fight with Natalie. This isn't me. She's my sister—the reason why I came to this school in the first place. We haven't argued since we were kids, and that was only because I accidentally threw a football into her birthday cake.

But right now, I feel like a complete asshole, letting out my frustration on her.

Natalie stares at me, taking in my words. "Oh, Jason." She walks over to me and softly places her hand on my forearm. "She's not Brian."

I collapse on the couch, elbows on my knees, holding my head in my hands, trying to breathe deeply to get control over myself. "He tried to rape you, Nat. And every time I look at her, I think of him and what he tried to do to you. It makes my blood boil to the point that all I see is red."

"Yes, he is her brother, but she is not him, and you are getting so blinded by rage that you are forgetting who she really is." She sits on the couch next to me, sighing. "Vanessa basically lost her only sibling. She has a mother who insults everything about her and a father who is too busy having an affair to pay any attention to his only daughter." She pauses. "We are pretty much the only family she has. And the two of you used to be really good friends. In fact, sometimes I would even find myself getting jealous of your friendship." She leans into the couch. "But this past year, you deserted her like I did the year before. She needed the both of us, and we both abandoned her."

Her words slap me violently across my face.

I abandoned her.

I abandoned my Vee.

What have I done?

Closing my eyes, I let out a deep breath I'd been holding in for far too long. My shoulders droop as I rest against the back of the couch, staring at the ceiling.

All this time, she thought I actually hated her.

I could never hate her when I've only ever loved her.

But I remember clearly when those words jumped off my tongue before I could stop them. It was a moment when I tried to convince myself that I didn't love the girl whose brother attacked my sister. My heart clenches with guilt, knowing she heard me tell the biggest lie of my life.

"I. Hate. Her." I spit the words out with vehemence, trying to convince myself I do. My hand wraps forcefully around my bedroom doorknob, needing to escape from this fight. Because the second those words left my mouth, it felt like all the oxygen had left my body. And I can't fucking breathe.

Nate's hand lands hard on my shoulder, gripping me in place. "No, you don't, Jason. And no matter how hard you try to convince yourself that you do, it won't work. Because you love her."

My knuckles turn white the harder I clutch the doorknob. My eyes burn as I pinch them shut, trying to erase his words.

"I don't." I shake my head adamantly. "I can't," I choke out, pleading with myself not to love her, but knowing my heart has only ever beat for her.

"Listen, I know you're my brother and just want to keep me safe, and I appreciate that, but Vanessa is my best friend, and she always will be. I'm not pushing her away again. It nearly destroyed me the first time." She pushes her hair back behind her ear. "Vanessa and I were able to mend our friendship and put that year behind us. Do you think you can do the same? Can you forget who her brother is? Because I bet that she misses having you in her life."

I turn my head toward her and see her eyes glossing over. "I fucked up." I run a hand over my face, feeling like shit which is what I deserve. "I owe her an epic apology." I place my hand on her knee. "And I'm sorry for dumping all of that on you. That wasn't okay."

She pats my shoulder and smiles. "I'll always put you in your place, Jason. That's what big sisters are for."

"Woah. Hang on. We all know I'm your *big* brother. Even if you're technically ten months older, I will always be physically bigger than you, making me the bigger sibling." I lightly shove her with my shoulder, making her laugh.

"You know, I'm really glad we ended up at the same school. I would have missed you if you went somewhere else." Her head rests on my shoulder.

A little ping zaps through my chest, and for the first time, I don't regret my decision to come to Linrey University. Hearing my sister tell me she would have missed me if I went elsewhere has wiped all previous doubts away, solidifying me being here beside her.

"Me too." I wrap my arm around the back of her, knowing at this moment I made the right choice.

"I'm sorry you never heard back from California. I know that was your dream school. But it was their loss and my gain." She looks at me with the brightest smile.

I've never kept a secret from Natalie, but this is one I'm taking to the grave.

"Hey, everything worked out the way it was supposed to." I rub the top of her head, messing up her hair like I did when we were kids.

She pulls away, laughing. "Okay. Never mind. I take back what I said."

"Nope. You can't take it back. I've got those words stored right up here for safekeeping." I point to my head, smiling.

She smooths out her hair. "So, how will you apologize to Vanessa?" she asks.

I scrape my palm over my stubble. "I'm not sure."

How the hell do I apologize for abandoning her? For letting her feel alone when I've always been right here.

Looking around their apartment for inspiration, I stop when I see the coat rack next to their front door.

That's it!

I jump up from the couch, quickly approaching the door.

"Wait, where are you going? I was just making some lunch if—"

"There's something I need to do," I blurt out, putting my hand on the doorknob.

"Okay," Natalie says. "But tomorrow night, Nathan, Paul, Vanessa, Sarah, and I are going to that new bar that opened down the street, *The Thirsty One*, if you want to come with us. It might be a good chance for you and Vanessa to become reacquainted."

"Actually, yeah. I think I'll go with you guys." I smile at her before saying, "I'll see you then."

I quickly make my way down to the lobby, a man on a mission, knowing I'll do whatever I need to do to make things right between me and Vanessa.

Because I will do anything for her.

I always have and always will.

Knocking on the apartment door, with the large white box in my hand, I feel ... Jesus, I think I'm nervous.

Definitely not something I'm used to feeling.

I know Natalie is out tonight having dinner with Nate, but it's not Natalie I'm here for.

It's Vanessa.

She opens the door with a smile, probably assuming it's Natalie, but the second she sees me, that beautiful smile fades.

"Hey, can I talk to you?" I ask. My gaze inadvertently travels down her body. She's wearing a baggy T-shirt and the tiniest pair of cotton shorts I've ever seen, and fuck me, she's not wearing a bra. God, this girl's body is made for fantasies.

But now is not the time for imagining her beneath me.

She pulls down on the hem of her T-shirt, appearing self-conscious in front of me, which I don't like. "Umm, sure." She opens the door wider, letting me in. "I'll be right back." She walks away, and fuck it, I can't help but stare at the perfectly round ass until she disappears in her bedroom. When she comes out a few minutes later, she's wearing a pair of grey sweatpants and a matching hoodie.

Message received.

"So, what did you want to talk about?" She motions for me to sit on the sofa with her.

"Well, first, I have something for you." I hand her the white box, watching her eyes widen.

She takes the box from me but handles it like it's about to explode on her lap. "What is it?"

I smirk. "Guess you need to open it to find out."

A tiny wary smile forms on her face. She lifts the cover off the box and digs through the layers of tissue paper before she sees the familiar red fabric, causing her mouth to hang open.

"It's not the exact same one you had before. But I had a picture on my phone of you, me, and Natalie when we were standing in front of a haunted house a few years ago, and you were wearing your old one, so I showed the sales lady, and we were able to find this one," I say.

She picks up the red peacoat as if it is the most breakable thing on this planet. Then she turns over the tag and sees the designer's name.

"Jason." She looks at me wide-eyed before looking right back at the tag in her hand. "This is Dior."

"Yeah, I'm not going to lie and pretend I know who that is, but the woman assured me you would. You know, since you always dress so nice and are into fashion." I shrug, hoping this Dior person is enough to win her over.

Her thumb circles one of the large black buttons, but suddenly she puts the coat back in the box, handing it back to me. "I can't accept this. I don't even want to know how much you spent on this, but whatever it was, it was too much."

I push the box back toward her. "Listen, Vanessa. I was a real asshole to you this past year. Giving you the cold shoulder, making you feel uncomfortable in your home." I look around at her apartment and then back at her. "I've been so confused after what happened to Natalie. I couldn't understand how she so easily forgave you, but now I know there was nothing for her to forgive because you didn't do anything wrong. And everything I said to Nate that night at my graduation party, well, I would do anything to take those words back."

I look down at the box. "I know that red peacoat was your favorite. You wore it any chance you had. So, please accept this as an apology, at least, until I can really think of a way to make things up to you." My eyes finally move up to hers, and I see them misting over. "I've never hated you. And I feel horrible that you heard me, in a complete moment of weakness, lie and say that I did."

Her lips scrunch to the side. Tears look ready to fall from her beautiful eyes any second. "I've really missed you, jerk."

"Come here." I open my arms wide for her, and she jumps in them willingly. "I'm so sorry, Vee."

"I know you are," she says into my shirt. "It's just a really shitty situation we were all thrown into, and I'm so sorry about what happened to Natalie. I truly am. I wish I—"

"Hey, there's nothing for you to be sorry about." I wipe the tears sliding down her cheek. "You are the best thing that ever happened to Natalie. Besides me, of course," I joke, which makes her grin, and we sit comfortably in silence for a moment. "So, does this mean we're back to being friends again?"

She tilts her head up to look at me. "Yeah. Looks like you're stuck with me." She pulls away from me, and I feel this weird ache inside me the minute her body is no longer in my arms. "You know, you could have just gotten me a new Jeremy Burns poster, and we would have been even. Would have saved you a whole lot of money." She bites her bottom lip.

"Pshh. If you think I'm buying you a poster of another man for you to get off to, you're out of your mind." She playfully punches my shoulder. "Ow. That's my throwing arm."

"I don't have his poster on my wall to get off to!" She's laughing, making my heart skip a beat.

"Oh yeah?" I counter, knowing otherwise.

"Well, maybe not just for that." She twirls a piece of hair, looking away from me shyly like I haven't envisioned what this girl looks like getting off a thousand times. Her eyes land on mine. "I watch football." She shrugs.

"Since when?" I ask curiously.

"Since you started playing. I never missed a single one of your home games with Natalie." A blush spreads over her cheeks.

"But I've been playing since I was a kid." Has she really been watching me play for all these years, but I was too much of an idiot to notice?

She turns away, probably trying to hide the pinkness covering her cheeks, and opens the box again to look at her new coat. "So, how did you even know what size to get me?" She pulls off her hoodie, stands up, takes the coat out of the box, and slides her arms inside each sleeve.

I reach out for her, buttoning the coat. "Just a lucky guess." I wink at her as I hook the last button and lean back to look at her, noticing that the coat fits her perfectly. Of course, I'm not going to tell her that the sales lady helped me pick out her size after seeing the picture of her in the original red coat.

She twirls, and the biggest smile appears on her face. "It's so much better than my old one. I love it. I'm going to wear it all the time."

"Good, because for what I paid for this, I better see you in it every damn day," I tease.

"Jason!" She picks up a pillow from the couch and smacks me with it. "You shouldn't have spent this much money on me. But I'm never taking it off, so I guess you can't have it back, anyway."

"You're worth every penny, Vee."

Her smile falls at the mention of her nickname. The name I used to call her all of the time but only recently let slip when I was holding her in the elevator.

And even though I'm still sitting and she's standing, we're at eye level. Her lips part, her breathing picks up, and the only thought that crosses my mind is wondering if her plump lips taste as sweet as they did that night four years ago.

The night that changed my life.

Neither of us can find it in us to look away, and Vanessa looks like she is about to take a step toward me between my legs, but then the door to the apartment swings open, and Natalie and Nate step inside.

"Hey, guys!" Natalie walks straight over to Vanessa, who has now taken a step back from me, looking flushed. "Vanessa, where did you get this coat? I love it." She grabs the ornate tag. "Oh my God. Dior?"

Vanessa looks back at me. "Your brother got it for me."

Natalie looks over at me, and a knowing smile appears on her face. "Well, he certainly has good taste."

"Obviously, unlike you." I stand and ruffle the hair on her head with my knuckles.

"Twice in one day. Really, Jason?" Natalie tucks herself behind Nate, who stands there laughing.

"What? I can't help it. You're the perfect height for it. It's too hard to resist." I notice Vanessa laughing, and it feels like old times with all of us together like this. "Well, I better get going. But I'll see you guys tomorrow night." I nod at Nate. "In the mood for some basketball tomorrow morning?"

"Sounds good to me." He plops on the couch, pulling Natalie down with him.

I walk out in the hallway and am about to open my door when I hear her.

"Jason, wait!" I turn around just as Vanessa wraps her arms around me. "Thank you." She looks up at me, smiling, and then parts, returning to her apartment.

And if that smile alone isn't worth the money spent on that coat, I don't know what is.

I'm wiped after a long day of football practice and playing basketball with Nate. But I promised Natalie I would go out with the group tonight, and having a few drinks to relax sounds like the perfect way to spend the night.

And if I'm being honest with myself, I'm mostly looking forward to spending my night with Vanessa.

I feel relieved that we're back to being friends again. I can't believe how much of an ass I've been to her this past year, and even though I spent a lot on the coat for her, it still doesn't feel like enough.

But I'll think of some way to make things right between us.

I open the door to Natalie and Vanessa's apartment, walking inside with a bottle of water in my hand. Natalie's back is to me, and I see from the bottle of wine beside them that they've each already had a few glasses. But just as I bring my water to my lips, taking a rather large sip, I hear Natalie say, "What do you mean you've never experienced an orgasm with a guy?"

I suddenly find myself choking on my drink, liquid running down the wrong pipe as I slam on my chest.

My widened eyes find Vanessa looking mortified, with her mouth hanging open and her hands covering her eyes as if trying to hide from this moment; from me. Her pale skin has turned the same color as her new favorite coat.

"What?" Natalie turns around, stopping when she sees me and realizes what she just said in front of me. "Oh, Jason. Hey. I didn't hear you come in." Natalie looks between me and Vanessa, remorse on her face. "Umm, any chance you didn't just hear what we were talking about?"

And as if an actual lightbulb turned on above my head, I now know exactly how I plan to make things up to Vanessa.

Nine

VANESSA

Sliding my ass onto one of the round red leather bar stools, I wave the bartender over with a flirty smile and watch as he saunters toward me.

"What will it be, gorgeous?" Not my type in the least, but hey, always nice to hear a compliment.

"I'll have a vodka soda." I hold out my fake ID for him to quickly scan over and watch as he walks away to create my beverage. The bartender pushes the drink in front of me just as someone to my left places a twenty-dollar bill on the counter.

"On me," says the mysterious man. He's tall, slender, and, unfortunately, has that know-it-all face I can't stand.

"If you insist." Never one to turn down a free drink, I twist on my seat to face him. "Hi, I'm Vanessa."

"I'm Derek." Yup, definitely an asshole name. "And you, Vanessa, are the sexiest girl in this bar." He takes the free stool beside me, invading my space, his knees touching mine. Not a great start, Derek.

"Oh, I don't think that's true. Last I checked, there are plenty of beautiful girls here tonight." I hold my own, but I can feel the heat creeping up my neck the longer he stares at me, making me uncomfortable. He'll probably change his mind about me when he starts noticing my flaws, and a part of me wants him to notice, so he leaves, no longer wanting his attention. But suddenly, a familiar, comforting presence comes up from behind me.

"Beat it. She's with me." I tilt my head to find Jason directing a deathly stare at Derek. Poor Derek. His lean body doesn't stand a chance next to Jason's large stature.

Derek looks between me and Jason and then shakes his head before leaving. Once he's gone, Jason takes the now-free seat beside me.

"Why are you cock blocking me?" I ask. I'm glad he scared Derek away, but I don't need him to know this.

"Well, first of all, you don't have a cock, so it's not called cock blocking," he counters with a shrug.

"Fine. Why are you pussy blocking me?"

He smirks. "You really think that was the guy who would be the one to finally make you orgasm? Come on, Vanessa, you have better taste than that. The guy looked like a total douchebag."

I cringe. "Jason, can you please pretend you never heard what Natalie said earlier?" I know I've been trying for the past hour to forget about it, but the horrified look on Jason's face after hearing Natalie reveal my little secret is now permanently ingrained in my memory.

"I can't." His grey eyes solely focus on mine, and I find it impossible to look away. "Besides, I think I know how I can make up for being a total ass to you." He pulls my stool closer to him so my legs are between his. His hands land on my knees, his thumb caressing my skin back and forth, sending a shock wave directly between my legs.

"H-how?" I ask, my heart thrashing in my chest. What the fuck is happening to me? I clench my thighs together, hoping to alleviate my throbbing core, but it's futile.

"Vanessa! There you are. I was looking for you." Jason removes his hands just as Natalie approaches, bringing Sarah along. "Come on. Let's dance!" She pulls me by the arm to the dance floor, away from Jason's gaze, utterly oblivious to what was happening between me and her brother.

Music has always been the thing to make me feel better. Make me feel comfortable in my skin. And right now, with the packed floor of people and strobe lights going off, I'm at my happiest as I try to forget about what just happened. Even if my body won't let me.

After about twenty minutes of dancing, Natalie and Sarah tell me they have to go to the bathroom. I hear them, but I keep dancing to the beat of the music, tuning out everyone and everything, being entirely in my element.

Suddenly, a large body stands right behind me, and I freeze.

"Keep dancing. It's just me," Jason says into my ear, pressing his chest into my back, our bodies molding together.

His hands slide down my torso until he finds a comfortable spot on my hips, pressing me firmer against him. The second my ass grinds into his very hard length, I feel a warmth spread between my legs.

He's just as turned on as I am.

His lips brush against my ear. "So, want to know how I plan on making things up to you?"

"What did you have in mind?" I'm facing away from him, but I know he can hear me.

He grazes his lips against my neck and over my shoulder, sending my pounding heart into overdrive. The palms of his hands slide down even further on my hips, reaching the hem of my dress and scrunching it up into his fists.

Is it hot in here?

"Let me be the man to give you what no other man has been able to," he whispers in my ear.

I tilt my head to face him, my lips part in surprise. We're playing in uncharted territory.

"What ... what do you mean?" I know what he means, but I need to hear him say it. Turning my head to the side, I make sure that both Nate and Paul are still situated at the booth in the back, completely unaware of the two of us.

He grins and then presses his lips to my shoulder before saying, "We both have needs. And since we're back to being friends, I say we add some benefits to this friendship."

"Like friends-with-benefits?" I ask, softly.

"Yeah," he says, very matter-of-factly.

"But Jason, we can't. You're Natalie's brother and—"

"No one needs to know. Especially not Natalie."

No one needs to know. Why does that turn me on?

His body feels so good against mine. I can't deny I'm curious, and I've been curious for a very long time. And did I mention he looks like freaking Jeremy Burns? But still...

I grip his hand, raising it higher on my thigh, bringing it closer to where I need him to touch me. *We're playing with fire, but Lord help me, I want to feel the burn.* "How do you know that you'll be able to..."

"How do I know I'll be able to make you come?" My cheeks redden, and it's not from the dancing. "Because I know you. You need to be with someone you trust and feel comfortable with. And right now, Vee, your body is telling me how comfortable you are with me."

Vee.

"But Jason—"

"Think about it," he whispers in my ear before disappearing into the crowd. A longing for him to come back pulls at my core.

"Sorry. There was a huge line. Took forever to get a free stall," Natalie shouts over the music as she approaches me with Sarah coming up behind her. "Hey, are you okay? You look flushed."

"Me?" *Well, your brother made me soaking wet without even touching me down there, something no man has ever been able to do, but yeah, I'm fine.* "I think I'm just tired. It's been a long day."

Sarah looks over at the booth where the guys are sitting, and suddenly, her eyes turn cold and sharp. I follow her hostile glare to see a group of girls standing beside Paul, and one of them has their hand placed on his arm, looking a little too comfortable. Sarah quickly shakes her head, feigning a small smile. "Let's meet the guys at the booth and call it a night." She grabs our hands, quickly leading us through the dance floor, crammed with sweaty bodies.

"Oh no. Nathan, I think I need to pee again." Natalie looks up at Nate, who smiles down at her.

"It's a good thing I love you," he tells her, tipping her chin up toward him and pressing a kiss to her lips. "Here are the keys, guys. We'll be right back."

Sarah and Paul left in Paul's car since there wouldn't be enough room for all of us, leaving just Jason and me standing alone next to Nate's car, neither of us saying anything.

Jason unlocks the car and then opens the back door. "Ladies first."

I slide in, and the second my ass lands on the leather cushioned seat, I realize how tired I actually am. Jason sits beside me, taking up most of the back seat.

"Be useful, and let me use your shoulder as a pillow." I lean my head against his strong arm, relaxing into him. But he lifts his arm, tucking me under it while he wraps it around me, holding me snugly against his body.

"Better?" he asks.

"Much better." I smile up at him, and then maybe it's the vodka or the lack of sleep, but I spit out the first thing that comes to mind. "I think..." I look down at my lap. "I'm broken."

His finger slides under my chin, gently lifting it until our eyes meet. "What do you mean?"

"It's just, why can't I..." God, I can't even say the word out loud. It's too embarrassing.

"Orgasm?"

I nod my head.

"Can you make yourself come?" he asks innocently.

Heat spreads up my neck as I nod my head.

"But you've never been able to come when you've been with someone?"

"No." I shake my head, embarrassed. "It makes me feel like there's something wrong with me."

"Vee, there's nothing wrong with you." His thumb glides across my cheek.

"How can you be so sure?"

He pauses, looks around, and then brings his eyes back to me. His hand finds its way to the top of my thigh. "Do you want me to prove it to you ... right now?"

Do I? Yes. Absolutely I do. But I'm going to be so embarrassed when this doesn't work—because it never has before. Granted, there have only been a couple of guys I wasted my time with, but every time I felt like a failure as I put on my Oscar-worthy, fake orgasm, performance of the year.

So, how could Jason possibly prove me wrong?

I timidly nod my head.

"Come here." He pulls me onto his lap so my back and head rest against the car door. He grabs his jacket from the car floor and throws it over my lower half. "Don't need anyone getting a view of this if they walk by." His hand slides under the coat, gripping the inside of my thigh, and fuck me, I hope he can't feel how bad I'm throbbing for him.

God, this is about to happen.

Jason is about to touch me in a place I've only ever imagined.

"But first," he looks me dead in the eye, "I need you to tell me what goes on in that head of yours."

Ok, that was not what I was expecting. "What do you mean?"

"I know there's nothing broken with your pussy, cause I'd bet my trust fund if I slide my finger in you right now, you'd be soaking wet for me. Am I right?"

I part my lips, ready to deny it, but what's the use? He'll soon find out exactly how wet I am for him. *Drenched.* "Y-yes."

A smirk finds its way onto his obnoxiously good-looking face. "That's what I thought. So, tell me, when you're with a guy, what are you thinking about?"

What do I think about? Easy. I worry about what the guy thinks when he sees me naked. The horrid face he'll make when he sees any of the stretch marks or cellulite on me. I hear my mother scolding me for putting on a few pounds. "Well, I ... I feel uncomfortable in my body." I bring my eyes down, ashamed to look at him after admitting this out loud.

"Vee, look at me."

After a second, I do.

"You have a body that any man would be lucky enough to worship." There's no humor in his voice as his lips brush against my ear, sending shivers down my spine. "So, let me worship you."

His hand glides up the inside of my thigh, reaching my panties. Our eyes never break as his middle finger pushes aside the fabric and then slides up and down between my wet folds, the anticipation driving me crazy as I grip his T-shirt. Without warning, his middle finger pushes inside me, causing me to roll my head back against the window, enjoying the feeling of the pressure inside me.

He brings his lips right next to my ear. "Your body would make a priest fall to his knees, begging God's forgiveness for what he wants to do to you."

His thumb starts stroking my clit as he adds a second finger inside me, and I feel ... I feel ... I feel something. *Oh God.*

His lips press against my neck, nipping, sucking, and licking, making my pulse race.

I tilt my hips up and spread my thighs out further for him to plunge deeper inside me, which is exactly what he does, finding that special spot.

"You remember that day before moving to Boston when you were lying outside by my family's pool? Goddamn, Vee, I wanted to fuck you right there and then. I wanted to rip that bathing suit off you and fuck you until you couldn't walk straight. I wanted you to feel the reminder of me between your legs for days. Seeing you in that little black bikini made me harder than I've ever been in my life." His fingers curl inside me, stretching me in the best way possible.

"Oh, Jason," I cry out. I've never experienced this before. This feeling he's giving me is putting every vibrator I've ever used to shame.

"And I'll tell you something else." His lips suck and nibble up my neck. "When I need a release, I use that image of you to get me off. And it works every time."

I'm taken aback. "You ... you think about me?" I ask breathlessly.

"Fuck, yes."

There's pressure building between my legs, a fire blazing inside me, and I feel so close to the edge, ready to unravel any moment. "Jason..."

He starts thrusting his fingers harder and faster inside me while his thumb continues to make little circles right on my clit, applying the perfect amount of pressure my body has been desiring forever.

"And I will prove to you." Thrust. "Over and over again." Thrust. "That you are not." Thrust. "Broken." Thrust.

I'm so close. So unbelievably close.

His lips move up to my ear. "You are so fucking beautiful, Vee."

I'm gone. Everything around me freezes as I squeeze my eyes shut, lost in this amazing but foreign feeling as a spasm of pleasure takes over my core, until all at once, I collapse against Jason's chest. Breathless. Exhausted. But feeling so fucking amazing.

And somehow, I knew it would be Jason who would give my body what it needed.

"That's a good girl. I knew you weren't broken." He sounds pleased with himself, making me smile against his chest. "I've got you." He brings the jacket up around me, covering my body for warmth, his arm keeping me secure against him. "Shit, pretend you're asleep."

"What?" I mumble, still lost in that post-orgasmic bliss.

I hear car doors open and immediately relax against Jason, doing as he says and pretending to be asleep.

"What's going on here?" I hear Natalie's tipsy voice ask.

"She wasn't feeling well. Thought she was going to get sick, so I wanted to make sure she didn't pass out next to me and choke on her own throw-up," Jason says.

"Aww, Jason. That was so nice of you. I'm so glad you two are back to being friends." Natalie sounds like she's about to cry.

"Okay, no more tequila for you," Nathan says with a hint of amusement.

"I think that's a good idea," she responds.

The car starts moving, and that's when I feel Jason slide his fingers out of me. I open one eye and look up at him as he licks off my arousal. I think I just almost came again from that sight alone.

Jason looks down at me and winks. "Looks like we are officially friends with benefits," he says just loud enough for only me to hear.

What did I just get myself into?

Ten

JASON

Thanks to my mom, cooking has always been one of my favorite hobbies. Whenever she was prepping dinner or getting a big feast ready for all to enjoy, she'd ask me to help her and play the role of her personal sous chef. Even now, at nineteen, I still enjoy cooking with her, which is why I find myself in the middle of my kitchen preparing a gourmet breakfast.

I'll say it. I miss the hell out of my mom right now, and cooking helps make me feel a little less homesick.

Knock. Knock. Knock.

Just like I knew there would be at some point this morning, there's a soft knock at my door.

"You can come in, Vee," I say over my shoulder. My eyes dart to my journal and the bracelet lying on top that is sitting on the kitchen island. I quickly grab for them, throwing them in a drawer before she sees them and asks questions she doesn't need to know the answers to.

I hear the door open and then close. "Wow, it smells amazing."

"Take a seat at the counter. I'll put together a plate for you." I cooked enough for both of us, certain she would be making an appearance this morning.

"Oh, I'm not hungry." I glance over my shoulder and see her eyeing the plate of home fries like she hasn't eaten a carb in a very long time. And she probably hasn't.

"Sit," I tell her.

"Bossy much?" she asks, pulling out a counter stool to sit on.

"Only when it comes to you," I retort. I turn around with both plates in my hand, sliding one in front of her. Her eyes grow wide from seeing the assortment of food. There are scrambled eggs, home fries, and maple hickory-smoked bacon. Oh, and fresh sliced strawberries because I know it's her favorite fruit.

"This is so much food. Are you expecting more guests?" she asks, grabbing the fork beside her, ready to take her first bite.

"Nope. Just got a big practice today that I need to be ready for, and I knew you would be coming over." I grab the orange juice from the fridge and pour each of us a glass before sitting across from her, noticing she looks like she just rolled out of bed. But in a cute way, of course. And the fact that she's comfortable like this in front of me makes me feel ... special. Her chestnut strands reside in a messy bun on the top of her head, her face is free of any make-up, and she's wearing an oversized T-shirt and a pair of cotton shorts.

I can't help but also notice the small dark circles under her eyes.

Was she overthinking what happened last night? Knowing her, probably. But I'll take care of that.

Her eyes move up from the plate to me, and she swallows. "How did you know I would be coming over?"

"We've spent almost our whole lives together. I knew you would want to talk about what happened last night." I shrug.

"Yeah, about that." She drags her fork over her food. I watch as an internal war rages on in her head. "Well, the thing is, we probably shouldn't do that again."

I knew this was what she would say. I'm also ready for all the excuses she'll be throwing my way, so I casually ask, "Why not?" I shove two pieces of bacon in my mouth, waiting for her to respond.

"It's just that, well, you're Natalie's brother, and I'm her—"

"That's bullshit."

"What?"

"You heard me. That's bullshit. I know it, and you know it." I take a sip of juice. "You're just looking for a cop-out for the real reason why you're scared to do this."

She looks at me like I've just hit a nerve, and her eyes glaze over, looking down at her plate.

"Vee, tell me honestly, are you scared about Natalie finding out, or are you scared about me seeing you naked?"

Her mouth parts in shock at my words. "Why do you have to be so blunt about it?"

"Admit it. It's one of the things you like about me." I wiggle my brows as I shovel some scrambled eggs into my mouth.

She shakes her head, squashes her lips together, and then slowly nods. "Okay. I guess it's the last part." Her fork goes down on a strawberry, bringing it up to her mouth, looking away from me.

I take one more big bite, knowing the time crunch I'm on before practice starts but also knowing how important this conversation is for us to have. Her eyes watch me as I get up from my seat and take two steps toward her until I stand beside her.

"You heard every word I said to you last night, right?" God, I meant every word, too—especially the part about using the image of her whenever I need a release. I even had to use it this morning in the shower.

"Yes, but I figured you were just saying those things to help, you know ... get me off." She bites her bottom lip, looking down at her plate.

I smirk. Only she would think I didn't mean any of it. She's the most self-conscious girl I've ever met, and I plan on changing that. "No, I didn't say those things to help get you off. Although, I now know you have a bit of a praise kink, and I plan on fully using that to my advantage."

Her eyes meet mine. "I do not have—"

I press my index finger on her lips. "Tell me you don't get wet when I call you a 'good girl.'" I look into her widening eyes. "And then tell me you didn't hit your peak last night when I called you beautiful." I wait for her rebuttal, but she says nothing. "Exactly."

I remove my finger, and she sighs. "I guess I kind of liked all the dirty talk you were throwing my way. No one has ever talked to me like that before." Her cheeks turn the lightest shade of pink, and damn if it doesn't make me instantly hard.

"Noted for next time." I smile at her, but her face falls.

"Jason, why would you want to be friends-with-benefits with me? I don't get it." She drops her fork on her plate, looking frustrated. But not with me, more like with herself.

"Is there a reason I shouldn't want to be?"

"Look at me." Her hand gestures toward her body. "I'm not exactly a stick."

"Personally, I don't want to fuck a stick. That sounds painful." It gets her to crack the tiniest smile. "I think you see yourself as some monster, and I want to help you see yourself through my eyes. You're beautiful, Vanessa. And no, I'm not just saying that to get you off." I cup her cheek with my hand, her eyes closing as I caress her skin with my thumb. "You are truly stunning. There isn't one thing about you that isn't. You've got the most gorgeous pair of bedroom eyes I've ever seen, and your curves..." I look her over and bite my bottom lip to keep myself in check. "Well, let's just say I'm dying to see what's under all those layers."

Her eyes open hesitantly. "I'm scared when you do see, you'll just be disappointed," she whispers, directing her words to the plate of food in front of her, not me.

"Hey," I tilt her chin up to look at me, "that's not possible, okay?"

She nods her head and bites her bottom lip. "But can I ask you something?"

"Anything."

"It's just," she looks away from me before continuing, "that day out by your family's pool when you told me to cover myself with a towel. Was it because you were embarrassed for your friends to see me?" She finally looks up at me.

I shake my head adamantly. "Vanessa, I didn't want my friends to see you because I didn't want you to be in their stupid fantasies. You looked like you belonged on the cover of Playboy, and I say that as a sincere compliment."

She blushes and then purses her lips like she is deep in thought. "Okay." Her finger traces back and forth on the counter in front of her. "I can't lie and say I don't want this, especially after last night." She smiles shyly, looking right at me.

"Oh yeah?" I ask, knowing she enjoyed herself.

"Oh yeah," she responds in a whisper, looking like the memory of last night is playing in her head this very second.

My hands grip her thighs as I whisper in her ear. "Knew you weren't broken, sweetheart. You just needed a man to do what a boy couldn't."

She clears her throat, shakes her head, and sits up straight, trying to appear as if my words don't affect her. I know better. "Yeah, well, if we're really going to do this, I think we should come up with some ground rules."

"Of course."

"Okay, the first one should be that no one can know about this. Especially not Natalie. I just got her back, and I'm not losing her again."

"That's obvious, but okay."

"Second, if we are sleeping with each other, we can't be sleeping with other people. That's just rude," she states, crossing her arms in front of her chest, looking annoyed as if I already broke this rule.

"I don't think you'll get much sleep with me." I wink. "But yes, agreed. No sleeping with anyone else."

"And the third one is the most important. This is strictly physical. We can't let feelings get in the way. If one of us starts having romantic feelings for the other, we end this," she says.

It's too late to say there aren't romantic feelings involved because they certainly are on my side, but I'm not admitting that out loud when she doesn't reciprocate those feelings.

"I'm flattered you think you're going to fall for me," I reply, placing the palm of my hand over my heart, quick to make a joke.

"Ha. More like the other way around." She rolls her eyes and crosses her legs.

"Okay, I've got my own three to add." I look down at my hand on her thigh and then back at her eyes. "We only do what you're comfortable with. If you only want to do other things besides sex, then I get it. It's not a big deal." I shrug. "And any time you're uncomfortable with anything, all you have to do is let me know."

"But I want..." She stops herself, biting her bottom lip.

"What do you want, Vee." I twirl a loose strand of her chestnut hair before tucking it behind her ear.

She closes her eyes. "I want sex. Well, what I mean is ... I want to have sex ... with you." Her skin heats up under my hand as her eyes flutter open. She looks down at her body with judgment in her eyes before looking at me. "I'm just nervous."

"I know you are." I pluck a strawberry off her plate, holding it out for her to take a bite, which she does. "But I'll do anything to help make you not nervous. If you need me to wear one of those inflatable T-Rex costumes while we have sex, then tell me, and I'll do it."

She laughs. "Please don't do that. I'll have nightmares for months."

"Okay. Someone's clearly not into role play." I tease. "But you should also know"—my thumb slides over her bottom lip, making her shudder—"I really want to have sex with you too."

She relaxes into my touch. "Oh yeah?" she whispers.

"Oh yeah." Goddamn, I wish I had time right now to show her how much I want her. But I'm not going to rush our first time together. I want to remember every single second of it. Forever.

She swallows. "The next rule?"

I brush a strand of hair away from her eye. "When you come over here, we eat. I don't care if it's one in the afternoon or one in the morning. You're going to need your energy with me."

She takes in my words and bites her bottom lip like I've hit a sore topic, which I'm sure I have. "That might be ... difficult for me." Her eyes meet mine, looking ashamed.

"You and me, we're going to work on that, ok?"

She twirls a piece of hair anxiously. "Okay. And your last rule?"

This is a hard one for me. If she can't promise me this, then there's no point for us to go into this little arrangement. "I need to know that you have absolutely nothing to do with your brother."

Her brows furrow. "In case you weren't aware, my brother is currently sitting in a jail cell."

"I'm well aware where he is. I did my time at the courthouse, standing beside Natalie the whole time—never leaving her side." Her eyes avert me, and I momentarily feel guilty bringing up that day, knowing she was there too, seeing firsthand what she did for my sister, but I need her to know just how important this rule is to me. "But I need to hear it, from you, that you have nothing to do with him. Not while he's in jail and not when he gets out of jail. Can you promise me that?"

She stares at me, showing no emotion, and it feels like forever before she finally opens her mouth and says, "I promise."

My shoulders relax. "Good." I rub my hand over my jaw, feeling relief from her promise.

"And Jason?"

"Yeah?"

"Can you promise me this won't ruin our friendship?" Her big brown eyes plead with me. "We were friends for so long, and then last year we weren't. We only went back to being friends two nights ago, and it will kill me to lose you again." She takes a deep breath. "Please promise me we'll always be friends."

God, I hate the word friends, especially when it comes out of her mouth. But knowing how much pain I must have caused her this past year by not being there for her hurts. And I deserve to feel that pain. But I will never abandon her again. No matter what happens. "I promise."

She nods with a smile. "Well, I guess it's official." She sticks out her hand for me to shake, but instead, I take her by surprise and wrap my hand around her neck, pulling her close to my face.

My lips brush against her cheek as I say, "Oh, I think we are way past handshakes at this point." I press my lips against her own, savoring the softness and taste of strawberries on her. Her lips part for me, letting my tongue find hers as I explore, and she reciprocates. Slowly, I pull away, watching her eyes flutter open. "Now, it's official." I cup her cheek with my hand, staring into her beautiful brown eyes. "You're mine until we end this. Understood?"

"Understood," she whispers in a daze.

Eleven

VANESSA

It's been one week since Jason and I came to our little arrangement. One week since he completely flipped my world upside down.

I hadn't seen him since that morning at his apartment, where we devised rules, and then he devoured my lips like it was the only thing keeping him alive. His lips were soft yet possessive, and I spent every night this past week tossing and turning, thinking about them, wondering when I would get another taste. But it wasn't just the thought of his lips that kept me up half the night. I couldn't stop thinking about how he easily brought me to orgasm. He dominated me in the back of the car, taking control, and then proved to me his words were more than an empty promise.

I lost my mind in that moment with him, and it wasn't until I got home that I realized not once while I was with him did I feel self-conscious or worry about what I looked like.

That was a first for me.

Granted, I was fully clothed, but still. Baby steps.

But over the past week, I had been busy with work, and I knew Jason had been living and breathing football, so I didn't think too much about why we hadn't seen each other in a week. It's not like we were starting

116

a romantic relationship. It's just a friends-with-benefits relationship. That's all.

I unlock the door to my apartment, feeling exhausted and very ready for a hot bubble bath. The school football game was televised tonight, which meant a packed bar with drunk guys ordering beers and chicken wings all night long. Not to mention there were a few crude comments about my work uniform.

I'll say it. Work officially kicked my ass tonight.

The only thing that kept me going was seeing Jason playing on the TV. Every time the broadcasters announced Jason's name, my head would snap in the direction of the screen, not wanting to miss a single second of him playing for the first time this season.

And damn, he knows how to throw a football.

I guess his hands have two things they're very good at doing.

As I step inside, I see Natalie and Nate cuddled on the couch, watching a movie. They both look up when they hear me shut the door behind me.

"Hey!" Natalie jumps up from the couch. "We were just wondering when you were going to be home. Jason just texted me."

Oh no. Wait. He wouldn't say anything to her. Would he?

"The football team won their game tonight, so there's a party going on at the football house to celebrate. He said we should meet him there." She looks at me with a hopeful smile on her face.

It looks like that bubble bath is going to have to wait.

And yes, a minute ago, I was complaining about feeling exhausted. And yes, my feet feel ready to give out at any second. But a part of me, okay, my pussy, is dying for another taste from Jason. "Sure."

"Yay! See Nathan. I told you she would come with us."

Nate looks at me with furrowed brows. "Didn't think football parties would be your thing?"

Shit. "It's not, but I umm ... could definitely use a drink. It's been a long day."

Not a total lie.

He nods, but I can't help feeling like he knows there's another reason behind me going. "Alright, well, looks like we're going out tonight," he says.

"Great. I just need to change. Be ready in five minutes." I walk into my room, close the door, and throw my bag on my bed, lying beside it. I pull my phone out of my coat pocket and realize I was so busy tonight I never checked it. As soon as I open it up, I have a few texts waiting for me, all from Jason.

Jason: There's a party tonight at the football house. I gave Natalie the address and I want you there.

Jason: Preferably wearing something with easy access.

Jason: Actually I have a better idea. No underwear.

Jason: Are you ignoring me?

Vanessa: Relax. I just got home from work. Confirmed wearing granny panties.

Jason: It's your choice.

Jason: But no underwear = a reward.

Jason: Granny panties = a punishment.

Vanessa: But what if I want to get punished?

Jason: Jesus woman. Are you purposely trying to get me hard?

Vanessa: Did it work?

Jason: I'm always hard when I think about you.

Jason: Text me when you get here.

Vanessa: What about Natalie and Nate?

Jason: Don't worry about them. They'll be too wrapped up with each other to notice when we disappear.

An hour later, we walk into the football house that's packed with people. Usually, it would feel a little overwhelming, but with Nate towering behind Natalie and me, we have nothing to worry about.

The music is blaring, people are dancing, and the atmosphere has a certain vibe that makes me feel like anything is possible. Anything, meaning feeling Jason's hands on me again—the only reason I came here.

"I wonder where Jason is?" Natalie asks, holding my hand to keep me snug by her side. She isn't a huge fan of parties anymore, not that I can blame her, but I know she wanted to be here to celebrate her brother.

"I see a group of guys from the team in the back. Let's head that way." Nate grabs Natalie's free hand and leads us toward the back of the house, only stopping to grab a drink in the kitchen. When Nate walks in the room first, some guys I recognize from the football team greet him with high fives and nods. "Have you seen Jason?" he asks one of the guys.

The guy tilts his head toward the corner. "Over on the couch."

We take a few steps around the crowd until we find a group of guys, Jason being one of them, sitting on a couch with beers in their hands, laughing and living off the high of winning tonight's game.

I can't help it, but I freaking smile just seeing him.

He's wearing dark jeans that fit his muscular thighs impeccably and a black T-shirt that outlines his perfectly contoured chest while showing off his defined forearms.

God, just looking at him makes me wet.

"I found Jason," Natalie announces excitedly.

But just as she pulls my hand to lead me toward him, a beautiful blonde skinny bimbo sits her ass on his lap and wraps her arms around his neck, taking him by surprise as she goes in to kiss him.

This bitch just fucking kissed him.

"Eww," I hear Natalie remark at the sight of her brother.

I can't breathe. A flash of heat spreads over my body, dampening my skin. My chest tightens as my stomach churns, ready to hurl today's food choices all over the floor. "I'll be right back. I need another drink." I separate from Natalie, but she grabs my arm to stop me.

"I'll go with you," she says.

"No. I'll be fine. Promise. Be right back." I turn and push past people to get out of this room as fast as possible. When I make it to the kitchen, I pour myself a glass of whatever is in the punch bowl and chug it in one sitting, all while standing next to an open window, allowing a breeze to cool me down.

Fuck him.

If he thinks he can have me and anyone else he wants at the same time, he has another thing coming.

But then again, it's not like we're in a relationship.

He's allowed to do whatever he wants, just like I'm allowed to do whatever I want. We only agreed that we couldn't sleep with other people, leaving other possibilities open. That realization creates a sour taste in my mouth.

Shit, maybe I should have been more specific with that rule. I shouldn't have said no to sleeping with other people. I should have been more explicit and said no touching, kissing, hooking up, or sleeping with other people.

Basically, all of the above.

An idea comes to me.

If he can have fun with someone else, why can't I?

I look over to the main room, filled with people dancing to the horrible techno music pumping through every speaker in the house. Making my way over, I see a tall, good-looking guy standing against the wall with another guy, enjoying their drinks.

Without letting myself overthink my next step, I walk right up to this stranger. "Feel like dancing?"

He smiles as he looks me up and down, making me feel like a piece of cattle up for auction. "With you, beautiful? Lead the way."

He puts his hand out for me to take, and I pull him to the center of the room, positioning my back right up against the front of his body. We instantly start swaying to the music. His hands grip me firmly, pressing my ass against him, making it very clear how turned on he is. There's a part of me that feels guilty for this, but the more significant part of me is reminding me that Jason currently has a Victoria's Secret model straddling his lap, not giving a fuck about me.

"How come I've never seen you around?" the stranger asks, putting his lips against my ear. His hot breath washes over me, smelling like Cheetos, and I have to contain my urge to vomit.

I turn my head away. "I just transferred to Linrey."

His clammy hands wander lower, gripping the bottom of my dress, and I realize this isn't what I wanted. Nothing about this feels right. I think I made a mistake.

He presses himself firmer into my ass, making me completely regret asking him to dance. "Well, I'm sure glad—"

Suddenly, a hand closes around my wrist, and I'm pulled away from the stranger and dragged through the crowd. I stumble and look up to see the back of Jason's head.

I try to pull from his grip, but it's useless. "What are you doing?" I hiss.

He doesn't acknowledge me and continues dragging me through the house and up the stairs. He stops in front of a door, opens it, and pushes me inside.

I trip over my feet, catching myself against the bathroom vanity. "What the hell, Jason?" I straighten out, leaning against the nearby wall.

He's facing the now-closed door. His shoulders are tense, and he's breathing erratically. "What the fuck do you think you were doing?" He turns to me with a stone-cold expression.

I cross my arms over my chest. How dare he! What was *I* doing? He has no right to care what I was doing while that *bimbo* was sprawled over his lap kissing him.

"What was I doing? Are you serious?" I scoff. "What the hell were *you* doing?"

He takes in my words, and a smirk appears on his stupidly handsome face as his shoulders relax.

"Is something funny?" I cock an unamused eyebrow.

"Were you jealous, Vee?" he asks.

"Were you?" I spit out.

"Yes," he responds with a shrug, catching me off guard. "Now it's your turn to answer my question. Were you jealous?"

Was I jealous? No. No way. Not possible. Not even going to wonder about that. "Me? Jealous? In your dreams."

He strides toward me, bracing his forearms beside my head, caging me against the wall. I inhale his scent, and my anger dwindles as lust takes over. "No." He shakes his head, bringing his mouth right up against my ear. "In my dreams, I'm fucking you every minute, of every, single day. I'm thrusting so deep inside your wet pussy, you scream out my name like you're praying to the gods for salvation." One of his hands slides down my torso to the hem of my dress, pulling it up to my waist. "In my dreams, I'm burying my head between your legs until you come apart on my tongue." His hand cups me, and his eyes widen. "No underwear?" he asks, his voice husky.

I shake my head, biting down on my bottom lip, unable to speak with his hand on me.

"You're such a good girl." His finger trails leisurely between my legs, making me whimper. "I was prepared to punish you after seeing that display downstairs, but I think you deserve a reward instead. What do you think?"

I nod my head adamantly. "Y-yes."

"You just need to answer one question for me, and then I'll make you feel so good, Vee." His middle finger hovers above my entrance, and the anticipation is killing me. "Were you jealous?" He stares into my glossed eyes, awaiting my response with an obnoxious grin.

There's no fucking way I'm giving him the satisfaction.

"No," I say firmly, feeling proud of myself.

"Hmm, if you say so." His finger plunges inside me, causing me to moan as I grip his shoulders for support. "You're soaking wet for me, sweetheart."

He adds another finger, pounding inside me, and it isn't long before I can feel the beginnings of the orgasm looming so close. Yes, this is the feeling I have been waiting all week for.

"You're really not going to say it, are you?" he whispers against my ear, nibbling at my lobe. His thumb creates little circles over my clit as he thrusts in and out at a maddening pace, making my knees weak.

I can't find words to speak, so I shake my head. No way. There was no way I was jealous when I saw that girl with the perfect tits and ass sitting so comfortably on his lap. And I definitely wasn't jealous when I saw her lips land on his.

"That's a shame," he says, immediately removing his fingers from inside me.

What? No! No! No!

"What are you doing? I was so close." I'm left aching, feeling like I'm about to combust at any second.

His lips brush against my parted ones as I pant with pleasure and disappointment. "I want you to think about this the next time you lie to me." He stands up straight, towering over me. He pulls down my dress before turning around and walking to the door. As he opens the door, he looks over his shoulder and says, "When you're ready to tell me the truth, you know where to find me." And then he disappears, leaving me a panting wreck, aching for his touch.

If I didn't love him, I'd hate him so much right now.

A few hours later, I find myself staring at my bedroom ceiling after tossing and turning, unable to shut off my brain. There's been an ache in my core since the moment Jason's hand left my body, leaving me ravenous.

Can girls get blue balls? Because I think that's what I have, and I know what I need to do to make this feeling go away.

But there is no way I'm admitting I was jealous.

I wasn't.

What was there to be jealous about?

It was just some girl sitting on his lap. A beautiful girl who molded onto his lap with her lips pressing against his, looking like they belonged together.

I bolt upright, breathing harshly.

My feet hit the floor beside my bed before I even think about what I'm doing. I open my bedroom door, peeking into the living room, ensuring Natalie or Nate aren't out there. As soon as I see that all of the lights are off and the coast is clear, I bolt through the apartment and out the door, finding myself standing in front of Jason's door with my hands clenched at my side.

What the hell am I doing?

I knock quietly on his door, unsure if he can hear me. I'm about to knock again, but the door swings open, and I find myself standing before a shirtless Jason—a shirtless Jason wearing only a black pair of boxer briefs, looking mouth-wateringly good.

My lips part as I stare at his toned chest, and my eyes linger down his six-pack and even further down to his...

"Like what you see?" he asks.

My eyes look up at his, and I lose my thought. "I came here to say..." But I can't say it. Why can't I say it?

"Did you forget something?" His eyes travel down to my bare legs, which, because I jumped out of bed in a hurry, I forgot to put on any pants. And I definitely didn't remember to put a bra on. Shit.

I pull down on my oversized T-shirt, looking down the hallway to make sure no one is getting a view of this.

He pulls on the center of my shirt, bringing me inside, and pushes me against the back of the door, caging me against his body like he did earlier. "You were saying?"

I take a deep breath, but I can feel my heartbeat racing. "I came here to say ... I ... *was* ... jealous." I look away from him, embarrassed.

His fingers grip my chin and turn my face so our eyes lock. "You had nothing to be jealous of. If you had stayed for one more second, you would have seen me push her off my lap. Maybe a little more forcefully than I planned, but the only girl's lips I wanted on me were yours." His thumb brushes against my cheek. "Besides, I promised you the only person I would be sleeping with is you. And that's exactly what I plan on doing."

I don't know why, but this makes my heart flutter.

"Speaking of sleeping with each other..." His hand slides down my body, gripping me around the waist, pulling me against him, letting me feel how hard he is for me. His lips lightly brush against mine, eliciting a tingle in my core. He looks down at my body before bringing his eyes back to mine. "You are an image I want engraved in my memory."

I bite my bottom lip, feeling heat spread up my neck from his words.

His large hand grasps my thigh, bringing my leg to his waist, but I keep my other foot firmly planted on the ground.

"Wrap your legs around me," he orders.

I shake my head. "I can't."

"Why the hell not?"

"Because I'm too heavy for you to hold. You'll hurt your back. And I'm not going to be responsible for ruining your career."

He shakes his head before putting his lips right next to my ear. "Someday, you're going to realize how beautiful you are. How every curve on this body deserves to be worshiped." He grips the back of both of my thighs and lifts me in the air, holding me against his chest. "Your body was made for me."

His mouth lands on mine fiercely as he carries me into his bedroom. My hands hold onto his shoulders as he gently lays me on his bed. I keep my legs wrapped around his torso, my core craving his touch. He breaks the kiss, bringing his lips to my neck, sucking and licking his way down. His hand gathers the end of my shirt, pulling it up my waist.

"Wait." I push his hand away.

"What's wrong?" His brows furrow as he looks up at me with concern in his eyes.

"It's just..." It's just that I'm scared.

Scared of you seeing all of me.

Scared, you'll take one look at me and change your mind about this whole arrangement.

Scared, you'll see my stretch marks and be repulsed by me.

"Vee,"—his hand cups my cheek—"I told you we are only doing what you're comfortable with. If you're not comfortable, then we can stop."

"No. I want to have sex with you. Believe me, it's all I've been thinking about, but it's just..." I look down at my stomach, which my T-shirt is now only partially covering. I close my eyes tight and take a deep breath before saying, "I'm scared you'll never be able to look at me the same way again."

"Why?" He tilts his head, waiting for my answer.

"Well, for starters, I don't look anything like the girl who so easily splayed herself all over you tonight. I have curves and stretch marks. I'm not ... I'm not beautiful." My hand, which I didn't know was balled in a fist as nerves overwhelmed me, is now wrapped in Jason's large hand. His fingers intertwine with mine, his thumb massaging the palm of my hand where my nails dug in, relaxing my muscles. Suddenly, he brings my hand to his lips, tenderly kissing the backside.

And unexpectedly, I feel less overwhelmed than I was thirty seconds ago.

Jason removes his hand and slides himself off me, standing beside the bed. "Come here, sweetheart." He holds his hand out for me to take.

I look at it apprehensively before placing my hand in his.

He walks us over to the other side of the room and closes the door, which displays a floor-length mirror.

Oh God. I hate mirrors.

"What are we doing?" I ask nervously.

He stands behind me and makes me face the mirror before us. "I want you to tell me what you like about yourself."

"What?" He can't be serious.

"You heard me. Tell me what you like about yourself." His eyes don't leave mine in the mirror.

"I umm..." I look at myself, but nothing comes to mind. God, how pathetic am I? I can't even pretend that there is something I like about myself. "I don't know." I look down, feeling so embarrassed, heat spreading over my chest in shame.

His hand wraps around the front of my neck and tilts my chin so I look back into the mirror. "Alright. Let's try this a different way. Tell me what you don't like about yourself."

"Jason..."

"I'm not giving you an orgasm until you tell me, and you should know I've been told I'm pretty stubborn, so I have no problem standing here all night with you like this." The smug look on his face makes me narrow my eyes.

"Okay." I look at myself, and it doesn't take long to think about what I don't like. Here goes nothing. "Well, I don't like the stretch marks on my thighs."

His hands run down both of my thighs. "You mean these thighs? The ones I'm dying to bury my head between?"

I timidly nod, but his words cause a slight pulsing between my legs.

"I umm ... I don't like my stomach." This is the part about myself I hate the most because no matter what I do, I can never make it flat and toned.

His hands slide under my T-shirt, and his lips land on my neck. "You mean this stomach?" His hands splay over my midsection, and he presses his hips into me. My eyes widen when I feel his very large erection pressing right up against my lower back. "The same stomach I plan on kissing every square inch of?"

I nod, my lips parted, still in shock at how hard he is.

He looks into the mirror, placing his chin on my shoulder. "Anything else?"

I sigh. There are at least a hundred other things I don't like about myself, but I'll settle with the big one. "You won't understand, but I don't like how big my boobs are." And yes, I'm sure I sound crazy, but any girl with big boobs knows what I'm talking about. Every shirt you wear makes you look like you're wearing a tent, every button-down top can barely stay buttoned, and don't even get me started on what happens on those hot, humid summer days.

Jason's hands still. "Are you joking?"

I shake my head.

His hands grip the bottom of my T-shirt. "Can I?"

I bite my bottom lip feeling nerves grip me, but again I shake my head, giving him permission to remove my top. He does it in one fluid motion, and when I look in the mirror, I find myself in only a black pair of panties, my back pressed against Jason's chest. His eyes burn into mine, the color changing from a light grey to a storm cloud grey. Feeling self-conscious, I start to fold my arms over my chest, but Jason grips my wrists and brings them down to my sides.

"No. You don't get to hide from me." His hands slide up my stomach and waist until he reaches my breasts. His large hands each cup one, and the sight alone makes me throb with anticipation. He lightly squeezes before the pad of his thumb slides over each hardened nipple. "They feel like they were made to fit in the palm of my hands."

My head rolls back against his chest as a moan slips through my lips.

"Look in the mirror," he orders.

I do. And it's then that I notice I look almost ... small compared to Jason. Not a word I've ever used to describe myself.

One of Jason's hands travels down my body while the other continues assaulting my hardened nipple. He cups me from the outside of my panties, instantly causing a pounding between my legs. His index finger creeps under the fabric, and then his whole hand finds its way underneath. Two of his fingers glide back and forth between my wet center.

"Jason ... please," I pant.

His fingers still above my entrance. "I know that wasn't easy for you. But I want you to know that every inch of your body is about to be worshiped like it should have always been." He plunges two fingers inside me, causing me to moan as my eyes roll back.

"Oh God, Jason."

"Have you been waiting all week for this like I've been?" He keeps thrusting in and out, faster and harder as his thumb finds my clit.

"Y-yes," I manage to reply.

"Every night since then, I've thought of only you. How fucking sexy you looked coming apart on my fingers."

"Jason ... I'm so ... Oh, right there," I plead, feeling so close to euphoria after teetering on the edge all night. A fire erupts in my core, sending tingles all over my skin. My breathing picks up as I lose the strength in my legs to stand. But Jason keeps me standing, with his free arm wrapped around my waist, holding my body tightly against his own.

His fingers repeatedly hit that special spot inside me, providing the all-consuming pressure my body craves. My legs begin to shake, and my whole body molds into Jason's for support as my eyes seal shut.

"Look at yourself."

I open my eyes, looking straight ahead.

"So fucking beautiful coming all over my fingers like a good girl."

Maybe it's his dirty words, or maybe it's the sight of me in the mirror being thoroughly dominated by Jason that finally causes me to fall apart.

I scream out for him as the all-consuming orgasm rolls through my core, taking over my entire body.

"I've got you," he whispers as his fingers continue thrusting inside me slowly until eventually stopping altogether. I lean against him, breathing harshly like I just ran a marathon.

"Holy shit. That was amazing," I say, nuzzling my head into his chest.

He grins triumphantly. "Now, what was it you said earlier? Something about how all you've been able to think about is having sex with me?" I look up, our eyes locking, before he spins me around and throws me over his shoulder, returning me to his bed.

Twelve

Jason

I toss Vanessa down on my bed, watching as she stretches out on her back, arms above her head, basking in her orgasm that's slowly fading away.

My eyes roam over every square inch of her perfect body. God, she's so fucking beautiful, and she has no idea. Why doesn't she see what I see?

Those plush pouty pink lips.

Those perfect tits that were made to fit in the palm of my hands.

And those chocolate brown eyes I could spend forever getting lost in. The same eyes that, at this moment, look to be in post-orgasmic bliss, unable to process what just happened.

She also has no idea how many orgasms I plan on giving her tonight, but she's about to find out.

"Take your underwear off and spread those legs wide for me, Vee. I want to see all of you."

She hesitates, clenching her fists above her. But I watch as she takes a deep breath, unclenches her hands, and then does as I say, giving me the best view of my life. Licking my bottom lip, I lean down, placing a tender kiss on the center of her stomach, her biggest insecurity, catching her off guard. I then move down, pressing soft kisses on the inside of her thighs, back and forth, as my hands grip her thighs in place.

"Jason…" she pants, grasping the sheets in her fists.

"I just need to taste you first, sweetheart," I say right before taking my tongue and swiping it through her wet center, tasting her arousal and savoring every drop. "Fuck, you taste so sweet." I know it was only supposed to be a taste, but I can't stop myself. I bury my head between her legs, pressing my tongue into her, unable to get enough. Eventually, I replace my tongue with two fingers, plunging into her. She gasps as she withers beneath me, her legs shaking, telling me she's so close to another orgasm.

"You like that?" I look up to see her mouth parted and her eyes sealed shut. A flush spreads over her cheeks and chest while those beautiful round tits heave up and down with each breath she takes.

"Y-yes," she gets out, shaking her head frantically.

"Look at me, Vee."

She opens her eyes, which are completely glazed over and tilts her head to lock eyes with me as I lean back down to suck on her clit.

"Oh God, Jason!" she screams out as the orgasm takes over her. She collapses back on the bed as I lap up the rest of her arousal until she lightly pushes at my head, unable to take any more, which makes me laugh as I pull away to look down at her. The sight of her smile catches me off guard. "No one's ever done that to me before." Interesting. Looks like we'll both share a first tonight. "Can we do that every night?" she asks innocently.

I chuckle, sliding off the bed. "I'll eat that sweet pussy out every goddamn day like it's my last meal." I walk over to my nightstand. "Now," I start to say, "get on all fours." I remove my underwear and grab a condom, quickly tearing at the wrapper and sliding it over my dick, ready to blow any second. I turn to stand in front of the bed, facing her.

Her eyes widen as they travel from my face down my torso until finally landing on my hard cock, throbbing to be inside her. She blinks a few times, unable to look away until I clear my throat to grab her attention. She's nervous.

I reach out to cup her cheek, bringing her eyes to mine. "Are you nervous?"

She lets out a shaky breath. "Maybe a little bit. It's just been a really long time since I ... umm, well." She closes her eyes and takes a deep breath. "Well, you know."

Yeah, I do.

"Hey, what did I say? We're only doing what you're comfortable with." My thumb glides across her cheek.

"No. No. I want this. I want you." Her eyes open, pleading for me to believe her, and I do.

I lean down, tasting her lips. "Then get on all fours, sweetheart."

She doesn't even hesitate before she rolls over onto her stomach and then lifts herself on her hands and knees, giving me her ass in the air for me to take and do with whatever I want. Fuck, I feel like I've waited so long for this. I bite my lower lip and lean down to kiss that perfect ass. The moan that comes out of her is so fucking intoxicating. Like rain hitting a windowpane. Or an ocean wave crashing against a cliff. And I can't take it anymore. I grab each of her ankles and pull her back so she's right up against the edge of the bed, lifting her ass back into the air so it's right up against me.

I want to bury myself so deep inside her that she thinks of only me for days.

"Goddammit. This ass is perfect." My hand cups her ass cheek, squeezing it before my palm slides up her back, right over her spine, to hold her in place. My other hand fists my hard cock, rubbing it through her folds and then lining up with her entrance, letting the anticipation build for the both of us. I lean my head down as close to her ear as possible. "Are you ready for me?"

She nods frantically. "Yes."

I feel like I've waited my whole life for this. Truth be told, I have.

I slowly enter her, inch by inch, cursing how tight she is, praying that I can last long enough to make this good for her. We both moan and groan as I bottom out inside of her. I notice her gripping the sheets, so I give her body time to adjust before moving slowly, finding a steady rhythm between us.

"You feel so goddamn good, Vee. You're doing such a good job, taking my cock like such a good girl," I praise.

I feel her clench around my dick, and I smirk, knowing it was those damn words. The girl needs to be praised, so you better believe I'll praise her any chance I can.

"Jason…" she moans. "More."

I'll give her more.

I pound into her faster and harder, holding her hips in a tight grip right up against me. She can't move even if she wants to. But I take it from her sweet moans and how she thrusts back on me that she has no interest in moving away from me anytime soon.

"Yes. Just like that. Please don't stop, Jason," she begs.

I feel so close to coming apart, but because I'm a fucking gentleman, I do everything I can to keep going so she finishes first. Everything, meaning like trying to think of every single vegetable I hate. Asparagus. Broccoli. Cauliflower. Beets.

Her body starts clenching, and she's gasping on the verge of an orgasm. Thank fuck.

But I don't like this because I can't see her.

I immediately stop and flip her over onto her back. She's panting, so close to the edge. I can see it in her glossy eyes and flushed cheeks. Looking down at her, I say, "You're a goddamn dream." I slide right back inside her, only having to thrust twice before she unravels for me to see. And fuck, is it a sight. Her eyes close tight as she grips the sheets, and her back arches from the bed as she calls out my name before finally collapsing, panting uncontrollably.

It was way better than I could have ever imagined.

"Oh God," she murmurs. Her hands come up to her chest as her round tits go up and down with each breath she takes.

The sight of her does it for me. I come quickly and powerfully, leaning down against her body for support as my whole body feels taken over by a current of ecstasy.

I'm breathing hard, sweat beading down my skin, trying to catch my breath. But I don't want to crush Vanessa underneath me, so I slide out of her, which causes her to whimper. I toss the condom in the bin and then hop up onto the mattress with my head on the pillow, but I realize Vanessa is still near the edge of the bed, now positioned in a ball. I grab her body and pull her toward me so she's right up against my torso. She turns her body to face me and places her head on my chest, where she can probably hear my heart pounding like a snare drum.

Lifting her head, she looks at me, mouth parting, like she wants to say something, but instead, she puts her head back down.

"What is it, Vee?" I rub my hand over her back, her skin so soft under my rough fingers.

She adjusts herself to lie more on top of me and then opens her mouth. "It's just that, wait, am I squishing you?" She starts raising herself off of me, but I push her back down.

"You were saying?"

She purses her swollen lips. "Well, has it ever been like that for you before?"

Do I tell her? No. Not yet.

"What do you mean?" My fingers travel lower over her body, reaching all the way to the top of that perfect round ass, cupping a cheek in my hand.

"Well, what just happened ... that was ... wow. Was it wow for you too?" She looks down at my chest, waiting nervously for a response.

"It was wow for me, too," I respond, leaning my head toward hers and kissing her sweet lips, devouring them until I can't get enough. But slowly, I lean back to let her breathe again.

She plops her head back on my chest and pulls the covers up around us. "I can't believe we just had sex. You know there's no going back now, right?"

"Even if I could, I wouldn't want to." I wrap my arm around her and feel her body melt into mine.

She yawns and closes her eyes.

"I'll give you a fifteen-minute break, but after that, you better be ready for more." I slide my hand down to her ass and smack it, causing her to yelp.

"More?" she asks with wide eyes.

"What? You thought we were only having sex once tonight?" I arch a brow.

"Well, I just thought you'd probably want me to go back to my own bed." She looks away from me and down at my chest, where her hand resides, tracing small circles over my skin. Why would she think that?

Within a second, I pin her underneath me, brushing my lips against hers. "You thought wrong."

She bites her lip, looking like she has a million anxious thoughts inside her head.

"What are you thinking about?"

She hesitates before asking, "Do you remember that night at my house a couple of years ago?"

How could I forget?

"Of course I do."

"Well, I never got to tell you who I wished my first time had been with." She blushes, looking away from me.

"Who, sweetheart?" I lightly grip her chin, tilting her head so she can look into my eyes when she says what I've been waiting to hear for years.

"You."

TWO YEARS AGO

I'm walking down the halls at school when a small body slams into mine. I instinctively reach out for the person, holding their shoulders upright so they don't fall back.

"Woah, are you okay?" But the second I look down at who just walked into me, my heart sinks.

It's Vanessa.

And God, I've missed looking into those beautiful chocolate-brown eyes.

But what catches me by surprise are the big tears streaming down her face. I reach up and wipe them away before they have a chance to fall any further.

"What's wrong, Vee?" Did someone hurt her? I can feel my insides coil at this notion, ready to put anyone in their place who did.

She steps away from me, out of my grasp. "No." Wiping at her face, she says, "I just have allergies. Sorry, I have to go."

She quickly moves around me, moving toward the exit of the school.

I've known her my whole life. She doesn't have fucking allergies.

The bell rings, letting me know I need to hustle to my last class. But as soon as I get out of football practice tonight, I plan on finding out what just made her so upset.

It's pitch black out when I sneak into the Gordon's backyard, walking around the rose bushes that make a path right below Vanessa's bedroom window. She has a small terrace attached to her room that overlooks the expansive backyard, which also makes for an easier way to get up to her room without getting caught.

I wrap my arms around the column, shimmying my way up until I'm close enough to the terrace to jump onto the ledge and hop over the medal barrier surrounding it.

Just call me Spiderman. I land firmly on both feet, wiping away at the dirt that made its way onto my jeans. Stepping directly in front of the French doors, I knock quietly. God knows I don't need her brother to catch me out here. He's entirely crazy and would probably kill me.

"Vanessa! It's me. Open up," I whisper-shout.

A chill sweeps over me as a gust of wind wraps around my body. It's fucking cold out tonight.

Finally, the door opens, revealing Vanessa in a little black satin nightie. Well, fuck me.

"Jason?" She tilts her head to the side. "What are you doing here?" She looks around me, appearing puzzled. "Did you just climb up here?"

"Yup. And my balls are freezing out here, so are you going to let me in or not?" I ask, avoiding her first question.

She takes a second to think about this but then steps aside to let me in, closing the door behind me.

"Will you answer my question now?" she asks.

I turn around to find her arms crossed in front of her chest, pushing up those perfect set of boobs she was blessed with. Lord, thank you.

But it's not her boobs that I can't stop looking at. It's the glassy eyes, red-rimmed eyelids, and dark circles that have me concerned. "I came to see if you're okay."

"Me? I'm fine. Why wouldn't I—"

She breaks. Sobs take over her body as she covers her face in her hands.

"Aww, Vee, come here." I hold out my arms, which she doesn't hesitate to walk into, as I wrap them tightly around her, holding her close to my body and rubbing her back soothingly with my hand. She feels tiny in my arms, making me wonder if she's lost weight recently. Something I've always worried about with her. "Will you tell me what's wrong?"

"It's just ... I don't even know." She takes a deep breath. "I think today at school, I might have hit my breaking point."

I pull back a little to look into her eyes. "Does this have anything to do with you and Natalie?" I've noticed the two haven't been hanging out with each other recently, which tells me something happened, but when I tried to ask Natalie about it, she just started crying and stormed off to her room.

She nods her head. "It's part of it." The tears really start falling from her eyes now. "I don't know why she won't talk to me."

"She won't talk to you?" This is news to me.

"She's ignored my calls and texts for weeks, and when I've seen her in school, she just walks the other way. I don't ... I don't know what happened." She sobs into my shirt. "I miss her so much."

"Ok, I'm sure it's nothing that can't be fixed. You two are best friends." The world might end if these two aren't friends anymore.

"Maybe," she whispers. "I just don't know what I did wrong. The last time I saw her was at the Halloween party at my house. I was so drunk. I'm worried I said or did something stupid, but even if I did, she won't tell me because she won't talk to me."

"You didn't do anything wrong. Maybe Natalie is just working through something and needs some time."

"Yeah, maybe." She sniffles.

I reach up, tucking a piece of her silky brown hair behind her ear. "What else happened."

She looks away, and her cheeks redden.

Two of my fingers softly grip her chin, tilting her face so our eyes meet. "You know you can tell me anything, Vee."

She bites her bottom lip. "I don't know if I can tell you this." She sounds like she's in pain, and I don't like it. Not one bit.

"Yes, you can—no judgment from me. We're friends, remember. We tell each other things. It's what we do. It's you and me." I smile down at her, and the gesture makes her soften.

"Okay." She looks away from me again, creating a barrier between us. "Well, I started seeing Logan recently."

"Logan Flaherty?" I ask, surprised. The guy is the captain of the football team and a total douchebag.

"Yeah, and umm," she takes a deep breath, "he had me come over to watch a movie last week." I don't like where this is going. "And well..." She closes her eyes and then, so softly that I can barely hear her, says, "We had sex."

An immediate ache penetrates me right in the center of my chest, feeling like there's a blade twisting inside my heart.

I wanted to be her first.

"Did you want to have sex with him?" I ask, trying to keep my voice calm even though the unexplained pain I feel is taking over.

Maybe I'm having a heart attack. That has to be the only explanation for this pain.

"I thought I did." Her whole body starts shaking, breaking my heart even further. "But everything about it was horrible." She folds into me, muffling her cries. "He knew it was my first time, but there was nothing special about it. And he didn't even ... take care of me during it." A pink flush spreads over her chest. "And after he told me he had to get to bed early, so I left, and then ... I never heard from him again." Her fingers grip tightly onto my shirt. "Today at school, I was walking down the hall getting to class when I saw his arm wrapped around some girl. I quickly turned down a hall to escape, and that's when I bumped into you." I hug her body tighter against mine. "I feel so stupid."

"Don't. You have nothing to feel stupid about," I reassure her. "Logan is a piece of shit. I'm surprised you even gave him the time of day."

I, on the other hand, will be giving him the time of day the next time I see him. Why the fuck would he do this to her?

"I just ... I just needed to feel ... like I was enough for someone." She looks up at me. "Pathetic, huh?"

"You're the furthest thing from pathetic, Vee." My thumb wipes across her cheek, destroying every damn tear.

Her eyes look right into mine. "I didn't even want him to be my first."

There's a pull between us, like two magnets needing to be connected at the hips.

"Who did you want it to be with?" I ask, running my hands through her hair. Every part of me hoping to hear my name spoken from her lips.

"I wanted it—"

A door shutting in the hallway breaks our trance. We both look over toward her bedroom door in a panic, seeing the light on in the hallway, but only a few seconds later, it's turned off as footsteps can be heard going down the stairs.

I let out a deep breath, my heart racing at the notion that we were almost caught.

But being caught doing what? The only thing I'm guilty of is comforting this beautiful girl clinging to my body like I'm the last life vest aboard a sinking boat.

Knowing nothing more than that can happen between us, I slowly unwrap my arms around her and take her hand in mine, leading her to her bed. I pull back the covers and wait for her to slide her body between the blankets.

"I should probably go, but promise me you'll let me know if you need anything," I say.

She nods and watches as I turn away, heading toward the door.

"Jason."

I stop, looking back at her.

"Will you ... will you stay with me?"

I know I shouldn't. She's my sister's best friend. And more importantly, she's my friend. And that's all we can ever be.

Friends.

But the longer I look at her, the harder it is for me to walk away.

So I take two steps over to her bed, remove my shoes, and then lay on the other side of her mattress, bringing the blanket up to my chest. We both lay there silently, inches away from each other, staring at the ceiling, and it's driving me crazy.

"Vanessa?"

"Yes?"

"I don't have cooties."

"What?" She tilts her head toward me, furrowing her brows.

"There's so much space between us."

"Oh. It's just we've never…" She hesitates.

"We've never what?"

"We've never slept together before." She bites her bottom lip, looking nervous. No, not nervous. She looks like we're about to do the total opposite of sleeping together. And how I wish we were. But she needs a friend right now, and that's exactly what I'll be for her tonight, even with a massive hard-on.

"Well, there's a first for everything." I wink, which makes her laugh softly. God, I love making her laugh. "Come here, Vee."

She smiles and inches toward me, cautious at first, but then finally places her head against my chest and snuggles against my body. Our free hands intertwine on my stomach, and I listen to her breathing even out. I'm staring up at the fake glowing stars on her ceiling, just about to close my eyes, when I see something on the other side of her room that surprises me.

"You can't be serious," I blurt out.

Her eyes open, and she sits up. "What?"

"Tell me you don't get off to a poster of Jeremy Burns?" The quarterback of the Cincinnati Bengals hangs on the back of her door, mocking me.

"Who I get off to is none of your business," she says, closing her eyes again and curling up closer to me. "Besides, he's hot as fuck."

"He's a total dweeb," I counter.

This gets her to shoot up. "How dare you insult him! Besides," she looks at the poster and then back at me, "you do realize you look exactly like him, right?"

Interesting.

Suddenly realizing her mistake, she rolls away from me, taking a pillow to cover her head.

"Vanessa?"

She makes no sound.

"I know you didn't fall asleep." I roll my body over so my chest is right up against her back. I lift the pillow from her face the tiniest bit, leaning in as close as possible to her ear. "Did you just admit that you think I'm hot?"

"Nope. No. No. I don't know what you're talking about." Her muffled voice comes through the pillow as she pulls it down tighter against her head.

I chuckle. "You've had a tough day, so I'll let it go this one time."

She groans. "There's no way you're ever going to forget this are you?"

"Nope." I smile, removing the pillow from her grip, knowing she won't need it anyway. "Now, come on. Let's get some sleep." I curl my body around hers, keeping her back right up against my chest, trying to ignore how good her ass feels against my dick.

She shifts beneath the covers, turning over to face me so that she can press herself into me as she uses one of my arms as a pillow, and my other arm wraps over her body with the blanket between us, keeping her safe. Her eyes close, and she looks like the real-life version of Sleeping Beauty, only with long dark strands of chestnut hair framing her face.

"Goodnight, Jason," she whispers, placing her hands on the center of my T-shirt, lightly gripping the material.

I press my lips to her forehead. "Sweet dreams, Vee."

Thirteen

Vanessa

It's been two weeks since Jason and I first had sex, and it has been the absolute best two weeks of my life.

Whether with his fingers, tongue, or giant dick, he gets the job done every time, leaving me in a blissful post-orgasmic state that I never want to end.

The man sure knows how to make me happy.

But right now, I feel the complete opposite of happy.

Hmm, what's the word I'm feeling? Oh right. I'm miserable.

"You're really not going to have turkey? It's a Thanksgiving staple," my dad mumbles to my mom as he continues driving toward my Aunt Tina's house for Thanksgiving dinner.

My mom pulls out her compact and fixes her lipstick. "I need to lose three pounds by next week. I'll just have some steamed vegetables."

My dad sighs and rolls his eyes. She's been like this their whole marriage. There's no changing her now.

"Vanessa, honey," my mom says, sweetly. "Make sure you skip dessert. That dress is looking a little tighter on you." She turns to face me, making a slight frown.

Gee, thanks, Mom. You always know how to give a compliment.

"Careful, Mother. You wouldn't want your face to freeze like that," I reply sarcastically.

I hear my dad snort, holding in a laugh as my mom turns to face forward in her seat.

I glance out the window beside me, waiting for this Thanksgiving nightmare to end. Because the sooner it's over, the sooner I can return to Boston.

A place that feels like home.

"If only Brian were here today," my mom remarks. Her words ignite a spark of guilt inside me. "I made his favorite kind of stuffing with the sausage he likes."

"I'm sure he'll be eating a good meal today," my dad assures her.

She scoffs. "In jail? I highly doubt it." She shakes her head. "This'll be our first Thanksgiving without him. It isn't fair that he's there, suffering like an animal behind bars." She slams her compact closed and shoves it in her purse.

"I know." My dad grips the steering wheel tighter. "It's not right what the Spencer family put our boy through. It was a mistake. Kids make mistakes."

Are they joking?

"You guys do realize he attacked my best friend, right?" I ask in disbelief.

"Vanessa, you don't know what you're talking about." My mom crosses her arms. "It was all just a big misunderstanding. Brian would never do what the Spencer's daughter claimed he did to her. She clearly had too much to drink that night. That's all there is to it."

They won't even say her name anymore. Absolutely unbelievable.

"Her name is Natalie. You've known her since she was a little girl. And she told the truth. Why is it so hard to believe that your precious son—"

"Enough!" my dad yells. "We will not have you talking badly about your own brother. We are all quite aware of how much you dislike him. You made that very evident in the courtroom."

An uneasy feeling sweeps through the car at the mention of that day.

My nails dig into the palms of my hands as I clench my hands into fists on my lap and take a deep breath, looking out the window, holding back unshed tears.

My parents will never forgive me for what I did.

"Oh good, we're here," my mom says as we pull into the familiar driveway.

Ten minutes later, I find myself sitting across the table from my mom and dad at my aunt and uncle's house, putting on a united front before everyone, even though they're far from it.

And the empty chair beside me is the one Brian would normally sit in. He would sneak me rolls under the table when Mom wasn't looking. And he would make me laugh when he knew I was on the verge of tears from a comment Mom made about me.

But now, the empty chair only suffocates me with guilt, knowing it's my fault he's not here.

"I hope you can live with the guilt."

"Vanessa, dear. Is that all you're going to eat?" My Aunt Tina asks, looking at my nearly empty plate. The table has platters of all the Thanksgiving essentials like turkey, cranberry sauce, rolls, green bean casserole, stuffing, etc. Everything that makes my mouth water. But knowing my mom would have a front-row view of my plate, I opted for a salad and steamed green beans—the only things on the table that she wouldn't be hard on me for eating the minute we leave here.

"Oh, Vanessa needs to watch her waistline," my mom responds on my behalf, causing heat to rush up my neck at the mention of my body.

"She doesn't look like she needs to lose a single pound to me. She looks like she could use a carb or two," my aunt counters, picking up a roll from the center basket and placing it on my plate.

I just love when everyone discusses my body as if I'm not sitting right here.

"She most certainly does not." My mom reaches over the table, grabs the roll, and places it back in the basket.

Aunt Tina stares at my mother, looking like she might murder her on the spot. *You go, Aunt Tina.*

"Now. Now." My father takes a sip of his wine. "Vanessa can make her own decisions on what she eats. She's a full-grown adult." His phone buzzes on the table in front of him, and he quickly grabs it before my mother can see the name on the screen. "Excuse me. I need to take this." He gets up from his seat, places his phone to his ear, and walks to the other side of the house.

Typical.

It's probably his assistant, also known as the woman he's having an affair with.

Wouldn't surprise me in the least.

"You always have to put your nose where it doesn't belong, meddling in other people's business, Tina." My mom eats a piece of lettuce, chewing on it longer than needed. It's one of the tricks she tried to teach me when I was a kid so that I would make myself think I was full when I was actually starving.

"Well, I'm sorry being concerned for my niece's health is considered meddling." She looks at me with sympathy but then immediately brings her glare back to my mom with daggers in her eyes. "It's Thanksgiving, for Christ's sake! Let the girl eat what she wants!"

"How dare you! I've only ever done what's right for my daughter! And she knows that!" My mom scowls, or at least she tries to. Having too much Botox jabbed into her skin over the years has made it impossible for her to show emotion, making her always appear indifferent.

"Does she? Because she looks about as happy as a kid who was just told their dog died!"

The two continue bickering as other family members join sides, which is my cue to leave. No one from the table notices as I sneak away, walking to the kitchen.

I lean against the marble counter, pinching the bridge of my nose, wishing I was anywhere else but here. It sucks not having anyone here who would have already silenced my mom's rantings about my weight, like my brother.

My brother.

Well, I guess there is one place I could go even though everything in me tells me not to.

Anywhere is better than here, especially if it means my mom won't be there to bully me.

I grab a Tupperware container and start packing it full of different foods until it's completely full. Discreetly, I grab my coat, order an Uber, and make my way outside. It'll take everyone at least an hour or two until they realize I'm gone anyway.

Fifteen minutes later, I'm walking into the Connecticut State Prison. I sit at a round table in what looks like a cafeteria but is instead a room used for family visits. I take my coat off, place it on the chair beside me and anxiously wait, drumming my fingers along the table's edge.

I know I shouldn't be here. Everything in me is telling me to get up and go. And the worst part is I promised Jason I had nothing to do with Brian anymore—I lied straight to his face. I can only imagine what Natalie would think of me if she knew I was here, sitting with a container of Thanksgiving food for my brother to enjoy. She would probably want to stop being friends with me. She would hate me, and I wouldn't even blame her.

But I came because as much as I feel guilty for being here, there's a part of me that feels guilty for *not* being here. He's my brother, and before everything took a turn for the worse, we used to get along. He used to have my back, especially when it came to my mom.

He was the only one in my corner who made sure she left me alone. When she had me on special diets, it really pissed him off. He'd go out of his way to buy me takeout at my favorite spots and sneak it in before my mom noticed.

But now I feel like I have no one.

And no matter what I do, coming here or not coming here, I'm in the wrong.

"Vanessa?" Brian asks in surprise, approaching the table. "What are you doing here?" He fills out the orange jumpsuit stretching over his muscles as he sits across from me.

I push the container of food toward him, avoiding eye contact. "I just wanted to bring you some of Aunt Tina's Thanksgiving food."

He rubs a hand over the top of his shaved head. "You didn't have to do that."

"I know, but I wanted to."

He watches me but then looks up at the white clock on the wall, noticing the time. "Why did you leave their Thanksgiving dinner? Shouldn't it still be going on?"

"You know how it gets." I wave my hand around, dismissively. "Mom and Tina started arguing, and I just couldn't stand to be there anymore."

"Arguing about what?" he asks.

I shrug my shoulders. "Me."

He furrows his brows and purses his lips before getting up and walking away, leaving me feeling like I shouldn't have come here. But seconds later, he returns with two plastic forks. "Here." He hands me one of the forks.

"Oh, I shouldn't," I say.

"Yes, you should. I know how Mom treats you, so you probably only had a salad while everyone else ate around you."

"I had green beans too." I don't mention that I never got to eat any of my food before I left, but I don't need to because the rumble my stomach makes is loud enough for anyone standing within ten feet to hear.

He pushes the container toward me, and I hesitate before finally taking my plastic fork and scooping up some stuffing and gravy, bringing it to my lips, savoring the taste in my mouth. "This is so good," I say through a mouthful of food. It's been a while since I've had something this tasty.

Brian takes a bite of food for himself. "Thanks for the birthday cookies, by the way."

"Yeah, no problem." I don't mention that the secret ingredient in the cookies I sent him a few weeks ago was pure guilt.

"You never answered any of my calls," he states.

I nod. "I know. I'm sorry. I just wasn't … ready to talk to you after everything."

The two of us eat silently for a few minutes until he finally speaks.

"How are your classes in Boston going?"

I swallow the mouthful of stuffing. "They're good. I actually just submitted some sketches and an essay yesterday for a design competition at The Met in February." I look down at the table, pulling at the end of my sleeve. "I don't know. It's a long shot. But I just thought I should try and see if I would be good enough for it."

"Of course, you'll get it," Brian remarks. "You're amazing at that stuff. You always have been."

I look at him. "You think?'

He grins. And it's the first time I've seen him smile in so long, giving me hope that maybe he's not mad at me anymore. "I know. You always used to draw or sew shit for hours when you needed an escape from Mom."

"Yeah. I guess I've had a lot of practice, thanks to her." I shrug my shoulders, realizing how sad and true that statement is. I look over at Brian, observing his appearance more closely. "You look good, Brian—healthier."

"I feel good," he responds. "Guess being on drugs wasn't really for me." He tries to throw it off like a joke, but it's not a joke to me.

"Brian, I'm sorry. I should have—"

"No, Vanessa." He shakes his head. "We're not going down that road again."

I knew Brian was taking drugs, and I never said anything. I never reached out for help when I found the pills in his nightstand because I didn't want him to be mad at me for tattling on him. I could have helped him; if I did, maybe he would never have attacked Natalie. And then he wouldn't be spending Thanksgiving here.

Keep telling yourself that.

There's an awkward silence between us as the tension between us begins to suffocate me so I spit out the first thing that comes to mind. "And Brian, I'm sorry for—"

"I don't want to talk about that, Vanessa," he warns, looking down at the container of food, shaking his head.

The harshness in his voice is not familiar to me. He sounds distant and cold. But most of all, he sounds hurt.

I nod, bringing my sleeve up to my eyes to wipe away at the single tear wanting to escape. "I know. It's just ... life is hard. You know? I wish I could rewind time to when we were kids. When things weren't fucked up." When *you* didn't fuck everything up. My voice goes soft when I say, "Because sometimes I feel so alone, and I can't help but miss ... my brother. You were the only one in the family who always had my back."

And I'm so fucking mad at you, I want to say, but I can't find the courage inside me to get out.

"Life is hard?" he questions bitterly. "Look around Vanessa." He gestures around the room. "This is my life now. I spend twenty-three hours a day inside. I take my life in my hands when I take a shower. And I sleep with one eye open, on a cot that smells like piss. And do you know why?"

I look away from him, fighting tears, knowing the answer. "Because of me," I say softly.

"Because of you," he agrees.

"But I had to, Brian. I did—"

"My own fucking sister testified against me!" he roars, alerting nearby guards to start advancing toward our table. "Do you know how much that hurt? I spent my life looking out for you. Protecting you. Being there for you. And this is how you repay me. By fucking me over."

A few tears slides down my cheeks at the admission of his words.

"I'm sorry." My chest tightens, knowing how much I've hurt him after everything he has ever done for me.

But I also know telling the courtroom about the ripped dress I had found in Brian's room was the right thing to do.

It was the only thing to do.

The morning after the Halloween party, I looked for Natalie in my house when she wouldn't answer my calls. She was supposed to stay the night, but when I woke up alone in my room, I had a bad feeling that something wasn't right. I checked every room in the house, saving Brian's room for last. I inched his door open, finding it empty and in shambles. So, I opened the door further to see his light knocked over, blood on his nightstand, and a black dress ripped to pieces. I had no idea at the time what I had found. It wasn't until a year later when all the puzzle pieces were put together, that I realized what happened. And when Natalie decided to press charges, I knew what I needed to do. I needed to testify against Brian.

So why am I always filled with guilt for doing it?

Because at the end of the day, I am the reason my brother is here.

"Do you know what my lawyer told me?" I look up at him, seeing him through blurry eyes, waiting for him to continue. "He said that if my sister had just kept her mouth shut, I would have gotten off. I would be a free man, not rotting away in this Hell hole."

The guards approach the table standing behind Brian.

"I should go," I say, wiping tears from my eyes.

"Yeah, you probably should." His eyes are glued to the table, no longer able to look at me.

I quickly stand, putting my coat on in a hurry.

The coat Jason bought me.

"I need to know that you have absolutely nothing to do with your broth-er."

Fuck, I think I'm going to get sick.

"Wait, Vanessa," Brian murmurs, his eyes meeting mine. He runs his hand over the top of his head and lets out a breath. "Thanks for coming."

I freeze in my haste, gulping at the lump in my throat as I look over my shoulder at him.

No matter what I do, I always feel like I'm doing something wrong.

Wrong for being here.

Wrong for not being here.

Giving a tight smile, I nod without a word.

The wind whips at me almost as a form of punishment as I walk out of the state prison, trying to keep the rest of my tears at bay. I button my coat all the way up, trying to distract myself from all my emotions.

You can't fall apart right now. Not yet.

Pulling my phone out of my pocket to order an Uber, I see Jason's name on my phone screen, causing my stomach to twist into thousands of guilty knots.

Jason: I saved you a piece of my mom's chocolate pie. I know it's one of your favorites.

I shatter.

Why did I visit Brian?

Because he's your brother.

But he sexually assaulted Natalie, your best friend.

But when we were kids, he was my protector.

He's a monster.

He'd check for monsters under my bed.

Why did he do it?

He'd hold my hand at the dentist, knowing how scared I was.

He's a selfish asshole.

He'd save me the last ice cream sandwich in the freezer.
You're the reason he's sitting behind bars.
He. Tried. To. Rape. Natalie.
STOP!

My palms press into the sides of my head, trying desperately to make the voices stop. I slide down a nearby tree, bringing my knees to my chest. Tears stain my cheeks as they stream down my face and onto my jacket.

You promised Jason you had nothing to do with him anymore.

God, I feel like I'm about to pass out.

You lied to Jason.

I can never come back here again. Ever.

Taking a deep breath, I look up to the night sky, wishing I could see even just one star to make me feel the slightest bit better. But the stars are completely hidden behind stormy clouds, leaving only an ominous sea of darkness above me and a pit of despair inside me.

Because I know that if Jason ever finds out about me being here, it's game over.

"Earth to Vanessa!"

"Huh?" I blink to find Natalie watching me curiously. "I just asked you, three times, if you wanted some popcorn, and you were in some kind of trance."

Last night I returned to my apartment after Thanksgiving break to find Jason ready to consume me like he hadn't seen me in years when it had only been one week. He left me with a sore reminder between my legs and a slight limp in my step, but I was not complaining.

Nope. Definitely not.

But as much as I love spending my nights in Jason's bed, getting ravaged in the best possible way, I also love my girl nights with Natalie, like the one we are having now with freshly painted nails and full bellies of takeout while we lounge on the couch in our pajamas getting ready to start our rom-com movie marathon.

"Oh, sorry. I was thinking about … the fashion competition. We'll find out in our next class if we made it to the finals."

I was *not* just thinking about your brother's dick. Nope. And I especially was not thinking about his head buried between my legs because that would be wrong. So, so wrong.

So, yeah, I definitely wasn't thinking about that.

Natalie gives me a sympathetic smile. "There's no way they won't choose you. You're going to win the whole thing. I just know it."

I pull the beige Sherpa throw over my legs. "I hope so. I could really use that scholarship money." I smile before adding, "Now, how can a girl get some popcorn around here?"

Natalie laughs. "Coming right up." She gets up from the couch and heads to the kitchen to make popcorn in the microwave. A few minutes later, she's walking over with two bowls—one for her and one for me.

Her smile is almost too big as she hands me the bowl.

"What?" I ask. Is there something on my face?

"Nothing." She shakes her head. "Well, it's just you've seemed like your old self recently."

"I feel like my old self," I reply, bringing a handful of popcorn to my mouth.

"And you look really good," she states.

I know what she means—I look healthy. Probably because, true to his word, every time I've snuck over to Jason's, he's made sure we always ate before or after our *sessions*. There was even one time we ate during a session, but we don't need to get into that. I've gained a few pounds and don't have to stand on the scale to know this. I can feel it in the way my clothes fit over my curves. And to be honest, I'm not entirely sure how I feel about that right now.

But all I know is that I feel desirable every time Jason's eyes are on me. I feel *beautiful.*

So maybe that's why I haven't felt the self-hatred that usually comes after I've gained a couple of pounds.

"When we first moved in, you just looked a little..." She runs her hand anxiously through her hair. "Well, what I'm trying to say is I'm always here for you. You know that, right?"

"Yeah, of course." I can feel my eyes watering, so I bite my bottom lip, gripping the blanket around me. "I know I haven't always had the best relationship with food, and if anyone is going to notice, it's you." *And your brother.* "But I am working on it." *Thanks to your brother.*

"I know you are." She smiles. "Just don't ever feel like you have to work on it alone when I'm right here. Okay?"

I nod, swallowing the lump in my throat. "Okay."

She sits on the other side of the couch and grabs the blanket closest to her.

"What about you? How have you been?" She knows what I'm asking without having to say it.

How has your anxiety been?

She twists a small silver ring on her finger. "There are good days and bad days. But I've definitely had a lot more good days recently. Thanks to therapy, I know how to be in better control of my bad days with coping mechanisms."

"And the therapy helps?" I ask. "You're okay talking to a complete stranger about this stuff."

She ponders my question. "At first, I was uncomfortable. Opening up and being transparent with someone you don't know is hard. But the more sessions I had, the better I was at getting everything off my chest because I knew it was helping me. I started to quickly realize my therapist was trying to help me, and I was only hurting myself if I wasn't being honest with them."

I nod, taking in her words. The idea of therapy has been in the back of my mind, especially seeing how much it helps Natalie, but it's daunting, putting your fears and insecurities out there for someone to judge you.

It probably wouldn't even help me.

It's too late for me—I'm a lost cause.

"Sometimes it's easier to talk to someone you don't know than talking to someone you've known your whole life," she adds. And as if reading my thoughts, she says, "And it's never too late to start."

"I'll keep that in mind," I say with a half-smile.

"And Nathan is just amazing about it, which helps a lot."

"That man worships the ground you walk on," I tease.

We both laugh, knowing it's true.

"I guess you're right. But the feeling is mutual." She wraps her arms around herself. "I love him so much that sometimes I'm worried it's all a dream that will end."

"No way. You guys are end game. If any two people on this earth were meant to be together, it's you two."

She blushes. "What about you?"

"What about me?" I ask.

"Is there anyone you have your eyes on?"

"Umm..." The guilt inside me builds to the surface, screaming at me to tell her the truth—convincing me that this is the moment to tell her about Jason. But the selfish part of me overrides the guilt, convincing me to keep this secret between Jason and I for as long as possible.

I look down at the blanket on my lap, unable to make eye contact with her as I lie straight to her face. "No. I'm just so busy with work and schoolwork." But besides the whole feeling-guilty-for-having-sex-with-her-brother-behind-her-back thing, there's something else I've been meaning to talk to her about—something that's been on my mind since I saw Brian on Thanksgiving. So, before she presses play on the remote, I reach over and place my hand on top of hers to stop her. She looks at me, head tilted to the side, and I spit out the words before I can stop myself. "Do you hate me because of who my brother is?"

Her mouth gapes open, brows raised, and she's stunned into silence. It takes her a few seconds to compose herself before she finally says, "What? Of course not! Why would you think that?"

I shrug my shoulders. "I wouldn't blame you if you did."

"Vanessa." She sits up, twisting her body to face me. "You're my best friend. You're the sister I never had. You were there for me in court, defending me because you wanted to, and I can never thank you enough for doing what you did. Nothing could ever make me hate you."

I wonder if she would feel differently if she knew about me visiting Brian. That fear causes my stomach to plummet, unleashing an extensive amount of guilt inside me.

I should never have gone there.

"It's just what he did to you was horrible. And sometimes, I worry you'll eventually resent me because he's my brother." A single tear slides down my cheek. "I can't ... I can't lose you again," I say softly.

"No, Vanessa." She grabs my hand, squeezing it in reassurance. "It was my fault for pushing you away after everything. The only one to blame for that is me. You had no idea what had happened. And I thought I was doing the right thing, but I wasn't, because it killed me not having you in my life anymore."

"It killed me, too," I whisper.

Our arms instinctively wrap around each other, clinging on for dear life as we shed therapeutic tears.

"We're stuck with each other for life, okay? Nothing will ever come between us again." Natalie rests her head on my shoulder, promising we'll be friends forever.

But what happens if she ever finds out about me and Jason?

Will she still feel the same way then?

Because I meant it when I said I can't lose her again.

Because me and her, well, we're not best friends or even sisters. *We're soulmates.*

I remember, clear as day, meeting her on the first day of kindergarten because that was the day my whole life changed. It was the day I met the yin to my yang. The vanilla to my chocolate. The macaroni to my cheese. The ... well, you get the picture.

Our phones both vibrate at the same time, causing us to part and reach for our phones.

Sarah: Hey, guys! It's lady's night at The Thirsty One. Get your fine asses over here!

Natalie looks up from her phone screen, wiping tears from her cheek. "What do you think? Maybe a drink would do us both some good tonight."

I tuck my hair behind my ear, already thinking about what to wear. "I think a drink with my best friend is exactly what I need right now."

An hour later, we walk through the bar doors, keeping our eyes out for Sarah, whom we find sitting alone in a corner booth. The second she looks up from her phone, her eyes meet us, widening with excitement as she waves us over.

"Hey, guys!" Sarah slides herself down the booth so Natalie and I can fit in. "I'm so glad you guys came. I just ordered a round of shots and an order of nachos for us!" She pushes two glasses of water toward us.

"Oh, perfect. We need a drink," Natalie says, squeezing my hand under the table.

Sarah looks between the both of us, wearing a frown. "Everything okay? You guys look like you were just crying."

"Couldn't be better," we both respond in unison, causing us to laugh.

"Here are your drinks, ladies. Enjoy!" The waitress slides a shot glass in front of me and Natalie and then places the plate of nachos between us. "Here's your soda water with a splash of cranberry." She hands Sarah the drink and then walks away.

"You're not drinking?" I ask.

"Oh, I wish. But I, umm, have to be up early tomorrow." She frowns but then picks up her glass, raising it in the air. "To being three, badass women, living in a world with too many men that think with their flaccid, shriveled, dicks and not their brains." Natalie chokes on her water, laughing. "And,"—she looks between me and Natalie, her eyes glossing over—"to making new friends."

"Are you trying to make us cry again?" Natalie dabs at her eyes as the three of us laugh.

I raise my shot glass in the air. "And to loving ourselves the way we deserve."

Natalie's glass taps against mine. "And to always being there for each other."

Sarah puts her glass down. "Shit. Now I'm crying."

The three of us burst out laughing before we down our drinks in one go.

And for the rest of the night, I push away any guilt I might feel over being with Jason, so I can greedily have a fun night out with my best friend and new friend.

A couple of hours later, after a few too many drinks, and way too many nachos that I'm definitely going to have to work off tomorrow, we decide it's time to call it a night.

"I'm just going to run to the bathroom. I'll be right back." I slide off the booth and walk toward the back of the bar, seeing the sign for the restroom hanging high on the wall above a hallway. But as I approach, I immediately stop. A guy and a girl are standing in the back, and my gut tells me something is wrong.

"Come on, baby. You've been giving me signals all night. So let's stop playing games and—"

"I don't know what signs you're talking about, but I'm not interested, so please let me go." The girl pushes against the guy's chest, but he doesn't budge. His body is blocking the only exit to get away from him, and as my eyes scan down, I notice his hand gripping her forearm.

"If you like it rough, that's all you had to say." He leans down, looking like he's going in for a kiss, but she quickly turns away from him.

Enough.

I know I should probably get one of the guys working behind the bar to help, but my feet move before I can stop myself. And the next thing I know, my finger is now tapping on this asshole's back.

"Umm, excuse me," I shout over the music.

The guy's body tenses, and he turns his head to the side to glare at me. "What?"

"I believe she said 'no,'" I say, matter-of-factly. The girl looks at me with widened eyes.

"This doesn't concern you," he says, turning his head back toward the girl.

My finger taps him on the back again more forcefully.

What the fuck am I doing?

The guy tilts his beet red face toward me, narrowing his eyes on me. Yup, I definitely have a death wish.

"Oh, I think it does," I say. "There's this thing called girl code, and when one of us sees a girl with a douchebag, who won't take the hint to back the fuck off, it's our job to intervene." I shrug my shoulders, noting the pissed-off look plastered all over the guy's face, getting redder by the second.

He turns his whole body toward me. "What the fuck did you just say to me?"

"You heard me." I cross my arms over my chest and stand my ground in front of him. He may be towering over me, trying to intimidate me, but I'm not about to back down.

No means no, and someone needs to teach this guy a lesson.

He raises his hand in the air like he's about to slap me, and that's when I realize I probably should have gotten someone bigger to teach him this lesson. I close my eyes and bring my forearms before my face like a shield in battle.

"Why, you little—"

His words are immediately cut off.

I wait one second, two seconds, and finally, three seconds before I open my eyes to find someone much bigger than this guy gripping the guy's forearm and pinning it against the wall in a death grip. When I tilt my head up, I'm met with a pair of stormy grey eyes, causing my heart to skip a beat.

Fourteen

JASON

"**I** *know* you weren't about to touch my girl, were you?" Anger radiates throughout my body as I grip the asshole's forearm, looming over him. Did he really think he was about to hit Vee?

My Vee.

I look down into her big, brown, doe eyes, feeling thankful the guys from the football team had decided to stop here tonight after our practice.

"Well, your slut needs to keep her fucking mouth shut and—" In one easy, swift motion, I have his arm twisted behind his back, pressing him forcefully against the wall. "Fuck," he hisses.

"What happened?" I ask Vanessa.

"He wouldn't let this girl leave." Vanessa tilts her head toward the girl standing a few feet away. The girl's eyes are brimming with tears, and her arms are wrapped around her body, appearing scared, which only pisses me off more.

I twist the jerk's arm harder, causing him to cry in pain. "You need to apologize—right, fucking now," I order.

"You can't be fucking ser—"

I bend his arm as far as it will go, watching the shoulder ready to pop out of its socket.

And I wouldn't feel one ounce of guilt if it did.

"Alright! Alright! I'm sorry!" he yells.

"What was that? I couldn't hear you over the music."

"I said, I'm fucking sorry!" He looks like he is about to cry.

Scratch that—he *is* crying.

I drop his arm and push him away from the girls, out of the hallway. "Get the fuck out of here!' He scurries off, heading straight for the bar exit.

He better fucking run.

No one lays a hand on my girl and gets away with it.

No one.

When I turn back around, I see the girl approach Vanessa and thank her with a hug before turning to me to say and do the same thing. She walks away, leaving just me and Vanessa in the dimly lit hallway.

Vanessa bites her bottom lip, looking down at the floor. "Your girl, huh?"

The words had slipped out before I could stop them, but honestly, I'm glad they did. "You caught that, huh?" She nods but doesn't look up, so I tilt her chin with my fingers. "No one is allowed to touch you except me, right?" My body cages her against the wall.

"R-right," she breathes. I know she can feel my hard cock pressing against her stomach. "Jason—"

My lips land on hers, hard and demanding. I haven't seen her in twenty-four hours, and it feels like I can finally breathe again.

She's seeped into every part of my mind and body like a drug I can't get enough of. And right now, I need a hit.

The taste of tequila fills my head with every inhale, intoxicating my mind with my favorite vision of Vanessa naked in my bed. I don't know how much time passes before we part, both of us gasping for air. I cup her cheek, taking in her flushed cheeks and glazed eyes.

"Have you been drinking?" I ask, pressing my lips to her neck, inhaling her addictive floral scent.

She nods. And then, as if a lightning bolt struck down, she pulls away. "Your sister ... umm, Natalie is here with Sarah. We were getting ready to go." She runs her hands over her hair, trying to smooth it out, hiding the evidence of our little make-out session.

"Ah, I see." I hate this part. The fucking hiding from everyone when all I want to do is claim her as mine. "How did you guys get here?"

"We took an Uber," she responds.

I rub my hand over my stubble. "Well, come on then." I turn and head toward the main room when she grabs me by the arm to stop me.

"What are you doing?" There's panic in her eyes.

"Relax, Vee." She looks anxious, and I hate that. "I'm just going to let the guys know I'm going to bring you girls home."

"But what if Natalie—"

"Hey." I brush some loose strands of hair behind her ear. "I'll take care of Nat, okay?"

She lets out a deep breath, nodding. "Okay."

My fingers intertwine with hers as I lead her to the booth where the guys sit. Approaching the table, I see Grant bringing his pint of beer to his lips before stopping at the sight of me and Vanessa. A big stupid fucking cocky smile spreads on his face.

It's disgusting.

"If it isn't the waitress." He places his pint on the table, and I give him my famous death stare. "Jason so rudely didn't introduce us last time we met, but I'm Grant."

Chris finishes eating the nachos in his mouth, wipes his face with the back of his arm, and then smiles, wiggling his eyebrows. "And I'm Chris."

Vanessa smiles shyly, but I can feel her body relax beside me. My hand remains firmly interlocked with her own, keeping her tucked into my side.

"It's nice to meet you guys, I'm Vanessa."

"And there's the name we've been waiting for." Grant smiles triumphantly.

Fuck you.

"Anyway." I run my fingers through my hair. "I'm going to give her a ride home, so I'll see you guys tomorrow at the game."

"Yeah, enjoy the ride, Vanessa," Chris says with a horrible attempt at a wink.

I smack him on the back of his head. "What's wrong with you?"

"A lot," Grant answers for him. "But it was nice to finally meet you, Vanessa. Take care of this big guy, alright?"

She smiles and nods, squeezing my hand.

The moment I turn toward the other side of the bar, I, unfortunately, have to release Vanessa's hand, leaving an ache in my palm where her touch once was. I look down at her to see disappointment cross her face.

I spot Natalie immediately and walk right up to the table. As I get closer, I notice her glossy half-closed eyes. She's never been able to keep her eyes open when she drinks. "What do we have here? Do I spy a drunk Natalie?"

"Jason!" she squeals. "What are you doing here?"

"I came here with some guys from the team after practice, and I was on my way to the bathroom when I ran into Vanessa." Well, shit. Now that I think about it, I never did get a chance to use the restroom. I look down at Vanessa beside me, but I can tell from her posture she's too nervous to look at me. "She told me you guys were just about to leave, so I thought I'd give you a ride home."

"Aww, that's so nice of you, Jason. Isn't that so nice of him, Sarah?" She leans her head on Sarah's shoulder.

"So nice," Sarah confirms with a smile, not appearing drunk at all. I look at the glass in front of her and notice it appears to be just water.

After finally getting the girls through the lobby of our apartment building, I leave Sarah to go with Natalie up in the elevator. I walk with Vanessa in silence toward the stairwell, knowing there's no chance in hell I can get her back on the elevator after what happened last time.

When we enter the stairwell, Vanessa looks down at her feet. "I wish I wore flats tonight."

She, in fact, did not wear flats but wore a pair of heels that are doing things to me. More specifically, to the man downstairs as my mind starts imagining her wearing only those heels in my bed...

Shaking my head, I crouch down. "Okay, get on."

"What?" she asks, looking at me like I've got three heads.

"I'm giving you a piggyback ride up the stairs."

"Oh, no. No." She walks around me, about to take the first step, but I stop her, placing my hand on her waist and bringing my mouth right next to her ear.

"You can either get on my back, or I'll bend you over this railing and fuck you until you can't walk at all. Your choice."

Her eyes narrow at me, but there's an internal conflict happening. She wants me to fuck her here right now—*that's interesting*. My lips curve up, knowing exactly what's going on inside her head.

"If I didn't know better, I'd think you want me to fuck you here. In a public place, where anybody could catch us." My eyebrow raises questioningly.

But as if to prove me wrong, she walks behind me, facing my back, and I crouch down for her. Her arms wrap around right below my neck, and just as I lift her in the air, she hugs her legs around my torso. My hands grip her thighs, holding her securely against my body.

"Was that so hard?" I tease.

"Keep walking," she mutters, nuzzling her head against my shoulder. We're just about to walk up the third flight of stairs when she quietly says, "Thank you."

"Anything for you, Vee." She presses her lips against my neck, and for a moment, I think about actually fucking her in this stairwell. "So, any plans tomorrow?"

"Umm," she adjusts her head on my shoulder, "probably just working on some schoolwork. Maybe clean the apartment."

"That sounds boring," I state.

"Yeah, well, someone's got to do it." She chuckles.

It's now or never.

"Maybe you should come to my game," I suggest.

"Your game?"

"Yeah, unless you have something better to do."

She hesitates. "You *want* me to come to your game?"

I smile at the way she enunciates, *want*. "Yes, Vee. I *want* you to come to my game." I squeeze her thighs in my hands. "Nate and Nat are going, so I figured you could sit with them."

"Okay. Yeah. I'd love to go." I can hear the excitement in her voice. "I don't have to wear blue face paint, right? Natalie made Nate wear it before, and getting it off was impossible."

I laugh. "No, you do not have to wear face paint."

She nestles her head into the crook of my neck, brushing her lips across my skin. "There's probably so many girls screaming your name in the stands. Do you want me to be one of those girls, Jason?"

My hands tighten possessively around her thighs. "The only girl I want you to be is the one who screams my name after the game when I bury my cock deep inside you."

Fall is in the final stages as an ominous winter presence can be felt lingering nearby. A brutal chill in the air whips at our faces as we run out onto the field. The trees in the distance surrounding the stadium have completed their transition into red and orange hues as most of the leaves spiral down to the cold, hard ground, getting ready for the first real frost of the season.

It's my favorite time of the year.

We all line up on the side of the field, ready to dominate the opposing team. The coach kneels in front of us, showing plays on his board that I have ingrained in my memory since day one of training camp this past summer.

I'm fucking ready.

The plan is for Grant to play in the first half of the game, and then I'll take over after halftime. The coach has been giving me a lot more playing time recently, knowing I'll become the go-to quarterback next year when Grant leaves, and I don't want to let anyone down.

My eyes scan the crowd, narrowing on the friends and family section. Immediately I see Nate and Natalie sitting huddled together. The poor bastard has blue paint on his face, which I'm assuming was, once again, Natalie's doing. But as I look to either side of them, I'm left feeling disappointed.

Vanessa isn't here.

Not like I have any right to be mad at her. It's not like we're a couple or anything. I just wanted a chance to see her face in the stands. I wanted to feel like I was making her proud.

The coach finishes talking, and the ref blows his whistle, signaling the start of the game. I turn around, storming toward the bench, and take a seat, running a frustrated hand through my hair.

Chris comes up beside me. "Everything okay, man?"

"Yeah, everything's great." I pick up the sports drink beside me and start guzzling down the contents to distract me.

"If you say so." Chris throws on his helmet and sprints off toward the center of the field, leaving me on the bench with my arms crossed in front of my chest while having a minor tantrum.

After spending the first half of the game looking over at the stands every five minutes to feel disappointed, I walk into the locker room with the rest of the guys while the coach tries to pump us up for the second half. It's currently a tied game, so he's giving it his all with this speech.

"These bunch of lazy pansies aren't going to know what hits them when we get back out there!" He stands on a chair bringing his fist in the air. "I want to see every one of you give one hundred and ten percent. I want this to be the game people will look back on and remember for years!" He points at each of us. "Do I make myself clear?"

"Yes, sir!" we chant in unison.

"Then get the hell back out there and remind me why you deserve to be on this team!" he roars.

Everyone hollers and cheers as they get up from the benches and enter the stadium.

"Hey, you ready, kid?" Grant runs up beside me.

"I'm ready," I respond.

Grant furrows his brows. "Remember, whatever is going on in here," he points to my head, "leave it off the field. Okay? This is your chance to show the coach and everyone else what you got."

I nod and sprint toward the field, ready to get this over with.

I know he's right. I should be thinking about football and only football at this moment, but I can't get Vanessa's damn big brown eyes out of my mind.

Without even thinking about it, I look up at the stands waiting for a final blow of defeat to spread over me, but instead, I catch myself staring at the most beautiful girl in the stands.

Vee.

She's jumping up and down with Natalie, wearing her red button-down coat, and cheering as the players make their way onto the field.

And goddamn, her huge breathtaking smile nearly stops my heart from beating.

She catches me staring and waves excitedly. I wave back, feeling an overwhelming need to win this game now more than ever.

I line up with the rest of the guys, anticipation tingling in my fingers, ready to get the second half started.

"Hike! Hike!"

"Hey, you coming to the football house with us?" Grant asks as he throws on a shirt. "It's going to be an epic night after today's win."

"Nah, I got other plans tonight." I look down at my phone screen, running my fingers through my wet hair.

Jason: Meet me on the rooftop in twenty minutes.
Vanessa: Yes, sir.

Grant chuckles. "Can't say I blame you. If my girl were in town, I wouldn't be going either." He throws his gear in his bag and closes his locker. "You did good tonight, Jason. Keep playing like that, and we'll have a guaranteed spot in the Rose Bowl." His hand lands firmly on my shoulder, giving a reassuring squeeze before he parts, making his way out of the locker room.

Tonight's win was one for the books, that's for sure. The score remained tied for almost the entirety of the second half as we all played the hardest we've ever played before, knowing a loss would pull us out of the finals. And with only ten seconds left in the game, there was chaos in my mind and unrelenting screams from the crowd as I gripped the leather ball firmly in my hands. The pressure in my chest magnified, everything around me appearing in slow motion. I looked into the audience, needing to find the one face that centered me in the madness, and there she was—jumping and screaming up and down with Natalie. Her smile and eyes lit up with the excitement tingling in the air. The moment my eyes locked with hers, I knew what needed to be done. I turned and saw our wide receiver, Graham, completely open, barreling down the field, so I took a chance. I did what most rookies would never do in my shoes. I threw a Hail Mary. And thank the Lord, it worked.

Throwing my sports bag over my shoulder, I head to my truck, getting congratulated by other members of the team on the way out. Their respect for me is felt permeating in the air. Something I haven't experienced since last year. And it feels really fucking good.

I step out of the elevator onto the floor of my apartment to grab the essentials before meeting Vanessa on the roof. Five minutes later, when I open the rooftop door, I find Vanessa leaning against the stone barrier, staring up at the night sky. She turns around at the sound of my presence, her chestnut strands blowing against the slight breeze, and a beautiful smile appearing, taking away all the oxygen from my lungs before feeding new life inside me. She has no idea what she does to my very being.

She's my whole world.

"So why did you summon me up here?" she asks with a hint of amusement. "I thought you would want to spend the night celebrating with your team. Not up on some dirty old rooftop."

I grin, walking toward her with a couple of thick blankets and two pillows in my arms. Her eyes sparkle with pleasure as understanding registers on her face.

The only way I want to celebrate today's win is with her. Only her.

"There's a meteor shower tonight." I spread one of the blankets on the ground and then place the two pillows on the edge. "I thought you might want to watch it." I lie on one side and wait for Vanessa to join me. Her body touches mine as she lies beside me, her hair fanning out around the pillow while our fingers interlock, both of us staring up at the clear night sky.

"Are you suddenly into stars now?" she asks.

I'm into you.

A breeze cascades over us, and I notice Vanessa quietly trembling, so I reach beside me for the second blanket.

"No. But I know you are." I spread the thick blanket over us and pull her body partially onto mine. It was dumb to bring a second pillow when I knew she would use my chest for support anyway. "You always have been."

Her finger traces little circles over my chest, and I wish I could remove my hoodie to feel her touch on my skin. "I used to have this bracelet with star charms on it. I had it for so long that I don't even remember who gave it to me. I just remember wearing it every day until one day, I lost it. It just vanished." Surprising me, she unbuttons her coat and pulls up the side of her shirt, displaying her waist. "That's why I got this tattoo. So I'd never lose them. They'd always be with me." My hand instinctively reaches for her, delicately tracing the stars tattooed on her ribcage, sending shivers over her body.

"I remember when I first noticed this tattoo when you were lying by the pool. I wanted to trace it with my tongue instead of my finger." I grin, watching her blush. "I might have, too, if you had let another moan slip out."

She lightly smacks my chest and pulls down on her shirt, snuggling into me, seeking warmth. Her eyes look up to find mine, and she hesitates before softly saying, "You were incredible tonight."

"Oh, yeah?" I wrap my arm around her back, sliding my hand under her shirt, caressing her bare skin.

"Don't act like you don't know it." She laughs against my chest. "It's because of you that they won the game." She shakes her head, lost in thought. "I don't know how to explain it, but when you're on the football field in that uniform, so focused and determined, taking charge over your team, it's ... it's ..."

"It's what?"

She bites her bottom lip before saying, "It's a turn-on."

I grip her waist, pulling her completely on top of me. My hands slide up to her face, cupping her smooth cheeks, our eyes connecting.

"Everything about *you* is a turn-on," I whisper, lifting my hips against her so she can feel the truth of my words.

One hand slides to the back of her neck, bringing her closer to me, while the other travels down her back to grip her voluptuous ass. My lips ghost over hers, taking my time, but she can't wait any longer and presses her luscious lips onto mine. Her lips part, allowing our tongues to connect as my hand snakes between our bodies so I can cup her core firmly. She moans into my mouth but then suddenly pushes away, smiling.

"I thought we came here to watch the stars, or was this just some evil ploy to trick me into having sex with you on the roof," she teases, her fingers raking through my damp hair.

I roll her over, pinning her beneath me. My forearms press into the blanket beside her head, holding me up above her. Her chest rises with each breath she takes, anticipation mounting between us. I brush some hair away from her eyes as I look down into those perfect chocolate-brown eyes that hold more power over me than she'll ever know.

My lips brush against her ear before nipping at her lobe. "We came here so you can watch the stars above us while I bury my cock deep inside you, and watch you come apart."

Fifteen

VANESSA

Do you ever have one of those days that feels like it will never end? Yeah? Well, today is that day for me.

And I'm so fucking over it.

I woke up on the wrong side of the bed. No, like literally the wrong side of the bed. After a pretty intense dream, I fell out of bed and realized I slept through my alarm. Not the best way to start my day, but I couldn't be late for class since this was the day I had been waiting for—the day we find out whose sketches and essays were enough to impress Professor Fabuleuse and be entered into the final round for The Met Future of Fashion event, along with the three pieces we will be responsible for creating in the next few weeks.

My pulse races at the thought of not being selected—at being a failure. A disappointment to myself.

You got this, Vanessa—deep breath.

I'm the last person entering the classroom, and I sit next to Brady just as Professor Fabuleuse begins speaking.

"Today is the day." She looks around at everyone with excitement in her eyes. "But before we get started, I have a special guest I would like to introduce to everyone. She is a dear friend of mine, and it is an absolute honor for me to introduce you to—" Oh my God. I see the elegant woman in the corner of the room stand, and my heart rate escalates. "Raquel Springs, the editor-in-Chief of one of the most famous fashion magazines in the world, *The Closet*."

The same magazine I've had a subscription to for as long as I can remember. Every month I'd cut out the latest fashion trends, taping them to posters and hanging them on my walls, looking on proudly at my work as if I was the one who created these original pieces.

Everyone breaks out into applause as Raquel smiles. "Thank you for such a warm welcome." She scans her eyes around the room. "As you all know, The Met Future of Fashion event is a significant event that only the most prestigious in the fashion world attend. Anyone who is anyone will be there." She gives a little smile. "It is a chance for the fashion world to celebrate and recognize up-and-coming talent. New blood, if you will. The event is a night that many of us look forward to every year—me included. And I have to say that after receiving a sneak peek of all the submitted drawings, I know that this year's will be no exception." She looks over to Professor Fabuleuse to take over.

"Yes, I have to agree with Raquel. The selection of sketches was quite impressive. And I think it's time we announce the five candidates who have made it to the final round. From there, you will have only a few weeks to create the three designs you have sketched, bringing them to life for the team at The Met to judge. Their decision will be made the day after Christmas so as not to ruin anyone's holiday beforehand. And if you win, you have a week to make any tweaks to your pieces before shipping your collection to the team at The Met to prepare for the show. I know this may seem daunting but believe me when I say the reward will be quite worth it. Not only will your pieces be displayed for some very important people to see, but this opportunity will open countless doors for you. It will also come with a substantial scholarship to help you in your future here at Linrey University."

Having doors opened for me would be amazing, but getting that scholarship money would take a weight off of me. It might even mean

I no longer have to work at the bar. Not that it's a terrible place to work. Rob is great, and so far, it's been easy sailing, but it is exhausting on top of balancing schoolwork.

"Ok, I don't want to be cruel and keep you waiting, so here are the five names." She clears her throat, and Brady squeezes my hand on the desk while we wait nervously. "Christina A., Joseph C., Brady R." Brady lets out a deep breath, and I smile at him. He deserves this. "Alexandra S., and last but certainly not least, Vanessa G."

"Oh my God," I whisper. My mouth opens in shock as my eyes involuntarily begin to tear up.

"We did it!" Brady squeezes me as I remain in shock. "We fucking did it!"

There's an overwhelming applause heard throughout the whole room.

"Congratulations on making it this far! And for those whose name was not called, please do not let this discourage you. But instead, let it motivate you. Learn from your classmates, and great things will come your way." She clasps her hands together, looking excited for everyone. Her phone rings, and she looks down at it on her desk before saying, "Okay, now please open your textbook to chapter seventeen, and I'll be right back." She turns and walks out the door with her phone in her hand.

I stare at Brady in shock. "Am I dreaming right now? Because this feels too good to be true. Pinch me." He pinches my arm lightly, and I yelp, making him laugh.

"Nope. This is definitely not a dream." He smiles and pulls out his textbook.

"Wow." I push my hair behind my ear and pull out my textbook, feeling so excited to start making my pieces with the special fabric I ordered, scheduled to arrive tomorrow.

I can't believe I did it.

My phone vibrates on my desk, alerting me with an email notification. I slide my finger over the message and wait for my email to display.

Oh no. No. No. No.

My heart drops when I see who it is from and what the subject line reads.

From: Threads N'More
Subject: Delayed Fabric

Dear Ms. Gordon,

We regret to inform you that the black (color code 001) floral silk fabric pattern (code 1EC39) is now delayed and will be unavailable for the expected delivery date. Please accept our deepest apologies for this unforeseen circumstance and a ten percent discount on a future order.

This can't be happening.

"What's with the face?" I hear Brady ask, but I can't comprehend what he's saying.

This fabric was everything.

The whole design of my entire collection centered around this fabric. It was expensive, but I used every dollar I had on it when I ordered it a month ago when I was assured that it would be here in time for me to use it.

"Hey"—Brady taps me on my shoulder—"what's wrong?"

I shake my head. "Sorry. I just got a weird spam email." Holding back the anxious tears, I turn my phone off and place it on my desk.

What am I going to do?

He furrows his brows at me but then looks over my shoulder, and his mouth falls wide open.

"What?" I ask.

"Vanessa, hi." I turn to see Raquel standing directly behind me.

"Um, hi. Hi, Mrs. Springs." I'm at a loss for words. What do you say when you meet your icon? I always thought I would be cool if this ever happened to me, but nope. Proven by my clammy palms and the stutter in my voice.

"Oh, please, call me Raquel." She smiles warmly at me. "I probably shouldn't be saying this, but I was very impressed with your essay and the collection you envision. Do you think you'll be able to pull it off?" Her eyes are eager with excitement.

I want to say no. To tell her I just found out that the fabric I have been waiting over a month for is no longer available, but instead, I say, "Absolutely!"

"Great!" she chimes. "Well, I can't wait to see it. I, for one, am very eager." She pulls out her business card that, like an idiot, I just stare at. "Please call me anytime you might have questions."

"Wow, thank you." I'm still staring at it, so thankfully, Brady takes it from her hand.

"She definitely will," he responds.

Raquel turns and walks away.

"Okay, now I know I'm dreaming." Brady lifts his hand to pinch me a second time, but I stop him. "Don't even think about it." We both start laughing. I look back at my phone, and dread fills me. What am I going to do? Well, I know what I'm not going to do. I'm not going to sit here and waste time. "There's something I need to do." I start packing up my books. "Will I see you later? My shift starts at five."

"Yup. I'll be there at the same time."

"Okay, great. See you then!" I jump out of my seat and practically run all the way to my apartment like a woman on a mission. Because I am one. I just hope it works.

"Thanks for all your help tonight," Rob says as I grab my coat off the hook, preparing to leave.

"No problem." I was only supposed to stay until nine, but they were short-staffed, so it's currently ten and I'm just now leaving. My feet ache, actually, my whole body aches, and I am more than ready to take a hot shower and throw myself into my bed.

I hear my phone beep and pull it out of my pocket to see I have a new voice message waiting for me. But when I see the familiar *"Connecticut State Prison"* contact, dread fills me.

"I hope you can live with the guilt."

My finger hovers over the little trash barrel icon, before firmly pressing down, deleting the voicemail.

"You okay?"

I look up to find Rob watching me. "Oh, yes." I take a deep breath, shaking my head. "Totally fine. I'll see you in a few days!" I walk around the counter and pass a couple of booths, putting one arm in my coat when a hand slides under my skirt, squeezing my ass, causing me to jump in alarm. I instantly turn around as his fingers slide down between my legs, and I back up against the counter, putting space between me and a guy sitting at a booth with some friends wearing a big cocky smile, proud of what he just did.

"What the fuck?" I demand, wrapping my coat protectively around my body.

"Oh, come on, you looked like you needed a little pep in your step there, baby." He laughs with his buddies, bringing his beer to his lips as he eyes me up and down suggestively.

My skin lights up in goosebumps as the hairs on the back of my neck stand, warning me to stay away. This creeper fucking touched my ass and was so close to touching more if I hadn't moved as fast as I did.

I feel like I'm about to get sick. I want to cry, but I don't want to give him the satisfaction.

"What's going on here?" I hear Rob walk up to my side. He steps around me and puts himself between my trembling body and this asshole.

"Oh, we were just having a little fun, weren't we?" The asshole looks at me to confirm, but I shake my head, my throat tightening as the tip of my nose begins to burn. *Don't cry.* As he turns his head to the side, I see a frightening-looking skull tattoo on his neck, sending shivers down my spine.

"No, we weren't." I reign in the quiver in my voice. "It wasn't fun for me to have your disgusting hand on my ass." I stare him down, feeling a little braver with Rob here.

"Okay, well, that answers my question." Rob puts his hand on the asshole's shoulder. "Come on. It's time for you to leave."

"What? Why?" His face is flushed as he slams his beer down on the table.

"Because you fucking put your hand on my employee, and that won't fly with me. So, I suggest you get up and get out of here before I show you what happens when I have to put *my* hands on *you*." Rob stares him down. "And don't even think about ever returning here because you won't be welcomed."

The man looks at his friends in disbelief as if groping a girl's bare ass is ok and he didn't do anything wrong. He stands up, looking at me up and down. "You weren't even worth this hassle." *Ouch.* "Better sleep with both eyes open."

"Okay, I've had enough of you." Rob drags the man by the collar out the front door and returns only a moment later, looking at me worried. "Are you okay?"

"Yeah, I'm fine." I button my coat all the way up, wanting nothing more than to be covered. I look around, noticing other patrons staring at me with pity, but all it does is embarrass me. I've never felt so humiliated before—so dirty. The first thing I want to do when I get home is jump in the shower to wash that asshole's touch from my skin.

"Is there someone you can call for a ride?" he asks.

Should I call Jason? No. It's a Friday night. He's probably out with his team at one of the frat houses. I don't want to bother him. Besides, it's not like I'm his girlfriend or something. I don't want to risk crossing that line. "No. It's okay. My car's right out front anyway."

"Let me walk you to your car in case that loser decides to stick around."

Thirty minutes later, I'm home. I feel like a dam ready to break, but I hold it together as I exit the stairwell.

You can't cry until you get into the shower.

Letting out a deep breath, I search for my keys to my apartment in my bag when my phone vibrates. I grab it, hoping it might be Jason, but I cringe when I see my mom's name on the screen. Stupidly, I open her message.

Mom: Hi, honey. Your father and I found an excellent deal on a two-week cruise. And with how stressful this past year has been, we figured this would be perfect for us. It leaves on Christmas Eve, so we won't be able to spend the holidays with you, but you'll have the house to yourself! How does that sound?

She's joking, right?

She just told me I'd be spending Christmas alone and wants to know how that sounds.

The dam breaks.

I bang my forehead against the door, feeling utterly broken.

Tears run down both cheeks, and I don't even care if anyone sees me. I drop my bag to the floor and bring my hands up to my face, my shoulders shaking. I need this day to be over.

Suddenly a pair of strong arms wrap around me, and I jump, spinning around to face a very worried-looking Jason. "Hey, it's just me." He pushes my hair out of my face. "What's wrong?" His hand cups my cheek, and I look up into his eyes, which show concern, and I don't know why, but that makes me cry harder.

I shake my head, and instead of saying anything, I bury my face into his chest and hold onto the front of his T-shirt for dear life, trembling against his body.

His embrace always feels like a warm bubble bath after a long strenuous day on your feet. It's heaven. And it's where I belong, especially right now.

He holds me silently for a few minutes. His hand gently slides up and down my back, before he pulls away to look down at me. "I think I know what will make you feel better."

"I'm too tired for sex right now," I respond.

He laughs. "No. Just trust me. Okay?"

"Okay," I say through a sniffle.

Sixteen

JASON

"Where are we?" Vanessa looks around the fifties diner, perplexed.

"It's called *Turn Back the Clock*, and they have the best milkshakes, so that's why we're here." I put my menu down as the waitress approaches our table. She's got a whole fifties ensemble going on.

Pink apron, big hair, big ... personality?

"Hi, you two. What can I get for you?" She pulls out a pad of paper and a pen from her apron.

"I'll have the vanilla milkshake. She'll have the chocolate milkshake, and we'll split an order of loaded fries, please." I hand her the menu.

"Coming right up, sugar." She turns and walks straight into the back kitchen.

"How did you know I wanted chocolate? Maybe I wanted strawberry." Vanessa folds her arms over her chest, pushing her perfect tits up and goddamn. Her cheeks blush when she sees where my eyes have wandered. "Eyes up here, sugar," she teases, pointing to her big brown eyes, and I laugh.

"Well, first, I know you. You love chocolate, so it was a safe bet. And don't even try to convince me otherwise. And two, if you didn't want me looking, then don't push them up like that in front of me. It's pure torture seeing those perfect tits and not being able to do anything to them from over here." I run a hand through my hair and move my eyes to the mini jukebox on our table. Trying to find anything more enjoyable to look at than her tits is proving impossible.

"So, it's a Friday night. Why aren't you out at a party or something?" She traces her finger back and forth on the table.

Why wasn't I out? Simple. Because I hadn't seen this girl sitting across from me for a whole week, and I had planned on showing up at her apartment, pounding on the door until she opened it so I could throw her over my shoulder and bring her straight to bed. But as luck had it, she was already standing outside her door when I got off the elevator. I didn't realize until she turned around that she was having a breakdown, and I didn't like seeing her like that—not one bit. So I brought her here, hoping to put a smile on her beautiful face, and find out why she was so upset.

"Didn't feel like it." I shrug my shoulders, leaving my answer vague. "But what about you?"

"What about me?" she asks.

"Why did I find you in tears at your front door?"

She looks down at the table. "I was just having a bad day."

"Do you want to talk about it?

"Do you *want* me to talk about it?" she asks, looking up at me curiously.

"I *want* to know what made you so upset." I look into her eyes, trying to let her know that I would do anything for her not to feel that way.

A slight frown appears on her face. "Well, this morning I found out that the fabric I need for my fashion project won't be delivered on time. So, I spent all afternoon calling and emailing every store in the country that might have it available and finally found a place. It will put a big dent in my wallet to get it shipped here fast enough for me, but I think it will be worth it. And then, at my shift tonight, some asshole slipped his hand under my skirt and squeezed my ass. He almost felt more too, but I—"

I put my hand up to stop her. "What?"

"Yeah, it kind of took me by surprise, and I wish I had been wearing full panties instead of a thong so that my skin would have had some kind of barrier from his hand, but then—"

I jump up from the booth, anger radiating throughout my body. "Who is he? Tell me right now, Vanessa! I will kick this mother fucker's ass for touching you!"

She tugs on my hoodie, bringing me back down on my side of the booth. "Sit down," she whisper-shouts, looking around to make sure I didn't just cause a scene, because lord knows this girl hates attention. "The manager threw him out as soon as it happened. It was just some drunk asshole who won't be allowed back." She strokes my arm on the table, trying to calm me down, but I'm fucking seething.

No one touches what is mine.

No one.

"Hey," she looks into my eyes, "take a deep breath." I realize I'm breathing erratically and sit back against the booth, rubbing my temple.

"Why didn't you call me?"

She looks at me, tilting her head. "Jason, we're not in a relationship. We're just friends ... with benefits." She shrugs. "Besides, I assumed you would be out tonight."

Not going to lie and say that didn't sting to hear.

"Listen, the keyword to the relationship we have going on here is *friends*. And I don't give a fuck if you think I'm out or not. If something like that happens, you call me. Okay? I'd stop whatever I was doing to come get you and make sure you're okay."

Her eyes don't blink as she takes in my words, but finally, she nods, looking down at the table. "When I got to my apartment, I was just about to unlock the door when my phone vibrated. It was a text from my mom, and that's when I could no longer hold back the tears. Not when I panicked because the fabric I needed was delayed, or when some asshole groped me, but when my mom texted me."

"What did she say?"

She waves a hand dismissively. "Nothing important."

"It must have been something if it made you cry," I quip.

"I'm just emotional." Her shoulders drop, appearing defeated. "It's nothing."

God, I would do anything to make this girl's day better.

I watch as she plays with the napkin before her, twisting it up and letting out her frustration, but I can see something brewing in her head.

"What are you thinking about?"

She looks up at me, dropping the napkin on the table. "Can I ask you something?"

"Anything." I run my fingers through my hair, taking a deep breath.

"Why did you and Grace break up?"

Okay, not what I was expecting.

I let out a sigh. "Why does it matter?"

"It's just ... I don't get it. You're the kind of guy every girl dreams of being with. You're funny, smart, protective, good-looking." She holds up her hand to stop me from saying anything. "Yes, I said it. Now get over it." I smirk. "I just don't understand. What happened between you guys?"

She wasn't you.

I stop myself from saying those three words.

Clearing my throat, I say, "Well, I guess when you put it like that, I am a pretty great catch." I chuckle. "But Grace and I..."

How do I tell her that, like an asshole, I only dated Grace to keep my mind away from her? That the moment I saw Vanessa a year ago at my front door with Natalie was when I realized Grace wasn't Vanessa and that no one would ever come close to making me feel the way Vanessa does, which is why I ended things with Grace the next day. I can't tell her any of this. "I guess it just fizzled out."

"I'm sorry." Vanessa's hand finds mine and squeezes it gently. I bring her hand up to my face and press it against my cheek, enjoying the feeling of her smooth skin on my stubble.

"Yeah, well, I'm over it." It should probably be concerning how over it I've been. I haven't even thought about Grace since we broke up. Last I saw from social media, she had moved on with a new guy at her school, which comforted me.

Because I want her to be happy.

My eyes lock with Vanessa's. "Okay, my turn to ask a question." She raises her eyebrows, and I place our intertwined hands on the table. "What's your fantasy?"

"Excuse me?" Her eyes widen, and she looks around, ensuring no one heard me.

"You heard me." I wiggle my eyebrows, rubbing the palm of her hand with my thumb. "Tell me that deepest darkest secret."

"No way." She takes her hand back and picks up an extra menu, pretending to be scanning it.

"Come on! If you tell me yours, I'll tell you mine."

She peers at me over the top of the menu.

"I knew that would pique your interest. Out with it." I intertwine my fingers in front of me, resting my elbows on the table, and give her my undivided attention.

She drops the menu in front of her and sighs. "Well, it's not really the normal type of fantasy that most people probably have."

"Let me be the judge of that."

She looks out the window beside us, hesitating, before finally saying, "I fantasize that someday I'll feel so comfortable in my skin that I'll be able to have sex with the lights on." She looks back at me, giving me a half-attempt at a smile, but I see the sadness overshadowing her features.

"Vee—"

"It's okay." She shakes her head. "I've been ashamed of my body for as long as I can remember. When I was younger, it was worse. I always felt ... repulsive—ugly. It's funny because I felt fat even at my skinniest. I felt like there was still more weight I needed to lose. So, I put myself on every diet you can think of, doing everything I could to stay a size two even when my body was never meant to be that size. But every time the number on the scale went up, I felt out of control. Like even though I had starved myself, I did something wrong. I did something in my life to make that number go up." Her finger draws little circles on the table as she looks lost in thought, and I wait for her to continue.

"My mom." She sighs. "Well, she's always been hard on me about my weight. As a kid, I think my mom was proud of me for being skinny, always signing me up for beauty pageants and showing me off to her friends when I came home with awards and ribbons. But when I got my curves, when I was no longer the perfect size two, it felt like she looked at me with only disgust in her eyes—like she was embarrassed, I was her daughter. She's never once used the word beautiful to describe me."

A tear makes its way down her cheek, and I can't stop myself as I reach across the table to wipe it away. The fact that any mother could make their daughter feel like this doesn't sit right with me. In fact, it has me fucking livid.

"My vision of myself has become so altered over the years that I don't even recognize myself anymore. Having my picture taken is a nightmare. And mirrors are my enemy. Whenever I look at one, I find something new about myself to hate. Something that I obsess over, needing to change. But no matter what I do, I've never been able to look in a mirror and truly like what I see. Even when people compliment me on something, I don't believe them. There have been girls who tell me they wish they had my body, but I always think they're lying to me or just trying to make me feel better."

Her hand clenches in front of her, alerting me to her self-consciousness as she bears her truth before me. Her nails dig into the palm of her skin, so I reach out, covering her hand in my own as I unclench her fingers, intertwining mine through hers.

"Sometimes I feel like a piece of glass. Like any moment, I'm going to hit my breaking point and shatter into a million pieces." She lets out a slow breath. "That's why I don't like looking in the mirror. Not only because I don't like what I see physically but because mentally, I see a fragile girl breaking, and if I shatter, I won't have anyone to help me put the pieces back together again. I'll be broken forever."

Her body starts to tremble, immediately causing me to slide out of my side of the booth and sit beside her. "Come here, Vee. You're not alone. I'm here." My arms wrap around her as she buries her head into my chest, crying silently into my shirt. My hand moves up and down her back in a soothing touch.

She lifts her head, wiping her tears away. "I'm sorry. That was so much to throw your way. I don't know what came over me."

"Hey, don't apologize. Don't ever apologize for letting me know how you feel." I push back her hair that's stuck to her damp cheek. "That's a lot for one person to feel, and I wish you had confided in me sooner, but I'm glad you did now." Her bottom lip quivers as she bites down on it, holding back more tears. "I know me telling you how beautiful I think you are won't magically make you see yourself through my eyes, but we'll work on it. Everyday. Okay? I'll do whatever you need me to do." She nods her head, comprehending. "I will never let you shatter, Vanessa."

She looks at me as if I am the only one in the world who understands her. Who sees her fears and insecurities but only recognizes the strength within her. The *beauty* within her.

"And if for some reason you do shatter, I will be there on my hands and knees, picking up every damn piece until I've put you back together again. Do you understand me?"

She rests her head on my shoulder. "Thanks, Jason. You're the only one I've ever said any of this stuff out loud to before. And it feels … freeing."

"Well, I wish I had known that you were going through all this growing up. I mean, I had my suspicions, but I didn't know the extent of everything."

"No one did." Her hand finds mine, and she interlaces our fingers. "That's why I want to be a fashion designer."

"What do you mean?"

"I want to be able to design clothes that make every girl and woman feel beautiful no matter what size they are. Girls grow up with the media in their faces every day, telling them what size they should be or how they should look. Living up to today's beauty standards is impossible, ruining the confidence in little girls who are comparing themselves to what they see online even though most of it is filtered and fake. So, I want to help as many girls as possible not to feel the same way I did while growing up. I want to help them feel beautiful in their bodies."

This girl beside me is something else.

I kiss the center of her forehead. "That's pretty incredible, Vee." My arm wraps tighter around her waist.

"Yeah, that fabric I mentioned earlier, it's for a pretty important competition that would guarantee me a chance to make my dream happen. So, I'm just really hoping everything works out. I really need this."

"There's no doubt in my mind it will. There's nothing you can't do, Vee," I assure her.

She wipes away the remaining tears on her cheek. "Okay, your turn."

"My turn for what?"

"Tell me your fantasy," she responds matter-of-factly.

I laugh. "Easy. I've always wanted to fuck a girl wearing my jersey."

"You've never done that before?" Her head tilts to the side, looking up at me.

How do I answer that without revealing the truth?

"Well, Grace never wanted to wear my jersey to games in high school—she said it wasn't her style." I shrug like it's no big deal, even though I remember how much it hurt seeing other players' girlfriends proudly wearing their jerseys.

"And there was no one else?" she asks.

I look at her, not ready to tell the full truth. "No."

She nods like she understands, and maybe she does.

"Jason..." She lets out a deep breath. "I just laid *everything* out to you, including that another man's hands were on me less than two hours ago. And well, the thing is … I really need you right now."

"I'm right here." I squeeze her hand, but she shakes her head.

"No." She looks at my chest and then glances up into my eyes. "I. Need. You."

I narrow my eyes on her, finally understanding what she's hinting at. Is she suggesting what I think she's suggesting?

Fuck.

I look around, noticing only two other people in the place, and they're both in a deep conversation on the other side of the diner, facing away from us. "Here?" I ask incredulously.

She purses her full lips, looking away from me. "It was a stupid idea."

I take two fingers, tilting her chin toward me. "Not stupid. Fucking amazing." My free hand slides up her thigh. "Is this what you wanted?"

She bites her bottom lip, and I can see her breathing increase, her chest moving up and down with anticipation. "Yes, but maybe a little more."

I play along even though I know exactly what she wants me to do. "Oh yeah? What does *more* mean?"

She looks up at me under those damn lashes and gently tugs on my right hand, pulling it higher up her bare thigh, under her skirt. Her eyes plead with me to take care of her, but I need to hear her say what she wants.

"Tell me what you want me to do to you," I whisper, my lips brushing against her ear.

"I want you to make me feel good. Make me forget about today and everything else." Her eyes have a longing in them when she whispers, "Please."

"You want me to make you come?" My fingers slowly crawl up her leg as my lips brush against her shoulder.

She whimpers and nods.

The bell above the door entrance jingles, letting me know someone has entered, and when I turn to check, it's a man and a woman making their way to the counter in the back. I look up to see if there are any cameras, and even though I don't notice any, I shift my body to block hers from anyone's view.

"Are you going to be a good girl for me and be quiet?" My fingers reach her panties, moving them aside.

She nods again, clutching onto my shirt. "Yes."

I kiss her forehead at the exact moment my middle finger slides into her wet pussy. She bites her bottom lip, holding in that moan that I would normally love to hear. But not in public. No one is allowed to hear her moans of pleasure except me.

My finger glides in and out so easily that I add another finger for more pressure. She spreads her legs further apart under the table, allowing me to reach deeper inside, curling my fingers when I get to that special spot that's making her eyes flutter closed. Her head shifts back against my arm, now supporting her upright.

"You're so fucking beautiful." I bend my head, gaining access to those luscious lips, and swallow the moan she lets slip out. Releasing her lips, I say, "When we leave here, I'm carrying you to my bed, stripping you naked, and kissing every fucking inch of that goddamn perfect body." My thumb starts to circle her clit, as I thrust harder and faster, giving her body what it wants. She begins to shake in my arms, fighting the orgasm that wants to consume her. "I've got you, Vee. You can let go. I'll catch you. I'll always catch you." The second my thumb presses down, she comes apart at my touch. I press my lips firmly against hers, keeping her quiet beside me. My fingers slow down until I feel the last of her orgasm wash over her, and then I gradually pull them out. She sags into my chest as I lick my fingers clean, enjoying her sweet taste. "Feel better?" I brush her hair away from her eyes and see a small smile form on her face. It's the first time I've seen her smile all night.

"Much better." She nods and slowly starts to separate from me, but I keep my arm wrapped behind her, keeping her as close to me as possible.

I hear footsteps walking toward us and turn to see the waitress coming our way, holding a tray with our order.

"Looks like you finished just in time." I wink and watch her cheeks burn up. God, I love doing that to her.

"Here you are." The waitress places everything in front of us. "Oh, you two are such a cute couple."

"Oh, we're not," Vanessa and I both say at the same time, but the waitress doesn't hear as she continues speaking.

"Well, let me know if you need anything else. Enjoy!" She smiles before turning around and making her way back to the kitchen.

We both laugh awkwardly at the "couple" comment.

Vanessa eyes the chocolate milkshake in front of her with skepticism as I reach for mine and finish half of it in no time.

"What's the problem?" I ask before shoving a few fries in my mouth.

"Nothing." She shakes her head, but I see worries floating across her eyes.

"Vanessa"—I cup her face and run my thumb across her cheek—"are you scared to drink it?"

She nods. "A little bit."

"It's okay. Why don't you start slow and take one sip? You don't need to drink the whole thing."

"You're right. I'm sorry. Sometimes it's hard for me not to look at something and see the number in my head on the imaginary scale go up." She reaches across and pulls the drink toward her. She takes a deep breath and then lowers her lips to the straw, and goddamn, now I wish I was that straw. She slowly takes a sip and then closes her eyes. "Wow ... this is ... amazing!" She looks at me and smiles, which freaking does something to me.

"That's my girl." I kiss her cheek and watch her take a few more slow sips feeling so damn proud of her.

Seventeen

VANESSA

*U*gh. *I hate being a woman.*

I'm lying in bed in the fetal position, holding onto my stomach for dear life because it's that lovely time of the month when I just want to cry for no damn reason and eat every piece of chocolate I can get my hands on.

Thankfully, Nate surprised Natalie with a weekend at a luxurious hotel on the water in Boston, meaning I have the whole apartment to myself while I make wild animal noises and suffer through every cramp coming my way.

Even better, Jason flew out yesterday morning for an away game and won't be back until this afternoon. So I'm pretty positive that when he gets home today, he'll go out with his friends to celebrate their win, which is fine by me. And that way, I won't need to explain to him why we cannot have sex tonight.

Awkward.

It's not like—

Did I just hear the apartment door open?

Oh my God, am I getting robbed?

Oh God. Oh God.

They can take whatever they want, but just please leave me my heating pad!

There's a soft knock on my door. Would a burglar knock?

"Vanessa? Are you in there?"

Fuck me.

What did I say about being positive Jason wouldn't want to hang out tonight?

I think I would have preferred it if he was a burglar.

"No," I yell.

"Can I come in?" Jason asks.

"No! No!" I panic. "I, umm, I don't feel well. So you should just not come in. Don't want you to catch this."

"You don't feel well? Do you need me to take you to the hospital?" There's concern echoing in his voice, which surprises me.

"Nope. Not necessary. I'll ah ... be fine in a day or two."

There's silence on the other side of the door.

Thank God, he left.

"Vanessa?"

Oh shit, the cramps are in full swing now. "Yes?" I manage to grit out.

"Are you on your period?"

"Oh my God, Jason, just please leave." I grab the closest pillow and smother myself, hiding in embarrassment.

"Okay. Okay. But you'll let me know if you need anything, right?"

"Right." I muffle my voice into my pillow. I hear footsteps walking away from my door, and it's not until I hear the apartment door open and then close that I feel like I can breathe again.

But a couple of hours later, when the pain gets so bad I can't even walk to the bathroom, I only want one person with me. So I reach for my phone on my nightstand.

Vanessa: Remember when you said if I needed anything to let you know?

Jason: What do you need, sweetheart?

Vanessa: I need you.

It only takes two minutes to hear the soft knock on my door again.

"Come in."

Jason walks into my room cautiously with a white bag in his hand and sympathy plastered on his face. "Aww, Vee, is it bad?"

I nod my head. "Yeah, it can sometimes get like this. I didn't want to bother you, but I just don't want to be alone."

He walks around the other side of my bed and sits beside me, taking things out of the plastic bag in his hand. "When you kicked me out, I ran to the closest pharmacy to get some things for you." He starts placing items on my nightstand. "I got a bottle of pain reliever, chocolate ice cream, which I already put in your freezer, a bag of chips, a chocolate bar, and then I even got this lavender massage oil that heats up when you rub it onto your muscles." He examines the bottle in his hand, looking like he has discovered the cure to every illness on this planet. "The pharmacist told me this stuff would do the trick. He called it liquid gold."

I stare at him in awe. "What … you … I don't understand."

"You do realize I grew up with a sister, right?" He looks down at me with his brows raised.

But why would he go through all this trouble for me?

"Now, where does it hurt?" He brushes my hair off my face, cupping my cheek while waiting for a response.

"My stomach and lower back are killing me," I admit.

"Okay, we can start with the front."

"What do you mean?"

"I'm going to rub this oil on you to help with the cramps." He tears the seal off the bottle and opens the cap, inhaling the lavender scent.

I cringe. "Jason, you really don't have—"

"I know I don't have to. I want to. Now, do you think you can lie on your back?" he asks.

I bite my lower lip, uncurl myself out of the fetal position, and situate myself on my back, taking a deep breath.

Jason puts a few drops of oil in his hands and rubs his palms together. "Can you lift your shirt for me?"

Why? So that he can get a full view of my stomach. Hell no! I start to shake my head to indicate *absolutely not*, but a bolt of pressure surges through my stomach at the exact moment I do, causing a tear to slip out of my eye. So I quickly lift my shirt, bringing the hem under my breasts.

Jason looks down at my stomach, and I wait to feel embarrassed, but the only way he's looking at me right now is like he wants to do everything he can to make me feel better. His palms glide onto both sides of my torso before pressing down and lightly massaging my stomach. "How is that?" he asks.

The warmth of the oil, combined with the pressure of his large hands, provides a much-needed feeling of comfort as the aroma of lavender drifts through the room, putting my mind at ease. "Really good."

He grins. "Good."

I close my eyes, melting under his touch. "God, Jason, I really love your hands."

I hear him chuckle, but then his hands slide lower, edging under the waistband of my cotton shorts. "You know, there are other things I could do to help you feel better."

"No. No, no, no." My eyes shoot open, and I wave my hands nervously in the air. He can't be suggesting what I think he's suggesting. Right? "Just keep doing what you're doing. It feels perfect."

"Yes, ma'am." He presses down firmly, and I swear I'm about to moan. "But just so you know, I've played football my whole life, and I'm not scared of blood."

I recoil. Why am I so awkward about this? "No, this is fine." If it's fine, why is my body screaming at me for turning him down?

"Okay. Turnover, sweetheart."

I sit up, facing him, his beautiful blue-grey eyes piercing my brown ones.

"Is this helping?"

I nod. "Thank you."

His hands brace my face. "Of course."

"So why aren't you out celebrating your win with your team tonight?" I ask.

He smirks. "Because I just spent the last twenty-four hours with them, and all I wanted to do when I came home was see you."

"Really?"

"Really." His lips brush against mine before consuming me in a kiss, making me second guess my response to his earlier proposition. "Now, lie on your stomach so I can take care of your back."

I turn my body away from him and position myself comfortably, or as comfortably as possible, on my stomach, waiting to feel Jason's hands on my skin.

His hands move smoothly over my lower back, providing a firm but gentle touch, which eases the discomfort and pain I have been dealing with. And just as his hands reach the lowest point on my back, I let out a moan. "Mmm, right there." His hands press harder into me, and I feel ... I feel ... horny? No. How can I be horny while on my period? That's not possible.

Body, please don't do this to me. We are not having sex while on our period, for God's sake.

But as his fingers sweep across my back, eventually coming up higher, closer to the sides of my breasts, causing goosebumps to spread over my skin, I can't take it anymore.

"Jason?"

"Mhm?"

"Remember that earlier suggestion you had?"

"Hmm, you'll have to jog my memory."

I know he's fucking with me, but I'm too damn horny to care.

"The one where you suggested that there were ... other things you could do to help me feel better?" I bite my lower lip before continuing. "I think I want to try that."

Jason's large hands freeze on my skin. "Are you sure? I don't want you to feel pressured. It was just an idea."

I turn over, his hands staying securely on my skin as I do. "I'm sure. But only if you're sure you don't care about..."

"I promise I don't care. Not at all. Not even the tiniest bit. Period." He smirks. "Yes, the pun was intended."

I smile before sitting up. "Okay, let me just run to the bathroom to ahh ... take care of things. I'll be right back." I hop off the bed, noticing that I'm starting to feel better, thanks to Jason's magical hands.

Unfortunately, when I walk out of the bathroom, I see Jason is gone. Did he change his mind? Shit, I knew this was a stupid idea.

"Back!" he says, coming through my bedroom door.

"Where'd you go?"

"Just needed to get some things." He spreads out a towel on my bed and then throws condoms on top of the nightstand. Why is the sight of him spreading a towel out on the bed embarrassing me?

I look down at the ground, feeling my heart pound.

"Vanessa?" I look up to find him sitting on the bed, appearing concerned. "Did you change your mind?"

"No. It's just..." I point at the towel.

"Oh, come here." He holds his arms out for me, and I walk over to him, standing directly between his legs. "I just don't want to ruin your blankets, that's all."

"Oh, that was a good idea." Why didn't I think of that?

"I'm a pretty smart guy." His knuckles run along my torso. "You ready for me to make you feel better?"

"Yes, please." His hands brace my face, pulling me in for a kiss as my body leans into him. I lift one leg, wrapping it around his hips as my other leg comes up to do the same, and finally, my ass makes its way onto his lap. As the kiss gets deeper, he positions my body on the towel, removing my T-shirt and laying my head on my pillow. He breaks the kiss, bringing his lips down my neck and across my collarbone, where he nips and sucks on my skin in between pressing feather-soft kisses to my body. Slowly, his hand slides down my stomach before finally reaching where I need him most.

My heart races as his hand slides beneath my cotton shorts and grips at the shorts and the panties, slowly sliding them down my legs until they're entirely removed and tossed to the ground next to my bed. Anticipation overwhelms me as his finger traces its way over my skin and down to my wet folds before finally entering me.

I grasp onto the towel beneath me, waiting for pain, but instead am comforted by the pressure his finger provides me. He gradually starts thrusting in and out, and I roll my head back against the pillow, feeling the build-up inside me.

Jason's lips nibble at the bottom of my ear. "Does this feel ok?"

"This feels amazing," I breathe out. "Don't stop."

"I won't." He keeps thrusting, adding another finger inside me, causing that sudden overwhelming feeling to build in the pit of my stomach. I'm sure he can feel my body tensing up, which is why he brings his thumb right on my clit, rubbing in tight little circles, making me unravel so fast and hard.

"Jason!" I cry out as my back arches off the bed, and an orgasm takes over me. I fall back on the bed, breathing erratically but feeling incredible.

"How do you feel?" Jason looks down at me, watching me with a tenderness in his eyes I've never seen before.

"So much better." And I really do. "But I want another one."

He smiles. "How could I possibly say no to you?"

"You can't," I tease.

Jason reaches for the condom on the nightstand, and I sit up in a panic. "Oh my God. Your hand!" There's blood on his hand. My blood. Oh my God. Oh my God.

"Hey, relax, Vee." He wipes his hand off on the furthest edge of the towel. "See, it's fine."

It's fine. It's fine. It's fine. But it's not fine. This is so embarrassing.

"Hey, do you feel good?" he asks, watching me breathe like a mad woman.

"Well, yes..."

"Then that's all that matters." Jason slides the towel to one edge of the bed and stands up, removing his clothes in one fluid motion.

Holy hell.

I will never tire of staring at that perfectly sculpted body.

Every chiseled ab looks like it was photoshopped on his torso, making my pussy throb at the sight of him.

He sits on the towel and then motions for me to come toward him, and I do, crawling over to him across the bed. Bringing me up on his lap, I look between us to see a very rock-hard cock pointing right up at me, ready for action. He slides the condom onto himself and then looks into my eyes, brushing stray strands of hair away from my face.

"Ready?"

"Yes." I lift my hips, giving him access to me. I feel the tip of his cock hit my entrance, and that's when I come down hard. We both gasp as his length fills me, stretching me out.

"You feel so damn good." Jason's fingers rake through my hair, giving him access to my neck, where he begins nibbling and sucking a path down my skin. "Like you were made for me and only me."

His words elicit a flutter in my core; every fiber of my being is ready to prove that I am made for him.

I gradually start to ride him, feeling pleasure building inside me with each bounce on his cock as he stretches me in the best possible way. I wrap my arms around his neck, pulling myself into him for support as his arms cradle me against his chest. His hands slide down my sides coming to my hips, where he grips me and takes over, lifting me up and down like nobody's business.

His eyes glaze over my body. "You're so fucking perfect, Vee." I arch my back at his praise, letting my head roll back, giving him access to my breasts bouncing in his face. He buries his face in the space between my breasts, where his tongue comes out to play, sending shivers over my skin. He tilts his head to the side, taking in one of my hardened nipples between his teeth, sending a zap straight down to my core.

"Jason..." I can feel the orgasm looming, building inside me, ready to erupt.

"I've got you, Vee." And he does, because when the orgasm hits me, I fold into him, burying my head into his shoulder, screaming his name like it's the last word I'll ever say.

The only thing I see is stars shooting across my closed eyelids.

Jason's body tenses under me before he finally comes, breathing roughly in my arms. We're both a hot, sweaty mess, holding tightly onto each other.

"Good girl," he whispers into my ear, making me instantly blush as his lips skim over my skin. "That was..."

"Wow," I finish his sentence.

His hand approaches my face, caressing his knuckles along my cheek. I break away from his shoulder to look at him. He shakes his head, lost in thought, before pressing our foreheads together. "Yeah, definitely, wow."

Bringing his hands back to my thighs, he grips me and stands, holding me to his chest.

"What are you doing?" I ask.

"We're going to take a shower. And then I will give you one more massage before I leave to let you sleep." He places me in front of the shower as he fiddles with the nob.

"Umm, do you think..." Why am I nervous to ask him? Oh, right. Because I don't deal well with rejection.

"Do I think what?" he asks softly.

I look down at the ground. "Do you think you could maybe stay tonight? You know, only if you want to, of course. If you don't want to, that's totally fine. No big deal." I wrap my arms around my waist, suddenly feeling self-conscious.

His two fingers lightly grip my chin, making me look up into his eyes. "Yes. I'll stay."

A smile breaks out on my face. "Okay."

He turns, stepping into the shower, holding out his hand for me to take.

And as I take his hand, I say, "Did you mention something about chocolate ice cream?"

I wake up with a body slightly on top of mine. A very large body that I'm having a hard time moving off of me so that I can breathe. But once I twist myself out from under Jason's arm and leg, I turn to face him, watching him sleeping peacefully beside me.

His hair is disheveled, his lips a little swollen, and his naked body next to my own is doing things to me that it shouldn't be doing this early in the morning.

"I can feel you staring at me," Jason grumbles with a smug smirk.

Busted.

A blush spreads over my skin as his eyes flutter open, looking directly at me.

"Good morning. How are you feeling?" he asks.

"Actually, I feel pretty great." I run my hand over my stomach, amazed that I no longer feel discomfort. He might have to start giving me special massages every month.

"It's my magic hands." He wraps his arm around me, his hand firmly on the middle of my back, pulling me right up against his chiseled chest.

"Magic hands, huh?"

His lips brush against mine. "Mhm. But I only use them for good. Like making you come over and over again."

My cheeks heat up, and I bury my head into his chest.

"Hey, I want a good morning kiss!" he whines.

"No way! I need to brush my teeth first." I move away from him, intending to go to the bathroom to brush my teeth, but instead, I get pulled back down to the bed. He pins me beneath him, with my hands above my head.

"I don't give a fuck about your morning breath." His lips land hard on mine, demanding I open for him, but I fight it, holding out until his tongue slides across my bottom lip, and I eventually cave.

After a few seconds, he pulls away. "Was that so hard?" His nose traces across my cheek as he makes his way to my neck.

I moan at the feeling of—

Knock. Knock. Knock.

"Vanessa? Are you up? I got something for you!" Natalie's voice comes from the other side of the door, and my heart stops working.

Jason's body stills as he lets out a quiet, "*Fuck.*"

We remain frozen, waiting for her to leave.

"Vanessa?" No luck.

I panic. "Sorry! I didn't hear you."

Jason shuffles off of me in alarm, falling off the bed.

"Vanessa, are you okay? Can I come in?"

"No!" I blurt out, jumping off the bed, looking around for anything to throw on. "I'm just getting dressed." Jason throws me his football T-shirt he wore last night, and I quickly throw it over my body, relieved that it flows almost to my knees. I take a few steps to the door and open it only a few inches so she doesn't see her brother now hiding on the other side of the bed.

"Hey," I say casually, looking completely normal.

"Are you okay?" Natalie furrows her brows at me. "You're flushed and breathing weirdly."

Okay, maybe I don't look completely normal. She knows. She definitely knows. Stay calm.

"Me? Oh, I'm fine. So what's up?" I lean against the doorframe, crossing my arms over my chest, trying to smile as my heart beats rapidly.

She stares at me, tilting her head. "Well, I got you something." Her eyes narrow in on the shirt I'm wearing. "Oh my God. Is there a guy in there?" she whispers, pointing to the Linrey football logo on the front of the T-shirt.

Shit.

"Umm, well, kind of," I say.

"Oh my God. I'm so sorry! Here take this." She shoves a bag in my hands. "Nathan and I were just getting coffee anyway. We'll be right out of your hair." She winks and turns, walking back toward the living room. "Nathan, let's go get coffee!"

"But we already got coffee." Nate sounds confused.

But the next second, I hear the front door open and close, followed by silence. Finally, I let out a deep breath and turn around to see Jason sitting on the edge of the bed wearing his sweatpants.

And it's making me wonder what it is about a guy wearing grey sweatpants that makes every girl completely turned on. Because at this moment, I am completely turned on.

I shake my head and walk over to him as I reach into the bag Natalie gave me and pull out a soft, maroon-colored sweatshirt with the words *I Love Boston* on the front, which makes me laugh. God, I love my best friend. But then, realizing what could have happened only thirty seconds ago comes back to me, causing my stomach to knot up. "So, that was close." I push my hair behind my ear, biting my bottom lip as guilt builds inside me.

"Hey, what's going on in that head?" Jason pulls me closer so I'm standing between his legs. I toss the bag and sweatshirt to the floor beside us.

"I feel guilty for lying to Natalie." I drop my shoulders. "She's my best friend, and it's like an unwritten rule you don't hook up with your best friend's brother."

"Do you want to stop this arrangement?" His question takes me by surprise.

He watches me silently, waiting patiently for a response.

My mind tells me to say *yes*. To tell him we need to stop this before one of us gets hurt. But my heart, and let's not lie, my pussy, scream for me to tell him I can't stop this even if I wanted to.

"No, I don't want to." I pull on the bottom of his T-shirt that I'm wearing, looking down at the ground. "Unless you want to?" Our eyes lock as every muscle in my body tenses, terrified of his answer.

The corners of his lips curve up. "No, Vanessa. I don't want to stop this." His hands pull on my T-shirt, dragging me closer to him. "But I don't ever want to be a source of your guilt or stress, so if this becomes too much for you, you'll tell me, right?"

"Right." Wrong.

He presses a delicate kiss to my forehead before pulling his T-shirt off my body as my arms go up into the air, allowing him to do so. "Okay, now get back into bed so I can fuck you before they get back."

Eighteen

Jason

"I'm open!"

I quickly pivot on my left foot, making it look like I'm going that way, throwing Paul off balance for a split second as I dribble to the right, and pass the ball to Nate. Nate dribbles toward the basket, only stopping when his buddy, Tim, blocks him from making a shot. Nate spins around him, leaps in the air, and shoots the ball looking to tie up the game, when out of nowhere, Paul slams the ball down to the concrete court.

"Better luck next time, suckers!" Paul exclaims with a victorious grin as he high-fives Tim.

"Nice one!" Tim reaches into his bag, pulling out a sports drink. "Now I see why the NBA is hounding you."

"Pshh. Playing against these two is like taking candy from a baby." Sitting on the closest metal bench near us, Paul laughs, stretching out his longer-than-life legs.

"You won by two points. Don't go thinking you're Lebron James," Nate adds as he plops on the grass, pulling out his hoodie from his bag. "Next time, Jason and I will be ready. Isn't that right, Jason?"

"Absolutely. We just had an off day, won't happen next time." I sit on the free side of the bench next to Paul, resting my elbows on my knees.

There's sweat coming out of every pore on my body, but this is what I live for. The high from physical activity. The adrenaline, pumping through me. Win or lose; it's addicting.

"Well, I have to get going, but Nate, are we still on for the batting cages tomorrow?" Tim asks, staring down at Nate.

"Yep. I'll see you there after my shift." Nate lies back on the grass, positioning his arms under his head as Tim runs over to his car.

"So, any plans for tonight?" I reach for the water beside me, bringing it to my lips in a hurry to quench my thirst.

"Nah," Paul responds. "Got the night off. Probably going to catch up on some TV." He slumps against the bench, looking up at the sky.

"No luck in the girl department?" I ask sympathetically.

"It's complicated." He runs a hand over his face, appearing like he wants to say more, but doesn't.

"How complicated?"

"Let's just say it's like Han Solo trying to stay away from Princess Leia. It's not possible."

"Who?" Both Nate and I ask at the same time.

"Oh, forget it. You two wouldn't know the Millenium Falcon if it hit you on the head." He sighs, resting his elbows on his knees and holds both sides of his face in his hands.

"Hey, big guy, cheer up. I'll come over tonight, and we can watch one of your nerdy shows." I would much rather have my cock buried inside Vanessa, making her come over and over again, but the guy clearly needs a distraction.

"Thanks, man. I'd like that." He pats my shoulder and looks over at Nate. "What about you, Nate? You in for a guy's night?"

"Nope." Nate pops the p and looks right at me. "I've got a double date tonight."

"What poor suckers did my sister convince to go out with you two?" I ask. Paul and I both glance at each other, breaking out into a fit of laughter. After finally catching my breath, I bring my water to my lips, amusement evident on my face.

Nate smirks. "Vanessa."

I spit out my water, some of it going down the wrong pipe.

Paul pats my back. "You alright there?"

"Yeah. Yeah." I wipe my mouth with the back of my hand. "Vanessa? But she's not even dating anyone." My eyes burn into Nate's. He must be mistaken. There's no way she's going on a double date with them.

He's wrong.

He has to be.

"No, she's not, which is why Natalie set her up with some guy from her English class. Said they would make a cute couple." Nate sits up, wiping the sweat off his forehead.

"And Vanessa agreed to this?" There's a vehemence in my voice that doesn't go unnoticed by both Paul and Nate, who look at each other before watching me with stupid grins on their faces.

"Well," Nate pulls his phone from his pocket, "Natalie was going to ask Vanessa while we were here, and seeing that she texted me saying, *'We're on for tonight,'* I'm going to guess she agreed." My blood is boiling. "You wouldn't have a problem with this, would you, Jason?"

The fucker is baiting me.

"No." I lean back against the bench and finish my water before continuing. "Vanessa's a single woman free to do whatever she wants. Why would I have a problem with it?"

"Interesting," Nate chimes.

Okay, I bite. "What's interesting?"

"Natalie is pretty positive Vanessa had someone in her room last week. She answered her bedroom door wearing a Linrey football shirt. You wouldn't happen to know of anyone on the team who she would be interested in?"

Paul's eyes widen as his smirk gets bigger.

Fuck. Nate fucking knows. But this can't get out. It will mess everything up between us.

I take a moment to answer, fixing my gaze on a nearby tree. The only leaves left on the tree are all a vibrant shade of red. The only color I see when I say, "Like I said, she's free to do whatever and whoever she wants."

No, she's fucking not.

I'm sitting on the black leather couch in Nate and Paul's house, silently losing my shit. My leg won't stop bouncing, and the inside of my cheek is starting to throb from chewing on it so much. Paul sets down two beers and a bowl of popcorn on the coffee table, completely unaware of the turmoil I'm experiencing. He picks up the remote, flicking through the channels.

"So, what should we—" He glances at me and arches his brows. "Everything okay? You seem tense?"

No, everything is not okay. Nate left a couple of hours ago to pick up the girls, and I'm losing my mind.

There is a part of my brain trying to remind me to calm the fuck down because, as I stupidly told Nate, Vanessa is free to do whatever she wants. She's single. She's an adult. And she's the one who agreed to go on this little date.

And if I'm being honest with myself, that's what's really bothering me.

She agreed to go on a date with someone else.

It fucking hurts even if she didn't intentionally do anything wrong.

We're not in a relationship. She's not my girlfriend.

But you want her to be.

But she can't.

She fucking can't be.

And no matter how hard I try, I can't make the questions in my head stop. Like, why didn't I man up and tell Nate she's mine? What was she wearing tonight? Would she laugh at this asshole's jokes? Would she be okay if he touched her? If he went in to kiss her, would she kiss him back?

Like I said, I'm going insane.

"No." I shake my head and jump to my feet, pacing the room. "Everything is not okay."

"Okay…" Paul shuts the TV off. "Want to talk about it?"

"I can't. That's the thing. I can't fucking talk about it."

Paul sighs. "Does this have anything to do with you and Vanessa seeing each other? And the fact that she's now on a date right now?"

I pause my steps, facing him. "How did you know?"

Paul huffs out a laugh. "It doesn't take a rocket scientist to know you two are … enjoying each other's company."

I let out a deep breath. "I'm so confused right now."

"Well, why don't you start from the beginning?" He brings a beer to his lips and relaxes on the couch. He pats the free cushion, insinuating I should sit down, and I do.

"You know we grew up together, right?"

"Right."

"But the thing is, me and her were always more than friends. Vanessa was always … the girl of my dreams." I can't believe I'm saying this out loud. "There's always been this invisible friendship line between us. We crossed it once when we were younger." I sit back, remembering that night like it was yesterday. Paul looks at me with wide eyes, so I clarify. "We were each other's first kiss." I shrug my shoulders like it was no big deal when I could never get that kiss out of my head. "But after that moment, she made me promise we would always be *just* friends." I pinch the bridge of my nose. The word friend seems to be responsible for some recent headaches in my life. "I abandoned her after everything with her brother came to light, and that's on me. I know I should never have done that, but I couldn't stop thinking about what Brian had done, and I let that asshole win even in jail by unintentionally letting him push me away from Vanessa. But when we became friends again, we kind of also became ... friends with benefits."

"And whose idea was that?" Paul asks.

A frustrated sigh leaves me. "Mine. I thought it was the only way I could ever have her while still being her friend."

I wait for Paul's judgmental comment, but he just sits there listening to me.

"We came up with some rules so neither of us would get hurt, like if one of us starts having feelings for the other, we end this."

"And now you're breaking that rule because you love her?"

"Is it really breaking it if I've loved her my whole life?"

Paul lets out a low whistle. "So, why don't you just tell her?"

"And risk losing her? No way. That risk is too big to take." I shake my head adamantly. There's no way I'm doing that.

I can't lose her.

"Did you ever think she might feel the same way?" Paul asks.

"No, I don't. She's made it clear several times that all she wants to be with me is friends. And I've promised her twice now to always be her friend no matter what. Just a fucking friend." I tug at the ends of my hair, feeling defeated. "Besides, even if I love her, I can't tell her."

"Why not?"

I shake my head, knowing I can't tell him. "You wouldn't understand." Paul looks confused, and I can't blame him. No one will ever know the real reason why Vanessa and I can't fall in love with each other, even if I'm already past that point. And I'm not about to say why out loud because I'll only sound crazy.

I even sound crazy to myself when I think about it.

"The point is I'm losing my fucking mind right now knowing she's on a date with some asshole who—"

"Actually, Ben's in my ASL class, and he's a really nice g—" I smack him with a couch pillow. "Ow!"

"As I was saying, I need to find them. Do you know where they went?"

Paul rubs his cheek dramatically. "Why should I tell you? You just hit me with a pillow. Could possibly be out for the rest of the season."

I raise the pillow in the air, and Paul raises his hands in surrender. "Alright! Alright! They went to that new Italian place down the street."

I know what place he's talking about since I drive right by it on my way to practice every day.

I leap to my feet and make my way straight to the door but freeze, turning back to face Paul. "And Paul, I know you're good friends with Nate, but please don't mention any of this to him."

He smiles reassuringly. "I won't. Scouts honor."

"Thanks, Paul. Sorry about tonight. We'll try this again next weekend," I state, anxiously zipping my coat.

"Sounds good. Now go get your woman." He waves me away, and I move through the door like my ass is on fire.

I don't know what I'm doing, and I don't have any idea what I plan on saying, but all I do know is that I need to get to my girl right fucking now.

I race to my truck and pull out, my tires screeching on the cement, leaving tire marks. I make it to the restaurant in ten minutes, and just as I pull into a spot near the front, I see the four of them walking out of the restaurant laughing.

My heart sinks.

The guy looks decent enough. Dark black hair, lean, skinny jeans—only a few inches taller than Vanessa compared to me, given that I'm at least a foot taller than her. Too big of a smile that spreads over his face when Vanessa says something.

I immediately hate him.

Maybe because he's the total opposite of me.

Is that what she wants?

Vanessa looks stunning, wearing a black knee-length dress under her favorite red coat. She's laughing along with what everyone else is saying, hypnotizing me with her smile as they all walk toward the cars. I swear I can see the hues of her beautiful brown eyes shimmering against the sun that is setting, casting a pinkish glow over her face.

The asshole has the nerve to put his hand on Vanessa's lower back, guiding her to Nate's car. She stops at the passenger door and spins to face him. Her lips move, saying something I wish I could hear before she reaches up and kisses the guy on his cheek, sending a harsh stab of ice through my erratically beating heart.

She kissed him.

Granted, it wasn't on the lips. But she kissed him. And she looks happy with him. She looks like she belongs with him.

Absentmindedly, I pull out of my spot and head toward my apartment, not wanting to witness another second of this.

I slump inside my apartment and lie face-first on my couch. What the fuck am I doing?

But I don't have long to think about this because only a moment later, there's a small knock on my door.

"Come in," I say, sitting up, reaching for the remote near me.

Vanessa walks in, slowly closing the door behind her. "Hey."

"Hey." I don't look at her as I aimlessly flip through the channels.

She sighs, sliding her coat off her shoulders and folding it in her arms. "I know you're mad at me, but I can explain."

"I'm not mad."

"Yes, you are. You're doing that thing where you get so tense a line forms between your brows, and your eyes are practically the color of a piece of charcoal." She raises one defiant eyebrow, crossing her arms over her chest.

Fuck. She knows me too well. I try to relax my muscles.

"It wasn't a real date." She sits on the other side of the sofa, giving me space. "Natalie asked me to go with them, and I couldn't come up with a reason not to go without looking suspicious, so I said yes."

I shrug my shoulders. "You can date whoever you want, Vanessa. Why should I care?"

Yeah, I regretted the moment these words left my mouth.

"You don't ... you don't seriously mean that, right?" she asks softly.

I don't say anything, staring ahead at the TV screen.

"Okay then. If that's how you feel." She gets up, making her way to the door, but I get up too, quickly moving without thinking. Her hand lands on the doorknob, opening the door only an inch before I slam it shut, keeping my palms on the smooth surface above her head, caging her in. My chest brushes against her back, and I feel her body shiver, the smell of her fucking floral perfume intoxicating me.

"No." I clench my jaw. "That's not how I fucking feel."

Her breathing is shallow as tiny goosebumps erupt on the back of her neck. I bring my lips down to her ear, grazing her skin with my teeth. "Do you think I liked knowing you were going on a date? That you were getting dressed up for him? Laughing for him? Kissing him on his fucking cheek?"

She gasps. "Were you spying on me?"

"I was going insane thinking about another man touching you, so I went to find you. I don't know what I planned on doing, but all I knew was that I couldn't sit around and wait any longer. So, I drove to the restaurant just in time to see the four of you leaving. To see your lips on him."

I'm angry.

No, I'm pissed.

But not at her.

Never at her.

I'm pissed at myself.

"Jason…" She spins around to face me, my chest against her soft breasts, backing her into the door. "I told him I had a nice time but didn't feel anything. I kissed him on the cheek to be polite, but there was nothing between us. I only went to throw off Natalie. That's why I said yes to going. I swear."

I press my forehead to hers. "It killed me. It was a fucking kiss on the cheek, and it still killed me."

"You trust me, don't you?" she asks quietly.

"With my life."

"Then please kiss me," she pleads.

"Only if you say it," I respond.

"Say what?"

"Tell me you're mine, Vanessa. I need to hear it."

The spot where my heart is currently pounding is met by the gentle touch of the palm of her hand. She looks up at me through her dark lashes, biting her plush bottom lip, revealing an expression of pure desire, and it's the most beautiful thing I've ever seen. "I'm yours, Jason."

My lips consume hers, needing to invade every part of her. Her fingers tangle in the back of my hair, pulling me into her while my hands slide down her waist, gripping her thighs and lifting her into my arms. I turn away from the door, planning to bring her to my bed, but I need her now. This very second. So instead of taking her to my bedroom, I use one arm to sweep everything off the kitchen island, pots and pans clattering to the kitchen floor around us as I lay her on the countertop.

I break the kiss, bringing my lips down her neck.

"Jason…" she breathes, our eyes locking. "Fuck me like I'm yours."

A groan escapes me from her words that have taken over me.

Fuck. Me. Like. I'm. Yours.

She is mine.

Her fingers stay intertwined in my hair as I savor every kiss down her neck. My hands grip the bottom of her dress, heaving it up to her waist. I look at her panties and notice how soaked they are between her legs. "Are you wet for me, Vee?"

She nods her head, spreading her legs wide open for me. "Only for you."

"Fuck," I hiss, pulling them off her body swiftly. I sit on the counter stool directly between Vanessa's legs, giving me a full view of what I want. Grasping her ankles, I pull her all the way to the edge so that her ass cheeks hang off the counter and her legs balance on my shoulders.

My lips press to the inside of her right leg, nibbling and sucking a path to her core. She shivers with each kiss, gripping the edge of the countertop for support. Her ass wiggles against the surface. I know she's looking for some friction to take care of that ache between her legs, and I plan on giving her exactly what she needs.

I lap up her arousal with one long leisurely swipe of my tongue between her center, watching her squirm with pleasure. "Is this what you want, sweetheart? To get fucked by my tongue until you come all over my face."

"Yes," she moans, shoving her pussy toward me, demanding my attention. "More Jason. Please," she begs.

I devour her. Feasting on her like a starved man. The idea that some other guy could do this to her throws me over the edge as I lick, nip, and suck, sending her to the brink of an orgasm at record speed. I plunge two fingers inside her, and she screams out my name as her muscles clench around me. She's so close that it only takes one more firm swipe of my tongue over her clit to make her completely come undone under my touch. She's panting, bringing her hands up to her chest, trying to catch her breath, but I need to see all of her. I come to her side, pulling the dress over her chest until it's finally off her. Bending down, I kiss the soft porcelain skin of her breasts spilling out of her bra.

"This needs to come off." My fingers hastily unclasp the bra in the front, and I immediately start sucking on one of her hardened nipples while she shimmies the bra off her shoulders. I release her nipple as she gasps and stand up straight to look down at her, completely taken aback by the sight of her. Tousled hair. Swollen lips. Creamy soft curves. Flushed cheeks. "You're so unbelievably perfect. My eyes never get their fill of you."

Her blush deepening makes my cock harden uncomfortably against my pants.

Grabbing a condom from my wallet, I unzip my jeans and let them fall to my ankles. I quickly roll the condom over my throbbing dick and then set her ankles on my shoulders as I run my cock through her folds, loving the anticipation building between us.

"Jason, please."

"You're mine," I say as I enter her in one hard thrust, the angle allowing me to go deeper than I ever have. "This ass." I grip her round ass, kneading my fingers into her soft skin. "This pussy." My hand cups her, pressing my thumb right onto her clit, creating a back-and-forth motion that I know she likes. Her head rolls back as she lets out a moan, gripping the counter's edge for dear life, trying to stay in place, which is almost impossible to do as I repeatedly thrust in and out of her at a mad pace. "This whole goddamn beautiful body is mine." My hands hold onto her waist tightly, bringing her flush against me. She watches me with glossed-over eyes as her tits bounce and her body begins to tremble.

She sits up, wrapping her legs around my torso, using one hand to hold her up while the other arm rests around my neck. Her eyes lock with mine, holding a silent conversation, reminding me she's mine, even if just for right now. She bites down on her bottom lip, hanging her head back as another orgasm approaches. My thumb provides just enough pressure on her clit, sending her into euphoria at the same moment I lose control, unraveling with her.

We sit like this for a few minutes, breathing erratically against each other. She brings her arms around my neck, holding onto me while I wrap one arm around her back, splaying my hand against her skin, and bring my other hand up to her face, tilting her chin toward me.

"You're never going on another date again. Are we clear?"

She agrees but says, "I don't even want to consider that a real date."

"Why?" I'm curious. Relieved but curious.

"Because I've never been on a real date before."

"Wait. Never?" Not that I like the thought of her being on a date with another guy, but the fact that she's never been on a real date before doesn't sit right with me.

She shakes her head. "No." Her head rests on my shoulder, and her eyes start closing.

"I take it you probably have to return to your place so Natalie doesn't think you're missing?"

"No." She grins. "She's staying at Nate's tonight."

"Well, in that case." I throw her over my shoulder and walk over to the couch, where I place her before heading to my room.

"What are you doing?" she asks, but I ignore her as I rifle through my bureau for a pair of sweatpants for me and a T-shirt for her. I grab my football T-shirt with my name on it, knowing how good she's about to look in this.

"We're going to have—"

My words cut off when I see her. She's wrapped in a blanket with my journal in her hand. The goddamn journal that I left out like an idiot, completely forgetting to put it away.

"Hey, Jason. What's this?"

Her eyes look up to me, but it's too late. The damage is done. Or is it? How much could she have read in the span of thirty seconds?

"It's nothing." I grab the spiral journal from her hand, trying to act casual as I place it in the drawer inside the coffee table.

"Was that ... a diary?"

"Nope." I sit on the couch beside her. There's no fucking way I'm telling her the truth.

"But it looked like a diary. There were dates in it."

"Did you read any of it?" I ask casually.

"Well, no. I didn't think I should."

Thank fucking God.

"Ok. Then you have no proof it was a diary. Here." I toss her the T-shirt distracting her. "We're having a sleepover."

"A sleepover?" She smirks, removing the blanket and putting on my T-shirt. And as sexy as she looks with nothing on, I can't help but stare at her wearing a shirt with my last name on it.

"What?" she asks, looking self-consciously down at herself. "Do I look okay?"

"Vanessa," my eyes travel over her body, "you could wear a potato sack and still look unbelievably beautiful."

She looks up at me with a breathtaking smile. And knowing I'm the reason for her smile makes me feel like the luckiest man in the world.

"Come here." I place my arm on the back of the couch, waiting for her to curl up to my side, which she does. The smell of that damn addicting scent I've become obsessed with hits me, and I need to know what it is. "Why do you always smell so delicious?"

She giggles. "It's my honeysuckle perfume. Do you like it?"

"Like it? Vanessa, it's like a shot of Viagra to my dick. Not that my dick needs it. Clearly evident from this evening." I wink at her, and she shakes her head laughing.

"So what does a sleepover with you entail?" she asks, snuggling against my side.

"Well, first, here's the remote. You find something we can watch. And I'll order some food to be delivered."

"But—"

"No buts." I look down into her eyes, cupping her cheek. "I know you didn't eat enough tonight. You don't like eating in front of anyone but me, so we're eating."

She purses her lips, but instead of protesting like I thought she would, she says, "Okay."

"No argument?"

"Nope." She shrugs her shoulders. "You're right. You're the only one I don't mind eating in front of besides Natalie. And I am pretty hungry." She smiles but suddenly drops her gaze. "I umm. Well, I don't want to make it a big deal, but I was talking to Natalie about her therapy, and she told me how much it helps her with her anxiety. So I thought that maybe I could find a therapist who specializes in ... body image issues and eating disorders," she quietly admits. "From what I've seen online, I might have ... well, actually, I know I have body dysmorphia, so I thought it might be worth a try."

"Vanessa." She looks up at me nervously. "I think that's amazing."

"Yeah?"

"Yeah." I'm so fucking proud of her. I tilt my head down to kiss her forehead. "That's my girl."

Nineteen

VANESSA

"That looks like a monkey's butt," Natalie remarks.

I tilt my head to the side, squinting as I look at the painting before me. The one I am currently working on, which is supposed to look like the sunset image the instructor has presented at the front of the room for us to recreate.

"Oh God. You're right," I reply, giggling. I reach for the glass of wine in front of me, hoping alcohol will improve my painting.

Natalie laughs but then slumps on her stool. "It's okay. Mine isn't much better." I take a glance at her easel.

"I think we'd make Van Gough roll over in his grave if he ever saw these." I bite my lip, holding in my laugh until we both finally lose it, gaining the attention of others in the room.

"Done!" Sarah declares, turning her easel to show us her work.

Natalie and I sit silently beside each other, our mouths hanging wide open.

"Sarah, that's beautiful!" Natalie gets up from her seat, stepping closer to the painting. "Where did you learn to paint like this?"

Sarah shrugs. "My mom taught me." She looks over the painting, looking lost in the colors and brush strokes as if seeing something else entirely.

"I'm surprised you don't do this professionally," I add. "People would pay a lot of money for a beautiful painting like that."

"Oh, I'm not that good," Sarah says, shaking her head.

Natalie and I give each other a look.

"You're wrong," I state, not wanting to see her diminish her own accomplishment. "You're very talented. And you should be proud of yourself."

Gee, look at me being the pot who calls the kettle black.

She looks at me with tenderness in her eyes. "Thanks, Vanessa." She glances at my and Natalie's paintings, stifling a laugh.

"Go ahead. Let it out," I say, smiling, throwing my hands in the air.

"I was just going to say I wish I could return the compliment." She loses it, laughing so hard that tears spill out of her eyes.

We all take a moment to contain ourselves, but it's easier said than done when I have to stare at my monkey butt picture in front of me.

"Refills, anyone?" The waitress at the art studio asks as she approaches our table with a bottle of wine in her hands.

"Yes, please," both Natalie and I say in unison.

"I'm all set," Sarah confirms, holding her sparkling water.

"Sarah, the place is called Wine and Paint Night. Not Water and Paint Night," Natalie teases.

"I know. Trust me, I wish I could join you guys, but it's just..." She pauses, lost in thought, before shaking her head. "I have to be up early again for work." Her shoulders drop.

"Hey, don't worry. Natalie and I will drink enough for the three of us," I tease, making her smile.

"Everything going okay at work?" Natalie asks, looking suddenly concerned.

"Oh, yeah. Yeah. Everything is fine," she replies with a smile that I know Natalie can see right through. She's always been good about seeing through people—one of her hidden talents.

"And you still like working for a bank?" Natalie asks, her brows furrowed.

"It's umm..." Sarah's smile falters, and her eyes mist over. "It pays the bills."

"Oh, Sarah." I get up from my stool and wrap my arms around her. "What is it?"

"It's nothing," she says, but the way she holds me tighter tells me it isn't nothing.

I pull away just enough to look at her, waiting for her to continue.

"It's just some asshole at my office." She wipes the tears off her face. "Nothing I can't handle." Her back straightens, trying to appear confident.

"Is there anyone in your office you can talk to about this?" I ask.

She looks at me, hopeless. "It's a company filled with rich old powerful men. It's also the boss's son. They wouldn't care or do anything about it. I would quit, but I umm ... I really need the money right now."

"You know. I know you don't know him very well, but if you ever need help, I know Paul would take care of things for you. He's a really great guy. He'd give you the coat off his back on the coldest day of the year," I say. He might be a teddy bear, but I have a feeling underneath that fuzzy exterior is someone very protective you don't want to mess with.

Her eyes momentarily widen, looking ready to shed more tears, but she clears her throat and shakes her head adamantly. "No. I got this. Really." She wears a forced smile. "Please don't say anything to him."

"I won't." I promise, even though everything in me tells me not to. "But if there is anything Natalie and I can do to help, you'll let us know, right?"

She nods as tears begin to stream down her face. "I'm sorry. I don't know why I'm so emotional."

I wipe her tears away and throw my arm over her shoulder. "It's Natalie's picture. It's so ugly it just makes you want to cry."

"Hey!" Natalie exclaims. "At least mine doesn't look like a monkey's ass."

"Touché," I say.

Natalie gets up from her seat, wrapping her arms around me and Sarah. "We girls have to stick together."

"I'm seriously so glad I met you guys," Sarah says softly through a quiet sob. "I don't know what I would do without you."

"Me too," I say as Natalie squeezes my hand.

"Thanks for coming with me." I glance out the passenger side window of Jason's truck as we make our way home to Connecticut.

"It's no problem. I was due for a trip home anyway." Looking over at him, he smiles, but then it drops as his brows crease. "Why do you seem tense?"

If only he knew.

"It's nothing." I rub my clammy palms over my jeans, feeling dread permeate through every pore on my body.

The fabric I've been waiting on was finally delivered a few days ago, and I should be back at my apartment working on my designs now, but instead, I find myself going to the one place that's only ever made me anxious. The place I always felt the loneliest. *My home.* I haven't been home since Thanksgiving, and was hoping to prolong my next visit for as long as possible, but I knew this day would eventually come. Besides, I didn't have much say in the matter. My mom called me for the first time in weeks to tell me she was redecorating the upstairs and needed me to move some of my things out of my room before the painters started working in the house next week.

Maybe this is her way of trying.

Maybe she's trying to redecorate my room for when I come home from school.

But as much as I try to convince myself of this, the bigger part of me, the part that has spent so much time being hurt by her, knows better than to think this.

You'll only get your hopes up, Vanessa.

We pull into the driveway, and as I jump out of Jason's truck, I reach for my overnight bag and make my way toward the front of the house. I notice dumpsters lining up on the side of the house, but my mom had only mentioned she was redecorating, not doing renovations. A knot builds in my stomach. Jason makes his way around the truck and walks along with me up the cobblestone path to the rather ornate and, in my opinion, tacky-looking door.

"Jason, if my mom says anything … out of line. Please just ignore her, okay?"

"Out of line?" His eyes narrow.

I place my hand on the doorknob, looking at him over my shoulder. "Just, please promise me?"

He looks agitated but says, "Okay."

I open the door and poke my head inside. "Hello?" As we make our way inside, I notice boxes and supplies everywhere. "What the hell?"

"Oh, good. You're here!" I view the top of the grand staircase to see my mom making her way elegantly down each step. "And you've brought Jason. Perfect. We're going to need some muscles." She clasps her hands to her cheeks, acting like Jason is God's gift to the world, and he displays a tight-lipped smile in return.

The man does not need an ego boost, Mom.

"Well, come on, you two." She pauses halfway down the stairs and motions for us to follow her. "Let me show you what needs to go!"

What needs to go?

We follow her up the stairs and down the hallway to my room, where I abruptly stop in the entryway. "What the actual fuck?"

"Vanessa! Language!" my mom scolds.

"Mom, you told me I needed to remove some things from my room before the painters arrived. You didn't tell me you destroyed my bedroom!" I'm in utter disbelief. I don't know if I want to cry or if I want to laugh at how this should never have been a surprise to me in the first place.

Trying my ass.

"Oh, you're being dramatic. It's not like you live here anymore anyway." She throws her manicured hands in the air. And I'm the dramatic one? "The painters are coming to finish the rest of the rooms next week. And I don't want your things to be in the way while they're here."

The walls are no longer a soft pink but a deep grey. All of my childhood boy band posters are gone, replaced with scenic landscapes. An elliptical and treadmill take over one side of the room. Yoga mats and weights are lined in one corner of the room, surrounded by candles and weird-looking chrome bells. Where is my room? Where are my stuffed animals? My bookcase. My ceiling stars. My favorite quilt my grandma made me. My diaries.

I'm suddenly enraged. My hands turn into fists at my sides, and I close my eyes, taking a deep breath.

"Where am I supposed to sleep when I come home?"

"Well, honey, you can just use one of the guest rooms," she responds, looking at me like I've lost my mind.

"One of the guestrooms?" I'm full-on pissed now. "Why didn't you do this to the guestroom?"

"Well, this room has the best lighting, you know that. Honestly, Vanessa, it's not a big deal. I packed all your stuff in boxes right over there, and there's more in the hallway. And your father already brought the dresser downstairs for you to take."

My blood pressure has hit its boiling point, and during all of this, I completely forgot that Jason was standing right behind me, witnessing this disaster, until he clears his throat.

"I'll grab the boxes for you and meet you downstairs." He takes the overnight bag from my hand, realizing I won't be needing it anymore, and then puts it on top of a box before picking up the whole thing like it weighs nothing, walking out in the hallway, leaving me alone with the woman who calls herself my mom.

Her phone rings, and she answers without giving me a second thought. "Hi, Karen." She goes out into the hall, but not before she looks at me up and down. "Stand up straight, honey, you're slouching, and you know that's not good for your waistline," she says on her way out.

My eyes start watering.

My own family doesn't want me. I mean, I always felt like they didn't, but this just confirms it.

And then a thought occurs to me.

I bolt out of my room and make my way down the hall hastily to Brian's room—well, the room that was his before he left for prison. I take a deep breath and slowly turn the doorknob. Right after opening it, I fall to my knees on the plush-beige carpet with a thud and cry into the palms of my hands.

They didn't touch anything in his room.

They've left it the same as if he still lives here.

They're waiting for him to come home.

Is this my punishment for testifying?

A pair of strong arms wrap around me, picking me up. My legs wrap around Jason's torso as he shuts the door behind us and walks us back to what used to be my room. Not anymore.

"Shh." His hand glides down my hair and up and down my back in a comforting caress. "I'm here. Let it out."

I bury my head into his shirt to muffle my sobs and wrap my arms tighter around his neck. "What did I do wrong?" I ask so quietly I'm not even sure he heard me.

"Nothing." He shakes his head. "Absolutely nothing." He sets me down on my feet and then moves his hand up to my chin, where he tilts it so our eyes lock. "You are perfect. And I'm sorry they don't see that, but I do, Vee. I see you." He pushes my hair behind my ear and then gently kisses my forehead. "Now, let's get you and your stuff out of here before I lose my shit in front of your mother."

It takes us about an hour to get everything out of my room and into Jason's truck, but when we're done, I search the house to find my mom in the kitchen to tell her we're leaving.

"Hey, Mom, we're going to get going now. We have a long trip back." I thought I would be spending the night here, but I guess I'll probably have to take the bus back to Boston since Jason will stay at his house.

"Are you two stopping at the Spencer's house?" she asks in the middle of food prepping her weekly allotted calories—something she used to drill into me.

Jason enters the room behind me. "Yes, we are going to head there now." He doesn't smile, and honestly, he looks mildly irritated.

"Perfect. I just made a chocolate cake." She places a large container in my hands. "Give this to Nancy and tell her I say hi, won't you?" She's probably trying to kiss Mrs. Spencer's ass with this. You know, since my brother attacked her daughter and all. "Vanessa, honey, try not to have any." She looks at my midsection. "I don't want it adding to the love handles you seem to have developed while being at school."

My mouth falls wide open as my whole body heats up in embarrassment. I'm used to her criticism about my body in private. But the fact that she just said that in front of Jason has me feeling absolutely mortified.

Jason moves around me and takes the container out of my hands. With fury in his eyes and a terrifying grin, he says, "Actually, I love Vanessa's love handles. It helps to have something to hold onto if you know what I'm saying." He gives me a wink before he kisses my temple and walks out of the house, leaving me momentarily stunned.

My mom appears as if she just saw a ghost but then quickly turns back to the counter, aligned with an assortment of chopped-up vegetables for her to continue sorting.

"Umm, bye, Mom." I quickly leave the house, not having a clue what to say, and head straight for Jason's truck. I jump inside and buckle up, feeling the tension suffocating me. "Jason, about what my mom—"

"Not right now," he says through gritted teeth. His hands squeeze the steering wheel as we back out of the driveway and head toward his parents' house, conveniently only ten minutes away. We drive in strained silence, and all I can think about is the latest insult my mom speared me with.

Do I really have love handles? Are they noticeable? I know I've gained a few pounds, but I hadn't noticed any extra weight on this part of my body. Maybe Jason didn't love them and only said that to piss my mother off. I reach for the hem of my shirt, wanting to lift it just a smidge to examine these love handles I haven't noticed before, but as my fingers grip the fabric, Jason's hand lands on mine.

"You're perfect," he whispers, looking straight ahead. He intertwines our fingers, placing them on his thigh for the rest of the drive, essentially shutting off my overthinking mind.

When we pull into his parent's driveway, he lets out a deep exhale. "Do you want to talk about it?" he asks, looking at me with pure sympathy in his eyes as I sit here feeling so fucking embarrassed.

I look down and shake my head.

"Vee?"

I look up at him. "Maybe later."

"Okay." There's silence between us. "Come here, sweetheart."

Immediately, I lean toward him and the moment his soft lips press against mine, I'm reminded I'm no longer alone in this world. And even if what we have is just a friendship, it's enough for me.

I think.

His lips part from mine as his thumb rubs against my cheek. "Let's get inside and have dinner. I'm starving."

"Well, okay, but I should probably make my way to the bus stop before it gets late."

"Why would you do that?" He arches a brow.

"In case you didn't notice, I no longer have a room to stay at. My bedroom is gone."

Jason laughs—a genuine no holds back kind of laugh.

"Why is that funny?" I press my lips together, annoyed.

"It's funny if you think I'm letting you take a bus all the way back to Boston tonight, alone." He laughs again as if hearing the joke for the first time, and I let him continue as I cross my arms over my chest, staring out the windshield. "Come on. I'll get your bag from the back. You're staying here tonight."

"What? I can't." I shake my head.

"And why not?"

"Well, because I've only stayed over when Natalie's here. Don't you think your parents will think it's weird if I'm here with you?"

"Absolutely not." He opens his door, hops out, and then grabs my bag and the cake from the back seat before coming around and opening my door. "You know they love you and don't care if you come here with me, Natalie, or by yourself. You'll always have a room here."

There's a silent *ping* where my heart beats.

I jump out and follow him to the front door, but he detours toward the trash barrel by the garage.

"What are you doing?" I ask as he lifts the lid.

He tosses the cake into the barrel. "Taking care of this."

I open my mouth to protest but stop myself.

He wipes his hands on his jeans. "Any objections?'

I shake my head and smile. "Nope."

"Good, because no one talks to you that way. Especially not your mother." He grabs my hand, leading me to the place I've always felt most at home.

Walking inside, it smells like heaven, if heaven is a room filled with all the Italian fixings one could ever desire. Someone should bottle this scent up and call it "*amo la pasta.*"

"Ah, Mom must be making Italian tonight. I told her we would be over for dinner." He rubs his stomach enthusiastically.

"And how did you know I would be joining you?"

He shrugs his shoulders. "Just had a feeling."

We make our way toward the kitchen, where the smells become stronger and more potent in the best possible way.

We quickly separate our hands before Jason declares, "Hey, Mom! We're home."

We're home. Why do those two words make my heart blissfully pitter-patter?

Mrs. Spencer stands on the other side of the kitchen island and turns around to face us. "Perfect timing, you two!" She wipes her hands on her apron. "Oh, Vanessa, I was so excited when Jason said you'd be joining us for dinner! I made your favorites, so I hope you're hungry!"

Jason and I look at each other with a knowing smile.

This is how a mom should treat you.

This is how it should feel when you come home.

This is called *love.*

Twenty

JASON

This is my ideal perfect night.

There's a fire roaring in the fireplace, a New England Patriots game on the flatscreen in front of me, and one of my mom's famous double chocolate chip brownies on a plate in my hands.

It doesn't take much to make me happy.

The only thing that would make this better is if—

"So." My mom enters the living room, making herself comfortable on the other side of the couch with a brownie in her hand. "I just got off the phone with Linda Gordon, we had a pretty interesting conversation. Want to tell me what you said to her?" she asks, most likely already knowing.

Would I take it back? Absolutely not. The horrified expression on that woman's face was something I'll cherish forever.

I grin. "Nothing that isn't true."

She rolls her eyes but smiles. "What am I going to do with you?"

I shake my head laughing, then sigh, crossing my arms over my chest. "You should have seen it, Mom. They basically kicked Vanessa out of the house. She had all of her childhood memories packed in boxes for her to take. All so they could have a workout room with *perfect lighting*."

I scoff. "Mrs. Gordon told her she could use the guest room when she visits, which is when I started to feel myself losing it."

Vanessa went upstairs after dinner. She was exhausted—I could see it in her eyes that she could barely keep open. I made sure she had everything she needed in the guest room before I made my way back downstairs and was comfortable in my current position.

I'm hopeful my surprise for her tomorrow night might be enough to cheer her up.

"Linda never mentioned this to me. Although, I suppose she wouldn't. She probably doesn't even recognize that she did something wrong." My mom rubs at her temple.

"Why are you guys friends with them?" I ask, getting straight to the point.

She chews on the brownie piece in her mouth before saying, "I don't know." She puts her brownie down on a napkin on the coffee table. "When we were all younger, everything seemed simple. We weren't trying to impress each other, we were just friends. But sometimes people change and—"

"And now you're kind of stuck in an uncomfortable friendship."

"I guess you could say that. I suppose after everything that's happened this past year, we've slowly started drifting from each other." She looks over at me curiously. "What did you say to Linda? Because she made it seem like you and Vanessa might have something going on between the two of you."

I take a bite of my brownie, refusing to answer.

"Listen, you don't have to answer that, but just know I'm not blind, and I see how the two of you look at each other." She reclines her side of the sofa and grabs a blanket between us to place over her waist.

I look up at the ceiling, closing my eyes. "She basically called Vanessa 'fat' in front of me."

My mom picks up the remote and puts the game on mute.

"What?" she asks, shocked.

"Yeah." I open my eyes, facing her. "She handed Vanessa a cake to bring here and told her she shouldn't have any of it because it would add to her love handles." I shake my head feeling pissed. Vanessa doesn't have fucking love handles. She has a waist, hips, curves, and everything that makes her perfect. And even if she does have them, who fucking cares? "And instead of exploding on her mother, I remained calm and just kind of insinuated that I liked Vanessa's love handles." I shrug my shoulders. "I guess it's not new for her mom to criticize her body."

My mom exhales. "I can't tell you how hard it is growing up and being a woman in today's society, especially when the one person who is supposed to make you feel confident and strong does the complete opposite." She shakes her head, crossing her arms over her chest. "Has Vanessa talked about this with you?"

"Yeah, she has." We still haven't talked about her mom's comment tonight, but I would like to. I immediately noticed when she went to lift her shirt in my truck to check for herself if she had damn love handles, and it made me so angry. Not at Vanessa, but at her mom, who so easily put a new insecurity in her head.

"Well, all we can do is be there for her. And I know she's lucky to have a friend like you in her life. Whatever the word *friend* may mean these days." She raises her brows in question.

"Mom!" I run a hand down my face. "Please don't make me regret coming home for the night."

She chuckles. "And what happened to the cake?"

"I threw it out."

"Jason!" Her voice is loud, but she's smiling, so I know she doesn't actually care.

"You know it's what you would have done."

"Like mother like son," she adds. "Is that the saying?"

"Looks like it is now." Laughter breaks out between us. "Don't worry. I won't tell Natalie that I'm your favorite."

She playfully smacks my arm. "I don't have favorites."

"Sure you don't…"

She takes another bite of her brownie and then relaxes in her seat. "Vanessa seemed pretty exhausted when she was here tonight. This all can't be easy on her. Especially on top of everything with her brother. I'm sure testifying against him has weighed heavily on her."

The mention of Brian makes me tense, but thankfully Vanessa doesn't have anything to do with him anymore. If she did, we'd never be as close as we are now.

"Yeah." I take the last bite of my brownie and put the plate on the table beside me.

"All I'm going to say, Jason, is if you hurt her, I will be forced to take you out of the will." She shrugs her shoulders as if it was an obvious statement.

"Jesus, Mom." I chuckle as comfortable silence falls around us. And then I look at her, knowing I need to ask. "How's Grandpa doing?"

She shows an encouraging smile. "He's okay, honey. I saw him this morning, and we had a nice time playing bingo. He kept asking about you, wanting to know all about your football season. He's so proud of you."

I swallow the lump in my throat, nodding. "I'm going to try to visit him soon. It's just…"

"I know, honey." She squeezes my hand. "It's not easy, but I know he'd love to see you."

I'd love to see him too. It just scares me, never knowing what kind of day it'll be when I see him.

It's either a good day, or a bad day.

There's no in-between.

And the last time I saw him was a day I try so hard to forget.

I clear my tightening throat, pushing away the melancholy feeling. "Now, back to the part about you taking me out of the will. What exactly am I going to inherit?" I joke, trying to lighten the mood.

"Who's getting taken out of our will?" my dad asks as he enters the room.

"Jason if he doesn't take care of our second daughter." My mom looks up at my dad, who kisses her forehead before taking the spot on the sofa beside her.

"Oh, I see." My dad winks.

"God, can the two of you please not make this weird?" I run an exasperated hand down my face.

"Who said anything about making this weird? We're cool, parents," my dad remarks.

"Oh, sweetie"—my mom pats my dad's forearm—"I'm afraid we're no longer 'cool' in our kid's eyes."

"Well, this is news to me." He pulls on the blanket over my mom's lap so she's forced to share with him.

"So, Jason, how is everything at Linrey going?" my mom asks hesitantly. She softly elbows my dad in his side.

"Yes. How is football going, kid?" They both give each other a *look* before staring at me.

"Fine." I narrow my eyes, glaring between the two of them. "Am I missing something here?"

My mom waves a hand around dismissively. "Well, you know how I would never invade my children's privacy?"

"By the way you're looking at me, I'm not so sure…"

She reaches into the coffee table drawer, pulls out a thick manilla envelope, and places it on the table. "Why didn't you tell us?"

It's my acceptance packet to the University of Southern California. *Shit.*

"I was doing laundry, and it was on the floor beside your laundry basket." She looks at me apologetically. "We know it was your dream school. You've wanted to play football for them since you were a little boy. So, why didn't you go?"

I sit up, pick up the packet, and pull out the acceptance letter. The same letter that offered me a starting position on—what used to be—my dream team to play for.

"I guess it wasn't my dream anymore." I give them a sheepish look, hoping they'll drop it, but they both wait for me to explain. I sigh. "I couldn't do it. I got the letter in the mail, and for five whole minutes, I was so excited, picturing myself leading the football team to victory as the starting quarterback. But then I realized that dream was on the other side of the country. Away from home, you and"—I close my eyes—"Natalie," I whisper, shaking my head. "After what happened to her, I couldn't leave her to be on the other side of the country. She's my sister, I'm supposed to protect her, but I failed her." I relax in my seat. "I wasn't going to fail her again. So, when the acceptance from Linrey came, I did what I felt I needed to do for my sister."

My parents are both quiet. And when I look at my mom, I see a tear rolling down her cheek.

"Does Natalie know this?" she asks softly.

"No. And please don't say anything. I don't ever want her to know." I rake my fingers through my hair. "Maybe at first, I regretted my choice. But it didn't take long for me to realize I made the right decision."

Because not only was I living just across the hall from my sister but also the girl I've loved my whole life. Proving everything happens for a reason.

"Jason"—my dad clears his throat—"don't think, for one second, you failed Natalie. What happened to her was not something in your control, son. And I'm proud of you for the decision you made, but I'm proud of you every single day for being the son that any father would be lucky to…" He wipes at his face. "Damn, here come the waterworks."

My mom smiles, grasping his hand. She looks from my dad to me. "As long as you're happy, Jason, that's all that matters to us. But make sure you're living your life for you, ok?"

I nod. "What makes me happy is being with my family; I wouldn't have it any other way."

I walk down the hallway and stop in front of the guest room door, tempted to open it and slide into the bed beside Vanessa. But I know she's had a long day and probably needs some sleep. Maybe even some alone time.

So instead, I make my way into my room, remove my clothes, slide under the covers, and finally close my heavy eyes.

The creek of my door has my eyes fluttering open, and I look over to see Vanessa silently walk in and softly shut the door behind her. She tip-toes over to my bed and stands beside it in nothing but an oversized T-shirt. Putting my hands behind my head, I look at her gorgeous body up and down. "And what do I owe this pleasure?"

She bites her bottom lip, and instead of saying anything, she gets onto my bed and under the covers. But she takes me by surprise when she gets on top of me, straddling my thighs. I glance up at her eyes, waiting for her to say something.

"I just wanted to thank you," she whispers.

I cup her cheek with one hand and let my other hand slide up her thigh, enjoying her silky smooth skin on the palm of my rough hand. "Thank me for what?'

"For standing up for me against my mom." She pulls nervously on the hem of her shirt. "No one has ever done that for me before."

I sit up, holding her in my arms.

"Hey"—I rub my nose against hers—"I would do anything for you. You know that, right?"

She nods timidly.

"Does your mom always talk to you like that?"

She looks down at her hands that lay flat on my chest. "She kind of caught me off guard today. She usually says things like that in private to me, but she's never said something like that in front of someone." She shrugs her defeated shoulders like it's no big deal when it's actually a very fucking big deal. Her mom shouldn't be saying shit like that to her.

"Have you ever talked to her about this?"

She huffs out a quiet laugh. "She wouldn't listen to me. You heard her telling me I was being dramatic today because she destroyed my bedroom to turn it into her perfect sanctuary. It only makes me wonder how long she has been waiting to do this. It's her world, and I was just a mistake thrown into their perfect lives. They were happy when they only had a son. I know they were—I see it in the family photos. And maybe when I was a baby, she tried to adjust to the idea of having a daughter, but the older I got, the harder on me she became."

My hand cups her cheek, her face leaning into me, her deep brown eyes well with unshed tears. "I think she's jealous of you, sweetheart. And that's not how a mother should be."

"Jealous? Of me?" She shakes her head adamantly, her chestnut strands falling in front of her make-up free face. "There's nothing for her to be jealous of."

"There is, actually." I lock eyes with this beautiful girl straddling my lap. "To be beautiful on the outside is easy. Women find ways every day to do that. Whether with needles, expensive lotions, surgery, you name it. But you, looking like this, with no hint of make-up on, wearing nothing but a T-shirt and your hair falling around you, are the most beautiful woman I have ever seen." She bites her bottom lip as her cheeks flush. "But these women can't buy what's on the inside. And you are, as corny as this is about to fucking sound, extraordinarily beautiful on the inside and the outside. You can't buy that kind of beauty." I hold her face in my hands, pressing a soft kiss to her lips. "You are so fucking perfect, and I will scream it at the top of my lungs if you want me to."

She smiles shyly, placing her hand on my bare chest.

"You know, my whole life, I've never felt good enough. It's been ingrained in me since I was a kid, causing me to see the worst in myself or compare myself to others. But I don't feel that way whenever I'm with you. I feel like I'm everything. I feel important. I feel … like I matter. And it's a really good feeling."

"I'll always be here when you need someone to remind you how much you matter because you matter so much, Vee. You matter to me."

I kiss her lips, savoring her sweetness. Her hands run down my chest before bringing them to the bottom of her T-shirt. She takes a deep breath, closes her eyes, and slowly lifts the fabric over her body, tossing the shirt to the floor, revealing all of herself to me.

There's not even a pair of panties for her to hide behind.

Goddamn. I'm so fucking proud of her right now.

She's beautiful. No, that word doesn't feel strong enough for her. It's like calling a star pretty when a star is more than that. A star shines, and that's exactly what she is doing now.

My Vee is shining.

I look down at her body, instantly getting hard for her, and from the little whimper she releases, she feels it too. She gently grinds against my hard length, causing a groan to escape me.

"I need you, Jason." She cups my face, waiting for me.

"I'm all yours, Vee. Only yours." I bring my lips back to hers but immediately freeze. "Shit."

Her grinding comes to a halt. "What?'

"I don't." I run a frustrated hand through my hair. "I don't have any condoms." Shit. I knew I should have left some here. Well, I still plan on making this girl in my arms feel so fucking incredible, even without sex. "We can still do other—"

"No." She shakes her head adamantly. "I'm on the pill, and I'm clean." She looks at me with pleading eyes.

"I'm clean too. We get tested with every physical at the beginning of the season."

She has no idea how clean I am.

She nods but doesn't make a move.

"Are you sure you're okay with this?" I ask. "Because there are plenty of other things I can do to make sure you leave this room unable to walk straight." It gets her to laugh.

"Yeah, I'm just nervous. I've never had sex before without a condom." She bites her bottom lip. "You'll be my first."

Fuck me.

My lips crash down on hers, consuming her as my fingers run through her hair. I break apart from her lips, pressing kisses down her neck and collarbone until I reach her breasts, finding pink aroused nipples that desperately need my attention. Her moans increase as I suck on one and use my fingers to play with the other.

"Oh God." Vanessa closes her eyes, grinding on me to find any source of friction.

"Are you wet for me, Vee?" While torturing her nipples, my free hand slides down to cup her over her core.

"Mmm," she purrs softly, eliciting my cock to throb beneath her, getting harder each time she rubs her pussy over my boxers.

But suddenly, her eyes shoot open, and she freezes, looking straight at me as she pushes herself away from me.

"What's wrong?" I ask, feeling very confused.

"Nothing." She shimmies herself down between my legs. "I just wanted to thank you properly." A devilish smile on her face makes me almost come as her fingers trail along the waistband of my underwear. She gently palms me over the fabric, making me groan uncontrollably from her touch. Her fingers slide beneath the fabric, and she pulls down, allowing my hard cock to spring free as she removes the boxers entirely from my body. "You look like you need help with this. Do you want me to make you feel good?"

"Fuck yes." I lie back, crossing my arms behind my head on the pillow, giving me the best view of what is about to be my new favorite show.

She fists my cock, licking her lips at the sight of me. And as if she can't wait any longer, her head bows down, and she takes me all the way in her mouth, instantly bobbing up and down.

My hips lift on impact, causing my cock to hit her in the back of her throat, but it doesn't deter her. If anything, it just makes her work harder. I grab her hair needing to touch her, my fingers stroking each silky strand, but I don't take control of this moment. This is all fucking her.

Her swollen plush lips wrapped around my cock are enough to make me lose it at any second, but I hold back, not wanting this to end.

"Do you like knowing you're the only one who can do this to me?" Her glossy brown eyes meet mine seductively as she places the palm of her hand against my balls, cupping them, and I let out a hiss at this incredible sensation. "You're the only one who makes me feel so fucking good, Vee. Only you."

Her thighs clench together at these words, and all I want to do is relieve that ache she's experiencing between her legs, so that's precisely what I'm about to do.

I lightly push on her head and slide out from under her.

She wipes at the saliva around her lips. "What are you—"

I flip her over, pinning her beneath me, not giving her a chance to stop me. My cock nudges against her entrance, eager to be inside her.

"It's my turn to make you feel good."

I slam inside her, watching her eyes roll back and her lips part, forming a perfect "O." I thrust in and out of her, fast and hard, feeling her muscles tense around me. She's just as close as I am, which leads me to believe she enjoyed that blow job as much as I did.

Suddenly, her hand reaches up, pushing at my shoulder so I land on the bed, and she's positioned on top of me, my dick still fully inside her.

"I want to ride you," she breathes.

Well, fuck me. I think I've officially died and gone to heaven.

"You want to take control?"

She nods nervously.

"Then let me see my girl ride me."

Her body, highlighted by the moonlight streaking through my bay window, is on complete display for my eyes and my eyes only.

She places the palm of her hands on my abs, steadying herself as she lifts her hips up and down, my hardened cock throbbing inside her. I look down at where I'm buried inside her, loving the sight of her taking charge of her pleasure—owning my dick. My eyes travel up her body, noticing how her back arches, pushing her round breasts in the air, bouncing with each thrust she takes from me.

"Oh God, Jason..." she pants in a hushed whisper.

Her glassy eyes flutter closed as her head rolls to the side, the dark strands of her hair cascading down her back.

This image of her will be burned into my brain for the rest of my life. I'll make sure of it.

My hands run up and down her thighs as she rotates her hips rougher against me, begging for that release looming inside. Her muscles grip me, and her thighs tense, hinting at the impending orgasm she's about to have.

"I need more, Jason. Please," she begs, her body beginning to shiver.

I sit up, wrapping one arm around her body, gripping her hip to bring her up and down at a deeper angle. My free arm snakes its way between us, so my hand can cup her pretty pussy, pressing my thumb right onto her clit in tight little circles, giving her just the right amount of pressure she was searching for. "Come for me, Vee."

And she does as I swallow her scream into a kiss and come at the same time as her, spilling inside her. I feel her body tremble against my own as we both brace onto each other during the aftershocks coming at us. Her chest rises and falls as she breathes hard, her body melting against mine. She buries her head into the corner of my neck, but I feel something wet fall onto my bare chest.

Is she crying?

I use two fingers to lift her chin, angling her head so our eyes meet. Her eyes shimmer with an overwhelming flood of tears, ready to break free. "Hey," I whisper. "What's wrong?" My fingers rake through her silky hair, pushing it out of her face. "Did I hurt you?"

"No." She shakes her head, a shy smile appearing. "I'm sorry. I'm just happy. So unbelievably happy." She looks up at me, our eyes locking, while a tear rolls down her cheek. My thumb brushes away the tear before it has a chance to get very far.

"You being happy, Vee, is the only thing I care about in this world."

Something shifts between us. And no, it's not my hard cock which is already ready for round two.

It's a change felt in the atmosphere. It's an electric shock running through every vital organ in my body. It's a constant pressure lurking beneath my ribcage. It's three words on the tip of my tongue trying to escape and be heard by the woman in my arms. But instead, I press my lips tightly together, holding in every emotion I feel while tightening my grip on her as she snuggles into my chest, closing her eyes.

A few minutes later, her breathing evens out, letting me know she's fallen asleep in my arms. I gently lay her body on the empty side of the bed and then make my way to the bathroom to get a warm washcloth. After taking care of her, I bring the covers up around her and kiss her forehead before I wrap myself around her body securely.

And as I tenderly place the palm of my hand on her chest, feeling her heartbeat steady, I know what this feeling is.

Love.

And yes, I've loved this girl my whole life.

But this kind of love is different.

Because in just a single moment, I went from loving Vanessa to being *in love* with Vanessa.

I am absolutely, completely, wholeheartedly *in love* with her.

And I am absolutely, completely, wholeheartedly screwed.

Twenty-One

VANESSA

"Jason?"

"Yes?"

"You missed our exit." I watch out the window as Jason continues driving past the exit we need to take to get to our apartment building.

"I know." Looking over at him, I see him smiling, focused straight ahead, driving to who knows where.

"Care to tell me where you're taking me then?"

"Nope."

"Do I at least get a clue?"

"Nope."

I place my hand on his thigh, slowly inching toward my favorite area. "How about now?"

"I sure as hell am not going to stop you." He grins. "But I'm not telling you anything."

I remove my hand and cross my arms over my chest. "Fine," I huff.

"You're cute when you pout," he states.

"I'm not pouting."

"Oh really?" His eyes quickly roam over my face before going back to the road. "So, what do you call that face you're making?"

"I call it the *this is what a girl looks like when she doesn't like surprises* face."

We stop at a red light, and he glances at me, tipping my chin toward him with his hand. "Do you trust me?"

I roll my eyes. "Yes."

"Did you just roll your eyes at me?"

I purse my lips. "Maybe. What are you going to do about it?"

He shakes his head, laughing. "It's a good thing you like the color red."

"Why?"

"Because that's what color your ass is going to be when we get home," he says, gazing straight ahead.

Fuck. Why did that just make me wet?

I cross my legs to clench my thighs, and Jason notices with a stupid knowing smirk.

The light turns green, and Jason pulls forward before taking a right into a parking garage where a large sign reads, "Boston Museum of Science."

"Why are we here?" Isn't this place for kids? Besides, I really need to get home to finish working on my designs before they're due in a few days. Just thinking about everything I have left to do makes my stomach plummet. I'm definitely going to be having some late nights with my poor, old sewing machine this week.

"You'll see oh, patient one." He parks his truck and hops out, coming right over to my side to open the door for me. Taking my hand, he leads me through the entrance and right past the ticket booth.

"Don't we need a ticket or something?" I ask, looking over my shoulder at the line of people waiting to buy their tickets.

"Not when you have connections." He winks at me, turning my insides into a swarm of butterflies.

We walk through the crowds of people, hand in hand until we finally stop in front of an entrance where a guy stands, looking like he has been waiting for us.

"Hey, Jax, thanks for this." Jason walks up to the guy, pulls an envelope out of his jacket pocket, and hands it to him.

"No problem. Enjoy the show." He opens the door for us, and Jason directs me through a dark hallway.

"Who was that, and what did you give him?" I ask, feeling hesitant about where we're going. Each step I take brings us closer to a large black door. There's nothing to give me any clue as to where the hell he's taking me.

"He's in my statistics class. I did a favor for him, so he did a favor for me."

"What kind of favor?" I ask.

"He's flunking the class, and I happen to be acing it, so I gave him my notes for the past couple of months to help him with the final coming up," he tells me.

"Oh." Jason's always gotten good grades in school, so this doesn't surprise me. He even saved me my sophomore year in high school by helping me pass geometry class. "But I don't understand. What favor did he do for you?"

We reach the door at the end of the hall. "Why don't you open the door to find out?" Jason ducks down until our eyes meet, and the way he's looking at me has my heart thundering against my ribcage.

Why am I nervous?

This is Jason.

My Jason.

But maybe that's the problem.

He's not *my* Jason.

He's my *friend* Jason.

I internally shake my head and place my hand on the door, slowly pushing it open, having no idea what to expect on the other side.

As I peek inside, my heart stops. "Jason?"

"Do you like it?" he whispers into my ear, wrapping his bulky arms around my waist.

"Do I like it?"

We're standing at the entrance of the planetarium, completely alone, shrouded in darkness. The only light source comes from the faux stars on the ceiling above us, looking eerily lifelike, as if we were in the middle of nowhere with only the stars to guide us. But my eyes immediately move to the center of the room, where I notice a blanket, two pillows, and a large white paper bag on the floor.

Jason takes my hand and guides me toward the blanket. He takes a seat and motions for me to sit beside him, so I do, like I'm on autopilot, still feeling shocked at where we are. His hands start rifling through the bag, pulling out what looks to be Chinese food containers.

"What is all this?" My voice comes out soft.

"Well"—he opens one of the containers and places it in front of me—"you mentioned you had never been on a real date before, so I wanted to do something about that."

The food.

The planetarium.

This is a date. Wait. No. That can't be right.

I shake my head. "But, Jason—"

"I know what you're going to say." His eyes snap up to my face. "You're going to say we're just friends, and I know that, Vee. Believe me, I do. And I'll always be your friend. But as your friend, it's my responsibility to take care of you. To make sure you know how you're supposed to be treated. How a guy should make you feel. So, for just tonight, can we be more than just friends?"

More than just friends.

More than being friends with Jason is what I've always wanted. It's what I've dreamed about since we were kids. But for tonight only? Will this be too difficult for me, knowing we'll return to being just friends the moment we leave this place?

But against my heart's better judgment, I say, "Yes. I'd like that."

Jason's mouth lifts at the corner as he pulls me into his arms for a kiss. A deep, sensual kiss that sends tingles down to my core, making me want more than I should in public, so I gently pull away. "Won't other people be coming in here?"

"No." He pushes a strand of hair behind my ear. "We have the place to ourselves tonight. In fact"—he looks at his phone—"the show should be starting in fifteen minutes." He hands me one of the containers, and I smile at him, appreciating everything about this night.

Fifteen minutes later, I'm lying on my back with a full belly, side by side with Jason, watching the show above us as stars fly on and off the screen. Our pinkies intertwine before Jason engulfs my hand in his own, pulling me closer to his side. He tosses my pillow and places his arm under my head. I prefer his bulky arm to a pillow, anyway.

"So, why did you choose the planetarium?" I ask, curious.

He turns his head, facing me. "Because when we were kids, you told me that the stars were the most beautiful thing you had ever seen and that they made you happy. So, I thought tonight you could spend it watching something beautiful that makes you happy, while I spend the night watching something beautiful that makes *me* happy—you."

I don't have to look in a mirror to know how pink my cheeks are. Thank goodness it's dark in here.

"Jason?" I turn my head on the pillow to face him. Our lips are so close, ghosting over each other.

"Yeah, Vee?"

"This is the best first date. And I'm really glad it's with you," I breathe.

"I'd do anything for you." His lips press against mine as his hand cups my cheek, his thumb caressing my skin.

Everything about this moment is taking my breath away.

The fact that he put thought into this night, planning everything without me knowing, makes me feel overwhelmed but in the best possible way.

Of course, I can't help but feel like Cinderella, waiting for the clock to strike midnight, thus ending the spell on this magical night of being more than just friends.

But if we're being honest, how is tonight different from any other night I spend with Jason? Or, for that matter, how is Jason different than what a boyfriend would be like? It's true I've never had one, but I would bet anything that the way Jason has been with me these past few months is exactly how a boyfriend is supposed to be.

He's the man I confide in.

The one who picks me up when I'm down.

The one who looks at me, making me feel nothing short of beautiful.

And the one who my heart beats for. Always has and always will.

Jason's lips part from mine. "Hey, there's something I've been meaning to ask you."

Maybe this is it. The moment he'll ask to make us more than just friends. Will I say yes? Do I want to be more than friends?

Abso-fucking-lutely I do.

"Yes?"

He lets out a deep breath. "Next weekend is the football banquet for the team before we head home for Christmas break. Would you ... would you want to go with me?"

My eyes widen, and my heart accelerates in happiness. Is he asking me to go as his date?

"You know, as friends, of course," he adds, sending my heart rate back down to its normal pathetic speed.

"Oh, umm, sure." I try to smile, but he can immediately sense my hesitation.

"Is something wrong?"

"Wrong? No." Yes, there is, but I'm not going to tell him I've been in love with him since we were kids and ruin this night.

"You can wear whatever you want. Well, it is a black tie event but other than that, you can wear whatever you want. I'll buy you anything you need, so you feel comfortable," he says, eyeing me warily, hoping that this is why I've turned quiet.

I smile. And weirdly enough, the thought of wearing a formal dress in front of people hadn't even crossed my mind like it usually would have in a situation like this. "I'll find something to wear."

"Okay." He turns on his side, wrapping his arm around my waist, his nose skimming up the side of my neck. "Are you sure everything is okay?"

"Yeah. I promise," I lie, pressing my lips to his, making a wish in my head that this night would never end.

"I don't understand why you can't tell him?" Brady sounds exasperated, and honestly, I don't blame him.

It's how I feel every time I think about the situation I've put myself in.

"Because." I sigh, resting my head against a pillow on Brady's couch where we are currently sandwiched together, both of our heads on op-posite sides, waiting for our face masks to dry. "If I tell him how I feel, everything will change between us."

"But isn't that the point? You love him. Capital L-O-V-E. The man deserves to know, at least."

"But what if he doesn't feel the same way about me?"

"But what if he does?" He removes the cucumber slices from his eye-lids, narrowing his eyes at me. "The man has spent the past few months showing you he has feelings, Vanessa. Comforting you in the broken elevator, forcing food down your throat, buying you that gorgeous coat, taking you on your first date, and now taking you as his date to his football banquet where he can show you off to all of his friends! Do you need him to spell it out for you?" His hands fly in the air dramatically.

"Yes, I do." Because I'm scared to lay it all out in the open for him only to reject me. "Besides, I'm not going as his date. We're going as just friends. He was sure to remind me of that when he asked."

"Psshh. A technicality." He eats one of the cucumber slices before continuing. "I guess the real question is how much longer will you go on being *just* friends-with-benefits when you want more than that? Because the only person you're hurting is yourself."

"I know. You're right. But I also don't want this to end either. I'd rather have him like this than not have him at all, which I know is messed up and delusional," I admit quietly.

"No. It's not. I understand. Really, I do. I just don't want you to get hurt, and that's all I see happening if you don't speak up for yourself."

He's right. Of course, he is.

But it's been a few nights since Jason, and I went to the planetarium, and I haven't figured out what to do.

If I tell him how I feel, it could go horribly wrong.

But if I don't tell him how I feel, eventually, I'll be the one getting hurt when he gets bored with me and finds someone else to occupy his time with.

Ugh, my stomach is in knots, and it has nothing to do with the Christmas cookies we ate earlier.

"And Vanessa?"

"Yeah, Brady?"

"When you win the fashion competition, I'm going to be so happy for you. You deserve it," he says matter-of-factly.

"Brady, I'm not—"

"You are Vanessa. And you know how I know that?" he asks.

My eyes narrow at him. "How?"

"Because to me, this was just something fun to do. And I'm thrilled to have made it this far. But you"—he smiles, reaching for my hand—"I watched you put your whole heart into this. And I just know with everything in me, it's going to be you. It has to be you."

My eyes water and I blink a few times to hold back the tears. "Thanks, Brady. But win or lose"—I squeeze his hand—"the best thing about walking into class on that first day was making friends with you."

Brady purses his lips, holding back tears.

"Hey, I thought you two were supposed to be out shopping and getting your projects turned in?" Brady's boyfriend, Gabe, walks into the apartment, looking between the two of us, laughing. His black hair is styled with no hair out of place, and his tan skin stands out against the white button-down shirt he has tucked into a pair of black pants. He rolls up his sleeves showing off very muscular forearms and a few hidden tattoos.

Well done, Brady.

"We had a very long day," Brady responds.

"I can see that." Gabe laughs, bending down to kiss the top of Brady's head, avoiding the wet mask on his face. "Hi, Vanessa. Always lovely to see you."

"Hi, Gabe." I smile.

"I'll have you know that after we turned in our designs for the competition, we then needed to find a dress for this one who will be attending the football banquet with her childhood friend slash friends-with-benefits slash soon-to-be love of her life."

"Brady!" I smack his leg beside me.

"You know, I was just going to turn on Yellowstone for the night, but this sounds more entertaining." Gabe sits on the leather chair opposite us.

I groan. "Do I really have to?"

"I'll sum it up," Brady offers, sitting up as if a bolt of lightning struck him as a smile plasters his face.

"You're enjoying my misery far too much," I complain.

"Oh, shush you. So anyway. This one," he points at me as if I'm not in front of them about to hear their gossiping session, "has been secretly in love with her childhood-friend slash best-friend's-brother, Jason. And a couple of years ago, her brother, well, he umm..." He looks at me, knowing immediately I don't want that part revealed. "He did something he shouldn't have, creating tension between the two families. So, because of association, Jason spent last year giving her the cold shoulder, but it was inevitable that their paths would cross because, not only do they now both go to the same school, but they're also neighbors. Eventually, Jason realized he had been treating her horribly for something she didn't do, and they mended their friendship. And when I say mended their friendship, I mean..." He wiggles his brows.

"Oh, I see..." Gabe smiles wickedly.

"Can we not?" I hide my face beneath my hands but stop, remembering the clay mask still drying on my skin. At least the mask is hiding how red my cheeks probably are from this conversation.

"Well, now our girl here has realized she's head-over-heels-in-love with this guy and always has been but doesn't know what to do about it."

"That is certainly a lot to unpack. You should have told me to have a drink first," Gabe says to Brady. "Actually, it sounds like we should all have a drink." Gabe makes his way to the mini bar in the corner of the living room and starts pouring liquid into three glasses. He turns around and hands one to Brady and then one to me before taking his own and sitting back on the chair. "Okay, where were we?"

"She needs to figure out if she is going to tell Jason how she feels," Brady sounds wound up, making me giggle.

"Well, what do you want to do?" Gabe asks me.

"I don't know." I take a sip of my drink, enjoying the slight burn from the alcohol as it slides down my throat. "I've spent the past few nights trying to decide, and I just don't know what to do."
My phone buzzes beside me. I reach for it, turning the screen on to see

Jason's name appear.

Jason: Are you coming over tonight?

Jason: Because I miss your pussy.
Jason: And your moans.
Jason: And that sexy body.
Jason: And those sweet lips wrapped around my dick.
Jason: And...
Jason: Oh fuck it. I miss you. Come over, please?

I can't help the smile that spreads over my face.

"And that right there is exactly why you need to tell him." Brady points at my face and then looks at Gabe for backup.

"He's right." Gabe shrugs his shoulders. "Isn't it better to know if he feels the same way about you than always wondering?"

"Yes." I sulk. "You guys are right. I need to tell him how I feel." Although, the thought of doing so makes me want to puke this very instance. "But I have to wait until after the banquet. I don't want to ruin that night for him."

"Deal," Brady and Gabe say simultaneously.

I tap away on my phone and hit send.

Vanessa: I'm at Brady's and will be leaving soon.
Jason: Brady sounds like a boy's name ...
Vanessa: You're very observant.
Jason: Who is Brady???
Vanessa: My friend from class. Are you jealous, Jason?
Jason: I'm not the jealous type. You should send me his address, and I'll show you how not-jealous I am.

An evil idea comes to me.

Vanessa: Just sent it to you.

I'm so freaking giddy and can't wait to see his "not-jealous" reaction. Knowing he is, in fact, jealous is completely turning me on.

Jason: I'll be there in ten minutes to pick you up.

"Well, it looks like you're about to meet Jason." I glance between Brady and Gabe. "He didn't seem thrilled I was spending my evening at a guy's house."

Brady looks at me, smirking. "Oh, you wicked thing."

A few minutes later, as soon as I finish washing off the face mask on my face, there's a knock at the door. I don't even want to know how fast he drove here.

"Should I open it, or should you?" Brady asks in a hushed whisper.

"Oh, you can handle him." I push him toward the door, ready for the show to begin.

Brady runs his hand through his hair, making it look disheveled, and then opens the door I find myself hiding behind. "Hey, you must be Jason." Brady deepens his voice a few octaves, and I have to cover my mouth with my hands to stop myself from snickering.

"Where's Vanessa?" Jason's voice is almost unrecognizable. It's deep and vibrating around me with a possessive undertone I've never heard before.

"She's umm..." Brady clears his throat, peeking quickly behind the door at me before folding like a cheap beach chair. "Shit. I'm sorry. I can't do this. He's so brawny and gorgeous when he's jealous."

I start laughing out loud, which causes Jason to move around Brady, finding me in complete hysterics.

Jason looks between Brady and me and then nods his head, understanding dawning on him when he realizes why I'm bent over laughing. A devilish grin appears on his face. "You think you're so funny, don't you?"

I can't speak as tears make their way down my cheeks, so I nod my head.

"Excuse these two." Gabe approaches Jason from behind. "I'm Gabe. This one's boyfriend." His head tilts toward Brady.

Jason shakes his hand. "Nice to meet you."

"And I'm the one you should, most certainly, be jealous of." Brady reaches his hand out to Jason, which causes a grin to appear on Jason's face.

"Nice to meet you, Brady."

I finally calm down, leaning against the wall for support, holding my stomach. "That was priceless."

Jason has a smirk on his face, but it's the kind that tells me I'm in for it as soon as we leave here.

"Well, Vanessa." His eyes scan me up and down, emerging prepared to devour me.

Yes. Yes. Yes.

"Are you ready to go home?" he asks.

I nod, losing the ability to speak under his guise.

He holds his hand out for me to take, and the second our fingers intertwine, a bolt of fire ignites in my core.

"You two have fun tonight." Brady winks as we make our way out the front door.

As we approach Jason's truck, he opens the passenger door for me. "You're going to pay for that little stunt when we get back to my place."

"But I thought you weren't the jealous type?" I tease.

He shakes his head in disbelief, his eyes the darkest shade of grey I've ever seen. And in the next second, he pushes me up against his truck, devouring my lips with his. His hips press into me, revealing how hard he is for me, and I let out a moan in approval, needing him right now.

He pulls away, both of us catching our breath as he presses his forehead against mine. "When it comes to you, Vanessa, I am always jealous."

Twenty-Two

JASON

The engine of my truck roars to life as snow falls from the bleak night sky. I crank the heat up as high as it will go and push the small, round button on the center of the console to turn my and the passenger's seat warmers on. After pulling out of the garage, it only takes me a moment to arrive in front of the apartment building.

Jason: I'm out front.

Suddenly, my eyes spot the bright red contrasting against the pure white snow. Vanessa walks briskly to my truck, bundled up in her favorite red coat with chestnut strands of brown hair partly hidden under a white beanie with this adorable little white puff on the top. She opens the passenger door, throws her bag on the floor, and slides inside, her teeth chattering as she places her hands in front of the vents, seeking warmth. Her fingers are shaking, so without hesitation, I reach over.

"Let me," I say, taking her hands in my own, swallowing them whole as I rub them back and forth.

"Thanks," she whispers, biting her bottom lip.

I smile, admiring her.

She's wearing a little more makeup than usual, accentuating her big brown eyes and luscious lips. She removes one of her hands from mine to remove the adorable white beanie, revealing dark strands of hair in loose curls framing her frame.

She looks like the only present I want to open on Christmas morning.

My eyes move down to her legs, where I finally notice she's wearing jeans and a pair of white sneakers. "Umm, I did mention this was a black-tie event, right?"

She playfully shoves my shoulder and removes her hand from my own. "Yes, Jason. I had to wear these to avoid looking suspicious when leaving the apartment. I told Natalie I was going to the library to spend the rest of the night working on finishing touches for my project even though I had already handed over my designs a few days ago."

"You did? That's great! How do you feel about it?" I know how hard she's been working on this, but I also know she is her worst critique.

She shrugs. "I don't know. I gave it my best and created something I would be proud of, so hopefully, they like what they see, but the decision is ultimately in their hands."

"And when do they let you know who won?" I ask.

"The day after Christmas."

"Okay, cool. I'll make sure my schedule is cleared so we can celebrate that night together," I insist.

"You don't even know if I won yet," she counters.

"Oh, but I do." I lean over to kiss her cheek, causing an instant flush on her face.

Her fingers lift the bottom of her jacket to access the button and zipper on her jeans, quickly undoing them.

Eyes widening in excitement, I clear my throat. "Umm, Vee. Are we having sex in my truck?"

She laughs, shaking her head. *Damnit.*

"No." She removes her sneakers before finally sliding her legs out of the denim. After reaching into her bag, she slides on a pair of black high heels that tie around the ankle with a satin ribbon.

I can't help it. My hand finds her bare thigh and caresses her silky soft skin. "You're being such a tease right now."

"I'm just trying to finish getting ready, and you're making this very difficult." Her breathing picks up the higher my hand travels.

"Fine. Fine." I remove my hand and place it on the steering wheel as I throw it in drive. "So, when do I get to see what's under the jacket?"

She smirks. "Not until we get there." Her eyes roam over me. "You should wear a suit more often." She licks her lips and reaches for me, pressing a hand on my thigh.

"Are you trying to make me crash?" I joke.

She lifts her hand, laughing. "No. You just look ... you look really handsome."

My hand finds hers on the middle console waiting for me. "I can't wait to tell you how beautiful you look when I see what's under there." I motion at her jacket, which remains completely buttoned, hiding all evidence of any form of dress she may have on. "Although, if you opted to wear nothing under there, that's fine with me too. In fact, I would prefer that." I wink, and she shakes her head, looking away from me to hide the blush that once again spreads over her face.

"Just keep driving," she says.

Grinning, I look straight ahead at the road, driving slower due to the snow. "Speaking of driving, are you sure you don't want to just hitch a ride home with me tomorrow for Christmas break?" I asked her a few days ago, but she merely shook her head and changed the subject, but I'm not too fond of her driving back to Connecticut alone, especially if it's snowing.

"No." She shakes her head adamantly. "I need to finish some things for school. I'll, umm, come home in a few days."

"But Christmas is in five days. Can't you give yourself a little break? I can think of several ways to keep you entertained when we're home." I wiggle my brows, and she rolls her eyes.

"I can't." She smiles, but the corners of her lips don't reach their full potential. Something doesn't feel right, but I let it slide for now.

A few minutes later, we pull up to the hotel in downtown Boston where the football banquet is taking place. The valet takes my keys as I grab Vanessa's hand, leading her inside and out of the cold.

Immediately, we're met with tonight's theme: Winter Wonderland. *How original?*

There are twinkling lights hanging from the ceiling, mounds of fake snow placed throughout, white tablecloths and chair coverings, and even a light display that makes it look like it's snowing inside.

"Well, we should go find what table—"

I turn my head with the full intention of finishing my sentence, but the moment I see Vanessa sliding out of her coat, I lose the memory of every word from the English dictionary.

She hands her jacket to the man standing near us at the coat rack and looks up at me nervously under those dark lashes. "Do I look okay?"

Does she look okay?

I can't think.

I can't speak.

I can only see her as everything and everyone around us blurs in the background, only having eyes for her.

My eyes travel appreciatively over the girl I'm in love with, taking in every square inch of her.

She's wearing a black satin dress that perfectly displays every single one of her curves. Every. Single. One. Two thin straps hang on the side of her shoulders, barely holding up the fabric that pushes up her breasts with a dip in the middle. Her body is the actual definition of an hourglass, and I'm already wondering how fast I'll be able to take this off of her tonight. *She's perfect.*

She clears her throat, releasing me from the trance I find myself in.

"Vanessa." I reach for her hand, pulling her up against me. I tuck a piece of hair behind her ear as I look down at her and say, "You are absolutely breathtaking." I know this dress is pushing the limits of her comfort zone. It shows more skin than she is used to, but goddamn, I'm so proud of her for being comfortable enough in her skin to wear this tonight. She smiles and stands on her tiptoes because I still tower over her even when she's wearing high heels and presses a sweet kiss to my lips.

This kiss isn't fast. It isn't dominating or met with urgency. It's slow and languid. It's just right.

It's a kiss that says, "*Let's never stop this.*"

But I quickly remind myself that we're just friends, and this kiss does, in fact, have to end. I pull away and look into her eyes. "Thank you for coming with me."

"Thank you for inviting me," she responds. A look in her eyes tells me she wants to say more, but instead, she purses her lips and looks out at the venue in front of us. "They did an amazing job." Her eyes dance across the scenery, taking in every piece of detail. "I love the snow."

"Well, if you want, we can go right back outside to see the real thing." I jokingly pull on her hand, making her laugh.

"No way. It's warm in here."

I wrap my arm around her waist from behind her. "It's about to get even warmer." My lips land on her neck before I can stop myself. She moans quietly, and I pull away, pleased, and take her hand. "Let's go find our table."

A moment later, we sit with the rest of the guys. Vanessa sits on my left, and Grant sits to my right with his girlfriend, Kayleigh, by his side. Chris sits next to her, going solo for the evening. And Graham sits next to him with his current date by his side. I pull Vanessa's chair closer to me, remembering how the guys couldn't keep their eyes off her when we approached the table.

Do I like that every guy in this room gets a view of her in this dress tonight? Absolutely not. But do I care more about the fact that she's comfortable enough in her skin to wear this? Yes. And that's what's important. I can tone my caveman tendencies down just for tonight because looking at her with that damn gorgeous smile on her face is all I care about right now.

She's happy, which makes me happy.

"So, you getting nervous for the big game?" Grant asks me.

"What big game?" Vanessa asks.

"It's not a big deal." I shrug my shoulders, trying to act casually about it. I was waiting to tell Vanessa at the right time, and I guess that time is now.

"Umm, newsflash. It is a fucking big deal!" Chris chimes into the conversation.

"This guy here is playing in the Rose Bowl Game on New Year's Day." Grant slaps my shoulder with his good hand.

"You're playing in the Rose Bowl game?" Vanessa's eyes widen, and her smile blooms even bigger if that's even possible.

"Yeah. All thanks to this guy injuring his hand the other day." I tilt my chin at Grant, and Vanessa suddenly notices the wrapping around his wrist.

"Oh my God. What happened?" Vanessa leans in closer to me, so she can hear Grant speak, but the smell of her damn honeysuckle perfume surrounds me, bringing my dick to life.

Down boy.

"Nothing too serious. I'll be perfectly fine by the draft. Thank God," Grant says. His girlfriend leans into his chest, looking up at him with eyes only for him. "Just a slight sprain, but I won't be able to play in the Rose Bowl game." His good hand cups his girlfriend's cheek. "Good thing I have such an excellent nurse to take care of me." He winks, and she smacks him lightly on the chest.

Everyone starts chatting amongst themselves when I notice the music change to a slow song. I look around, seeing couples leaving their tables to gather on the dance floor, swaying to the melody.

Vanessa watches them with eager eyes. She's always loved to dance, which is why my hand reaches out to her, waiting for her to take it.

"Dance with me?"

"I thought you'd never ask," she answers.

She places her hand in mine, and I lead her to the center of the dance floor. I hold her right hand in mine, bringing it up to my chest while my left-hand travels down her back, stopping when I reach as low as I can in public, pushing her body against mine. I'd love for my hand to keep going down, but the only thing that keeps me in check is knowing I'll have her ass in my hands as soon as we get out of here.

Vanessa stares up at me, disbelief floating in her eyes.

"What?" I ask.

"It's just ... football is your dream. You work so hard, and this is such a big deal. I'm so ... I'm so proud of you, Jason."

"Yeah?" I raise my brows. Why did hearing her say that make my chest tighten? Maybe I have a heart condition that I need to get checked out.

Her cheek presses against my chest as we both move to the music. "Do you remember the first time we danced together?" she asks.

"Hmm, remind me." I remember every single moment with her, so how could I ever forget the first time I held her in my arms? But I want to hear her version of that night, so I wait for her to tell the story.

"We were young. Maybe around twelve or thirteen. And it was at your grandparent's fiftieth wedding renewal." My body tenses at the mention of my grandparents, but I quickly shake it off before she notices. "You were running around with all the other boys, causing too much commotion for all the poor old people there." She giggles into my chest.

"In my defense, I was bored as shit."

She shakes her head. "Well, finally, your mom had had enough and made you sit at the table beside me. And if I remember correctly, one of your cousins came over to see if I wanted to dance with him. And you'll have to refresh my memory, but what did you do then?"

I smile, pressing my lips onto the top of her head before saying, "I lightly hit him."

"No. No. You full-on punched him." Her laughter becomes contagious. "And you said, and I quote, '*she only dances with me.*'"

I shrug my shoulders.

"You grabbed my hand and forced me out onto the dance floor just to prove a point to your cousin even though you had no idea what to do," she says.

"Hey, the little fucker had to learn. I make no apologies."

"And when I asked you why I could only dance with you, what was your response?"

I sigh, remembering every word I had said and wishing I could take them back. "I said because we're friends. And that I was the only boy *friend* you were allowed to have."

I'm fucking removing the word friend from the dictionary.

"That's right." She sighs. "I've never actually ever had a boyfriend. But I've always had you. Well, almost always." She looks away, reminding me how much I hurt her this past year.

I bring my lips next to her ear. "I'm so sorry, Vee."

"I know." Her body relaxes into mine. "You know, your stuttering stopped around that same time." She looks up at me curiously. She was the only one who never made me feel bad for having a stupid stutter. I used to go to bed crying as a kid, frustrated that I couldn't talk like other kids my age.

"Yeah. I had been working with a specialist for a while."

She ponders this but then says, "But even after your stutter stopped, you still always called me Vee."

"Well yeah."

"But why?"

"Because ... it made me feel closer to you, having a nickname that only I was allowed to use on you," I admit.

Her lips part, and I lean down to kiss her, but the song ends, causing the room to go quiet, so we both smile awkwardly at each other and turn toward our table, where we find our dinner plated for us.

"So, how long have you two been dating?" Kayleigh asks, looking between us as we take our seats.

"We're not," we both say at the same time.

I remove my hand from the back of Vanessa's chair and clear my throat. "We're friends. Just friends," I emphasize.

Just friends, I remind myself. Always just friends, no matter how in love with her I might be.

You don't want to hurt her, Jason. You're doing the right thing.

"Oh, I'm sorry." She looks back and forth between the two of us. "You two just seemed so close I thought there was more to it than that."

I gaze over at Vanessa, who is now looking anywhere but at me. Her fingers squeeze the napkin in her hands, strangling the fabric as if trying to take the life from it.

"Hey." I reach out and tilt her chin so that she has no choice but to look at me, and when I do, I'm hit with two big brown eyes looking ready to cry. "What's wrong?"

"It's nothing." She tries to smile, but she can't fool me.

"It's not nothing. Talk to me." My thumb strokes her cheek.

She takes a deep breath. "I think we should talk about—"

Her words cut off as the coach's voice echoes in the space, ready to start his speech. The lights dim, and Vanessa faces away from me, looking intently ahead at the front of the room. And as I stare at the back of Vanessa's head, noticing the tension in her neck and shoulders, I'm left wondering what the fuck did I do wrong?

The whole car ride home was quiet. Insufferably quiet.

I did something wrong. I know I did, but I have no idea what.

We walk into my apartment, and I can feel the tension in the air, thick and suffocating. And I can't take another minute of this.

"So," I place the Rookie of the Year trophy on the counter and open the freezer to grab some ice cream, "want to tell me what's wrong?"

She nods her head, but her mind is elsewhere, overthinking something. But I can't figure out what the fuck she's overthinking.

I grab the bottle of whip cream, knowing she likes it as a topping on her ice cream. "Do you want whip cream on yours?"

She finally looks at me with the saddest pair of eyes I've ever seen.

"Vanessa, you're killing me here. What did I do wrong?" I ask, running my fingers through my hair, ready to pull at the ends in frustration.

"We can't do this anymore," she speaks to me, but it sounds distant, like she's talking to herself.

"Can't do what?" My heart thuds in my chest, knowing what she is referring to but refusing to believe this is it. That this is the moment when it all ends.

She shakes her head, looking away. "You and me. We can't ... we can't keep doing this." Her voice comes out choked, sounding overcome with emotions, and her shoulders drop, making her appear so fragile.

I place the bottle of whip cream on the counter a little more forcefully than intended. "And why the hell not?"

Her eyes lock with mine. "We said when this started that if one of us started getting feelings, we would stop this, and I ... I need ... I need us to stop this." She sniffles, wrapping her arms around her waist over her red coat.

My world stops spinning.

She has feelings for me.

Does she love me the way I love her?

Maybe I should tell—"

No!

You can't do that, Jason, and you know why.

Fuck! I won't hurt her, which means I can't tell her how I feel.

Because the thought of *him* reminds me why I can't tell Vanessa how in love with her I am. I won't put her through that.

I unclench my jaw, scrubbing my hand around the back of my neck. "If that's what you want to do, then okay." I immediately regret the words the second they leave my lips.

No, it is not fucking okay.

She stares at me, waiting for me to come to my senses, but I can't. I care more about her than I'll ever be able to tell her, which is why the moment she turns and reaches for the door, I don't stop her. I don't yell. I don't say anything.

I let her go and watch as my whole heart walks out my door with tears streaming down her cheeks.

It's Christmas Eve, and I don't feel much like celebrating. In truth, if I could spend the day in my room alone, I gladly would. I don't need a big feast or presents to open. There's only one thing, well, one person I need, and she's not here.

Because I'm a fucking coward.

These past few days, I've played the part of the happy brother and son. I helped my mom bake Christmas cookies, assisted my dad with hanging the lights outside, and even sat through a nauseatingly sappy Christmas movie with Nate and Natalie while I third-wheeled.

Just thinking about that again makes me want to gag.

I roll over in bed to look at my phone for the hundredth time this morning, hoping to see Vanessa's name, but I'm only left disappointed.

I fucked up.

No matter what I do, I'm left hurting her.

If I don't tell her how I feel, then I've hurt her more than I can imagine, leaving her feeling rejected as she walked out my front door sobbing.

If I tell her how I feel, there's a possibility that years from now, I'll be the source of her pain. I'll break her heart. I'll be the reason for her demise.

And I can't fucking do that.

I've been trying to convince myself I'm doing the right thing by not telling her how I feel, but is it really the right thing when every cell in my body is screaming at me to say those three words to her?

I love you.

And I don't want to lose her.

I can't lose her.

I need her like the sun needs the moon. For without each other, neither exists.

But that's the thing.

I don't want to go back to us being friends.

I want Vanessa. I want all of her. I want her contagious laugh and her pouty lips. I want her deep blushes and lip-biting. I want her insecurities and fears, her hopes and her dreams. I want every damn thing she has to offer.

I want her to be mine.

But there's something I need to explain to her so she understands my hesitation. Well, more like there's *someone* I need her to meet officially.

And maybe when she meets him, she'll understand.

Or maybe she'll just think I'm crazy.

I run a frustrated hand over my face. "Dear Santa, give me a sign. Help me out here, big guy. What should I do?"

With nothing but silence following my question, I jump out of bed, throw on a hoodie and a pair of sweats, and walk down the stairs to the kitchen. I hear my mom on the phone nearby, but looking around, I notice no one else seems to be up. So I grab a bowl, a box of cereal, and the milk, then sit at the counter. I scoop a heaping pile of cereal into my mouth as my mom enters the kitchen, looking concerned.

"What's wrong?" I ask through a mouth full of cereal.

She places the phone on the counter and then looks point blank at me. "I was just talking with Linda Gordon. I called her to wish her a Merry Christmas, and apparently, she and her husband are leaving today for a two-week cruise."

I swallow the cereal as what my mom just said hits me in the chest with a weighted thud.

"So, where is Vanessa?" she asks.

"She said..."

I need to finish some things for school. I'll, umm, come home in a few days.

She never left Boston, and she was never going to.

I curse under my breath and jump up from the counter stool.

"Jason!"

I turn around to see my mom looking ready to cry. "Bring her home."

And I know when she says home, she means here—the place where Vanessa has always been a part of this family.

"I'm on it." I grab my keys and make my way to my truck sitting in the driveway. My heart pounds as I turn the key in the ignition and back out of the driveway. There's just one place I need to stop on the way to Boston, so this girl always knows she has a home with me.

Twenty-Three

VANESSA

*M**erry Christmas Eve to me.*

After setting up a small, plastic tree in the corner of the living room, I decorated it with a string of popcorn and cranberries and added some tinsel to make it shine. I then baked Christmas cookies and selected my top five favorite Christmas movies to play during my solo Christmas movie marathon that I'm about to start.

God, I'm pathetic.

I sit my ass down on the couch with a warm cookie in my hand and pull down my oversized T-shirt to cover my bare thighs. And yes, I'm still in my pajamas because why the hell not? It's not like I have anyone to impress today. So, I cocoon my body in the soft plush blanket beside me, trying to feel any solace of warmth.

When I was a little girl, I remember spending Christmas Eve curled up in front of the roaring fire in our living room while my father read '*Twas The Night Before Christmas*. It was always my favorite tradition before my family became broken.

Before my father stopped caring.

Before my mother became cruel.

Before my brother became a monster.

And even knowing how horrible he is, I can't help but feel bad about where he's spending his Christmas.

"I hope you can live with the guilt."

No!

Don't go down that path, Vanessa. Not today.

He got what he deserved.

I internally shake my head, ridding myself of old memories, and find the remote beside me to start the first movie of my all-day marathon—*Home Alone*, obviously.

It's time to make my own damn traditions.

But just as I press play, there's a knock at the door.

Hmm. Glaring at the door, I wish I had x-ray vision so I wouldn't have to get up after getting nice and comfy, but I don't. So, I wrap the blanket around my body and then hesitantly walk toward the door.

Who the hell could it be on Christmas Eve?

I brought James down a plate of cookies earlier. Maybe it's just him saying thanks.

I press my eye to the peephole. *Shit*. It's not James.

"Vanessa, I know you're in there, so don't bother pretending you're not," Jason declares from the other side of the door.

I don't want to see him. After the other night, I honestly never want to see him again. I stood in front of him, vulnerable, admitting I have feelings for him, and he did nothing. Absolutely nothing.

He didn't stop me.

He didn't run after me.

He just let me go.

And it hurt.

It really fucking hurt.

My fingers massage my temple, holding back the fresh tears that want to be released. He doesn't get to show up whenever he feels like it. I was perfectly fine here on the couch with my stupid little tree and my movie marathon before he came here.

But was I fine?

And how would he even know I'm here? Maybe if I just tiptoe back to my room and wait him out, he'll eventually leave.

"I didn't want to do this, but you've given me no choice. If you don't open this door in five seconds, I'll start singing Christmas carols because I know how much you love atten—" I cut off Jason's shouting and pull the door open as fast as I can before he makes good on his promise. I'm ready for him to have a snarky comeback like he usually does, but instead, his eyes travel from me over to my pathetic-looking Christmas Tree and then back to me. "What are you doing here, Vee?"

My shoulders drop in defeat. "Trying to make the most of my Christmas." Embarrassment washes over me like a cold, unpleasant shower, so I look anywhere but at him.

"Why didn't you tell me?" he asks softly.

"What's there to tell?" I wrap the blanket around me tighter. "My parents chose a two-week cruise instead of spending Christmas with their only daughter." A tear slides down my cheek at the pain I feel from my confession being said out loud for the first time.

Jason steps closer to me, but I immediately recoil, still feeling too fragile to be near him.

"I'm taking you home," he says matter-of-factly.

"Home? Jason, didn't you hear me? My parents left this morning for a cruise. Why would I want to go to their house to spend Christmas alone when I don't even have a bedroom to use anymore? I don't ... I don't have a home." My throat tightens painfully. "I don't have a place where I belong." As hard as I try to stay strong, more tears manage to make their way down my face, so I drop my eyes to the floor.

"You belong with me."

I tilt my head up, furrowing my brows. "With you?"

"Yes."

"Really?" I scoff. "Because you made it pretty damn clear how you feel about me when you let me walk right out your door."

It was a blow to my extremely fragile ego.

And I won't put myself in a position like that again.

He runs a frustrated hand through his hair, pinching his eyes shut before opening them and looking directly at me. "You don't understand." He shakes his head. "I wanted to run after you. I wanted to beg you not to leave, but I was..."

"You were what?"

He looks up at the ceiling. "I was scared."

"Scared of what?"

"Of this." He motions between the two of us, locking eyes with mine. "I don't want to be your friend anymore. I can't fucking be just your friend, Vee. I need more. I need all of you. I need you." His glossy eyes are breaking my heart. The last time I saw Jason cry was when we were just kids.

I take a step, filling the space between us. My hand rests on his heart, feeling it beat wildly against my palm, mirroring my own. Closing my eyes, I take a much-needed deep breath, knowing what needs to be said. "I've always been yours, Jason."

Jason's lips land hard on mine, overwhelming me as he steps inside and slams the door closed. I let the blanket fall to the floor as my hands wrap around his neck, pulling him toward me.

His lips part from me, his forehead pressing against mine. "It's you and me, okay?" The palm of his hand cups my cheek, his thumb wiping away all the tears from my face.

"You and me," I repeat breathlessly.

His fingers slide through my strands of hair before twirling a piece between his fingers. "You're spending Christmas with my family—your family. They've always been your family." He plants a soft kiss on my forehead. "We need to leave soon, though, to make it back for dinner with everyone, but there's ... there's someone I'd like you to meet on the way home. It's really important to me."

"But Jason," I look down at myself, "I'm a mess."

"Hmm," he ponders, looking down at me. "You are a bit of a dirty girl. Guess we should probably clean you up in the shower before we go."

"Why do I have a feeling you're only suggesting that to have shower sex?" I arch a brow, crossing my arms over my chest.

"What? Shower sex?" he gasps. "I wasn't even thinking that. But since you brought it up…" He reaches down, snatching me at the waist, and throws me over his shoulder.

"Jason!" I squeal before he puts me in the shower and scrubs me clean. Twice.

Peering out the passenger window, I find myself mesmerized by the beautiful winter wonderland everywhere I look, with fat snowflakes falling all around us. While the guy I love with every cell in my body holds my hand tenderly in his own as we make our way home to Connecticut.

Home.

I'm learning the word means more than just having four walls around you.

Before we left my apartment, I grabbed the present I bought for Jason a few weeks ago out of my closet and snuck it into my overnight bag while he waited in the living room. I really hope he likes it, but I'm worried he won't. Maybe he'll think it's stupid.

As if sensing my mood, Jason brings my hand to his lips and lightly kisses each knuckle before placing our intertwined hands back on the middle console.

His eyes stay on the road straight ahead, but the smile on his face tells me he's feeling the same way I am. Looking out the passenger window, I notice we just missed our Greenwich exit.

"Jason?"

"Yeah?"

"Where are you taking me?" He takes a turn off the highway and looks over at me.

"You'll see."

"Are you kidnapping me?"

His eyebrows raise. "If I was kidnapping you, I would have tied you up, put a blindfold over those pretty eyes, and then threw you over my shoulder, bringing you to my car against your will. But as I remember it correctly, you came with me voluntarily."

I bite my bottom lip. Why did the thought of him doing that to me just turn me on?

His eyes narrow over at me. "It kind of seems like you want me to kidnap you?"

"I don't know why you would think that." I unbutton my coat, feeling a sudden heat washing over me. "Is it hot in here?" I press the button on the door beside me, causing my window to slide down an inch. The cold air quickly whips inside.

"Uh-huh." Jason looks back at the road, but there's an obnoxious, knowing smile on his face.

I close my window, instantly feeling the effects of the cold air, and then turn up the music. The song *Snowman* by Sia starts to serenade us through the speaker.

I lean back in my seat. "I love this song. I love the snow. I love Christmas. I love—" I instantly stop myself. Oh my God. I can't believe I just almost said, "*I love you.*" Real smooth, Vanessa. "Everything about this time of year."

"You know what would make it even better?" Jason asks.

"What?"

He pulls over to the side of the road. "Put your gloves and hat on." He turns up the music, zips up the front of his jacket, and jumps out of the car, leaving his door open.

"What are you doing?" I ask, knowing he can't hear me over the music. I quickly place my white beanie on my head and adjust my gloves on each hand.

He opens my door and holds out his hand for me to take. "Dance with me?" he asks.

My heart thunders in my ears, noting the bright blue of his eyes at this moment. The most beautiful color I've ever seen in my life.

Maybe even my new favorite color.

I can't help the smile that takes over my face as I take his hand. He leads us to the front of his truck, where he places his phone down on the hood and hits record, saving this memory. The music engulfs us as the snow falls heavily around us. We're the only two idiots out here right now with no other cars on the road. I'm freezing from my head to my toes, guessing it won't take long for my lips to turn blue, but the second Jason steps in front of me, placing his hand on my lower back over my coat, an inferno lights within me. I'm at eye level with his chest, watching as each breath I take comes out in a vapid puff of smoke. Looking up at him, I place one hand on his shoulder as he takes my free hand in his.

That's the moment everything blurs around us.

He swings me in his arms, holding me tightly against his body. Our feet leave an unintelligible trail in the snow, proving our dancing has no rhythm or rhyme. Neither of us knows what we are doing, and we probably look like absolute fools, which is why we both start laughing hysterically.

This is the best moment of my life.

Before the song ends, Jason spins me away from him and then twirls me right back, braced against his chest, bringing his lips down on mine for a raw and utterly perfect kiss.

Twenty-Four

JASON

Every part of me is anxious and riddled with nerves as we near our destination.

I've never taken someone to meet my grandpa before. Especially because you never know what kind of day he will have. Some days are good, and some days, well, let's just say they're not so good. Natalie came for a visit a week ago, and unfortunately, it was one of the not-so-good days. But my mom and dad came by yesterday to see him, and she told me he was having a good day, so here's hoping it continues for us.

We pull into the parking lot of the Sunset Assisted Living facility, and I glance over to see Vanessa taking in the building.

"Why are we here?" she asks.

I park the car and turn off the engine. "Because my grandpa's here, and I'd like you to meet him if you're okay with that?"

She looks from me to the front of the building and then hesitantly back at me before slightly nodding. "Okay."

We both step out of the car, and I walk around the front of the truck to take her hand in mine, walking us right through the parted doors directly to the reception desk. The place is decked out for Christmas. Colorful lights are sparkling throughout, and a giant decorated Christmas tree is in the corner of the game room. But as nice as this place is, because, of course, my parents have him in the most luxurious assisted living facility in the state, it's still lonely for someone staying here, especially over the holidays.

"Jason! What a lovely surprise," Sandy, the woman who greets me from behind the counter, says. She's always been the first face I see when I visit here, which hasn't been in a while because of what happened the last time I was here.

"Hey, Merry Christmas Eve, Sandy." I walk right up to the desk, guiding Vanessa along with me.

"And who is this beautiful young lady?"

"Sandy, this is my girlfriend, Vanessa." I watch as Vanessa's cheeks redden. She's going to have to get used to me calling her that because I plan on telling the whole goddamn world that she's mine.

"Hi, Sandy. It's nice to meet you." Vanessa smiles warmly.

"Well, don't tell me someone tied down this man?" Sandy smirks. "Good job, girl. Keep him in line," she teases.

"Hey, I'm always on my best behavior," I counter.

"Mhm," Sandy muses. "It's lovely to meet you, Vanessa." Her eyes meet mine. "I take it you're here to introduce her to your grandpa?"

"Yeah, that's the plan." I take my free hand and run it through my hair. "How is he today?"

"He's good. I saw him earlier playing chess in the game room, but I think he's in his room now reading."

"Okay, good." That's a weight off my shoulder. "Well, we'll stop and say bye on our way out."

"Yes, you make sure you do!" Sandy demands as I lightly pull on Vanessa's hand and lead her down the hallway.

I know Sandy said he's having a good day, but I should probably warn Vanessa in case things go south. "So," I take a deep breath, "my grandpa came here almost a year ago because of Alzheimer's. Some days he's completely fine, and you would have no idea there's anything wrong with him. And other days..." I trail off, not knowing how to tell her.

How do you describe the feeling of watching the man you've always looked up to completely forget who he is? How do I explain that even though he taught me everything I need to know about football, he sometimes forgets who I am? Or that sometimes, he forgets that his wife, of over five decades, is no longer alive. I clear my throat hard, holding in the emotions that come with these visits.

The last time I was here, I had to physically hold him down for the nurses to sedate him after he got all worked up, forgetting where he was and who he was. I had to hold back the tears as they plunged the syringe into him and watch as he cried out for his deceased wife to save him before finally collapsing onto his bed.

It was one of the worst fucking days of my life.

Vanessa squeezes my hand, bringing me out of the trance. "It's going to be okay, Jason."

Her words immediately put me at ease.

We walk up to room sixty-five, and I gently knock on the door. "Come in," I hear from the other side. I open the door to find my grandpa reading a book in his leather recliner. "Jason!" he exclaims. Okay, it's going to be a good day. Everything is going to be okay, just like Vanessa said.

"Hey, Grandpa!" I walk in, removing my hand from Vanessa's so I can take my coat off and help Vanessa with hers. It's close to a thousand degrees in here, but that's how he likes it.

"And who do we have here?" he asks, admiring Vanessa.

"Grandpa, this is Vanessa, my girlfriend," I offer proudly.

"Girlfriend, huh?" my grandpa asks.

"Hi, it's nice to meet you, sir," Vanessa responds.

"Sir? I like this girl." My grandpa chuckles and looks over to me and then back at Vanessa. "But I haven't been called 'sir' since I was in the army. You can call me Arthur, darling. Now tell me, what is someone as beautiful as you doing with this shmuck?" My grandpa's head jerks in my direction.

"I've asked myself that same question every day." Her arms cross over her chest, and she rolls her eyes dramatically.

"Hey, I didn't realize it was gang up on Jason day." I cross my arms over my chest, mimicking her, causing them to laugh.

"It's lovely to meet you, Vanessa. Come sit over here." My grandpa motions to the sofa beside him, and we both walk over to take a seat. I place my arm on the back of the sofa directly behind Vanessa, keeping her as close to me as possible.

"Now, why do you look so familiar?" He narrows his eyes, trying to look closer at her face as if he's seen her before. Oh no. Is he having a relapse? Please, no. Not right now with Vanessa here.

Vanessa jumps in. "We've seen each other in passing over the years. I was even at your vow renewals almost seven years ago. We've just never been properly introduced. I'm best friends with Natalie."

"Ah, I knew I recognized you," he replies, nodding as if remembering her face. I'm instantly relieved. "But again, you're so beautiful, and he, well..." He waves his hand at me dismissively. "Let's just say he didn't get my good looks."

"Funny, old man. I look exactly like you did at this age. There are photos to prove it," I quip.

"Pshhh. Those photos are so old they're probably warped. Trust me, Vanessa. He wishes he looked like me when I was that age." He winks at her.

I place my hand on her shoulder, pulling her into me. "Don't even think about it. She's taken."

Vanessa shakes with laughter and nervously pushes her hair behind her ear as her cheeks turn the faintest shade of pink from the attention.

"You look just like my wife, Barbara, did at your age." He rests his hands on the arms of his recliner and looks over at a framed picture of my grandma on the table beside him. "She was absolutely beautiful. And her smile? It was my favorite thing about her." His finger taps the leather before he says, "She was the love of my life."

"She always had my favorite cookies ready for me whenever I came over to visit," I add. Sometimes I swear I walk into a room and smell the aroma of those damn chocolate chip cookies.

He chuckles softly. "Yeah. She always did know the way to any man's heart was through his stomach—even her grandson's. She loved you and Natalie so much." He clears his throat as his eyes gloss over.

Vanessa reaches her hand out, placing it on top of his. "She sounds like a lovely woman. Do you have any stories you could share? I'd love to hear about her."

The biggest smile spreads on his face, and goddamn, it makes me all warm and gooey inside to see. My hand slides down from her shoulder to the top of her back, where I trace a heart with my index finger.

I love this girl so much.

"I'd love to," he responds.

About an hour later, after my grandpa tells us stories that even I haven't heard before and, of course, made sure to include some embarrassing ones involving me, I look at my watch and realize we should get going, so we make it in time for dinner. I wish he could come with us, but I know in his condition that it's not possible.

"Well, I hate to break up the party." I stand up straight, stretching, looking over at my grandpa. "But we need to get going, or we'll be late for dinner. Natalie, Nate, and my parents will stop by tomorrow to see you. I don't know what it is, but Natalie said she can't wait for you to open your Christmas present from her." I put out my hand for Vanessa to help her up. This isn't the easiest couch to get out of or the most comfortable, as proven by my now aching back.

"Good. Good." My grandpa scratches his head, looks at the door, and slowly all around the room with bewildered eyes. His jaw opens, looking on the verge of saying something, but then closes.

Oh no.

Vanessa stands, smiling at him, oblivious to the turmoil going on inside his head. "Well, it was really nice meeting you. I had a lovely time, and I hope you have a wonderful Christmas."

"Christmas?" he asks.

"Yeah, tomorrow is Christmas." She looks at me in confusion.

"Hmm. I wonder if Barbara knows that," he considers. His eyes snap up to mine. "Where is Barbara anyway?"

My throat goes dry. This is the part I dread about visiting. Seeing him perfectly fine one minute and then, as if someone snapped their fingers, he's gone the next. Completely forgetting what day it is. Who we are. And the fact that his wife, the love of his life, died eight months ago.

"Grandpa, how are you feeling?"

"Grandpa?" he questions. "I'm sorry, but you must have me confused with someone else." He rapidly looks around the room, appearing ready to get out of his chair and storm the place down. "Where am I?"

This isn't good.

Vanessa puts her hand on his shoulder. "Hi, I'm Vanessa. I was just going to get some tea. Would you like one?"

"Yes. Tea would be good. Thank you." He nods, sinking back into his chair and raising his hands to his temple. "Just have a slight headache. I'm sure Barbara will be back soon."

"Yes. Well, we'll go get you that tea. Everything will be okay." She smiles at him warmly, and his shoulders relax.

"Thank you, Vanessa." He returns the smile, looking serene.

"Of course." She grabs a blanket from the sofa and brings it over to him, spreading it over his lap, and then hands him the remote to the TV. "Stay here. We'll be back with your tea, Arthur." She bends down and kisses his cheek, wiping away any worries he may have had ten seconds ago.

She takes my hand and leads us toward the door.

"Bye, Arthur. It was nice seeing you today." I hold back the tears, feeling my throat constrict and my nose burn.

"Thank you for visiting, Jason." He smiles at me and then turns his attention to the television.

I'm caught off guard by the use of my name, but we walk out into the hallway quietly and head straight to the reception desk.

"Hey, Sandy." I rub my hand over my stubble, disappointed with how the visit ended. "Unfortunately, it looks like he's about to have an episode. He's calm, but he was wondering where my grandma is." I drop my shoulder in defeat.

"Aww honey, I'm sorry. I'll send one of the nurses to his room to check on him."

"Can you make sure they bring him some tea, too?" Vanessa asks. "I promised him I would bring him some."

"Of course," Sandy replies. "You two go have a nice Christmas. You know he is safe in our hands, Jason," she assures me. "And you know he wouldn't want you to spend your Christmas moping when you have your beautiful girl beside you."

"Per usual, you're right, Sandy." I lift my lips, giving a slight smile. "Can you make sure someone calls the house to let us know how he's doing later?"

"Sure thing. Now go along. I'll take it from here."

Vanessa and I walk out to the car silently, holding hands. It's stopped snowing, but it's still freezing out, so when we get into the truck, I immediately turn the heat on, giving it a few minutes to warm up.

Vanessa turns to me. "Jason, I'm so—"

"You were amazing," I interject, spinning in my seat to face her. "You turned that whole situation around. I've never seen that happen before."

She shrugs her shoulders like it was no big deal, even though it was. "I just try to put my feet in other people's shoes. I think we all need to feel like we're not alone."

"Is that how you feel?" I ask, pushing a dark strand of hair behind her ear. "Alone?"

"I did, yes." She nods. "But I don't feel that way anymore." She looks into my eyes, the corners of her full lips tipping up.

I bring my lips to hers and kiss her, but she places her hands on my chest and gently pushes back.

"What's wrong?" I ask.

"It's just ... can I ask you something?"

"Anything."

"The journal I found ... is that why you write in it?"

I wasn't expecting that.

I take a deep breath before I explain this to her, hoping she doesn't think I'm crazy. "When my mom explained to me what was going on with my grandpa, I felt helpless. I mean, this man is the reason I play football. He taught me how to throw the perfect spiral. He practiced drills with me in my backyard until the sun went down, and even then, he made my parent's string lights on the patio so we could still play late in the night." I laugh, remembering that day. "I wanted to be able to help him after everything he's done for me. So, I spent hours researching Alzheimer's, but always coming up with the same results." I let out a shaky sigh. "There's no cure that will be able to save him from this disease." I look away from her and sit back in my chair. "There were other things I came across while researching." I rake a shaky hand through my hair.

"Some studies believe Alzheimer's is known for skipping generations. Some feel strongly that if a certain gene is passed down, it will increase the chances of a person developing the disease in the future. And other studies disagree with everything. There are no affirmative answers, and it's fucking overwhelming, to put it lightly." I look at Vanessa, her eyes watering. "I don't want to forget anything. Not one damn thing. So, ever since that day, I've been writing in a journal. Maybe it seems girlie or whatever, but it's the only thing I can think of that might help if this ever happens to me."

"Oh, Jason." Vanessa climbs over the middle console and positions herself on my lap, straddling my legs. "I had no idea." She buries her face into my shoulder as I wrap my arms around her.

"Hey, it's okay. I didn't mean to make you cry, sweetheart."

She pulls away and looks up at me. "Can I ask you one more question?"

"Of course."

"What happened to your grandma?"

I chew on the inside of my cheek before speaking. "About eight months ago, she passed away. The doctors said it was a heart attack, but I know it wasn't."

"What do you mean?"

I wipe away a single tear rolling down her cheek. "She died of a broken heart." My eyes gloss over, but I clear my throat before continuing. "You see, we moved my grandpa to this place right after Christmas last year. Things had just been getting too much for my grandma to be able to help him. So they both moved here. But one day, he woke up and had no idea who he was sleeping next to. She realized then she wouldn't be able to stay with him anymore, and so she made the hardest decision she ever had to make. She moved out of their room and into the room next to his. But seeing him in the hallways on days when he had no idea who she was, well, I think it just was too much for her. It broke her heart."

She cups my cheek in her hand, and I gladly mold into it. "I'm so sorry, Jason."

I close my eyes, savoring the warmth of her touch as cold tears trail down my cheeks. "When you told me you have feelings for me, it scared me. That's why I stood there like an idiot, not running after you. Because all I could think about was that someday this might be us. And I don't want that life for you. I don't want to be the reason for your heart breaking, Vanessa."

She presses her forehead to mine. "You can't live life worrying about what might happen tomorrow." Her small hands grip my shirt right over my pounding heart. "It's you and me. Those were your words. Remember?" A slight smile tugs at her lips, appearing hopeful. "We only get one life to live. So, will you live for today with me?"

I brush my lips across hers. "For you, I would do anything."

Twenty-Five

VANESSA

An hour later, we pull up to Jason's house, and I feel nerves spread uncontrollably inside me. Why am I nervous? These people are my friends. No. They're my family.

"Relax." Jason's hand clutches mine, resting on top of my thigh.

"Easy for you to say." I take a deep breath. "What is everyone going to think?" I pinch the bridge of my nose, closing my eyes for a second as I try to take a deep breath.

"Well," Jason starts, "my parents already knew something was going on between us." My eyes widen at this revelation. "And I'm pretty sure Nate has his suspicions."

"How?" I flop my head back against the headrest. "We were so careful."

"I guess we weren't as careful as we thought." He shrugs his shoulders with a smirk. "I think the only one in the dark is Natalie."

"Great." I sigh, squeezing the back of my tense neck. "The one person in that house who means the most to me." I look down at our connected hands. "She's going to be so mad at me for lying to her. What if she doesn't like the idea of you and me together?"

He unbuckles his seat belt and faces me. "I can't say for sure how she will handle the news. She loves us both, but this might be a lot for her to ... digest in one sitting."

I can feel my heart racing with uncertainty. There's no knowing how this will go, and I don't know if I'm ready to find out.

"Do you think..." I let out an unstable sigh. "Do you think we could wait until the day after Christmas to tell everyone?"

Jason's brows lower, his eyes narrowing on me. "You want to wait? Did you change your mind about us?"

"No! No!" I shake my head adamantly. "Absolutely not. I just..." I look through the foggy window at his house. The house where my best friend currently is, having no notion of anything going on between me and her brother. And it makes me sick to my stomach thinking of springing our news on her the day before Christmas. "Natalie is my best friend, and I don't want to ruin her Christmas." I look back at Jason, hoping he'll understand.

After a moment, he nods. "Okay, I get it." He leans forward, kissing my forehead, relief flooding me. "When you're ready, we'll tell them." His lips move to mine, soft and sweet. "God, I can't wait until this is out in the open so I can kiss you whenever and wherever the fuck I want."

"Wherever, huh?" I raise a brow, feeling a little mischievous. "Like here?" I part my legs and place his hand right over the front center of my jeans.

"Oh Jesus, sweetheart. Don't bring your sweet pussy into this now, or I'm never making it inside." He rubs his free hand over his stubble, biting his lip and looking down at my lap. "But maybe we have a few minutes to—"

"See you inside!" I yell as I jump out of the car and run to the front door at a record speed, laughing loudly. But I forgot I was racing a college athlete, who makes it over to me in no time, tackling me into his arms and gently pushing me against the front door.

"Your pussy is going to pay for that later," he whispers roughly into my ear, his chest pressed firmly against my back as his hand snakes around my waist, cupping me between the legs. His fingers start massaging right over the inseam, and a little moan slips out of my lips. He always knows how to make me feel good.

"Is that a promise?" I turn to face him, running my hand down his torso, making my way to the front of his jeans, and finding him rock hard for me. Just the way I like him.

He lets out a groan, pushing into my hand. "You love that you make me so damn hard. Don't you?"

"Oops," I tease, removing my hand from him.

Jason adjusts himself and grins. "Don't 'oops' me. You did that on purpose, and you know it."

I shrug my shoulders. "Guess you'll never know." I wink and turn, wrapping my hand around the doorknob just as his hand comes down to give my ass a firm tap, causing me to release a little squeak.

A throat clears behind us, causing my whole body to freeze.

Oh shit. Who the hell just witnessed that show?

Timidly, I look over my shoulder to find Nate standing a few feet away from the porch steps with grocery bags in his hands, seemingly bewildered, his eyes scanning between me and Jason.

"Umm, Nate. Hi. I didn't, umm. I didn't see you there." My pulse speeds at the thought of him telling Natalie what he just saw. And my skin ignites, altering to a deep shade of red, knowing what he just saw and heard. But maybe he didn't? "Have you been there very long?"

Please no. Please no. Please no.

"Long enough to know there's more than a friendship going on between the two of you."

Well, I think I'm just going to wander off in the snow and die of embarrassment now.

"Shit," Jason whispers, raking his fingers through his hair. He steps in front of me as if shielding me from Nate. "Listen, Nate. Vanessa and I are..." He looks over his shoulder at me to make sure it's ok to say what he is about to say, so I nod. There's no point in lying after the front row showing he just got. "We're together."

Nate is stone-faced, staring at us coldly until finally, a hint of a smile breaks out on his face. "I know."

"You know?" I ask, rearing back.

"Yeah, I thought you did, asshole." Jason shakes his head but smirks. "Didn't appreciate the double date stunt, by the way." He wraps his arm over my shoulder, pulling me to his side.

"What can I say? I thought it might push you in the right direction." Nate shrugs nonchalantly. "So, when are you telling Natalie?"

Jason and I look at each other.

"About that..." I start to say.

"You are telling her"—Nate's eyes bounce rapidly between us—"right?"

"We will. I promise. But I don't want to say anything until the day after Christmas. I don't know how she'll react, and I don't want to ruin her Christmas, so please don't say anything, Nate," I beg.

He runs his free hand over his face, looking in disbelief. "You want me to lie to my girlfriend." He looks at Jason. "Your sister." And then looks at me. "And your best friend. For two nights?"

"Not lie, per se." I peek up at Jason and then back over at Nate. "Just maybe don't mention anything about what you just saw."

"I don't like this," Nate says.

"I know, but—"

"But she's your best friend. And she's his sister. Don't you think she might be happy for the two of you?" Nate asks solemnly.

Honestly, I'm not sure. I know she loves us both separately. But together? I don't know, and I'm not ready to find out just yet.

"Please trust me on this, Nate," I plead. "I just want us all to enjoy Christmas together."

Nate thinks about it and sighs. "Fine." With his free hand, he points a finger at us. "But the day after Christmas, you guys are telling her, or I will. I don't like keeping a secret from her. We don't do that."

"We will. Maybe we can all go to dinner and tell her then?" I look at Jason for confirmation. "And after we come home from dinner, we can let your parents know."

Jason's eyes connect with mine. "That sounds great to me." He leans down, pressing a kiss to my temple.

"Alright." Nate groans. "Now, I'm going to walk through this front door and forget about everything I just saw and everything we just talked about." He walks up the steps, walks around the both of us toward the door, but then stops with his hand frozen on the door handle. "If there is one guy I trust not to hurt Vanessa, it's you, Jason. So don't make me regret this," he says, glaring over his shoulder at Jason before entering the house and closing the door behind him.

"Well, that was interesting." Jason squeezes my shoulder, probably sensing how anxious I feel as guilt nips away at me. "Hey, everything will be fine. I promise. And no matter how things go, I'll be right by your side. I'm not leaving you, Vee."

Taking a deep breath to calm my mind, I stand on my tippy toes and press my lips to his. "Thank you."

We enter the house, which looks like a freaking Christmas movie set. There are lights and garland strung throughout, ornaments hanging from the ceilings, fake snow scattered over shelves and corners of rooms, and of course, a Christmas tree that would put the one in the White House to shame.

Mrs. Spencer has truly outdone herself.

My eyes widen as I take in everything, and then my nose goes up in the air, smelling the aroma of freshly baked cookies. And knowing Mrs. Spencer, she probably quickly put together a batch of my favorite cookies because that's the type of mom she is.

"Oh my God. What is that amazing smell?" I ask as we make our way into the kitchen.

"Vanessa! I'm so glad you're here, honey!" Mrs. Spencer finishes plating the last cookie from the tray in her hands and walks right over to me, wrapping me up in her arms and squeezing all the air out of my lungs.

"Thank you for having me," I politely respond.

She pulls away, her hands clutching my arms as she focuses on me. "You know I love you like a second daughter. This home is your home too. How many times do I have to remind you of that?" I swear her eyes are misting over, making my eyes blur.

"You know, I'm here too, Mom." Jason cuts in and scoops his mom up in a giant hug.

"Yes, Jason. You're kind of hard to miss," she jokes. "I swear I constantly have to make more cookies because you and Nate are like human garbage disposals."

"Hey, you should take it as a compliment that your cookies are so delicious." He parts from her and walks right over to the tray of cookies she just set aside. "In fact, I think I should try one of these just to make sure they're okay." He tosses one in his mouth before she can stop him. "Yup. Delicious."

Mrs. Spencer shakes her head laughing. "Well, Vanessa, I made your favorites, chocolate crinkles. Please help yourself before this one eats them all."

"Don't mind if I do." I side-check Jason out of the way and pick up a cookie, taking a small bite. "Wow, these are amazing." I lick my lips to get all the sugar off.

"You missed a spot." Jason's thumb runs over my bottom lip slowly until I clear my throat, reminding him that his mom is standing only a few feet away, observing this whole exchange.

Keeping our hands off of each other for the next couple of days is certainly not going to be an easy feat.

She looks between me and Jason, smiling. "So, did you guys hit any traffic on the way home? I thought you would have been home sooner."

I don't think it's a great idea to tell her that her son insisted on us having shower sex before we left, which might have contributed to our delay.

"I wanted to stop by and visit Grandpa on the ride home." Jason shoves another cookie in his mouth, licking the sugar off his fingers.

Mrs. Spencer looks at me and then back at Jason, something tender in her eyes. "Oh, how was he today?"

"He was umm..." Jason clears his throat.

"He was good." I reach into the cabinet to grab a glass and place it under the sink faucet, turning the water on until it's filled. "He, unfortunately, lapsed toward the end of our visit, but we managed to keep him calm. The nurses said they will call the house later today to let you know how he's doing."

"Well," Mrs. Spencer wipes her eye, "I'm really glad you got to meet him, Vanessa. He's a pretty great guy and means a lot to all of us."

"I'm really glad I did too. Even just meeting him briefly, I can see why he means so much to you all."

My heart twists at knowing how important it was for Jason that I met his grandpa. It was a gesture that spoke louder than three words ever will and a moment I will never forget.

I take a sip of my water, feeling Jason's eyes on me, so I turn to find him watching me in what I can only describe as in awe.

"What?" I ask.

"Nothing." He runs his hand over his stubble, looking away from me. "So, Mom, do you need help with anything?"

"I would love it if you could help me make the lasagna."

"Sure thing." He turns toward a little closet and pulls out a pink apron, making me laugh. "What? Have you ever tried getting marinara sauce out of your shirt? It's impossible."

I shake my head, grinning at this idiot. "Is there anything I can help with?"

"No. No. I'm just so glad you're here, honey." She gives me a warm smile. "Natalie is in her room, wrapping presents."

"Great." I smile at Jason, who winks at me as I turn, making my way toward the grand staircase and up to Natalie's room.

"Knock. Knock," I say as I enter Natalie's room, finding her sitting on the floor with wrapping paper, ribbons, and gifts placed around her.

"Vanessa!" She jumps up and hugs me tightly like we didn't just see each other a few days ago. "Why didn't you tell me about your parents going on vacation?" she asks with a slight frown. She parts from me, sitting back on the ground and patting the space next to her for me to take.

I sit down and lean against the side of her bed. "I don't know. I guess I was kind of embarrassed about the whole thing." My finger twirls a red ribbon on the floor beside me.

"Vanessa." Natalie places her hand on my shoulder. "I'm your best friend. You can tell me anything."

I nod my head, feeling my tongue ready to reveal my secret to her but knowing I can't. Not yet.

I told Jason I wanted to wait until after Christmas to tell Natalie because I didn't want to ruin her Christmas, and that part is true. But I also wanted to wait because I need to do something before Jason and I make it official. Something that I have put off for too long, and it's the first thing I plan on doing the morning after Christmas.

"I know," I say.

"I, for one, am so happy you're here, celebrating Christmas with us. And I can't believe Jason drove back to get you, but I'm so glad he did." She bumps my shoulder with hers. "I tried not to take it personally that you texted Jason to come get you because your car wasn't working, and not me. But then again, I don't drive, so I won't hold it against you, but know if you ever need me, I will drive for you."

"Wait, I didn't—" But I stop myself. Mrs. Spencer must have told Natalie I texted Jason asking for a ride, so she didn't think it was odd that her brother just left like a man on a mission to get me.

Mrs. Spencer knows.

Ugh. I can feel my cheeks heating up.

"I'll remember that for next time," I reply.

"Since you're here, want to help me wrap some things? I kicked Nathan out to watch football in the basement with my dad because I need to wrap his gift next."

"What did you get him?" I ask.

She stands up and opens her closet, dragging out a large basket. "I got him a whole bunch of things for his boat. Like cleaning supplies, a scope monocular, a damage control kit, a waterproof speaker, boat rope, and my personal favorite, a Captain's hat that says, 'Captain Nathan.'" She lifts the hat from the basket and puts it on, laughing. "Do you think he'll like it?"

"I bet if you wear just the hat to bed with the boat rope in hand, he'll love it!"

We both keel over, laughing so hard tears are coming out of my eyes.

"Wait! Let me get my Bluetooth speaker to play Christmas music while we wrap. I'll be right back!" She places everything on the floor before me and strolls out her door.

In the corner of my eye, I spot a blue T-shirt on the floor near me in a box. I hold it up to see the words *"My Favorite Grandchild Got Me This Shirt"* and start laughing. Jason's going to have some competition.

I get up to look out the big bay window in her room and sit on the bench in front of it. The snow is falling slowly to the ground, covering all of the trees, making everything outside look like it came straight out of a scene from a Hallmark Christmas movie.

It's perfect.

Everything is perfect.

Twenty-Six

JASON

Everyone is seated around the long rectangular oak dining room table, enjoying all of the delicious food made by yours truly. Okay, well, maybe I only helped to chop and peel vegetables for my mom, who then used them to prepare everything, but it still counts.

Our Christmas Eve family dinner grew last year when we started a new tradition, which included having Nate's family join us. So, across from me sits Natalie, Nate, his mom, and her boyfriend, Mark. To my right is Vanessa, secretly holding my hand under the table as we speak. To my left is Nate's younger brother, Nick, and at the ends of the table are my mom and dad.

"Jason, can you pass the rolls?" Natalie asks, forcing me to separate my hand from Vanessa to get my sister her damn rolls.

"Sure thing." I pass the basket and then quickly bring my hand back under the table, finding a small soft hand waiting for me.

"Vanessa, I made one of your favorites, risotto cakes." My mom hands the plate of them over to me to pass to Vanessa.

"Oh, Mrs. Spencer, you spoil me." Vanessa's eyes light up as she takes the plate from me and then puts two on her plate.

That's my girl.

"So, what does everyone have planned for winter break?" Nate's mom asks, looking around at everyone.

"Nathan and I are going to spend a few nights in Vermont to go skiing." Natalie beams, looking at Nate.

"Hopefully, the weather cooperates. It looks like that area might be getting more snow than expected," Nate adds. "Guess it wouldn't be the end of the world to get snowed in with this one, though." Nate squeezes Natalie's hand that rests on the table beside him.

Seeing Nate and Natalie holding hands freely on the table in front of everyone makes me envious, while Vanessa and I keep ours interlocked, hidden under the table.

"Oh, how romantic!" Nate's mom replies.

"I think I'm going to be sick," Nick responds to the lovey-dovey display across from him before shoveling some lasagna into his mouth. Damn, this guy can eat.

"Since when do you ski?" I ask Natalie. I've never seen my sister pick up a pair of skis, let alone know how to put them on.

"Well, technically, I won't be skiing. But I will be reading a good book in front of the fire while Nathan skis."

"That doesn't sound like much fun," Mark says.

I laugh as I butter my roll. "Oh, believe me when I say there's nothing more fun for my sister than reading a book."

"Speaking of books, how is writing going?" My mom takes a sip of her wine, looking at Natalie eagerly.

"Actually," Natalie looks at Nate and then back at my mom, "I didn't want to say anything yet, but I guess this is as good of a time as any. I'm getting published in the spring!"

Everyone goes around congratulating Natalie, and I can't help but feel so proud of her, knowing the journey she's overcome.

"I'm so proud of you, honey." My dad pats Natalie's shoulder, and I'm pretty positive his eyes are watering.

"Natalie, that's amazing!" Vanessa removes her hand from mine, gets out of her seat, and walks over to Natalie, embracing her in her slender arms. "I can't wait for us to celebrate!"

"Pretty soon, you both are going to have things to celebrate," I add before taking a sip of water.

"Both of you?" My mom looks at Vanessa and then directly at me with, I think, concern in her eyes. Wait a second … yup. There is definitely the look of, *Oh dear God, Jason, what have you done?* I've seen this look so many times before, but what would she think I did to cause Vanessa to celebrate someth—

My eyes land on Natalie's hand that absentmindedly remains on Vanessa's stomach as they pull apart.

Oh fuck.

She thinks Vanessa's pregnant.

I nearly choke on my water, and when I look across the table at Nate, he seems like he wants to wring my neck between his hands, clearly coming to the same conclusion as my mom.

God, does no one have faith in my ability to put a condom on?

Well, not like we've been using them recently … but that's beside the point.

Pounding on my chest, I clear my throat quickly to clarify so my mom doesn't pass out in front of everyone and Nate doesn't murder me on Christmas Eve.

That would kind of ruin the festive mood.

"That's right," I interject. Vanessa sits beside me, unaware of the murderous stares I'm getting. "Vanessa will be finding out soon if the designs she entered in a school competition will be chosen to be featured at The Met in a couple of months."

I look at Nate with a face that says, "*Give me some credit.*"

Nate brings his drink up to his mouth to hide the stupid smirk on his face.

"Oh, my goodness." My mom's shoulders drop as relief hits her. Did she just fucking wipe sweat from her brow? "Vanessa, that is wonderful! When will you hear from them?"

Vanessa's cheeks redden from being put on the spot. "I should be getting notified the day after Christmas to let me know either way."

"We are so proud of you, kid." My dad looks like he's about to cry again.

Hold it together, man.

"Thank you," Vanessa says, looking at everyone before her eyes finally land on me. "But speaking of big news, I think there's something Jason wants to share with everyone." I know she's only doing this to get the attention off of her and onto me, which I don't mind at all.

I grin." Yeah, actually." I look between both of my parents. "I'm playing in the Rose Bowl game on New Year's Day."

"What?!" my parents exclaim in unison.

"Yeah. Grant, unfortunately, hurt his hand and doesn't want to risk injuring it more before the draft, so I'm going to be the starting quarterback."

"Oh, Jason." My mom is full-on sobbing, causing me to immediately get up from my seat and tackle her in a tight embrace.

"I hope those are happy tears, Mom."

"They certainly are." She wraps her arms securely around me. "We are just so proud of you. You've worked so hard for this."

The next thing I know, I have another set of arms wrapping around my shoulders.

"I'm so proud of you, Son."

"Thanks, Dad."

"Grandpa would be really proud of you, too," he adds, causing the bridge of my nose to sting. Goddamn allergies.

"Me too," Natalie says as she joins the family hug.

I'll say it. I love my family.

I look up to see everyone else smiling at us. "Well, I'm going to part ways now before this gets really awkward for everyone."

"Five more seconds," Natalie pleads, squeezing me tighter.

After five more seconds, we finally separate, and I return to my seat. Everyone starts talking about upcoming trips and topics they've seen highlighted in the news, but the only thing I hear are the words being whispered softly beside me.

"I'm proud of you, Jason."

My eyes lock with hers, wishing I could kiss her right this damn second in front of everyone with no cares in the world.

The only reason I'm not is because I know she wants to wait. I know she's more concerned about hurting her best friend on the other side of the table than being happy, so that's what we will do.

We'll wait.

But you better believe that in two days, I'm telling the whole goddamn world that this girl is mine.

I drop my napkin on the floor and twist my torso to reach for it, which brings my lips closer to her ear. "Keep your door unlocked tonight. I have something to give you." She raises her brows in question, biting that damn luscious bottom lip. Her mind is definitely in the gutter right now, and I freaking love it. "Okay, I have two things to give you, but only if you're a good girl and keep your door unlocked for me."

She gives a slight nod and takes a sip of her drink, trying her best to look casual. When I sit back upright in my chair, her hand slides on the top of my thigh, waiting for my fingers to interlace with hers, which is exactly what I do.

I tip-toe down the hallway on the carpet, which is easier said than done when you're over six feet tall and over two hundred pounds of muscle. And like the good girl she is, Vanessa left her door unlocked for me. Slowly turning the knob in my hand, I quickly enter the room and find her sitting on the guest bed in an oversized T-shirt, looking sexy as fuck with a perfectly wrapped box on her lap.

"Hey," she says softly with a heart-stopping smile.

"Oh, were we supposed to get each other gifts? I had no—" I pull my hand from around my back, showing a small blue box, instantly causing her smile to get even bigger.

I sit on the bed beside her, my eyes transfixed on the large box resting on her thighs. I really want what lies underneath the box between those luscious thighs, but I'll do my best to be patient. I place the small box beside me, hoping she'll like it. It's something I had thought about getting her weeks ago, but it wasn't until this morning that I knew for sure I needed to get the last part of it, which is why I had to take a quick detour to the hardware store on the way to get her today.

"You open your gift first," she requests, placing the box on my lap.

"If you insist." Quietly, I tear the wrapping paper off and remove the lid. My fingers slide over the fabric and lift it out of the box, observing my name on the back of the Linrey University football jersey. The identical one to it is hanging in my closet at my apartment. "Umm, Vanessa, sweetheart. I hate to be the one to tell you this, but I already have this same jersey with my name on it."

She laughs quietly. "No. This jersey is for me, but also for you. You told me you always wanted to umm ... fuck a girl wearing your jersey, and well, I want to be that girl." She suddenly turns shy and looks down at the blanket, pink creeping up her neck.

"Vanessa." Her eyes meet mine. "I fucking love it."

"You do?" she asks, emerging relieved.

"Yes. I'm already picturing you in this, and goddamn..." I bite down on my fist. "Maybe you should put it on now, and we can give it a test ride."

She playfully punches my shoulder. "No way. Natalie is right across the hall." I pout, but it isn't enough to convince her otherwise. "Okay, my turn. Give me. Give me."

She reaches for the box beside me, but I snatch it and hold it out of reach from her grasp. "Tsk. Tsk. You didn't say please."

"Please, Jason," she whispers, giving me those damn puppy dog eyes. Her hands rest on my thighs as she leans in closer to me.

I kiss her forehead and wrap my fingers around her wrist, placing the box in the palm of her hand.

She looks at it questioningly, and I know exactly why. "Don't worry. It's not a ring."

Not yet, anyway. But someday, I will present her with the same blue box with the biggest diamond my future NFL contract will buy me.

She smiles and then opens the small blue Tiffany's box revealing a silver keychain. And on that keychain hang three silver star charms, mimicking the ones tattooed on her ribs, along with a silver key.

"Jason." She looks up at me, waiting for an explanation.

Shit. Maybe this wasn't a good idea.

"I'm sorry, if you don't like it, I can—"

"No." She shakes her head adamantly. "I love it." Her fingers run over the edge of the key. "Is this for your apartment?" Her eyes shimmer, eventually releasing the first big tear.

I wipe away the tears descending down her porcelain cheeks. "Yes. I want you to always feel like you have a place to go. A place to call home. As long as you have that key, you have a home with me ... fuck, I didn't mean for that to rhyme."

She jumps into me, wrapping her arms around me, pulling me against her. Her pretty tear stained face buries right into my chest. "Jason, this means so much to me. I don't even know what to say."

"Then don't say anything, Vee." I kiss the top of her head and hold her tighter in my arms. There is nowhere else I would want to be right now. This girl is it for me. There's no question about it. She's the one. She's my endgame.

She pulls her face away from me, her eyes locking with mine, and I'm positive that we both say those three words to each other without actually saying them out loud.

Or at least I do, anyway.

I love you.

Twenty-Seven

VANESSA

"Okay, you can do this," I repeat out loud to myself for the third time like a lunatic as I stand outside the Connecticut State Prison, trying to muster up any strength I have inside me for what I am about to do.

Rubbing my hands together for warmth, keeping the small gift tucked into the crook of my arm, I look up at the ominous sky, covered with dark grey clouds, hoping it's not foreshadowing the outcome of this visit. Each shaky breath I take comes out in a puff of smoke. It's freezing, but I've been standing here for ten minutes, too nervous to walk through the front door, knowing I will never walk through them again.

This is going to be harder than I thought.

Yesterday was one of the best Christmases I've ever had. Actually, it was the best Christmas I've ever had.

Jason and I walked down the grand staircase to find everyone else waiting for us around the Christmas tree, surrounded by beautifully wrapped presents. Natalie and Nathan sat cuddled up on the floor, exchanging gifts with one another. Mr. and Mrs. Spencer sat on chairs beside each other, holding hands, and Jason and I made ourselves comfortable on opposite sides of the sofa, pretending we didn't just spend the night wrapped around one another.

Everyone was laughing and tearing wrapping paper off gifts like it was a competition. Mrs. Spencer even handed me a heavy box with a tag that said *To Vanessa, Love Your Second set of Parents*. I teared up reading the tag, and when I tore off the wrapping paper, revealing what was inside the box, the waterworks set in full motion. They got me a top-of-the-line sewing machine. No more having to use the third-generation crappy one in my room that was barely hanging on by a thread. Pun, definitely intended. It's a gift I'll cherish forever.

But the gift that means more to me than any other gift I've ever received is the key to Jason's apartment because it feels more like the key to his heart.

It's his way of saying he wants this. He wants me.

And more than anything, I want to be his.

We spent the day decorating Christmas cookies with Natalie and Nate before they left to visit Arthur Spencer on their way to Nate's aunt and uncle's house, where they would spend the night. Once they left, Jason and I put a Christmas movie on and watched until we couldn't keep our eyes open anymore. He carried me up the stairs and tucked me in his bed, where he snuggled up beside me. And I fell asleep feeling no longer alone but utterly and hopelessly loved.

But now, it's time for me to put that feeling of bliss aside so I can do what I came here to do.

I got this. I am Vanessa freaking Gordon. I can do th—

My phone vibrates in my coat pocket, interrupting what was about to be my optimistic and confident *"can do"* speech. I reach for it with my free hand while my other hand holds onto the neatly wrapped box, but I don't recognize the New York number on the screen, so I put my phone back in my pocket until it hits me.

New York!

Fumbling like a mad woman, I bring my phone to my ear. "Hello?"

"Hey, Vanessa! It's Raquel! Is this a bad time?" she asks.

I look up at the prison sign above me. "No. No. Not at all. How are you?" My pulse hammers in my chest. If she called me, then that's good, right? I mean, if they wanted to reject me, they would send me an email ... right?

"Well, you know, I ate way too much for the holiday, but nothing a juice cleanse can't fix." She laughs, and I join in, even though the thought of going on another juice cleanse makes me want to vomit. *Been there, done that.* "But anyway, I wanted to call and give you the good news over the phone." My heart no longer hammers in my chest. It's straight-up thundering.

"Y-yes?" I choke out.

"The other board members and I voted and unanimously have picked your designs to be featured at *The Met Future of Fashion* event!"

"Oh my God." I can't breathe. Did I hear her right? "I won?"

"Yes! We loved everything about your designs and what they stand for. Your use of fabrics, along with the precision and techniques you used with the cuts and layouts to provide a stunning silhouette to any body size, absolutely impressed each of us. And it would thrill us if you agreed to be the featured designer representing Linrey University."

Wow. "I just don't even know what to say. This is..."

"Oh, please say yes!" she encourages on the other end of the phone.

"Yes. Yes! Absolutely yes!" A smile breaks out on my face. This is really happening.

"Wonderful! Well, I have to make the next train and don't have the best service in the subway, but I will have my assistant send all the information over to you, including the information regarding the speech, and I will be sure to get in touch with you soon. Please call me if any questions come up, okay?"

"Yes. Definitely. Okay. Will do. Wow, I mean ... thank you." My words come out jumbled. I can barely think straight, let alone sound like an intelligent human being, when her words come back to me. *Information regarding the speech.* Hold up! "Umm, Raquel, did you say something about a speech?"

But there's no answer.

I look at my phone to see the call has disconnected.

Oh no. No. No. Speech? I can't give a speech in front of hundreds, if not thousands, of people. But I shake my head, trying to forget about the word *speech* and instead focus on the positive.

I won.

My dream is coming true.

My mouth remains wide open in complete shock, staring at my phone in my hand, wondering if that phone call even just happened or if I just made it all up in my head. To double-check, I scroll through the call log and see the New York number. *Holy shit.*

I'm floating on cloud nine.

That is, until the door near me opens, and an officer walks out, reminding me where I am and why I came here. He smiles as he passes me, walking toward his patrol car.

I take a deep breath, shove my phone in my pocket, and push all thoughts of the competition to the back of my mind while tightly holding the present in my hands.

You can do this, Vanessa. It's time to say goodbye.

I square my shoulders, open the glass door, and march to the reception desk to sign in.

A few minutes later, I sit at the cafeteria-style-looking table and drum my nails along the solid surface. It's been over a month since I've been here, and I wasn't planning on coming back, but after spending yesterday surrounded by people who love me and show me what it means to be a family, I decided it was time to come back for closure.

Because I need to say *goodbye.*

Brian walks out with a guard escorting him to the table. He's lost a little weight while being here, but he won't have much longer before serving his time and can return to eating real food.

"Vanessa. I didn't expect to see you here." He sits down across from me. "Where are Mom and Dad?" His eyes wander around the room, expecting to see them.

He doesn't know.

"Oh, well … they decided to spend Christmas on a cruise." I shrug my shoulders, and Brian narrows his eyes at me.

"They didn't spend Christmas with you?"

I shake my head.

"You spent Christmas … alone?" he asks, pity echoing in his voice.

"No, I umm … I spent it with the Spencer's." My eyes dart down at the table and then back at him.

He nods. "I see." He runs the palm of his hand over the stubble on his face.

"Yeah." There's silence surrounding us so I push the present I brought toward him. "I got you this. It's just something small."

He looks at it questioningly.

"You didn't need to get me anything," he points out.

"I know." I let my shoulders drop and force a tight smile. "Just open it."

Stay strong, Vanessa.

He slowly undoes the bow and then rips the wrapping paper from the box, removing the lid to reveal the gift inside. He looks at me and then back down at the item before picking it up. It's a framed picture of the two of us when we were kids, playing at the beach, back when times were simple.

It used to be one of our favorite things to do together. Mom and Dad would take us to their Cape house, where Brian and I would spend hours on the beach until our skin was pink and our hair smelled of the ocean water.

We were all happy then.

"Why did you do it?" I look down at the table, asking the question that's been on my mind since I found out the truth about that night.

"Vanessa, if you came here to try and make me feel bad—"

"No." My eyes move up to his. "I'm talking now. Not you." Adrenaline courses through my veins as anger radiates throughout me. "You made me think it was my fault that you ended up here. Your last words to me, before they brought you here were, 'I hope you can live with the guilt.'" I shake my head. "Those words imprinted on my heart, my soul, and guess what? It fucking worked. You got what you wanted. You guilted me into believing that it was all on me. But it fucking wasn't, Brian." My heart hammers in my chest, letting out everything that I've been holding inside. "I never wanted to believe that you were capable of doing what you did. I couldn't. Because you were the only person in our family who always had my back. The only one who was always there for me. And I would think there's no way he would do that. No way. It's not possible. But you did. You fucking did."

Tears stream down my cheeks, and I wipe them away as fast as I can, hating how much this is affecting me. "You tried to rape my best friend." I pause before repeating, "You tried to rape my best friend! And the day you did that, you broke us. And I will never forgive you for that." My nails dig so hard into my palm that a tiny drop of blood slides down my wrist but I keep going. "These past few months, I needed my brother. And I believed it was my fault that you were here but it wasn't. It wasn't my fault." I look straight into his eyes when I say, "I don't have a brother anymore. I'm just sorry it took me this long to realize that." I shake my head, fury overtaking me at the thought of his actions. For attacking Natalie. For trying to make me believe it was my fault he's here. "I came here today to stand up for myself. Because I know that what I did was the right thing to do. Testifying against you in court was the best decision I've ever made in my life." My eyes burn into him as he narrows his eyes. "I refuse to be a part of your life anymore and for the first time, I'm doing what's best for me."

For so long I saw him as the hero in my story. I saw him as the guy who would do anything to protect me and keep me safe. And maybe that's why I never saw him clearly. My vision was so clouded with all the good memories we shared that I never saw him for how he was portrayed in other people's stories.

The *villain.*

So why is it so fucking hard for me to do this? Why am I crying?

Because even though you're doing the right thing, you're losing your brother.

Brian leans back in his chair, crossing his arms. "Well, I have to say I didn't know you had that in you." He lets out a deep sigh. "Listen, Vanessa, the only thing I want for you to be is happy. I'm the one that fucked up. Not you." My eyes widen, shocked that he's finally owning his actions. "If I could change things, I would. I know that now. Maybe being off the drugs has helped me see that, or maybe just being in a cell most of the day has given me time to think about what I did." He shrugs. "Either way, I know things won't be how they were when I get out of here. I was kind of already expecting you and me to go our separate ways."

I close my eyes and nod. Am I doing the right thing?

Yes, Vanessa. You are.

"Vanessa." I open my eyes, looking at him through blurry eyes. He reaches across the table for my hand, but I unconsciously pull it back. "Can you promise me one thing, though?"

"What?" I ask.

"Don't let Mom get to you. You don't need to lose weight. You're perfect. And if she tells you otherwise, then tell her to fuck off, okay?"

I let out a frustrated laugh. "I'll try to remember that." I wipe the tears from my face with the sleeve of my coat. "Well, I guess this is good—"

"Don't say it." He slowly shakes his head, his eyes watering, looking ready to shed tears that he won't release. "For what it's worth, I love you, little sister. Even if it hasn't seemed like it recently, I do and always will."

I bite my bottom lip, trying to hold in every emotion, but it's useless. He's expecting me to say those three words back to him, but I can't. I won't. He lost my love the day he attacked my best friend. And he will never hear me utter those words to him again.

So, instead, I give a slight nod, buttoning my coat as I walk out of the visitor room, never looking back.

Only looking forward.

After stopping in the bathroom on the way out to make sure I don't have mascara running down my face, I push open the main door and walk outside, appreciating the cold air engulfing me from every angle.

There's a lot of guilt inside me, eating away at me, but I know I did the right thing. If anything, I can say I'm proud of myself for what I just did.

I love Jason, and I want to tell him that tonight but I didn't want this secret to keep me from doing that. But now, I feel ready to say those three words to the man I've loved for as long as I can remember.

I pull my phone out of my pocket and look down at it to see what time it is when I walk into a hard surface, causing me to fall back until two arms grip me, holding me upright.

I shake my head and look up to find Jason staring down at me. "Oh, God, Jason, you scared me." I smile but notice his face is stone cold. And his usual beautiful eyes are burning into my own. "Wait..." Realization dawns on me. "Why are you here?"

"I followed you." He removes his hands from me and takes a step back—the distance he puts between us creates an unholy amount of anxiety inside me.

"Why ... why did you follow me?"

"I left this morning to get us each a coffee. On my way back, I saw you driving Natalie's car, so I followed you, thinking you were just running an errand and I could surprise you with the coffee. But when you pulled out of town, heading toward the state prison, I thought, there's no way that's where my Vee is going." He shakes his head, looking down. His voice is rough, sending a chill throughout my entire body. "But look where we are." He gestures his arms out widely for dramatic effect as he laughs cruelly. "You came to visit the man who tried to rape my fucking sister."

"Well, yes, but you don't understand I came to—"

"You don't have to explain anything. I saw you walking through those doors with the Christmas present in your hand."

"It's not what you think." I shake my head, feeling like everything is about to crash down on me.

"Answer me this," he challenges. "Was this your first time coming here? Or have you been here before to see him?"

"I-I've been here before but—"

"Give me the key," he demands.

"What?" My lips part in shock. *No. No. Please don't do this.* I feel my heart thrash in my chest, predicting his next words.

"I want the key to my apartment back." He holds his hand out, waiting for me to give him the key. "You won't be needing it anymore."

Tears begin to sting my eyes. "Jason, if you would just let me exp—"

"No." He adamantly shakes his head. "I trusted you. And you promised me you had nothing to do with him anymore. But you lied to me. You chose him when you walked through those doors." His eyes pierce mine with fury, detaching himself from me. "I don't want to see you ever again."

My heart *cracks*.

Invisible shards of glass pierce every inch of my skin, penetrating any semblance of happiness I felt before coming here today.

How did I lose both my brother and the man I love in the course of five minutes?

I chose you! I want to scream at him, but I don't.

Fresh tears surge down my face, but I don't fight them. I let them take over as I pull my wallet out of my pocket and retrieve the key. I place it in his hand before he clamps his fingers around it and spins away.

"Wait!" I yell after him. He probably thinks I'm going to beg him to change his mind—but I won't give him that satisfaction.

He turns around and cocks an eyebrow as I boldly step toward him. I remove everything from my pockets and quickly unbutton my coat. God, I am going to miss this beautiful piece of armor. I shove it off my arms in one go and hand it over for him to take.

"Here. I don't want this anymore." He makes no move for the coat and stares at me, making me timid under his glare. "Take it!" I scream through a sob. But he remains frozen, so I throw it at him, watching as it hits him and then falls to the ground between us.

"You told me that you never wanted to be the reason for breaking my heart, but you just did. You successfully just broke my fucking heart." I shove past him, heading straight over to Natalie's car, which I borrowed to get here.

He doesn't run after me.

He doesn't yell for me to stop.

As I back out of my spot, I watch him in the rearview mirror remain in place, staring at the red coat on the ground. And just as he looks up, his eyes locking with mine in the mirror, I accelerate out of the parking lot to get the hell back to Boston.

I'm hibernating on the sofa in the living room, in the same pajamas I've worn for the past two days, with my two favorite guys beside me—Ben and Jerry—while I binge-watch a collection of sappy movies, causing me to cry until there's practically no liquid left in my body.

Pathetic.

The apartment door opens, and I turn my head quickly, hoping to see the face I've been seeing only in my dreams this past week, but instead, I'm met with Nate's. "Oh, hi."

"Don't sound so happy to see me," he jokes.

"No, sorry. I am." I rub away at the fresh tears on my face, hoping he didn't notice them. "What's up? You know Natalie is at her therapy appointment, right?"

"Yeah, I just dropped her off." He sits on the other side of the sofa, resting his elbows on his knees.

"So, why are you here?" I ask, trying not to be rude, but he's interrupting the pity session I have scheduled for the next few hours.

"Because a little birdie told me she's worried about her best friend." He observes me as if I might break at any second.

And maybe I will.

"She's worried about me?" I ask. I thought I had been doing a good job hiding my feelings from Natalie, but evidently, I'm going to have to try harder. "I'm fine." I wave my hand awkwardly in the air. "I'm ... totally ... fine," I manage to get out, my throat tightening and my eyes blurring with each second.

You know that moment when someone asks how you are when you're clearly not okay, and then no matter what you do, you can't stop the tears from pouring out of your eyes. That's me right now.

"Then why do you look like you're about to cry?"

The floodgates open. "It's this damn movie." I point to the TV screen, tears cascading down both cheeks. "She can't remember him. She forgets him every day, so he films their life together, and she watches the movie every morning. He just ... loves... her ...so ... much." The sob gets so bad that I get the hiccups.

"Vanessa?"

"Yeah?"

"Come here." Nate's arms open wide for me, and I jump in them without a second thought. His hand rubs up and down on my back soothingly as I find breathing almost impossible. "You know, you're the sister I never had, right? That means I'm your fucking big brother, and I don't like seeing you like this. So, can you tell me what happened?"

I sniffle, wiping my face with my T-shirt as I pull away. "I messed up, and now he hates me."

"Who? Jason?"

I nod, looking down at my hands, gripping his shirt.

"What happened? Because you two looked like you couldn't keep your hands off each other when I saw you."

"Yeah, well." I look away from him because how the hell do I explain the friends-with-benefits concept to someone who feels like my brother? "You promise you won't think less of me?"

"There's no judgment here, Vanessa." He watches me cautiously.

I swallow. "Well, we sort of had a friends-with-benefits arrangement." I look to find judgment on his face, but there is none. "And we came up with rules, so neither of us would get hurt. But I ... I lied to him." Nate waits for me to continue. "You see, he asked me to promise him that I had nothing to do with Brian anymore, and I told him I didn't. But the truth is, I saw Brian on Thanksgiving. I went after I couldn't take his empty seat at the dining room table beside me anymore. It just kept reminding me what I did and that he wasn't there to have my back like he used to be because of me."

I look away as tears start rolling down my cheeks, realizing Nate must be so disappointed in me—he hates Brian just as much as Jason does. "This past year, I've felt so confused and ... guilty. I wouldn't let myself believe my brother had it in him to do what he did. It was hard for me to wrap my head around." My shoulders start shaking, thinking about my last conversation with him. "I know that testifying against him was the right thing to do, but no one tells you when you testify against a family member what the long-term impact of that will do to you. It has slowly been killing me with guilt, thinking I was responsible for him being there. For putting my brother behind bars." I hide my face behind my hands. "I'm so sorry. I probably sound like a horrible person for still caring about him after what he did to Natalie."

"Hey." Nate's hands wrap around my wrists, removing them from my face. "I can't even imagine the turmoil you've been through with everything that happened. And I wish you would have felt comfortable enough to tell me this. Because no matter what, Vanessa, I'm here for you. Do you understand me? None of what happened was your fault. It was Brian's and Brian's alone."

I nod, taking a much-needed deep breath before I continue. "It was on Christmas Eve that Jason and I finally realized we wanted to be more than just friends, and after spending Christmas with everyone showing me what it's like to have a family that loves me, I knew what I needed to do. I needed to say goodbye to Brian." I close my eyes, guilt over taking me. "He's my brother, but I chose Jason. And I'll always choose Jason. So, I went to the prison the day after Christmas and told Brian I couldn't be a part of his life anymore. He said he just wanted me to be happy. And even though I felt guilty, I was proud of myself for ending things between us because as much as I did it for Jason, I did it for me. It was the right and the only thing to do."

I take a deep breath. "But when I walked outside, Jason was there. He had followed me to the prison." I wrap my arms around myself tightly as my whole body trembles. "He was so mad. He told me he trusted me and that I lied to him because I chose Brian over him. He told me he never wanted to see me again. He wouldn't let me explain, but maybe he's right. I mean—"

"Woah. Take a deep breath." Nate's hands land firmly on my shoulders, keeping me upright.

I close my eyes but can't make my heart stop racing.

"It hurts too much, and it's my fault." I throw myself back into Nate, my body convulsing in sobs. Tears are raining down my face, and it feels almost impossible to catch my breath.

"Shh. It's not your fault. I need you to breathe, Vanessa. Can you take a nice deep, slow breath for me?" His hand rubs little circles on my back, waiting for me to calm down.

I take a deep breath, then another, and finally another before I feel like I can breathe normally again. "I'm sorry."

"Don't be sorry. You didn't do anything wrong."

"Didn't I, though?" I ask, truly feeling like I did.

"No, you didn't." He runs a hand through his hair. "You've been in the middle of everything this past year. You're Brian's sister, you're Natalie's best friend, and you're in love with Jason. Am I right with that last one?"

I don't need to think about it because it's how I've felt for a long time. "Yes," I whisper. "What I'm about to say is going to sound totally corny, but ... he's my moon." I shrug my shoulders, looking down as my cheeks heat up. "When I look up at the night sky, the only thing I see is the moon, shining bright amongst a sea of stars. And with Jason, when he's in a room full of people, he's the only one I see. The only one I've ever seen."

He nods in understanding, not making me feel stupid for admitting that out loud. "Jason is not going anywhere, Vanessa. And do you want to know how I know this?"

I look up at him curiously.

"Because you might look at him as if he's your moon, but he looks at you as if you're his whole damn world. He's only ever had eyes for you."

"Really?" I sniff, reaching for the closest blanket to wipe my eyes dry.

"Really." Nate squeezes my hand reassuringly before reaching for the remote beside me to change the channel. He probably doesn't think that watching a rom-com is the best idea. He's right.

"But what should I do?"

"You should do nothing." He shakes his head. "Let him have his tantrum, and soon enough, he'll realize he was wrong for what he said to you. He'll realize he should never have put you in a position where you had to choose between your brother and him." He sighs, raking his fingers through his dark brown hair. His frustration is not going unnoticed.

"Are you mad at me?"

"Vanessa, I could never be mad at you." He shakes his head. "The whole situation with Brian is hard for me, too, sometimes."

"It is?"

"Of course. Your brother was the first friend I made when I moved to Greenwich. We were best friends for so long that it was difficult for me to understand that he could do what he did to Natalie. And sometimes, I find myself missing him, but then I realize I miss who he was when we were younger. Not the man he became."

"I know what you mean." I miss my brother. The one who played with me on the beach and always made sure I had enough food to eat. I don't miss the man currently sitting in a jail cell. "I'm sorry for venting all of this out on you."

"I'm the one who asked you to." He grins.

"Well, thanks. I do feel a bit better now." I lean back into the couch, feeling emotionally exhausted from everything.

"You should because a little birdie also told me you won the fashion competition you had been working so hard on." He wears a proud smile, looking like the brother I need in my life.

"Yeah, I did. They overnighted my pieces a few days ago, so I have a couple of last-minute touches to make tonight, but then I'm going to ship everything out to New York tomorrow morning so they have everything they need for the show."

"Isn't it over a month away?" he asks.

"Yeah, but there are other students who won from other schools, and a lot goes into an event like this, so they like to stay on top of everything, which means getting them the final products a month in advance so they can ensure no issues arise. God forbid, a button is missing, or a hemline is too short."

Nate laughs. "That's great, Vanessa. Really. I'm proud of you."

"Thanks, Nate." It feels good to hear him say this to me, but there's really only one person I want to hear those words from.

"Well, tomorrow Paul and I are having a little party at our house for New Year's Eve, and you better be coming with Natalie." He tilts his head, noticing my hesitation. "Jason won't be there. He'll be on his way to California for his game."

"Oh, right. The Rose Bowl game." I feel relieved that I won't risk running into him but also disappointed. "Okay, I'll be there. But Nate, can you please promise not to say anything to Jason about what I've told you?"

"Yeah, of course."

Twenty-Eight

JASON

I press play for the thousandth time, torturing myself as I stare at the phone screen in my hand.

It's the video of Vanessa and me dancing in front of my truck while the snow falls softly around us, providing the perfect backdrop. The song, *Snowman* by Sia, is a faint whisper in the background, both of us laughing like kids as I hold her body securely against mine, doing our best to sync our steps with the music but failing miserably.

Why am I doing this to myself? Putting myself through my own personal form of Hell.

I toss the phone to the other side of my bed, where I have spent most of my time since returning to my apartment for football practice a few days ago. The Rose Bowl game, the biggest game in my career so far, is in two days, and I can't let anything distract me.

But all I keep thinking about is Vanessa.

The way her body felt in my arms as she fell asleep in my bed.

The way her contagious laugh made me instantly smile.

The way her lips tasted so damn sweet, making me feel like I could never get my fill of her.

The way her confidence had grown these past few months and how goddamn proud I am of her for it.

But then I think about what she did.

She lied to me.

She promised me she had nothing to do with Brian anymore, and she fucking lied to me. My chest tightens at this realization.

How many times had she visited him?

Why did she visit him?

Did she forgive him for what he did to my sister?

I rub at my throbbing temple, a migraine forming with every wounding question.

We were finally together—me and her—no longer just friends. Or even friends with benefits, for that matter. But for whatever reason, she chose him. The moment she crossed the threshold into the prison was the moment she chose her asshole, psycho brother over me.

And it fucking hurts.

I run my hands over my head, frustration taking over me because this isn't how things were supposed to go. We were supposed to be together. Me and her. Forever.

I sit up and drag myself to my bathroom, hoping a shower will do me good. If even just to help make me feel alive and less zombie-like. Maybe it'll even lessen the pain I feel permeating around my heart.

But ten minutes later, as I wrap a towel around my waist, I still feel just as miserable as before. I swipe a hand over the fogged mirror to reveal bloodshot eyes and deep dark circles. I look how I feel.

Heartbroken.

I hear my front door slam open and jump back in alarm.

Who the fuck is that?

Walking out of my room, I find a very rigid and uptight Nate barreling inside.

Oh great. He's probably pissed because Vanessa and I never told anyone about us like we promised. But guess what, Nate? The joke's on you since there's nothing to tell anymore.

Because Vanessa and I are nothing anymore.

Nothing.

"Listen, Nate, I don't have time for this right now," I say, my fingers brushing through my wet hair. I'm tired. No, I'm fucking exhausted. I haven't been able to get a decent night's sleep since Christmas, and I don't have any energy for what he's about to throw my way. "I need to pack for my flight tomorrow." I grab my blue duffle bag lying on the chair near me, turning to make my way back to my room.

"What's wrong with you?" he demands, his eyes searching me for an answer he won't find.

"Again, I don't have time." I reach into the cabinet for some aspirin. This headache is just getting worse by the minute.

"She's broken because of you."

My hands freeze in the middle of opening the bottle. So, he didn't come here because we didn't tell anyone about us. He came here because he knew there was no longer anything to tell.

But did he say she's broken?

I shake my head. "What happened between me and Vanessa is none of your business."

"Yeah, well, it became my business when I sat with her on the couch, holding her shaking body in my arms, watching tears fall down her face. Trying to talk her down from a panic attack because she thinks she's the one who messed up and feels horrible about it, but in reality, it's you who fucked up for making her feel this way in the first place," he shouts.

Like an ice pick to my heart, a stab of pain hits me fast and hard. I massage the center of my chest. "I'm the one who fucked up? You don't get it," I scoff.

"No, you see, the thing is, I do get it, Jason. Because we both love Natalie, and we both love Vanessa."

I look at him like he's crazy, not wanting to admit my true feelings for Vanessa out loud as I advance toward my bedroom, wanting this conversation to be over. Because maybe if I don't say it, I can make the pain disappear.

"You love Vanessa. Don't even try to deny it," he affirms.

"So, what if I do?" I roar, turning to face him. "It's over! She made her choice when she went to see her scumbag of a brother. She knows how much I hate him. What the thought of him does to me. She knows what he did to my sister, and she still chose him!"

"She fucking chose you!" Nate shouts, his chest heaving up and down hard. "You asked her to choose between you and her brother. Maybe not in those words, but you did when you told her to promise she had nothing to do with Brian anymore. And if the roles were reversed? Who would you choose if Vanessa had asked you to choose between Natalie and herself?"

"It's not the fucking same thing!"

"It is Jason. You asked her to do the impossible when you should have given her time to come to terms with everything on her own. You asked her to choose between her brother and the guy she loves. And guess what? She chose you when she should never have been put in a position to choose between you two." He shakes his head, clearly frustrated. "That girl has craved a family her whole life—a real family. Not the one she was dealt. But still, she walked into that prison and told her only brother goodbye because she chose you. And when she walked outside, feeling guilt-ridden for what she just did, you stood there and broke her."

My mouth parts, but I can't find words. I rub the back of my neck, squeezing the tense muscles. "She went there to say goodbye?"

Nate takes a deep breath. "Yes."

I sit on the counter stool beside me, running my hands over my face. "I didn't ... know." I let out a frustrated sigh. "Natalie is my sister. I would do anything to protect her, but I couldn't protect her from Brian, and because of that, I feel like I failed her." I look down, my throat tightening. "I never wanted to hurt Vanessa, but when I saw her walking into the prison with a gift in her hand for him, all I saw was red." I remember waiting outside for her, stewing like a volcano, ready to erupt.

"I know, but Jason, you didn't fail Natalie. You never have." Nate pulls out one of the counter stools across from mine and sits. "How do you think I feel knowing I was right downstairs when she was attacked?" He looks up, shaking his head, appearing disappointed in himself. "You and I have a lot in common, including doing anything and everything we can to keep those we love safe. And I know you wouldn't intentionally hurt Vanessa. But you did." He places his elbows on the countertop, intertwining his hands before him.

"That girl testified against her own brother. Do you have any idea what that did to her? Or the amount of guilt that she's felt because of it? But she did it because she knew it was the right thing to do and because she loves you and Natalie. But she's been blaming herself for where Brian ended up, living every day with guilt eating away at her. And these past few months, she's had a tough time letting go of who Brian used to be, to who he became. It wasn't that she missed him. She just missed having someone in her corner. She missed having a brother. And it took her time to really see who he was because she knew once she saw him clearly, she'd need to say goodbye to the last person in her family who actually gave a shit about her." He sighs. "You and Natalie have an amazing family. You have two parents who love you both so much, and I think sometimes, growing up in such a close family, you overlook what the word family might mean to others."

I cross my arms over my chest, letting his words sink in. *Family.* A word that can mean something different to everyone. A word that I only ever associate with love. But to Vanessa, maybe it doesn't hold the same meaning. Maybe the word family only brings her pain.

I clear my throat hard, feeling a slight tingle at the tip of my nose. "I miss her so fucking much it hurts. But I don't know if I can look at her for the rest of my life, knowing her brother will always be a thought in the background of my mind. Someone who will always come between us."

"I think you're worried the thought of him will be there, but I can promise you that it won't. Because you love her so much, your mind won't let you see anything else but her."

"How can you be so sure?" I ask.

He takes in my question, slowly nodding his head. "How have you felt not being with her this past week?"

"What?"

"Tell me."

"Don't psychoanalyze me right now, Nate," I huff.

"I'm trying to help you, Jason. So work with me here," he says, sounding exasperated.

"Like I can't fucking breathe," I snap. "Like I wake up every morning living in a nightmare where I'm not with her anymore. A nightmare where I can't hold or kiss her any damn time I want. It's torture. It's like I've lost all purpose for everything, including football, the one thing I've cared about the most in my life. And my lifelong dream of being in the NFL feels like a distant memory because it means nothing anymore. It means nothing without her." My breaths are coming out rough and uneven. "I fucked up. Is that what you want to hear? I threw away the best thing that ever happened to me because I refused to listen when she tried to explain to me what she was doing." I look down, slamming my fist on the counter. "And I know now that she deserves better than someone like me."

Nate has the audacity to fucking laugh at my confession.

"I'm so glad you find this funny," I bite out.

"Oh, believe me, I don't." He grins, his chuckle slowly fading. "But what you just said is one of the biggest excuses a guy can make. And I only know that from firsthand experience."

"What the hell are you talking about?"

He rolls his eyes as if I should know the answer to his riddle. "If you think she deserves better, then be better. It's really that simple."

I let his words seep into my skin. Can it really be that simple?

"How the hell do I do that?"

Nate looks down at his phone before looking at me. "Well, I need to get to work, so it looks like it's up to you to figure that part out on your own." He gets up, pats my shoulder reassuringly, and then turns toward the door. "All I know is that you have a girl right across the hall from you who described you as being her moon. The only thing she notices in a night sky filled with millions of stars is you."

The door closes behind Nate, and I'm left not knowing what to do.

How do I apologize to her for making her feel anything less than my whole world?

How do I tell her I'm so in love with her that every day on this Earth without her feels like a waste of a life?

And then it hits me like a ton of bricks to the face.

I jump to my feet, walk into my room, grab sticky notes off my desk, reach under my bed for the box labeled *"private,"* and pull out my thick journal. The same journal I've been writing in for the past year, documenting every important memory to me. Past and Current. Flipping through the pages, I note every entry mentioning Vee. Every page filled with a memory of Vanessa that I never want to forget.

Because I love this girl like the moon loves the stars.

Infinitely.

Eternally.

Every night until their last fleeting moment in the universe.

But what Vanessa doesn't know is that a moon needs his star to shine. To breathe. To exist. And if I am her moon, she is my star, and everyone knows that the two can't live without each other.

And I can't live another fucking day without her.

Twenty-Nine

VANESSA

Sleep is a funny thing.

It's something that our mind and body needs to survive—to remain a functioning human. But when our hearts are broken, sleep becomes an impossible task. As we lay in our beds, closing our eyes, waiting for sleep to take us to a faraway place, our heart reminds our mind why it is that we cannot sleep in the first place, which then causes the overthinking to begin, which then causes our bodies to toss and turn looking for comfort from anything. Maybe even a warm body that no longer lies beside you.

It's a vicious cycle.

Stretching out on my bed, I stare out the window beside me as the sun makes its way up into the sky, waking all of Boston. I have zero motivation to get out of bed and would stay in it all day if I didn't have to get my pieces for my collection to the post office and if I then didn't agree to go to the New Year's Eve party at Nate and Paul's house tonight.

I groan in frustration. Why did I say I would go?

So that I could watch everyone else have a great time with their significant others before eventually getting swept into a romantic embrace as the bell strikes midnight. I must be a masochist. It's the only valid reason as to why I agreed to go.

I roll out of bed and trudge toward the shower, hoping a steaming hot shower will help make me feel alive. Thirty minutes later, after showering and throwing on a pair of jeans and a T-shirt, I grab my winter puffer jacket, missing my red peacoat.

Don't cry. Don't cry. Don't cry.

You can make it through one day without crying.

But as I notice the rumpled Linrey University football T-shirt on the floor by my bed, the notion of not crying seems impossible. So, I quickly grab the boxes on my desk and head to my car, making it my mission to get away from anything and everything that reminds me of Jason.

My mission proves to be impossible when the first snowflakes fall from the sky above me, reminding me of Christmas Eve when Jason pulled over to the side of the road only to get out of his truck to ask me to dance with him. My eyes water at this memory, but I shake my head to stop it. I will not cry today because I have things to do this morning, and I will not let the thought of him distract me.

I'm the first person in line, dropping off my packages, and after making the man behind the counter promise me on his life that all of my boxes would get to New York City safely and in one piece, I finally leave. The snow has picked up since I've been in the building, so I throw on my gloves and hat and go to my car, where I discover it's hidden under a fresh layer of snow. I stupidly don't have a snow brush in my car, so I use my arm to wipe off as much as possible, ensuring I clear the windshield enough to see while driving.

The second I sit my butt onto the cold leather seat, I turn on the seat warmers and blast the heat inside, keeping my hands in front of the vent for a few minutes before pulling out of the parking spot. There are not many people on the roads because of the snow, and as I make my way closer to campus, I can feel my tires skidding here and there against the ice forming on the pavement, so I drive almost too slowly, keeping a firm grip on the steering wheel.

The last thing I need is to start the New Year in the hospital.

I come to a stop at a red light as the song on the radio changes to *Snowman* by Sia, and I can't hold back the tears anymore. They pour from my eyes one by one as a silent sob grips my throat, taking over my body. My forehead falls against the steering wheel, and my hands clutch at my shirt right where my heart thunders beneath my skin. It hurts. It fucking hurts so much, and there's only one person who can make the pain go away.

But he won't because he never wants to see me again.

A horn blares behind me, and when I look up, I find the light has changed from red to green. So, I quickly wipe away the tears rolling down my cheeks, step on the gas, and return to my apartment.

Walking through the hallway, I find myself stopping in front of Jason's door. I stare at it, wondering if he's on the other side. Wondering if he would even open the door if I knocked. I raise my hand to the door, ready to rap my knuckles against the wood, but I stop myself and place the palm of my hand against it, knowing I can't.

It's over.

Taking a deep breath, I turn around, take a few steps, pull out my key and make my way inside my apartment, closing the door behind me but not before taking one last look at Jason's door over my shoulder.

"Hey! I was wondering where you were." Natalie's on the couch, still in her pajamas, with a stack of pancakes in front of her and some reality show on TV.

"Hey, yeah, sorry." I unzip my jacket, shake off the snow, and hang it on the wall beside me. "I just came back from the post office. I needed to get my pieces shipped to New York."

"But I thought the show isn't until Valentine's Day?"

"It's not, but it takes time. They need the pieces in their hands to ensure no changes are needed beforehand. Everything needs to be perfect."

"Ahh, well, there are pancakes on the counter if you want any. I figured we should load up on carbs before tonight." She chuckles.

"Good idea," I reply softly, making my way into the kitchen with absolutely no appetite.

"Hey, I almost forgot. Jason stopped by here about an hour ago looking for you."

My hand freezes on the fridge door. "He did? What for?"

Stay calm, Vanessa.

She finishes eating the bite in her mouth, each second passing, sending me into a state of panic. "No idea. I asked him why he needed to see you, and he just said he'll try again when he gets back, and then he left." She shrugs her shoulders.

"Where did he go?" I ask. Maybe he went back to his place. If I go there right—

"He left for the airport with his team. His flight leaves this afternoon."

"Oh." I missed him, and now he's gone.

"Is everything okay?" Natalie watches me carefully as I realize I'm staring at the pancakes in a daze.

"Yeah." I push my hair behind my ear. "I just didn't get much sleep last night, so I think I'm going to hop back into bed so I'll be ready for tonight." I put on a fake smile, hoping she doesn't see through it, but of course, she does. She's my best friend.

"Okay, but you know you can talk to me about anything, right?" She puts her plate down, gets up from the sofa, and walks over to me. "You've seemed a little off since Christmas." She looks at me, waiting for a reply, and I want to tell her, but what do I even say? Because there's nothing even going on between me and Jason anymore. We're nothing. And he never wants to see me again.

His words.

"Sorry, I don't mean to be." My throat tightens. "It's just..."

"Life," she finishes for me.

I nod, unable to find words.

Her slender arms wrap around me. "How about tomorrow we have a girl's day. No boys allowed. Just you and me. What do you think?"

I show a weak smile as a tear slides down my cheek. "I'd like that a lot."

"Okay, perfect." She squeezes me tightly before letting go. "Now, go get your butt in bed, and I promise tonight will be a night we'll never forget."

Natalie and I walk through the house's front door, immediately met by Nate, and I can't shake the feeling that I shouldn't be here.

"Well, aren't you two a sight." Nate spins Natalie in his arms before bringing her against his chest and placing a tender kiss on her lips.

I pull down nervously on the hem of my dress, worried it might be showing too much of my thighs. Maybe I should have worn something looser and not as form-fitting.

I never worried about what I wore when I was with Jason.

But here, now, I'm second-guessing everything about tonight.

I shouldn't be here.

"Hey," Natalie lightly smacks Nate's chest, "you're supposed to wait until midnight."

"No way, beautiful. I would never be able to last that long. Besides, that was just a taste of what's to come later." He pushes her blonde hair behind her ear, staring lovingly down into her eyes.

Man, I feel single.

"Hey, Vanessa. Want a drink?" Paul appears beside me, holding out a red solo cup for me. "It's your favorite."

I take it from him and see the familiar cranberry color liquid inside. "Thank you, Paul. Always such a gentleman."

"Anything for you ladies." He takes a sip from his cup and then looks at Nate and Natalie, still staring into each other's eyes. "Hey, love birds. You're supposed to wait until midnight."

Natalie giggles and pulls slightly away from Nate. "I tried telling him that, but he wouldn't listen to me."

"How do you put up with them?" Paul asks, looking at me.

"Aww, I think it's cute." And I really do. I just wish I had someone who wrapped me up in his arms like that too.

Someone, meaning Jason.

But instead, I find myself feeling something I haven't felt in a while.

Alone.

"Hey, guys!" Sarah approaches us looking stunning in a short sparkly silver sequined dress that puffs out at her waist, showing off not only the floral tattoos on her arms but on one of her thighs as well. Her jet-black hair falls down her back in waves, and her makeup is the definition of flawless.

"Oh my God, Sarah, this dress is everything." I twirl my finger for her to give a spin and watch as the lights reflect on her dress, making her look like a sexy disco ball. And it seems like I'm not the only one who notices, as Paul's eyes seem unable to leave her. "Don't you think she looks hot, Paul?" I lightly shove my elbow into his side.

"Yeah. Yes. Yes. Definitely. You umm, you look really beautiful, Sarah," Paul splutters like a fool.

Sarah blushes. "Thanks, Paul."

Nate catches on and looks between the two. "So Sarah, who'd you come here with?"

"Oh, no one." She shakes her head.

"Really? What a coincidence because Paul's not here with anyone either. Right, Paul?" Nate arches his brows.

Poor Paul almost chokes on his drink. "Right," he says.

For a man who looks the part, he sure as hell doesn't know how to act the part. But it's one of the things I've always liked about him. Natalie calls him the perfect teddy bear, and I think she's right because he's freakishly tall, adorable, and has a soft center.

I notice Sarah finishes whatever is in her cup, and I swoop in to help the man. "Hey, Paul. It looks like Sarah could use a refill."

"Yeah, of course. I can get you whatever you want." He motions for her to follow him to the kitchen, and she does. As they walk away, he looks back at me and mouths, "*Thank you*," which makes me smile.

Hey, even if I'm not getting my midnight kiss tonight, it doesn't mean I don't want others not to.

An hour later, the party is in full swing. People are filling all of the rooms as music blares from speakers and drinks get passed around. Sarah and Paul are on one of the sofas sitting pretty close together as they talk, and Natalie and Nate are dancing in the middle of the crowd beside me.

"Hey," I tap on Natalie's shoulder, "I'm just going to run to the bathroom."

"Okay, do you want me to come with you?" she asks.

"No. Keep dancing. I'll be right back."

She smiles as I wander toward the first-floor bathroom, but when I see the line in the hallway, I quickly turn toward the stairs, knowing I can use a perfectly good bathroom in Nate's room. Quickly I climb the stairs, like a girl on a mission, and when I turn the corner, I slam directly into someone.

My eyes pinch shut as I bring my hand to my head, rubbing at the spot on my forehead where I just collided into a man's chest. "Oh my God, I'm so sorry."

"Well, look who we have here."

I open my eyes and see a man standing directly in front of me, looking like he knows me. But do I know him? I scan his face, noting a familiarity, but no name comes to mind.

"Do I know you?" I ask, adjusting the chain strap on my dress.

"You mean to tell me you don't remember this face? Now that's a damn shame. I thought I was more memorable than that." He grins, rubbing his hand along his jaw. It's not until he turns his head slightly to the side that I see the familiar skull on his neck and am immediately assaulted with the vile memory of his hand on my ass.

Oh, shit. This isn't good.

"What are you doing here?" I look around the hall to see if anyone is nearby, but it's just the two of us up here.

"What? Not happy to see me?" He steps toward me, and I recoil, taking a step back. "You know, you got me kicked out of Winners permanently. Haven't been allowed to step foot in there with my friends." He shakes his head.

"Maybe that will teach you to keep your hands to yourself then." I cross my arms in front of my chest, standing my ground with this asshole, unwilling to show him the terror coursing through me.

"No, you see, the only thing it taught me was that I should have put you in your place that night for making such a big deal out of fucking nothing," he hisses like a snake with vengeance on the tip of his tongue.

My heart races as he takes another step toward me, and I take one back, now standing directly in front of the staircase.

"Get out of my way." I try to move around him to get to Nate's room, where I can lock myself safely inside, but it's useless. He grabs me forcefully near my shoulders, making me shriek in pain, but no one can hear me, with the music blasting out of every speaker. I try to wiggle free, hit, kick, or do anything, but he's too strong. His ice-cold black eyes stare into mine, and my heart plummets, knowing what's coming next.

"Sweet dreams," the asshole says right before lifting me and throwing me down the stairs.

The last thing I remember is that free-falling feeling you get in the pit of your stomach just as the rollercoaster dives straight down, right before my head slams against the cold hard ground.

Thirty

JASON

The Linrey University football team is currently crammed together like a pack of sardines in a tiny waiting area located by one of the gates in Logan Airport as our flight has been delayed over and over again because of the damn snow. Not only is the snow pissing me off because I've had to sit here for hours, but it's also reminding me of dancing with Vanessa, worsening my mood.

Not to mention, there's way too much testosterone in this small space.

I spent last night staring at the ceiling, unable to get Vanessa out of my thoughts because I know I royally fucked up, and I'm scared shitless that she won't give me a second chance. Not that I deserve it, but I'll do whatever she needs me to do to prove how sorry I am. If she wants me to get on my knees and beg for forgiveness, then that's what I'll do. But please, God, let me get a second chance with the girl of my dreams.

Let me prove to her that I will never let her shatter.

I will be the man she deserves.

I will be better for her.

I will love her always. Even if I can't remember anything one day, I know I will still love her with every part of me.

Because she was never just my friend.

She's the love of my life.

I know that now.

And that's exactly what I planned on telling her this morning not long after the sun rose, when I stormed over to her apartment, looking for her, only to be met with a very confused Natalie, who told me Vanessa wasn't home.

I was vague about why I needed to talk to Vanessa and quickly made my way out before she became suspicious. But as I stood outside the apartment building, watching the time on my phone, hoping she would make it home before I needed to catch the team bus for the airport, my heart sank, knowing I needed to leave. So that's what I did. I made it to the bus just as they were pulling out of the lot and knew that my begging for forgiveness would have to wait until I got back because this wasn't something I could send over a text or even say over a phone call.

But if she tells me to fuck off, I can't say I blame her.

I hurt her. No, I *broke* her. I did the one thing I promised I would never do to her.

I broke her heart.

In a world where she is constantly being let down by those she loves, I did the same fucking thing. I am no better than the others who have let her down.

My hands clench into tight fists as I try to take a deep breath. The small star charm on the bracelet in my clutch stabs the palm of my hand, a drop of blood poking through my skin. I need to see Vanessa now, which is impossible as I'm reminded by the irritating voice on the intercom letting people know what gate is boarding.

Surprise. It's still not ours.

"Well, this fucking sucks," Grant grumbles as he slides into his seat next to me with a slice of pizza in his hand. "I could be out with my girl tonight celebrating New Year's Eve, but instead, I'm stuck here with you fools for God knows how long."

"You don't want to celebrate the New Year with me, Grant? I'm hurt." Chris readjusts the bag under his head, which he's using as a pillow by my feet, before crossing his arms over his chest.

"Not a chance in hell," Grant responds before shoving the pizza in his mouth.

"What about you, Jason? You got someone you'd rather spend the night with? Maybe a cute waitress?" Chris asks, waggling his brows.

I sigh. "I don't know if she'd want to spend it with me, but I sure as hell wish I was spending it with her." I place the bracelet back in my pocket and take my air pods out of my bag, ready to drown out everyone around me.

"Ohhh, what did you do?" Chris sits up, looking eagerly for a juicy story he won't get.

"I fucked up."

"What? Did you cheat on her or something?" he asks.

I shoot up in my seat, anger taking over me. "No, I didn't fucking cheat on her. I would never do that!"

Chris stifles a laugh.

"And may I ask what the fuck you think is so funny?" I stab him in the chest with my index finger, watching him fall back on the floor.

He wipes pretend tears from his eyes. "You have it bad, my man."

"So what if I do?" I lean back in my seat, placing my air pods in my ears to drown out Chris's annoying laugh.

"Well, I, for one, am happy for you, man." Grant pats my shoulder before resting his head against the wall and closing his eyes. "Don't any of you mother fuckers draw on my face, or there will be hell to face. Understood?"

"Yes, sir!" Chris immediately responds.

The first song on my playlist begins but suddenly goes quiet, alerting me I have an incoming call. It's Nate.

I tap on the green answer button.

"What's up, Nate?"

"Hey, did your flight leave yet?" he asks, tension releasing in his voice.

"No. Our flight has been delayed all day. We're still waiting to get out of here." Something is wrong. I can feel it in my gut. "Why?"

"Okay, listen, I don't mean to put you in a tough spot, but I thought you should know…" He pauses, scaring the shit out of me.

"Know what, Nate? You're freaking me out here."

"She's okay, but there was an accident—"

"Who's okay? What the fuck is going on?" I shoot up in my seat for the second time, my heart thundering in my chest. Grant and Chris glance at each other, appearing concerned by my outburst.

"Vanessa was pushed down the stairs. She's okay. She's sleeping. Natalie and I are with her at Mass General, but she was banged up pretty good. The doctor said she might have a concussion, but they have to run some tests, and she's a bit bruised—"

I don't hear the rest of his words.

Someone fucking pushed her down the stairs.

My heart is pounding so loud that it's physically impossible to hear him.

I disconnect the call and jump to my feet, searching for Coach. When I spot him at the end of the aisle, I bolt over to him.

"Coach, there's been an emergency, and I need to leave—right now," I rush out, my throat feeling constricted.

He looks up from the book he's reading with furrowed brows. "What?"

Grant approaches me from behind. "What's going on, Jason?"

"I need to go!" I have to get out of here. Every second here is a second away from Vanessa.

"What kind of emergency is it?" Coach tilts his head calmly.

"Listen, Coach, with all due respect, kick me off the team if you need to, but I need to get to Mass General now. My girl is there, which means I need to be there too and—"

He raises his hand to stop me from speaking. "And this girl, is she worth you not playing in the Rose Bowl game? Is she worth putting your future on the line?"

"I don't have a future without her, Coach." I take a deep breath. "I know the second I walk out of here, I'm letting the team down, and I'm sorry, but I..." I pinch the bridge of my nose, fighting the onslaught of tears, trying to escape. There's no fucking way I'm crying in front of my coach. "She's my world. If anything happens to her, I will never forgive myself."

Coach nods his head in understanding. "Well, you're crazy if you think I'm kicking you off the team when you're the best one we got. I'm not that much of a horrible guy. I have a heart, too, and understand what it means to love someone."

Grant's hand lands on my shoulder with a thud. "We got this, Jason. We can play Mac and Bailey as quarterbacks for the game. Get out of here to go be with Vanessa."

I glance at Coach for the final approval.

He nods his head. "Get out of here before I change my mind."

"Yes, sir." I turn around and quickly make my way for the exit, but as soon as I step outside, I see it's a fucking blizzard. "Shit!" I pull at my hair. How the fuck am I going to get to her?

I grab my phone from my pocket, hoping and praying that someone on Uber will be crazy enough to drive in this weather, but there isn't anyone. Not a single soul.

Fucking. Fuck. Fuck!

My finger hovers over the map icon before finally pressing down and typing out Mass General. *Three and a half miles away.* I look out at the snow falling hard, completely covering the ground, and let out a deep breath, seen in a thick puff of smoke. I don't have any other option.

Putting my phone in my bag, gloves on my hands, and a hat on my head, I brace myself as I start running through the storm. I run through the bone-breaking cold and the harsh winter winds nipping at my exposed skin. And I run until I feel only numbness invading every inch of my solid body. But I run, knowing with everything inside me, I need to get to my girl, and nothing, not even a Nor'easter blizzard, will stop me.

I charge through the hospital entrance, my pulse racing with each step I take on the checkered linoleum floor. The heat inside thrashes at my frozen body as pain emits throughout me, especially my feet, that I wasn't even sure I could feel just a moment ago.

My body slams into the receptionist's desk, snow falling off of me, giving the woman on the other side a fright as I ask for the information I need. When I get off the elevator on the fourth floor, I head down the hall to find room four hundred and ten and force open the door.

Air rushes out of my lungs at the sight of Vanessa.

She's lying on a hospital bed, her eyes closed. A white blanket covers her waist, revealing her upper body in a soft blue hospital gown. She's hooked up to an IV, and a monitor on the furthest side of her bed beeps steadily, reassuring me she's alive. My eyes travel up her body, noting a beige bandage wrapped around her left wrist and a smaller bandage taped to her forehead next to a minor bruise partially hidden by her hair covering the side of her face.

"Fragile" is the only word that pops into my head.

"What the fuck happened to her?" I roar through tender lips.

Natalie, sitting in the chair closest to Vanessa, sobbing as she holds onto Vanessa's hand, jumps at the sound of my voice. Nate is standing behind her, with his hands on her shoulders, as he looks up at me calmly, expecting this reaction from me.

"Jason?" Natalie's voice sounds surprised to see me. "What are you doing here? You're supposed to be on your way to California." She looks over her shoulder at Nate, confusion written all over her face.

Nate runs a hand through his hair. "I called him." He lets out a deep breath before continuing. "He needed to know because I would feel the same way as him right now."

"What do you mean?" she asks, looking between the two of us.

God, I hate keeping secrets from my sister and can't do it for a second longer.

"Because I am in love with her," I admit, feeling a weight lift off my chest at this confession. I step inside the room, removing my jacket, bag, and gloves, dripping a mixture of snow and sweat on the floor, and stand beside the bed, looking down at Vanessa. My icy hand brushes a silky strand of her chestnut hair off of her face, revealing a bluish bruise near her eye, and she turns into my hand, snuggling into my palm, providing some much-needed warmth to my skin.

"Wh-what?" Natalie's eyes widen at this revelation.

"Listen, I'll explain everything to you later. I promise. But right now, I need to know what happened." I look between the two of them, waiting for answers.

Natalie appears shell-shocked but eventually blinks a few times, processing my words. "Well, we were at the party at Nathan and Paul's house, and Vanessa went to go use the bathroom, but it was taking a while, so I went to go find her, and when I headed toward the stairs, she umm ... she... she was lying unconscious on the last step and there was blood ... so much blood ... so I screamed, and when I looked at the top of the stairs, I saw a guy about our age standing at the top before he took off down the hall." Tears stream down her cheeks as she looks down in disbelief. "The only thing I remember about the guy is a skull tattoo on his neck. I have no idea who he is. I've never seen him before." She lets go of Vanessa's hand and raises her hands to cover her face. "I should have gone with her."

"Shh. It's okay, baby." Nate runs his hands up and down Natalie's arms, soothing her. He kisses the top of her head before reaching for the thin blanket on the chair beside her and wrapping it around her body.

Fury pumps vigorously through every vein in my body, pushing me to the edge of insanity.

I will find him. And I will make him pay.

No one gets away with hurting my girl.

"What did the doctor say?" I ask, trying to reign in my rage as I take Vanessa's hand in mine, my thumb brushing over her smooth skin.

"They ran a few tests to ensure there was no internal bleeding, and thankfully there was none. She's on some pain meds now, which is why she's sleeping. They bandaged a gash on her forehead, and her wrist might be sprained," Nate explains. "She also has some bruising forming on her ribs. Nothing is broken, but she will be uncomfortable for a little bit."

The sight of a slight blue mark on her skin at the edge of the hospital gown sleeve catches my attention, so I pull it up to reveal a bruise that looks like a handprint, and I can no longer reign in my wrath.

"Who the fuck did this to her?" I remove my hat, running a shaky hand over my hair. "What the fuck!" I turn around and slam a hole into the wall before I can stop myself.

Nate's over by my side in a second, pulling me away.

"This isn't going to solve anything." He moves me down into a chair. "Listen, Paul is at the house now trying to find out anything he can. When Vanessa wakes up, she might know who it is, but until then, you need to calm down and be here for her."

My elbows land on my knees, and my head sinks into my hands as I squeeze my eyes shut.

A delicate hand lands on my back, rubbing up and down, and I open my eyes to see Natalie beside me.

"Jason," she looks at me as if seeing me for the first time, "how did you get here?"

I rub my hands together and bring them up to my windburn cheeks. "I ran here."

Her mouth parts, her eyes widen, and her eyebrows shoot up to her hairline. "From the airport? But that's over three miles away, and it's a blizzard out there."

"Believe me, I know."

Natalie stands, gets a blanket from the other side of the room, and brings it over to me, wrapping it around my shoulders. She sits back beside me, taking my hands in hers, rubbing them between her palms. "You're freezing. You're lucky you didn't get frostbite."

I'm not entirely sure I didn't, but I don't mention this to her, not wanting to add to her anxiety.

"I needed to be here," I say, not regretting my actions.

I would do it again if needed because I would do anything for the girl sleeping quietly in the hospital bed before me. *Anything.*

"She's going to be okay," she says reassuringly. "She has to be." Her voice cracks as she speaks, and I realize my sister feels as helpless in this situation as I do.

"Come here, Nat." I open my arms for her to lean into, and I hold her tightly, needing comfort from my sister as much as she needs it from her brother.

"Jason?"

"Yeah?"

"I need you to find who did this to her." Her eyes, the same color as mine, look up at me pleadingly. She's sending me a silent request, and the message is well received.

"I will. I promise."

She buries her face into my shirt, sniffling and still holding tightly onto my hands, doing everything she can to keep me warm. "Mom and Dad are on their way. We couldn't get a hold of Vanessa's parents, so I didn't know who else to call, but—"

"Hey, it's a good thing you called Mom and Dad. You know she's their favorite daughter," I add to lighten the mood because as much as I feel like an inferno has been ignited inside me, I hate nothing more than seeing my sister like this.

She lifts her head from my shoulder, showing a hopeful smile through her tear-stained cheeks.

I push her hair back, and she leans against my shoulder as we both look over at Vanessa.

"I always knew you loved her."

"You did not," I retort.

She lets out a soft laugh. "Did too."

Nate, who I didn't even realize left the room, hands me a steaming cup of coffee, which I gladly accept. The hot liquid, rushing down my throat, provides warmth to my entire body, making me feel more alive with each sip. He then lifts a picture and a tac from the wall beside him and moves it to place over the new hole I created.

"Thank you," I say.

He nods and takes a seat on the other side of Natalie, putting his arm on the back of her chair.

The three of us sit silently, waiting for Vanessa to wake up.

Thirty-One

VANESSA

There's a rhythmic beeping coming from the left of me, thankfully waking me from my nightmare. My eyelids flutter open, but when I look around at the dimly lit room with white walls and breathe in the antiseptic scent, I realize I'm not in my bedroom. I'm in a hospital. Which means the nightmare wasn't a nightmare. It was real.

And the aches and pains that are currently traveling over my body are further proof of this.

Panicking, I try to sit up, but a large hand gently but firmly lands on my chest, pressing me down.

"Hey, Vee. You're okay," Jason says softly as he stands up from the chair beside my bed, bringing his face closer to mine. Deep bags are under his eyes, and his hair looks like he's repeatedly run his fingers through it. But the only thing that stands out to me is my favorite color. The almost blue, but not quite grey, eyes that stare into mine.

"Jason?" Tears form behind my eyes. "Where ... what?" I'm so confused. I look around, and my eyes catch on the site of Nate sleeping on a chair with Natalie curled up on his lap, sound asleep.

"Shh. I've got you." His arms wrap around me tightly, lifting me so my head rests against his chest. "I'm here, and I'm not going anywhere."

Okay, I must be dreaming. Because the last time I saw this man, he told me he never wanted to see me again, but here he is, holding onto me like he never wants to let go.

The tears tumble forcefully from my eyes. I reach my hand to my face to wipe them away, but Jason beats me to it.

"Jason, I'm so sorry for—"

"No." Jason cuts me off and pulls away to look down at me with his eyes locked onto mine. "You have nothing to be sorry for. It was all me, Vanessa. I should have never put you in that situation. I'm the one that is sorry." He lightly rubs my back, his strong hand splayed out, securing me to him. "But let's talk about this later, okay? I need to take care of you now."

I nod, too tired for the conversation we will eventually need to have. My eyes gaze down at the small space between us. "Do you think you can fit up here with me?"

His eyes scan the bed or, more specifically, my body. "I don't want to hurt you, Vee."

I stick out my bottom lip and flutter my lashes.

He doesn't hesitate as he slides in gradually beside me and positions himself on his side, placing his left arm under my head for me to use as a pillow. I turn on my side to face him, being cautious of the IV in my hand, and he pulls the blanket up around my waist.

I grip at his shirt, trying to anchor myself to him, but I'm hit with a sharp sting in my left wrist and caught off guard to find it bandaged. "What happened to me?" I ask. I remember going to the party and leaving Natalie and Nate to use the bathroom, but after that, it all becomes blurry.

He sweeps my hair away from my face, tucking it behind my ear. "I was hoping you could tell me that."

I try to remember, focusing on every detail of last night. It's like watching your favorite movie, but vital scenes to the plot are missing.

And I'm coming up blank. There's no reason I can think of as to why I'm currently in this state.

"Natalie said she saw you lying unconscious on the bottom step of the stairs at Nate's house." He watches me carefully. "She said she saw blood, so she screamed, and when she looked at the top of the stairs, she saw a guy standing there."

I purse my lips, scrunching my brows. "I don't remember." I let out a deep breath before rolling my lips. "This is so frustrating."

He wraps his arm tenderly around my waist, his hand planted firmly on my lower back. "She mentioned something about seeing a skull tattoo on his neck. Do you know anyone who would have that?"

"A skull tattoo. No." I softly shake my head. "I don't know any—" I shoot up, ignoring the pain, my heart racing as the encounter with the asshole from the bar comes back to me. The image of his dark, murderous eyes, as he threw me down the stairs projects into my head, and I see the scene play out perfectly. He gripped the top of my arms painfully hard. He sneered at me as he said, *"Sweet dreams."* And then, finally, he lifted me like I weighed nothing and tossed me down the stairs, watching me with an evil smirk, finding pleasure in the pain he was about to cause me.

Jason sits up beside me. "What is it?"

"It was him." I'm breathing fast, feeling as scared as I was at that moment.

"Who?" He looks down at me patiently, grabbing onto my hand.

"The guy from Winners. The one who ... the one who touched me." I grip the hospital gown, feeling suddenly suffocated by fear. "He was mad. He said he hasn't been allowed back to the bar, and he was going to teach me a lesson." I look up into Jason's eyes, seeing a wrath in him like I've never seen before.

But he hides it from me as he calmly lays back down, bringing me with him. "It's okay, Vee. I'm going to take care of everything." I don't know what that means, and I don't think I want to know either.

I nuzzle into him, his arm holding onto me protectively, calming my racing mind because I know I'm safe with him. "How did you know I was here?"

"Nate called me when I was at the airport and—"

"Wait! Your game. You're supposed to be in California." My stomach plummets, realizing he's not there.

"No." He shakes his head. "I'm supposed to be right here with you."

"But it's the Rose Bowl game. This is the biggest game of your career." Guilt builds inside me. Why did he come here? He should be in California, following his dream.

"I don't care about that. I only care about you." His hand moves up to my face. "When I got the call from Nate, everything around me just stopped. I was so scared, Vanessa." His eyes mist over, causing mine to do the same. "I was scared I was never going to see you again. I was scared I was never going to be able to see that beautiful smile. But most of all, I was scared I would never be able to tell you that I love you."

My whole world stops moving. Every breath I take sounds thunderous in the silence surrounding us.

"You love me?" I breathe.

His hand leaves my body to retrieve something from his pocket. My heart goes into overdrive when I see the silver chain with the "V" and star charms dangling from his fingers.

"Jason?"

He places the bracelet in the palm of my hand, wrapping my fingers around it, and my heart stops beating.

"That night in the closet, the stars were aligned for us, Vee. We were just too scared to see it," he whispers.

JASON
FOUR YEARS AGO

It's a Saturday night, which means as a fifteen-year-old guy, I should be spending my night playing video games or throwing a football around with some friends. But no.

Instead, I find myself, against my will, at a birthday party for my buddy Alex, pretending to be having a good time, but really, all I've been doing every five seconds is making sure Natalie and Vanessa don't get themselves in trouble.

And maybe I'm not here against my will, but I'm only here because I heard Vanessa tell Natalie she is hoping to get her first kiss tonight.

Fuck that.

No one is kissing her tonight.

Not while I'm here. That's for damn sure.

But knowing Vanessa has never kissed anyone does something to me.

I feel ... possessive. A feeling I only experience when I think about Vanessa. Especially when I see guys at school drooling over her curves like she's some shiny new toy for them to play with. *Assholes*. They'll never be good enough for her.

At this point in the night, there's a bunch of people swimming in the indoor heated pool, Natalie being one of those people. But Vanessa said she forgot to bring a bathing suit, which means she is currently sitting on a chair opposite me, a little too close to my soon-to-be ex-friend, Alex, who has his arm wrapped around the back of Vanessa. She's laughing at everything he says, like he's tonight's entertainment, and it's really starting to piss me off.

I crush the empty cup in my hand, only seeing red.

"Hey, why don't we play seven minutes in heaven?" Lindsey, the class bimbo, asks everyone in the room. She stares at me for a little too long for my liking. I'm in no mood to be locked in a closet with someone for seven minutes. Only an idiot would agree to this.

"I'm in," Vanessa responds.

Well, shit, it looks like I'm going to be an idiot tonight.

"Me too," I counter, staring at Vanessa, who hasn't even looked my way, too busy making eyes at Alex.

After a few more people agree, we all sit in a circle on the living room floor, and someone places a bottle in the middle.

"Well, seeing that I'm the birthday boy, I guess I'll spin first." Alex reaches over, takes the bottle in his hand, and looks at Vanessa with a stupid grin before spinning. It feels like an eternity watching it rotate until it slowly stops, pointing directly at Vanessa.

No fucking way.

This has to be rigged.

My mind sprints a mile a minute. I can't let this happen. Vanessa is not having her first kiss with my best friend. I pull my phone out of my pocket and type like a madman.

"Looks like you're the lucky one," Alex says to Vanessa. She blushes. She actually fucking blushes.

They both stand as Alex reaches into his pocket, which is currently vibrating. He looks at the screen and then immediately over at me.

"Hey Vanessa, I'll meet you in the closet. You go first. Keep the lights off," he says, eyes locked on me.

"Okay," she responds, tucking a strand of silky brown hair behind her ear.

Alex looks down at his phone and types. Within seconds, my phone buzzes.

Alex: Don't mess this up.

That's my cue. I walk down the hall to the closet where Vanessa is currently inside.

Nerves invade every cell of my body.

This must be how guys feel when they run out of a football stadium and onto the field for a Super Bowl game. There's no other way to explain this feeling.

It's game time.

My clammy hand lands on the doorknob while my other hand presses down on the light switch on the wall, shutting off the lights in the hallway so she doesn't see me when I enter. I take one last final breath and open the door, revealing a small space shrouded in darkness. Taking a step inside, I immediately feel her presence next to me as I shut the door, closing us in. My bulky football body occupies most of the tiny space, cramming her small frame against mine.

Every sense is in overdrive.

I hear her quick breaths.

I smell her floral perfume cascading over me.

I feel her nerves radiating off her body as her chest presses against mine, her heartbeat imitating my own.

And I'm so ready to taste those damn lips for the first time.

"H-have you ... ever kissed anyone before?" she asks nervously.

She doesn't know it's me, though, so I answer in a deep voice, trying to sound more like Alex. "No."

I feel her body relax at my answer as she lets out a relieved breath.

My hand reaches up, and I do something I've always wanted to do every time I've seen her. I run my fingers through her hair, tucking a piece behind her ear, and then leave my hand lightly wrapped around the side of her neck as my thumb rests on her pulse, beating rapidly. I lean down, finding her lips easily from the rapid breaths she's taking, and gently brush mine over hers.

"Wait." She presses her hands on my chest. "I can't ... there's someone else. I'm sorry."

I lean back. "Who?"

"I'd rather not say." She's quiet, and her body's trembling against mine.

I reach for the string hanging near my head and pull on it. The small space awakens in the amber hue the bulb above us gives off.

Her eyes squint at first but then widen as she looks up at me.

"J-Jason?" she gasps. "But how?"

I ignore her question and give her one of my own. "Who did you want Alex to be?" I ask, staring down into those perfect chocolate-brown eyes.

She bites her bottom lip, looking up at me under those dark lashes, not saying a word.

"Tell me, Vee." I place my hand on her hip, keeping her right up against me because it feels so good having her this close to me. Who knows when I'll ever have a moment like this with her again?

"I can't say because it can't happen." Her eyes shimmer, exposing tears ready to break free.

"Why not?" I ask her.

"Because I don't want to ruin two friendships." She looks away, breaking eye contact.

"Talk to me. *It's you and me.* We tell each other everything."

"That's exactly it, though. If we kiss, that means I lose you as my friend. And if Natalie finds out we kissed, I'll lose her too. I can't lose the both of you," she sniffs.

"You won't lose either of us. Ever." I cup her cheek, her eyes looking up at me. "And I promise you'll never lose me."

A single tear slides down her cheek, breaking my heart.

I didn't mean to upset her. I just wanted to seize my moment. To make sure her first kiss was with me. Because I want all of her firsts, and I want her to have all of mine. But the turmoil inside her ghosts over her face, and I don't want to be the reason for her agony.

"I'm sorry, Vee." I pull away from her to look down into her sorrowful eyes. "I heard you tell Natalie that you were hoping to get your first kiss tonight, and I wanted it to be with me." I feel heat spread from my chest to my cheeks at this admission.

"You did?" she asks quietly.

"Well, yeah." I shrug my shoulders like it's no big deal. But I know she's right. It will be a big deal. If we kiss, it will change everything, and I don't want to lose her as my friend. She's the only one who has ever put up with my shit, and I need her to keep me in line. "Come on, let's get out of here." I take a moment to tuck a piece of hair behind her ear, knowing I will never have an opportunity like this again, and then turn to reach the doorknob.

"Jason?"

"Yeah?"

The moment I turn back to face her, her lips land on mine, and time all but freezes around us. I'm too stunned to move. This is a moment I've dreamed about for years, and the taste of her lips on mine is blowing every fantasy I ever had out of the park.

It takes only seconds for my body to respond to hers. Her fingers clasp onto my shoulders, and the palm of my hand presses on her lower back, pushing her against me. She moans softly into my mouth, melting into my body, and before I know what I'm doing, I reach down, gripping both of her hips and lift her in the air, pushing her against the wall as her arms and legs wrap tightly around me.

"Jason," she pants.

"Do you want me to stop?" I whisper, kissing my way down her neck, sucking on her skin to mark her as mine.

"No," she breathes, shaking her head adamantly. "I want more."

My lips return to hers, devouring her, knowing this will be our first and last kiss all in one.

Knock. Knock.

"Hey, Natalie is walking around looking for you two." Alex's voice on the other side of the door ends this unforgettable moment between us.

"Shit," Vanessa murmurs at this sudden realization that only a door divides us from Natalie, who is now somewhere in the house searching for us.

Slowly, I bring her back to the ground, watching as she smooths her hair and fixes her lip gloss. She's fidgeting and looks nervous at the prospect of being found by her best friend, aka my sister.

"Hey." I place two fingers on her chin, tilting it so our eyes lock. "It's going to be okay."

She nods, and an adorable smile appears. "So, was that a good first kiss?" The prettiest shade of pink covers her cheeks, waiting for my answer.

"That, Vee," I run my thumb under her eye where a smudge of mascara sits, "puts every first kiss anyone on this earth has ever had to shame." I smile back at her, wishing we could stay in this closet for the rest of the night because I know the minute we walk out this door, we go back to being *just friends*. Reluctantly, I reach for the doorknob. "I'll go first so Natalie doesn't see us together. Wait a few seconds before coming out."

"Okay," she says. "Wait, Jason!" I tilt my head to find her staring at the floor before finally looking right at me. "Promise me we'll always be friends?"

I smile even though my heart crumbles at the word *friends*. "Yes, Vee. Always."

I walk out of the closet, looking both ways to make sure no one is in the hall. When I see the ghost is clear, I step out of the fantasy world where Vanessa was mine and back into a world where we can only ever be *just friends*. Sighing with a heavy heart, I make my way down the hall toward the food lining the counter in the kitchen. But when I take a few steps, I hear a soft jingle. My eyes look down to the floor, finding a bracelet. I bend down to pick up the dainty silver chain, examining the "V" charm and the stars hanging off it.

Her bracelet must have got stuck onto my shirt during our kiss.

I know I should give it back to her. But for whatever reason, I can't find it in me to do that.

I hear the door to the closet open and turn my head to see Vanessa looking both ways. When her eyes catch mine, a beautiful smile makes its way onto her face, and I hope I can remember this moment for the rest of my life.

I place the bracelet in my pocket, keeping it as a little souvenir for this moment—the best moment of my life.

I'll give her the bracelet back someday. Maybe not today or tomorrow. But when the moment is right. When the two of us can be more than just friends, that's when I'll know I can give it back to her.

And as much as it pains me to be just a friend in Vanessa's eyes, I know it's what she needs me to be. And I'll always be there for her, however she needs me.

Because that's what you do when you love someone.

VANESSA
PRESENT DAY

"I thought I lost it forever." I stare up at him, completely stunned. "That night at Alex's house was the last place I remembered wearing it, but I didn't realize until a few days later that it was missing." My fingers run smoothly over the charms, each one still perfectly intact. "Why didn't you give it back to me?"

Jason sighs, running his fingers through his hair. "Walking out of that closet, knowing we would be going back to being just friends after that kiss, was one of the hardest things I've ever had to do. But I knew you needed me as a friend, and as much as that pained me, I would be whatever you needed me to be to stay in your life." He lowers his head closer to mine. "That bracelet stayed a constant reminder to me that *we* had a moment that changed my life. And I was going to do anything I needed to get you back in my arms like that again—to make you mine again." His lips curve up. "That night was the best night of my life."

Tears stream down my cheek as I feel the impact of his words.

"Don't cry, Vee." Jason's thumb wipes away the tears falling down my face.

"I just ... I just wish I could turn back time. I wish we could go back to that night and have left that closet as more than just friends," I murmur.

He grins. "You and me, we were always more than just friends. I just had to wait for you to realize that on your own."

He's right.

This guy was always more than just a friend.

He's my whole world. My moon. My universe. My ... whatever I needed him to be.

"So, I guess the real question is, how did you get Alex to switch places with you?" I smirk, staring up into his eyes.

"I told him I'd kick his ass if he even put one finger on you."

We both laugh. Jason kisses my forehead and brushes strands of hair away from my eyes. "I love you, Vee. Always have. And always will." He wraps an arm over me, avoiding the area where I'm tender. "It's you and me."

I burrow into his hold, my head on his chest, ensuring myself that this isn't some kind of dream I'll wake up from, finding myself alone. "I love you, Jason. Always have. And always will."

Thirty-Two

JASON

It doesn't take long for Vanessa's eyes to flutter closed and for her breathing to even out as she falls asleep in my arms. My fingers comb through her soft dark strands that cascade down her back in lush curls as her head softens against my chest for support.

I'm so relieved that she will be okay, but when I think about some motherfucker laying his hands on her and purposely pushing her down the stairs, I feel ready to punch another hole through the wall. But instead, I take a deep breath and kiss her forehead, thankful to have her in my arms in one piece.

My head rests on the pillow, closing my eyes, when I hear the door to the room creak open. I look up, expecting to see a doctor but find Paul slowly entering the room, quietly closing the door behind him not to wake anyone.

"Hey man," Paul whispers. "Can we talk?"

I peek down at Vanessa, who is out like a light, and carefully remove myself from under her, bringing up the blanket around her body to keep her warm. She nestles into the thick mattress, whimpering softly in her sleep.

Paul and I walk out into the hallway, where it's eerily quiet, but that's probably because of what time it is.

"What's up?" I ask.

"I got a name and an address," Paul says, getting straight to the point.

I nod in understanding. "And you're sure it's him?" The last thing I want to do is beat the crap out of the wrong guy.

"I'm positive." He rolls his shoulders before stretching his neck, appearing tense. "When Natalie told us about the skull tattoo on his neck, I mentioned it to a few people at the house to see if anyone knew who he was. I finally found a girl who did. She wasn't a fan of his, so she pulled up his social media for me to see. His name's Roger." Paul pulls up the guy's info on his phone and shows me the picture of him that perfectly displays his skull tattoo for the world to see.

I'm going to kill him.

"Does Vanessa know this guy?" Paul asks, scrolling through the images on the guy's profile.

"Yeah." The palm of my hand scrapes across my fresh stubble as I breathe deeply. "One night, while she was leaving work, she walked by him, and he grabbed her ass. The manager threw him out and won't let him back in. I'm guessing tonight was his way to get revenge."

Little does this asshole know he made a huge mistake when he touched what is mine.

"What the hell?" Paul's eyes widen.

The door to Vanessa's room opens, and Nate exits with furrowed brows looking between us. "What's going on?"

I sigh. I know him. He's going to try to be the voice of reason right now, but the only voice of reason I hear is telling me to beat the crap out of this guy. "We know who did this to Vanessa, and I'm going to pay him a little visit." Nate opens his mouth to speak, but I cut him off. "And before you tell me not to do this, just ask yourself what you would do if this were Natalie?"

He stares between us but then shows an amused smirk. "I was only going to ask whose car we are taking?"

Slowly, my lips curl up, glad to always have him by my side.

"We got to make this quick, though. I don't want Vanessa waking up without me by her side," I add.

"Yeah, Natalie's still sound asleep too."

"Alright, boys, let's go find our new friend Roger," Paul says as he struts before us, leading the way. Nate and I are well over six feet tall, but damn, I feel small walking beside Paul as he ducks under the hallway corridors.

I take a deep breath, feeling unhinged. We're standing in a sketchy as fuck neighborhood, but with Nate and Paul standing behind me, I feel ready for war. I look over my shoulder at them, and they both nod, letting me know they're ready.

My knuckles slam on the door before me repeatedly until it swings open, presenting Roger on a silver platter in front of me. He's wearing basketball shorts and socks with ruffled hair, making him appear as if he just rolled out of bed in complete panic.

"Who the fuck are you?" Roger asks, squinting his eyes in the darkness.

"Me? Oh, I'm about to be your worst fucking nightmare." My fist connects with the side of Roger's jaw, sending him backward. Quickly, I get a second hit right into his nose, which snaps from the impact. I'm no doctor, but it's definitely broken.

He stumbles down to the ground, groaning as he holds onto his broken nose. He spits blood out of his mouth, spattering the beige carpet, and looks up at me as he crab walks backward on the floor, away from me.

"You broke my fucking nose," he wails, clutching his face.

"Yeah, well." I shrug my shoulders nonchalantly. "I would say that still doesn't make up for what you did."

"Listen, if I owe you money or something. I don't have it right now. But I can—"

"I'm not here for money, Roger." I shake my head, anger radiating throughout me. "I'm here to make sure you never put your hands on my girl, again." I step inside Roger's apartment with Nate and Paul coming up behind me.

"How do you know me?" He looks at the three of us towering over him. Poor Roger. He doesn't stand a chance. Nate and Paul didn't come here to hurt him. They only came here for intimidation. Back up, if you will. But I came here to cause him pain. He thought he would teach Vanessa a lesson, so I'm here now: teaching Roger a lesson he'll never forget. "And what girl? I think you have the wrong guy because I didn't sleep with anyone tonight!" he screams at me like I'm in the wrong here.

Tsk. Tsk.

"I didn't say sleep with. I said you put your hands on my girl." I sound calm, but I am far from it. "You remember, don't you? The beautiful brunette you threw down the stairs just a few hours ago?"

Roger's face pales, confirming he did throw my girl down the stairs.

"Or how about when you put your hand under her skirt and grabbed her ass while she was at work? You must remember that, at least. It's pretty hard to forget an ass like that. Am I right?" I clench my jaw. All I see is red, feeling like a bull about to charge.

"He did what?" I hear Nate's anger flare at the mention of this, making it sound like he's ready to destroy Roger. But that's my job. Not his.

Roger swallows. "Listen—"

"Which hand did you touch her with?" I ask.

"W-what?" Roger stutters.

"Don't make me repeat myself." I shake my head, disappointed in his response.

Roger unconsciously glances down at his right hand on the floor, and that's the answer I need. Before he has a chance to realize his mistake, I slam my foot down hard, feeling a crunch under my shoe as I continue to apply pressure. Roger screams out in agony, probably alerting the neighbors, but I doubt anyone would come to help his sorry ass. I remove my foot after feeling satisfied and watch as he lifts his lifeless hand, cradling it against his chest. The way it limps to the side tells me it's broken.

Good, he'll have a broken hand to match the broken nose.

"Your whore was not worth this shit," Roger spits out as he stands and walks away from me.

I don't think. I charge at him like I'm on the football field, slamming his weak body into the wall and pinning him with my hands tightly wrapped around his burly neck. Blood pours out of his nose and down his face looking like a rapid river with no structure.

"If you ever lay a finger on her again, I will personally come find you and kill you." He tries grabbing at my hands with his one good hand, squirming under my grip, but I'm stronger than him and a hell of a lot more pissed off, so his attempts are futile. "Tonight is just a warning. Do you understand me?"

Roger opens his mouth, gasping for air, nodding profusely.

"I didn't quite hear you. I'm going to need you to speak up." I loosen my grip just the tiniest bit around his throat.

"Y-y-yes," he manages to let out a choked gasp.

I feel his pulse hammering away under my fingers, knowing that if I continue to hold him here, I have the power to destroy him. The power to make sure nothing happens to Vanessa ever again.

A firm tap on my shoulder takes me away from that path.

"It's time to go," Nate states.

I release Roger, letting his body flop to the floor, and watch as he gasps for every morsel of air he can get into his lungs, knowing he'll never bother Vanessa again. He rolls on his side, coughing as he reaches up to his now bruised neck.

"Nice meeting you, Roger."

The three of us walk back into the frigid night air toward Paul's car. I look up at the picturesque night sky above us, noting the moon's fullness with more stars than I've ever seen, wishing Vanessa was here to see this with me. Paul stops me just as my hand reaches for the back door handle.

"Hold on." He stands outside the car and leans inside, reaching into the passenger seat glove box, and brings out a water bottle and wipes. "Use this for your hands."

My eyes instinctively move to my hands, which I hold up in front of my face for a better look. Blood is smeared on my palms and knuckles, but it's not mine. Taking the bottle of water and wipes, I clean my hands as best I can, knowing as soon as I get back to the hospital room, I'll need to scrub them clean before I touch Vanessa.

"Are you okay?" Nate asks, standing outside the car, watching me with concern in his eyes.

Am I?

I hurt the one woman in the world I love more than anyone or anything else in my life. I'm about to miss the biggest game of my career so far. And then, to top it off, the image of Vanessa lying bruised and fragile on a hospital bed because I wasn't there for her will forever be ingrained in my memory.

I'm not okay. Not by a long shot. But I know what will help.

"I will be, once I'm with her."

Softly and carefully, I slide my body on the bed beside Vanessa's, doing everything I can not to wake her.

After Paul dropped us back off at the hospital, Nate and I returned to the room to find Natalie and Vanessa still sound asleep. When I stepped out of the bathroom, after thoroughly scrubbing my hands raw, I witnessed Nate gingerly lift Natalie in his arms before sitting down and placing her on his lap with a blanket wrapped around the two of them. He kissed her forehead and then closed his eyes as he quickly drifted asleep, holding her tightly against his chest.

It's true what they say. No guy will ever be good enough for your sister. But that rule doesn't apply to Nate. Because he isn't just some guy, he's a friend, the brother I never had, and a part of the Spencer family, whether he likes it or not.

He's the guy my sister is going to marry. There's no doubt in my mind.

Vanessa quietly whimpers, nuzzling into my body. I hold her tighter to my chest, wishing I knew what she was dreaming about.

"Jason?" she murmurs, stretching out beside me, her eyelids fluttering open.

"I'm here, Vee. Go back to sleep. I got you." I run my hand comfortingly up and down her back.

"Will you stay with me?" she asks softly, already closing her tired eyes. Her fingers clutch onto the fabric of my shirt, right above my heart.

The heart she owns in every sense of the word.

"I will stay with you forever as long as you let me," I respond, watching the corners of her lips curve up the slightest bit before she falls back into a deep slumber.

I press my lips carefully against her forehead.

"I will never let you shatter."

Thirty-Three

VANESSA

Familiar voices echoing nearby wake me as I make my way out of a dreamish haze with a substantial warmth wrapped around my body, keeping me safe. My eyes flutter open, finding myself in the same hospital room I had fallen asleep in, only this time, Jason is sleeping soundly beside me. Well, actually, snoring beside me, but either way, he's asleep. His muscular arm is secured around my waist, keeping me close to him.

Protecting me.

"Oh, good! She's awake!" I hear a whisper-yell from the end of the bed, and when I look down to see who it is, I'm hit with an onslaught of emotions.

"You're here?" I ask, clearing my tightening throat.

Mr. and Mrs. Spencer look at me with concern etched all over their faces, except for the slight smiles that indicate relief at seeing me. I'm so overwhelmed by the love I feel from these two people. Something they have continually shown me my whole life.

"Of course, we're here!" Mrs. Spencer walks over to the side of the bed, handing me a plastic cup of water for me to take, which I do. "We left the house the second Natalie called us, but unfortunately, it took us some time to get here because of the snow."

My eyes glaze over. They're here. They've always been here for me. But where are my parents?

Mrs. Spencer notices my dismay and knows right away what I'm thinking. "Oh honey, I called them, but they're still on their cruise. They said they'll come to see you the second they dock."

I nod, taking a long sip of my water. I had completely forgotten about their damn cruise.

Mrs. Spencer places a hand on top of mine that lays flat on the blanket covering my stomach. "You will always be our second daughter. When you need us, we will always be here. Whether you like it or not, you are a part of this family." She flashes a smile even though her eyes look ready to unleash tears. "Do you understand me?"

I suck in my bottom lip, feeling like a dam is about to burst.

"Besides," Mr. Spencer cuts in, "looks like someone's got to keep this one in line for us." There's a warm smile on his face as his head tilts toward Jason's rather large frame taking up the majority of the bed. I'm suddenly hyper aware that these two have caught me in bed with their son. Even if it is just a hospital bed, it's still a freaking bed.

Fuck.

"Oh, he umm, Jason was just—"

"Vanessa, it's okay. If anyone is going to date my son, I'm so happy it's you." She gives me another smile before squeezing my hand and letting go. "And we are so relieved you're okay. When Natalie called me, we were both absolutely beside ourselves." A tear manages to escape from her eye, sliding down her cheek until she quickly wipes it away. "But the second we got here, I spoke with one of the doctors on call who told me what had happened and..." She takes a deep breath. "We can discuss that later, but I want you to rest now. Do you need anything? How are you feeling?"

"I'm okay," I tell her. "Or at least I will be." And it was the truth. Physically, I'm sore and achy, but mentally, I'm feeling better because of who's beside me. We still have a lot to talk about, but the fact that he abandoned his chance at starting in one of the biggest games of his career so far to make sure I'm okay says more to me than any words ever will.

I glance over at Jason, still sound asleep beside me. I have no idea how he hasn't woken up during this conversation. He must be exhausted.

Mr. Spencer clears his throat to get his wife's attention. "Why don't we go to the cafeteria and see what we can get everyone for breakfast, dear?"

"That sounds like a good idea." She turns back to look at me, her eyes shimmering as a relieved smile blooms over her flawless complexion, and she looks between me and Jason. "We'll be right back."

After they exit the room, I turn into Jason's embrace, snuggling closer to him. I breathe in his familiar, comforting scent as I rest my head on his arm, peering up to admire him as he sleeps.

Jason's eyes pop open. "Phew, they're gone." He stretches beside me as a sly grin spreads across his face.

"Are you kidding me? You were awake the whole time. Why didn't you say anything?" I quietly demand.

"My parents just found me in bed with you. There's no way I was going to say anything. Besides, you had it handled." He chuckles, so I lightly punch his shoulder, only to be met with soreness in my wrist, forgetting that it's partially taped up.

"Shit," I hiss, cradling my hand to my chest.

Jason's eyes widen, and he sits up, gently taking my hand. "Where does it hurt?"

"The palm area near my thumb." I watch his thumbs massage into the skin, tenderly pressing down, releasing the built-up pressure.

"How does that feel?"

"Really good." My voice comes out breathy sounding, probably because I haven't felt his magical hands on me in a whole damn week. A warmth rushes through me, burning where his fingers touch me, but in the best way possible. My eyes catch on Jason's knuckles, appearing swollen and bruised.

"Jason!" I use my free hand to reach for his. "What happened to your hand?" I gently run my fingers over his skin, noticing how fresh the bruise seems. This hand is his career. He needs it to make his dreams of playing in the NFL come true, so why would he risk injuring himself like this?

He doesn't make eye contact with me when he says, "I won't ever let anything happen to you, Vanessa."

His words are a promise to me.

I place my palm on his cheek, which he leans into, closing his eyes. When he opens them, he looks directly into mine, and I suddenly understand why his hand appears damaged. "You found him?"

He nods, continuing to rub my injured hand gently. "You don't ever have to worry about him again."

I'm momentarily stunned. My eyelids blink fast as I'm hit with a multitude of questions. When did he even have time to do this? How did he even find him? And most importantly, why?

"But football is the most important thing in your life," I exclaim. "You need your hand to play football. Why would you have risked—"

"Because football isn't what's important to me. You are." His stormy eyes lock with mine. "Nothing is more important to me than you. And if kicking some loser's ass is what I have to do to keep you safe, then that's what I'll do, Vanessa. I would do anything for you."

I roll my bottom lip between my teeth, nodding as I try to hold back tears. He really would do anything for me. Including risking his dream, the thing he's worked his whole life for.

He's such an idiot. But he's my idiot.

"I know we have a lot to talk about." Jason wipes away a tear on my cheek that manages to escape. "But let's wait until we can go to my place for some privacy, okay?"

"Okay." I look up at him, lustfully biting my bottom lip.

He smirks. "Do you want a kiss, Vee?"

A blush spreads up my neck, exposing my thoughts.

He lightly places my hand on my lap and then brings both of his hands to cup my face, brushing his lips over mine. "God, I missed you." His lips crash onto mine, taking the oxygen away from me as a pulse beneath my rib cage pounds with an astonishing amount of intensity. I open up for him, letting our tongues rekindle as my good hand grips his shirt, pulling him closer to me.

A muffled sob breaks the spell, and we pull apart. I look to my side and see Natalie sitting on Nate's lap, crying into her hands while Nate rubs her back.

"Natalie? Are you okay?" I ask hesitantly.

"Me?" She waves a dismissive hand in the air. "I'm just ... I'm just." She wipes away at the tears streaming down her face.

Oh no. She's mad at me. She's mad about me and Jason. I should never have kept this from her. She's my best friend, and I lied to her. I'm a horrible person. I don't deserve someone like her in my—"

"I'm just so happy that you two found your way to each other." She smiles through the tears, looking right at me, and I can't stay in this bed any longer. I pull the covers off, jumping out slowly until my sock-covered feet touch the floor. Natalie quickly gets up from Nate's lap, and after we both take two steps, we are embraced in each other's arms, holding onto the other like it's the last time we will ever see each other.

"I'm so sorry I didn't tell you." I sob into Natalie's hair, clutching onto her.

"No! There's nothing for you to be sorry about." She squeezes me tighter.

"I love you," we say in unison.

We stay like this for several minutes, neither of us saying another word.

Knock. Knock.

We break apart, looking at the door to see Paul standing in the door-way, making both of us instantly smile.

"Sorry to interrupt, ladies," Paul starts to say before we both hurry over to him and wrap our arms around him. He uses one arm to wrap around my side while holding a bouquet of yellow flowers up in the air, ensuring they don't get squashed.

"Here we go again," I hear Nate say. "Natalie, what did I tell you? You aren't allowed to hug this man like he's a damn teddy bear."

"I second that for you, Vanessa," Jason remarks.

"Oh, stop." Natalie's arms only wrap tighter around Paul. "You're just jealous because he's our favorite."

She's baiting Nate, and it works.

"I think the fuck not." He scoops her away from Paul, causing her to laugh in his arms as he brings her back down onto his lap on the chair.

"You know there are two other chairs in this room," Natalie says.

"I know. But you're staying right here." He nuzzles his lips into her neck, pressing a kiss before they look lovingly into each other's eyes.

"I think I'm going to be sick," Jason says, running a hand over his face.

I unwrap my arms from around Paul, looking way up to meet his eyes. "Thank you for coming."

"Well, we just wanted to stop by and make sure you're okay." He hands me the beautiful bouquet, the floral scent making me feel more at ease. *Oh, Paul.*

"We?" I ask.

Sarah, who I didn't see standing behind Paul, moves around him, approaching me. "Oh my God, Vanessa, I was so worried!" She wipes a small hand over her red-rimmed eyes. "Paul brought me ... home last night, but I just couldn't sleep, and well..." She wraps her arms around me. "I'm so glad you're okay."

"I'm fine. I promise." I squeeze her tight, so glad that Sarah is now someone I can call a close friend. It also doesn't go unnoticed that she's wearing a pair of leggings and a *very* oversized Linrey University basketball sweatshirt.

"Well, looks like there's a party going on in here." A deep male voice comes from behind us. I part from Sarah to see a doctor with grey hair and a warm smile standing in the doorway. "Hi, I'm Doctor Masen. I saw you last night when you came in and just wanted to see how you're feeling."

"I'm feeling like..."

I've got my best friend and the brother I always wanted sitting on one side of the room.

I've got my new friends standing behind me.

I've got my second set of parents in the cafeteria, getting us breakfast.

And I've got the guy I've been in love with my whole life sitting on the bed beside me.

"I've never been better."

Thirty-Four

JASON

We enter my apartment, and I immediately walk Vanessa to my room, so she can lie in my bed and get comfortable. Natalie had brought her a change of clothes to the hospital, so she's wearing a pair of leggings and one of my oversized black T-shirts, which tells me my sister is more than okay with the idea of us together if she's dressing her in my clothes.

She looks tired. So unbelievably tired. I pull back the covers for her, watching as she winces, adjusting herself onto the mattress, and it fucking kills me, making me wish I could have a round two with Roger.

"Is there anything I can get you?" I ask.

"No. I'm fine." She looks at me with a half-smile, trying to convince me she's alright, but I know otherwise.

"Yeah, I'm not buying that." I sit on the bed beside her, tucking a strand of chestnut hair behind her ear, carefully avoiding her bruise. "Do you want to talk?"

She looks down, fidgeting with the blanket.

"If you're too tired, I can let you sleep, and we can talk later."

"No. I'm ready to talk. But first," her eyes meet mine, "I think we should talk about the elephant in the room."

My brows crease in confusion.

"Was it just me, or does it seem like something might be going on between Paul and Sarah?" she asks.

"Oh, Jesus." I laugh, running a hand over my face. "After everything you've been through, that's what you want to talk about?"

"I knew it! You thought something was going on between them too!" She beams, proud of herself for detecting the love match.

"I mean"—I adjust the pillow behind her, fluffing it to perfection—"I might have had my suspicions. But I think her showing up at the hospital wearing his clothes kind of let the cat out of the bag."

We both laugh until she flinches with pain, grabbing at her waist.

"How bad does it hurt?" I note the time on my phone. "The pain medication is probably starting to wear off. Do you want to take more?"

"I'm fine." She closes her eyes, but when she opens them, a single tear manages to escape.

"No, you're not, Vee."

"You're right. I'm not." She closes her eyes, shaking her head.

I get up from her side of the bed and go to the other side to lean against the headboard. As gently as possible, I grip Vanessa at her hips and pull her back so she rests against my chest, between my legs. She twists her body to the side so that her head rests on my shoulder. My arms wrap protectively around her, feeling her body tremble.

"I'm here." I rub small circles on her back, trying to calm her as I kiss her temple delicately.

She lets out a slow breath. "I want to talk first," she whispers into my chest.

"Okay." I push the hair away from her eyes as she tilts her head, looking up at me, sorrow filling her big brown eyes.

"I can't even begin to tell you how confused I've been." She closes her eyes for only a moment and takes a deep breath. "But I know I should never have had any contact with Brian. And I'm sorry."

"No, Vee—"

"I need to say this."

I silently nod, giving her the floor.

"You have to understand. My whole life, I never felt like I had a family—a real family. A family that loves me. And don't get me wrong, I know I'm lucky that I grew up with a roof over my head and parents who would buy me things merely to make themselves feel like they were doing a good job at being parents. But I have a mom who criticizes me about everything, a dad who is never there for me, and the only brother I have royally fucked up, leaving me to feel … alone. Especially after these past couple of years when Natalie wanted nothing to do with me and then when … you wanted nothing to do with me."

Her eyes avert me, looking toward the window facing the Charles River, and my whole heart fucking breaks at her admission. "I saw Brian on Thanksgiving because I missed … my brother. Or what I mean is I missed the brother I had when I was a kid. It wasn't that I missed *him*. It was that I missed having someone who was there for me." Her fingers scrunch the fabric of my shirt, fidgeting restlessly. "I would do absolutely anything for Natalie and I know that I did the right thing, but after I testified against Brian, I felt so guilty. I convinced myself that I was the reason why he was in jail. He blamed me. My parents blamed me. And I blamed myself." She looks up at me hesitantly, embarrassment washing over her. "But I need you to believe me when I say I know what Brian did was wrong. It makes me nauseous even thinking about it. And I never want to see him again. I want nothing to do with him ever again." Tears pour from her eyes. "I know he's a monster. I do. I just wanted so hard to believe that he wasn't," she whispers.

"Hey, I know." I wipe her tears away with my thumb. Every single one of them spears me in the center of my chest.

"When I saw him after Christmas, it was only so I could say goodbye." She takes a moment to breathe. "The gift you saw me bring him was just a picture of me and him when we were kids at the beach. That's it. Just something for him to remember me by. But I'm so fucking sorry, Jason.

I should never have seen him." Her body begins to shake violently in my arms.

"Woah, sweetheart. I need you to breathe for me. Let's take a deep breath together, okay?'

She slowly nods her head.

We both breathe in as I rub her back and finally let it out together.

"Okay, let's do it one more time," I say.

We do it again, and I can feel the shivering in her body start to subside. I lift the blanket, bringing it up around her waist.

"You have nothing to be sorry about, Vee. You didn't do anything wrong. I was such an asshole to you. I promised you I would never hurt you, and look what I did." I rub my forehead feeling frustrated with myself. "It's just ... I am always going to hate Brian. My feelings for him will never change. After what he did to my sister, all I want to do is..." I look down into her eyes, stopping myself. She doesn't need to hear me say I want to kill her brother when she already knows this. "Well, you get the point. So, when I saw you going into the prison to see him, I just lost it. I wasn't thinking straight. I didn't give you a chance to explain. And I'm so sorry that I hurt you, like so many other people in your life have. And I will never be able to forgive myself for that." I lean back, closing my eyes, shame washing over me.

"Jason."

I open my eyes, seeing my favorite color before me.

"I'm not saying what you did was okay, but I think we both messed up, and all I want to do is forget about that day. Do you think we can do that?"

"I will do whatever you want, Vee."

She hesitates before saying, "I want you to tell me that when you think of me, you don't think of Brian. That you won't hate me someday in the future because your judgment is clouded from the anger you feel toward him. Can you do that?"

Her sad eyes melt my beating heart.

"When I think of you, I only think about spending the rest of my life with the girl of my dreams."

"Really?" she asks, tilting her head.

Instead of answering her, I reach into the drawer in my nightstand, pull out my journal, and place it on her lap.

"You weren't wrong about this being my journal. Although, let's please not call it a diary. I have my dignity to uphold." I grin, looking at her smile.

"Why do you have all these tabs in it?" she asks.

"Well, I went through it and tabbed every entry that was a memory with you. A memory I never want to forget."

She looks up at me with glassy eyes. "Jason..."

"And one more thing." I pull the key out of my pocket, placing it on the journal. "This is yours. I should never have taken this back from you." I shake my head. "Keep it safe, Vee."

She picks up the key, looks at it with shimmering eyes, and then puts it on the nightstand beside her before reaching into her pocket. "I want you to keep this." She pulls out the bracelet I gave her back in the hospital, handing it to me.

"But it's yours. I was way overdue on giving that back to you."

She shakes her head. "You said that that night was the best night of your life. But it was the best night of my life too. And I want you to keep it, knowing that."

She places the bracelet in the palm of my hand, and I wrap my fingers gingerly around it. "Thank you," I say.

She looks down at the journal, her fingers trailing over the edge.

"You can read it while I make us something to eat, okay?"

She nods, not looking away from it.

I kiss her forehead and slowly slip out beside her, replacing my body with a pillow to support her. I make my way to the kitchen to whip up a couple of grilled cheese sandwiches, making Vanessa's extra cheesy the way she likes it.

Holding two plates, I walk back into my room, thinking I've given her enough time to read most of it, at least if not all. "Lunch is ser—" Tears are streaming down Vanessa's face. "Woah. Woah." I place the plates on my bureau and stride right over to the bed, kneeling beside her. "What's wrong? Are you hurting?" My hands cup her cheeks, my thumb brushing away her tears, one by one.

"It's just," she says through a sob. "You wrote about everything. Our first kiss ... the night you snuck into my room ... the day you gave me my nickname ... the night we laid under the stars ... the first time we had sex ... even the moment in the elevator." She grips my wrist, pressing her cheek into my palm as she closes her eyes. "Everything." Her eyes open, looking at me like I'm her whole world.

And maybe I am.

I know she's mine.

"There isn't a single moment with you that I don't want to remember," I tell her honestly.

She leans toward me, her eyes closing as her sweet lips press against mine. This kiss is honest and raw. The two of us need each other more than we've ever admitted, and it's evident now.

I pull away, rolling our foreheads together. "Say you're mine, Vanessa."

Her lips curve up. "I'm yours, Jason."

I brush my nose against hers, wrapping my fingers gently around her neck, my thumb resting on her pulse point. "It's you and me. Forever."

"It's you and me. Forever," she whispers.

Knock. Knock. Natalie pokes her head inside my apartment.

"Who's hungry?" she asks.

The door swings open, with Nate walking right behind her, holding bags of food.

"Hey Vanessa, how are you feeling?" he asks.

She looks at me, smiling. "Pretty good, thanks to this one." She winks, snuggling closer to me on the couch.

"Glad to hear it," Nate responds, placing the bags of food on the kitchen island. Natalie watches us, looking like her face might crack from smiling so hard.

"What's wrong with your face?" I quip.

"I just love this," she says, waving her hand toward us.

I look down at Vanessa. "Yeah, I guess I love this too." Vanessa's cheeks turn the faintest shade of pink.

"And how are you feeling, Jason?" Natalie asks, observing me. Vanessa peers up at me with furrowed brows.

"I'm fine," I state.

"Well, I'm glad to hear it. But next time you decide to go for a run in a blizzard, maybe you should—"

"Why were you running in a blizzard?" Vanessa asks, appearing confused.

"I umm..." I shoot my sister a, *"thanks a lot,"* look before saying, "There were no cars available to get me to the hospital from the airport, so I ran there."

Vanessa's eyes widen, her mouth parting in shock. "You ran all that way in a blizzard to get to me?"

I press my lips to her ear so only she can hear me. "There isn't anything I wouldn't do for you."

She turns her head locking eyes with me. "You really do love me." It's not a question. It's a fact. And she's right. I absolutely do.

"Always have and always will," I remind her, pressing my lips to hers. After a moment, I pull away, pushing a strand of her chestnut hair behind her ear, watching a smile make its way onto her face.

"Always have and always will," she repeats softly, making me grin.

"Well, I hope everyone is good with Chinese food," Natalie announces, taking the containers out of the bag and placing them on the counter. "Paul should be here shortly, he had an appointment he had to go to first."

Vanessa clears her throat, sitting up and looking directly at Natalie. "Actually, I was wondering if we could talk before we eat."

Natalie tilts her head. "Of course."

Vanessa removes herself from me, leading Natalie to my room, where they shut the door behind them.

"What's that about?" Nate asks.

"You know, Vanessa." I walk over to the food by Nate. "She wants to apologize to Natalie for seeing Brian. I told her she didn't need to, but she insisted. She doesn't want anything between them."

Nate nods, understanding. "She always worries about everyone else." He scoops food onto two plates—one for him and one for Natalie. So I do the same for Vanessa, knowing exactly what she likes. "So, how are you feeling about missing the big game?"

"Honestly"—I let out a deep sigh—"it sucks, but I wouldn't have done anything differently. Vanessa needed me, so that's where I needed to be. With her. When she needs me, I'll always be there for her." I look at the time on my phone. "Looks like the game should be starting in an hour."

"Should we watch it?" Nate asks.

"Nah, I'll be too stressed and don't want to make Vee anxious." Feeling famished, I stuff a scallion pancake in my mouth before saying, "Thank you for being at the hospital and taking care of her before I could get there. I really appreciate it."

Nate nods. "We're family. It's what we do." He gives me a firm pat on the shoulder and says, "And how are things between you and Vanessa?"

I grab two crab rangoons and some veggie lo mein from a container. "We're good. Really good." I look over at him. "We laid everything out for each other and left no secrets unturned." Well, there is one small secret to tell her, but I'll let her know when the moment is right.

"I'm really glad to hear that," Nate says, looking ... like he's about to cry.

"Nate?"

He looks between the containers of food in front of him. "What?"

"Are you crying?" I ask, biting back a laugh.

"What? No!" His forearm swipes across his face. "I'm not fucking crying, Jason. I'm just happy for the two of you. I..." He drops the serving spoon back into the container, his hands going up in the air. "You know what? Fuck it. I'm man enough to admit I'm crying. Vanessa is the sister I never had, and I'm relieved she's with a great guy like you, asshole."

"You think I'm ... a great guy?" I ask in disbelief.

"Did you miss the part where I called you an asshole?"

"Oh, I heard it. But I also heard you call me a great guy." I flash a smug smile.

We turn our heads as Natalie and Vanessa walk out of the room, wiping tears off their cheeks but thankfully smiling as they hold onto each other. Am I the only one not crying right now?

"What's the big smile for?" Vanessa asks me.

"Oh, just because Nathan Thomas thinks I'm a great guy."

He punches me lightly in the shoulder, saying, "I take it back."

We both laugh. The truth is, I'm grateful that Nate is in my life and, because of Natalie, will always be in my life.

"Wow, everything smells so good." Vanessa walks up to me, and I wrap her in my arms, kissing her forehead.

"I made you a plate with your favorites."

She looks it over with an approving smile. "You did good."

Natalie and Nate walk to the living room, sitting around the coffee table. "What movie should we watch?"

Knock. Knock. Paul pokes his head inside. "Do I smell Chinese food?"

"Yeah, man. Come grab a plate." I sit on the couch with Vanessa beside me, holding her plate for her while she gets comfortable.

"Is it okay if I grab two plates?" Paul walks in, with Sarah following closely behind him. Yeah, these two definitely have something going on.

I look over at Nate, who bites his lip, looking up at the ceiling like he knows something.

"Sarah!" Vanessa and Natalie say in unison.

"Is it okay that I'm here? I don't want to interrupt if—"

"You're always welcome here," Vanessa adds, making Sarah smile.

As Paul and Sarah get their food, Vanessa discreetly whispers in my ear. "Do you think they're fucking?"

I almost choke on my food, which makes her laugh. Shaking my head, I chuckle. "Maybe you should ask them."

"Maybe I will," she responds, looking over at them. "Hey, Sarah?"

Oh my God, she's actually doing it. No ... she wouldn't. Would she?

Vanessa looks at Sarah as she says, "I love your shoes. Where did you get them?"

After Sarah tells her, I kiss her neck and whisper, "Once you're healed, you're paying for that."

She turns to face me, licking her lips. "I'm already looking forward to it."

"Oh my God, Vanessa," Natalie gasps, her eyes widening. "I just realized that when you guys get married, we'll be actual sisters!"

I fully choke on my food this time. A piece of rice is making its way down the wrong pipe. Vanessa pats my back as I lean over the side of the couch, bringing air back into my lungs.

"Easy, Natalie. Don't want to kill your brother before he graduates." Nate wraps an arm around Natalie's shoulder, laughing at my near-death experience as he brings his drink to his lips.

"Keep laughing, my friend," I say. "Especially because I heard Mom tell Dad that she can't wait to see how cute Natalie and Nate's babies will be."

And just like I expected, his eyes widen as he spits out his drink.

"Yeah, that's what I thought." I laugh, bringing a scallion pancake to my mouth. I freaking love Chinese food.

"Well." Paul sits on the arm of the chair across from us, and Sarah sits in the chair, appearing uneasy. "Speaking of babies..." He looks down at Sarah, who anxiously bites her thumbnail before looking up at him, nodding. "We're having one!"

"Having what?" Natalie asks, looking between the two of them.

"A ... baby," Sarah says, taking a deep breath, looking nervously around the room at everyone.

We're all in stunned silence.

If my napkin fell to the floor right now, you would hear it kind of silence.

That is until my Vee opens her mouth.

"Looks like that answers my question."

"What was your question?" Paul asks.

A huge grin spreads over her face. "I was wondering if you two were fucking."

The silence is taken over by laughter from all of us. Sarah hides her face behind her hands, her shoulders shaking from how hard she's laughing.

"Holy shit, Vanessa." Paul wipes a tear from his face, smiling hard. He looks ... genuinely happy. Happier than he's looked in a while.

I look at Nate. "You knew, didn't you?"

He shrugs his shoulders. "He left some baby books lying around our place. I had my suspicions."

Natalie is the first to stand, followed by Vanessa, who both hug and congratulate Sarah.

"How far along are you?" Vanessa asks, looking at her completely hidden stomach under the Linrey University basketball sweatshirt. The same one she wore to the hospital.

Sarah looks at Paul first before saying, "Five months."

We all look at each other, doing math in our heads. And I'm no math expert, but that would mean they definitely knew each other the day they pretended they didn't four months ago.

"Wait, so that means…" Natalie begins to say.

"It's a long story," Paul says, wrapping his arm around Sarah and pulling her in for a kiss, leaving us all speechless.

Thirty-Five

VANESSA

It's been almost two weeks of no sex, and I'm dying. Like actually dying. Someone please write my obituary because I feel my demise coming if I don't get some action right now.

Jason won't touch me because he's too scared to hurt me and says my body needs time to heal. But my God, that's all I've been doing is resting. Well, that and starting my first therapy session, which essentially went a lot better than I anticipated. It even pushed me to have a long overdue conversation with my mom regarding her years of body shaming remarks directed at me. She believes she only ever did what was best for me and ended the conversation by telling me about a new diet pill I should try, at which point I promptly ended the call, feeling only pity for her.

Some people will unfortunately never change.

But anyway, the point is that physically, I feel perfectly fine.

And what I need is Jason.

Specifically, I need him hard and ready to fuck me.

The Met Future of Fashion event is in a few weeks, and it's all I've been able to think about. Nerves eat away at me every night, causing me to toss and turn, unable to shut my mind off, which is why I've spent every night in Jason's bed, nestled against his chest.

What if someone doesn't like my designs? What if I get horrible reviews? What if they hate me? What if I mess up my speech, stumbling over every word like an idiot?

It's always the same worries keeping me up, but Jason has been there every night for me, shutting my mind up with a deep kiss before pulling away, snuggling beside me, and leaving me wanting more.

And I've had enough of it.

So as I lay sprawled out on Jason's bed, wearing the red peacoat that Jason kept safe for me during our week apart, with only his jersey on underneath and a pair of black high heels, I wait with anticipation as each second passes, knowing he'll be home any minute.

And how do I know he'll be here any minute?

Well, I might have texted him saying there was an emergency and he needed to come home right away.

What? He gave me no choice. It's a sex emergency.

I hear the door to his apartment open and then slam closed as he comes barreling inside.

My stomach twists into excited knots.

"Vanessa!" He roars in a panic. "Where are—"

His words are immediately cut off when he enters his bedroom, finding me resting back on my elbows as I tilt my head, my hair fanning over my shoulders.

"Hi," I breathe.

His mouth hangs open, and he can't take his lustful eyes off of me.

This is exactly the reaction I was hoping for.

Finally, he clears his throat, shaking his head. "Vanessa. Is this the emergency?" He brings his fist to his mouth, biting down on his knuckle. "Goddamn, sweetheart."

I slowly sit up, trying to be as sexy as possible with my movements as I turn around, unbuttoning my coat, letting it slide off my body, and then sitting on my calves near the edge of the bed, showcasing his last name on the back of the jersey. "I thought maybe we could make your fantasy come true tonight." I glance over my shoulder, eager for him to come over to me, and ever so slowly, he does. "After all, your team did win the Rose Bowl and we haven't even properly celebrated."

I feel his breath on my neck as he leans down, placing a kiss on my skin. His fingers trail down over the fabric until they get to my waist, gripping me tightly. His lips brush against my ear, sending shivers down my whole body. "Take it off."

I'm momentarily confused. "What?"

"I want you to take this off."

I twist the tiniest bit in his grip to have a better look into his eyes. "But I thought your fantasy was to fuck a girl wearing your jersey?" Does he not want to create this fantasy with me? I bite my lip, pulling down on the hem of the jersey, feeling self-conscious as heat burns up my neck.

He smiles before kissing my lips softly, making my insides ignite. His lips part from mine, but he stays close to me, holding my body against his own. "It was, *before I saw you*."

I bite my lower lip, holding in the onslaught of emotions about to overtake me.

He sweeps my hair away from my neck, pulling the jersey collar to the side, giving him access to my bare shoulder, where he presses his lips on me. "Every." Kiss. "Single." Kiss. "Beautiful." Kiss. "Inch of you." His hands, currently gripping my waist, move down to the hem of the jersey, lifting the material. My arms voluntarily raise so he can remove the jersey from my body and throw it on the floor beside us. "The only fantasy I have now is seeing you exactly like this every night for the rest of my life." His hands clasp onto my waist, turning me around to face him. He then raises one of his hands to cup my cheek, which I automatically lean into, closing my eyes. "There's something I need to tell you."

My eyes pop open, noting his mixed expression. "What is it?" A new set of nerves unleash inside me.

He lets out a deep breath, regarding me carefully. "You were my first."

"First, what?" I ask, feeling confused.

He narrows his eyes at me. "My first..."

I blink a couple of times, utterly taken aback. No. That can't be what he means. Can it? "You mean ... you were a virgin when we first had sex?"

That's not possible.

He nods his head.

"But what about Grace?" Why wouldn't he have had sex until now?

"Nope," he responds.

"But Natalie told me about the time you caught her stealing condoms from you." She told me how mortified she was and thought she would die of embarrassment.

"How do you think I knew she took them? She took the box out of the drawer of my nightstand and then left it on top of the nightstand for me to find. I assume she was in a hurry." He laughs.

I tilt my head. "There was no one else?"

The pad of his thumb runs across my cheek as he shakes his head. "No. I mean, Grace and I did ... other things, and I thought about having sex with her, just to do it, but it never felt right." His shoulders lift and then drop. "I guess I was waiting."

"Waiting for what?" I ask.

The most stunning smile appears on his handsome face. "For you, Vee. It's always been you." His beautiful eyes pierce mine, telling me more in just that one look than any words ever could.

A tear slides down my cheek, and he wipes it away. "Oh, Jason. I didn't know—"

"Hey, I didn't tell you to make you feel bad. I told you because I don't want any secrets between us. *It's you and me.* And it always will be." He cups my face, bringing his lips to mine.

But I pull my lips away from him, needing to confess. "I wish you had been my first."

He shakes his head. "For the longest time, I thought being someone's first was important. But with you, I learned it wasn't about the firsts. It's about the lasts. *You might have been my first, but I want to be your last. That's what's important to me.*"

I purse my lips, my throat tightening. "I'd really like that."

"I hoped you would." Jason smiles before looking over his shoulder and then back at me. "Do you trust me?"

"Of course." I don't hesitate.

He leaves me, walking to his door and closing it so that the full-length mirror displays all of me as I wait for him on his bed, so I instinctively look away. His eyes linger appreciatively over my naked body as he approaches me, kneeling on the bed behind me, pressing his chest into my back. I tilt my head toward him, but he shakes his head. "Look straight ahead."

A knot twists into my stomach. We played this game before, and I didn't like it.

"Jason..."

"Trust me," he pleads.

I close my eyes and turn my head directly toward the mirror, ready to note everything I hate about myself. Ready to fight back tears that will inevitably fall down my cheeks, feeling defeated by the mirror once again.

Vanessa: 0
Mirror: 1

Taking a deep breath, I open my eyes, fear gripping my insides, telling me to look anywhere but at the mirror. But when I look straight ahead, I'm fixated on the image before me. I don't shrink away, cowering at what I see. Instead, I tilt my head, observing myself in the mirror as if seeing myself for the first time.

Jason grips my hips, keeping me right up against him. "Tell me what you see."

I let out a shaky breath. "I see a girl who for so long struggled at seeing herself properly. A girl who didn't know how to believe in herself or love herself." My hands slide up my thighs and over my stomach, noticing the softness with appreciation instead of disgust. "I see a body that keeps me safe and healthy. A body that I will work on loving more with each day." I lock eyes with Jason in the mirror. "I see me."

Jason tilts my chin, angling my lips toward him so that he can kiss me softly.

"I know I won't feel this way every day," I admit. "I'll still have days where I'm terrified to look in the mirror, but having you to look in it with me makes it less overwhelming, knowing I don't have to do it alone."

Jason presses his forehead to mine. "You are nothing but perfection. And on the days you see yourself as anything less than that, I will be right by your side, helping you see yourself through my eyes."

I rub the tip of my nose over his. "Promise?"

"I promise." His fingers slide through my hair, gripping the back of my neck, bringing my face toward him for another kiss before he parts from me, walking over to the light switch.

"Wait," I say.

He peeks over his shoulder, his hand merely an inch from turning the lights off.

"Keep the lights on," I tell him.

Jason turns around with the biggest grin as he walks over to me. "Now, lie back so I can get a good look at my girl."

Epilogue

Vanessa

FEBRUARY 14TH

It's the perfect winter night.

The stars look almost too enticing as they shimmer and twinkle against the backdrop of the night sky, almost as if they know tonight is for me.

I step out of the black escalade in awe of what is before me, *The Metropolitan Museum of Art*. There are celebrities lined up outside, walking the carpet as lights flash all around us from the cameras of several photographers. Anyone who is anyone is here, and they're here to see my designs.

Someone pinch me.

Jason steps out of the car behind me. "Are you ready, beautiful?" His fingers intertwine in mine. The black custom suit he wears highlights his muscular physique in all the right places, making him look like his calling is to be in the next James Bond film.

I squeeze his hand. "I think so."

"Hey, you got this, Vee." He raises his hands to cup my cheeks, his thumbs running smoothly across my skin right before he presses his lips to mine. "It's going to be impossible to keep my eyes off you tonight."

His gaze lingers over my floor-length, red, satin dress, his hand curling around my side so his fingers can skim along my bare back.

"Then don't," I whisper, brushing my lips against his.

He takes a deep breath. "If we don't get inside now, I'm going to make the driver take us straight back to the hotel room so I can tear this dress off you."

I gasp. "You wouldn't dare. This is a borrowed Valentino gown."

"You know, I don't know who that is." He laughs, looking admiringly down at me. "But what I do know is that you are putting every star to shame tonight."

My cheeks warm up, probably matching the color of my dress. Jason had insisted I take a coat with me, seeing that it was the middle of winter in New York, but I didn't want to hide behind my armor. Not tonight. Tonight is my night. Besides, it might be only thirty degrees out, with snow covering everything around us, but just being in his presence always keeps me warm.

"Thank you for coming with me tonight," I say.

"It's you and me. Always." He places his hand in mine. "Shall we?"

I nod, letting him lead the way up the steps to the front entrance of The Met. We walk further into the building, admiration and nerves taking over me as I glance around at the exquisite building filled with people dressed to the nines. It doesn't take long for us to find the entrance straight ahead, but when my eyes lock on the door, my body comes to a standstill, freezing in place.

"What's wrong?" Jason's eyes mirror concern.

"What if ... what if everyone hates my designs? I put my heart into this, and I don't know what I'll do if they hate it." I look away from him, embarrassment eating at me.

"Hey," he tilts my chin up with two fingers, "there is no doubt in my mind that everyone will love it. You are so unbelievably talented, and Vanessa, no matter how tonight goes, I'm so incredibly proud of you." My heart bursts at hearing those words come out of his mouth.

"You, putting something out there for others to judge, puts you in a very vulnerable position. But here you are, looking so fucking beautiful and ready to do anything you set your mind to do." He brushes a loose strand of hair away from my eyes, putting it smoothly back in place. "They chose you for a reason. You deserve to be here right now. And I am honored to stand by your side tonight, watching you get the recognition and praise you deserve."

I carefully wipe under my eyes, hoping to avoid making a mess of my mascara. "Why do you have to be so damn sweet?"

He leans down, his lips brushing my ear, speaking only loud enough for me to hear. "I was going to mention that you'll be getting even more praise when we get back to our room tonight."

"Promise?" I breathe.

"Only if you're a good girl," he whispers, straightening up.

Fuck me. Why do those two words have such a damn effect on me?

I take a deep breath, smooth down my dress and look him dead in the eye. "Let's do this!"

"That's my girl!"

We walk hand in hand toward the door, and as we approach, the security guard smiles, takes our invites, and opens the giant door for the two of us. As we step over the threshold, applause breaks out. I look around, wondering what everyone is cheering for, when Jason leans down and says, "They're clapping for you, beautiful."

For me?

My eyes widen as I take in everyone getting up from their chairs to stand and clap ... for me. Tears make their way to my eyes, and I quickly wipe away at them as I smile, the biggest smile I've ever shown in my life.

Looking around, I have the most surreal experience as I see my designs showcased on a few models throughout the room, intermixed with the winner's designs from the other schools as well. Girls of different sizes wear my pieces, accentuating their figures in all the right places as they walk throughout the room. They're freaking gorgeous.

I'm unsure where we're supposed to go, but thankfully, Raquel approaches us. "Vanessa! Everyone loves your pieces. I've had so many people begging for your information. Raving over your designs." She hugs me tightly. "You should be so proud of yourself."

Looking up at Jason, I say, "I am." Because for the first time in my life, I truly am. And maybe hearing Jason tell me how proud he was of me was like taking that first sip of your morning coffee with a good book in your hands; perfection. But right now, I know that what matters most is how proud I am of myself, and that is not something anyone will ever be able to take away from me.

"Well, let's get you guys to your seats." Raquel motions us toward a table, and as we get closer, I think I am about to cry all over again.

"Surprise!"

Natalie, Nate, Paul, Sarah, Brady, and Gabe sit at the table before me, making my heart swell.

"You guys came?" I ask in astonishment, looking up at Jason with so many questions.

"I might have known they would be here." He winks.

Natalie jumps up from her seat, looking beautiful in a soft pink floor-length dress with a slit down the side. "We wouldn't have missed this for the world," she says before embracing me.

"God, I'm so glad you're here." A tear slides down my cheek, and as we part, she wipes it away before it ruins my makeup.

"My turn." Nate moves around Natalie, wrapping his arms around me, picking my feet off the ground. "I'm so happy for you," he says, placing me gently back down.

Finally, Sarah, Paul, Gabe, and Brady each hug me and congratulate me, and when I finally make it to my seat beside Jason, I'm so overcome with emotions that I place my head on his shoulder.

"You okay?" he asks.

"I honestly couldn't be better. This might be the best night of my life."

He tilts his head and whispers, "Are you sure it wasn't the first time you came all over my fingers in the back of Nate's car?"

I giggle as a blush spreads over me.

"I don't even want to know what you just said to her," Natalie says, leaning into Nate's chest.

Nate kisses the top of her head. "That makes two of us."

"Not me! I want to know everything!" Brady places his elbow on the table, leaning onto his hand for support.

"Leave them alone. They're in love." Gabe pulls Brady's chair closer to him.

"So, Vanessa." Sarah smiles at me, her black dress showing the beautiful growing baby bump. "Are you ready for your speech?"

I gulp. I completely forgot about the inevitable speech. My throat goes dry as I reach for my glass of water.

"Our girl Vanessa is going to kill it up there," Paul announces, his hand placed protectively on the back of Sarah's chair.

I try to smile, but I can feel my hands beginning to shake, so I hide them under the table on my lap, where Jason's hand is already waiting for mine.

"Don't be nervous. You got this." He gives me reassuring eyes, squeezing my hand.

"I don't know. Maybe this was a bad idea. Maybe—"

"Pretend it's just you and me," he says matter-of-factly.

"What?"

"When you get up there, pretend it's just you and me. Can you do that?"

"I-I think so." I nod, taking another sip of water.

"Good evening, ladies and gentlemen." A familiar voice echoes through the speakers letting everyone know that it's time for the event to begin. I look up at the stage to see Raquel standing in front of the audience addressing the enthusiastic crowd.

Oh shit. It's time.

"We'd like to welcome everyone tonight and thank you for attending The Met Future of Fashion event."

A loud applause erupts through the room.

"The fashion departments at the schools participating in this prestigious event have held a close relationship with The Metropolitan Museum of Art over the years, and it is evident in each and every one of our students who strive for perfection—knowing that it might, someday, land their work here for all to see and admire. It is a dream that one can only obtain from hard work and true talent—turning a piece of fabric into a piece of art. It's not something that just anyone can do, which is why we find ourselves here, tonight, for this annual event that started over two decades ago. To honor students in this room who have created something so unique and special that it deserves to be seen in this significant building." Her eyes roam around the room, smiling at familiar faces. "We would like to start this evening by introducing you to the winner from Linrey University." My heart plummets to the bottom of my stomach. "And I must say that what impressed us most about the winner this year wasn't just her stunning pieces, but it is what these beautiful designs stand for. The meaning behind this collection brought some of the judges to absolute tears, and when you hear the words from our talented winner, you may want a box of tissues nearby."

A low laugh resonates through the crowd.

Oh God, I think I'm going to be sick.

Raquel's eyes somehow find me in the crowd, and I clutch my stomach.

"So, without further ado, I am both honored and thrilled to introduce you to this year's Future of Fashion award winner, representing Linrey University, Vanessa Gordon." She claps along with every one of the thousands of people in the room, and that's my cue to get up, which I do, just on very unsteady legs.

Thankfully, I make it to the stage without having a Jennifer Lawrence moment by tripping up the stairs. If I did, I would have to move to another county, which sounds like a lot of work. But instead, I find myself hazily accepting the award from Raquel with a warm smile as she motions for me to stand in front of the podium.

It's the moment I have been dreading for months. Having everyone's judgmental eyes on me, scrutinizing everything about me when they don't even know me.

Okay, Vanessa. You can do this.

But the second I look out into the audience, with the lights beating down on me, I freeze up. All words leave my brain as I forget why I'm even standing up here in the first place until a subtle cough catches my attention, and my eyes lock onto him.

Jason.

I watch as he mouths, *"It's you and me."*

And suddenly, everyone else in the room disappears.

And the only guy I see is the same guy I've been in love with my whole life.

The guy who loves me for me, no matter what size I am, reminding me why making this collection was so important to me in the first place.

Deep breath, Vanessa. This is for every woman out there who doesn't see how beautiful they truly are.

"I'd like to start by saying, 'Thank you' to everyone at the Linrey University fashion department for providing me with this amazing opportunity. Standing here tonight, I am so deeply overwhelmed at the notion that you thought my designs were worthy of being displayed in one of the most influential and prestigious museums in the world, the Metropolitan Museum of Art."

Everyone in the audience politely claps.

"Being a woman is hard. And being a woman, looking in a mirror, is even harder." I look out into the audience, noting all eyes in the room are on me. "We live in a world where we are constantly bombarded with criticisms regarding our appearance. A world that glorifies superficial facades and praises the use of filters and editing apps to make us appear more *appealing* to the human eye." I place my palms on the podium, grounding myself to this moment. "Little girls grow up looking to influencers on their social media to show them what to do to look *prettier* when the reality of it is, they're being lied to. Because that little girl is already going to grow up beautiful without the help of make-up or extensions or weight loss supplements, she just needs to look inside herself a little bit harder." I let out a deep breath before continuing.

"But as a woman standing here before you, who grew up constantly questioning my worth because of my body's size, or who let worrying about my body's size hold me back from living the life I should be living, I know that is something easier said than done. And unfortunately, it's not only the media that likes to critique us. Sometimes, many of us find critics in those closest to us. Those who think they're doing what's best for us by letting us know when we've gained a few pounds—letting us know ways to improve ourselves. When instead, the only thing they are doing is traumatizing a little girl who once didn't give a second thought about her body. And now she can't stop looking in the mirror, finding something she hates about herself. Creating a monster in her head that makes her believe the size of her body is the only thing about her that matters. Newsflash"—I pause for emphasis—"it fucking isn't."

A roar of hollers and cheers is heard throughout the crowd.

"So tonight, I present to you my pieces that represent just a portion of my collection that I plan on expanding called, *'Love Your Body.'* A collection created with the goal of helping girls and women of all ages feel beautiful in their skin no matter what size they may be. But most importantly, I stand here tonight to tell you that looking in the mirror isn't as scary as we let ourselves believe. And sometimes, with the right person beside you, it can even be liberating." I look over at Jason, and even in the distance, I can see his eyes glossing over, which causes mine to do the same. "No matter what society says, we are beautiful, we are fierce, we are smart, we are courageous, we are confident, we are brave, and we are women."

Chairs are heard scraping against the floor as the crowd stands to their feet, cheering at the end of my speech.

I feel like I'm on cloud nine.

I did it.

I didn't stumble over my words. I didn't get sick in front of a room full of people or forget how to speak. I actually did it.

One second, I'm smiling, with tears spilling down my cheeks, and the next, I'm being pulled into a familiar warm embrace. "That's my fucking girl." Jason's lips land on mine, claiming me in front of everyone, causing the applause in the room to intensify. He pulls away, grinning, moving his lips next to my ear. "I'm so proud of you."

I'm proud of me, too, I think right before gripping his shirt and bringing his lips back on mine, feeling like a woman on top of the world.

This moment proved to me that I can do anything I set my heart out to do. I just need to believe in myself. But most importantly, I need to love myself the way I deserve.

But if there is a day where I feel like I can't. A day when my own insecure thoughts are too much for me to handle on my own, it feels pretty damn good to have him by my side, knowing he'll always help me see myself through his eyes.

Because as our lips part and I pull back to look up into Jason's currently bright blue eyes, I know that this man, the man I'm so head over heels in love with, will never let me shatter.

The End.

THANK YOU!

Thank you for reading Before I Saw You!
If you enjoyed this love story, I would be forever grateful if you could
leave a review on the platform of your choice. Your support means so
much to me and helps spread the word to other readers!

And stay tuned for ...
Paul and Sarah's love story!

BOOK 3
COMING 2024

She has a secret that's going to change his life.
There's just one problem.
She can't tell him.

ACKNOWLEDGEMENTS

If you're reading this — Thank you! Thank you! Thank you! From the bottom of my heart, thank you for giving my story a chance.

To my twin sister, Amanda — Thank you for everything, including our daily phone calls. I love you.

To my mom and dad, I love you both and, once again, hope you never read this book.

To my alpha reader, Grace — Thank you for showing BITY and BISY so much love. I can't wait to take a picture with you and BITY on the top of the Eiffel Tower!

To my beta reader, Amanda — Thank you for always being so supportive and showing my books so much love! I feel so fortunate to be able to call you a friend!

To my beta reader, Ashley — Thank you for your continual love and support for both BITY and BISY. I am so glad we found each other on Bookstagram, and I'm already looking forward to sending you the next book in the series!

To my editor, Caitlin Lengerich — Thank you for helping me perfect my story and making it the best it can be!

To my cover artist, Kate from Y'all. That Graphic — Thank you for once again making me the most beautiful cover I could have ever imagined. I'm already looking forward to the next cover!

To every single person who reads my books and then turns to Instagram, TikTok, Goodreads, etc., to spread the word — Thank you! Your words are why my books get into the hands of more readers, and I can't thank you enough for your love and support!

ABOUT THE AUTHOR

Ashley Elizabeth is an author of steamy contemporary romance. Her books will always tell a love story with just the right amount of spice and, most importantly, end with a happily ever after. When she's not reading a romance novel or overthinking everything, you can find her at Starbucks, keeping them in business, or watching Jurassic Park for the thousandth time with her fur baby, Bailey.

Keep in touch with Ashley Elizabeth

Instagram: @ashleyelizabethauthor
Goodreads: goodreads.com/ashleyelizabeth
TikTok: @ashleyelizabethauthor

www.ingramcontent.com/pod-product-compliance
Lightning Source LLC
Chambersburg PA
CBHW030057310726
48970CB00004B/1049